"*Little shrew!*"

"*Large Tyrant,*" she returned equably, but marvelling at the change laughter wrought in him.

The hushed silence, the dim arboreal light enfolded them. Carruthers drew her close, and kissed her.

It was a kiss that bore no resemblance to those that Brooks Lambert had shared with her. Carruther's hands were like iron; his mouth was hard and fierce and hungry. She felt crushed and half smothered, and something else . . . something powerful and primitive.

THE TYRANT

Patricia Veryan

*Book III of
"The Golden
Chronicles"*

FAWCETT CREST · NEW YORK

A Fawcett Crest Book
Published by Ballantine Books
Copyright © 1987 by Patricia Veryan

Library of Congress Catalog Card Number: 86-26223

ISBN 0-449-21666-7

This edition published by arrangement with St. Martin's Press, Inc.

Manufactured in the United States of America

First Ballantine Books Edition: March 1989

For Kit and Bill M.
true friends and compatriots

THE TYRANT

ᘒ *Chapter 1* ᘒ

England,
July 1746

The seamstress who had worked for many hours on the exact fit of the stomacher and the precise falls of the pleats at the back of the pink taffeta *robe a la française* would have thrown up her hands in horror could she have seen her peerless creation on this warm summer evening. For the Watteau pleats trailed in the dust, the laces were crushed, and the lady who wore the delicious gown was seated on a rustic garden bench, a willing captive in strong military arms.

Drawing back sighfully from those same arms, Miss Phoebe Ramsay raised her elegantly powdered head, and guilt came into her eyes. They were green eyes, wide and thickly lashed, set under delicately arching brows and enhanced by an enchanting, full-lipped face. Miss Ramsay, a true connoisseur might argue, did not possess pure classic beauty. Her mouth, sweetly as it was curved, had neither a pouting nor rosebud quality, and her nose, although small and delicate, had a slightly retroussé tilt. The true connoisseur would have been laughed to scorn: Miss Ramsay was widely held to be a true Fair, and much admired in both London and Surrey.

"Brooks," she said, placing one little hand against the broad chest of her ardent companion, "how wicked we are! I should not meet you alone like this—much less kiss a gentleman to whom I am not officially betrothed."

Captain Brooks Lambert wasted not a second in seizing that mittened hand and pressing it to his lips. "Only because Fate has been so dashed uncooperative," he said indignantly. "Two years I've worshipped at your shrine. And I doubt I've seen you alone above a dozen times in all that while, and then but for a few stolen minutes!"

"And most improperly," she said with a dimpling smile.

1

"Besides, I was at Seminary, and then Cousin Nathaniel was killed, and we were in black gloves for a year."

"And just when I *might* have been able to see you," he appended glumly, "I was off to the Rebellion."

She shuddered. "Those awful Jacobites! What a nightmare it was! I was fairly terrified for your sake."

He kissed the hand he still held, and said smilingly, "And I, sustained through it all by the knowledge that at home waited the lady who puts the smile in my world. Even if I was sent off without her promise."

"With my prayers," she said, "for you are very dear to me— No, Lamb! How grateful I am that this wretched war is over and done with."

"Over," he said with sudden grimness, "but not done with."

"Do you mean because of what the Duke of Cumberland is doing? They say the MP's and the Upper House wanted it, but I cannot believe they meant him to be as cruel and ruthless as we hear. Have you met him?"

"Oh, yes. A grand fellow, for such a youngster."

"He is? But they say his reprisals in Scotland are unspeakable. And to hunt down and slaughter these fugitive Jacobite gentlemen seems so—"

"Fiddlesticks! The Scots and their fellow-travellers followed Charles Stuart willingly enough. What d'you suppose they'd have done if *they* had been the victors? All they live for is to fight— if not us, then they slaughter each other! I'd like to have seen some of these mealy-mouthed clemency merchants had Bonnie Charlie led his murderous Highlanders into London! We gave 'em a lesson they'll not soon forget, I can tell you! There'll be no more Stuarts on the throne spouting their rubbish of King by Divine Right, and an end to the parliamentary process! Could I but lay my hand on some of the English Catholics who fought for him, or who now shield his wretched fugi—" Here, catching sight of the troubled look in his love's eyes, he went on quickly, "Sorry, my dearest. There speaks the soldier, and I should not sully your dainty ears with such gruesome subjects. Now, Phoebe, give me an answer, I beg you. Unless . . . Is there, perhaps, someone else?"

She faltered, "Why—I, I have a lot of—"

"Of admirers," he interposed, frowning. "How well I know it! But is there one amongst them whom you like better than you like me?"

He looked so anxious, and she eyed him fondly. Insofar as

personal attributes went, Captain Lambert was a most worthy aspirant for her hand. He was well-born, tall, perfectly proportioned, and extremely good-looking. His fair hair, well powdered, waved thickly from a noble brow, below which dark blue eyes were set wide apart and fringed with long dark lashes. The nose was straight, the mouth well shaped and quick to smile, the chin firm. It was indisputable that she cared for no man as much as she cared for him. He was brave, devoted, and unfailingly gentle with her. And Grandmama had often told her that the great loves she read of in books were seldom found in real life. Perhaps her deep affection for Brooks *was* love, and it was just silly romancing to wait for the soaring, worshipful adoration she so yearned for; that blessed moment when she would *know* that this was the perfect mate for her, however imperfect he might be in little unimportant ways; that this was the one, the *only* love. Thus, stifling a sigh, she replied softly, "No one, dear Lamb."

"Well, there you are, then," he cried, triumphant. "Phoebe, my love, my own, I will cherish you always, and do my damnedest to make you happy! I swear it!"

"I know you will—would, but—"

"But!" he exclaimed impatiently. "Always that accursed *but*! What if your papa accepts the next old duffer who jingles his money-bags?"

Angered, she stood and drew herself up. "I see no cause for such a vulgar remark!"

"Oh, do you not?" he cried, rising to take her by the shoulders. "Do you fancy I'm unaware of why I'm not considered a good catch? I could provide well for *you*, my dearest. But not restore your family fortunes. A penniless captain of hussars don't suit your papa or your grandmother!" Releasing her, he sighed and added reluctantly, "Not that I can blame 'em."

Phoebe bit her lip. What he said had an element of truth. Were she to go to her papa or to her formidable grandmother and plead to be allowed to marry Brooks, they'd likely agree, for she knew how dear she was to them. But she knew also how desperately her father hoped that she would make a match that would, to an extent at least, ensure the future of her brother and sisters.

Lady Eloise Ramsay had presented Sir George with six tokens of her affection, one of them stillborn, and another succumbing at the tender age of three to an attack of measles. The survivors were as healthy as they were handsome and, despite occasional

3

lively quarrels, were a fond and close-knit family. Sir George had inherited a comfortable fortune, and both his country seat and his Town house on Clarges Street were spacious and luxurious. Between poor investments, a scoundrelly solicitor, and the extravagances of his charming wife, however, Sir George had, as the saying went, "brought a palace to a pigsty," and while there was as yet no cause to be concerned for their daily bread, or to fear the roofs might be snatched from over their heads, penny-pinching had become the order of the day.

Sir George, craggy, kind-hearted but hot-tempered, who revelled in the life of a country squire and was not much given to introspection, now passed many a sleepless night worrying for his family's future. By contrast, Lady Eloise scarcely gave the matter a thought save when Sir George interfered with her plans to play silver loo, and adamantly forbade her the indulgence of any more gaming. ("Not even for *farthing* points!") "Your papa, Phoebe," my lady advised her eldest daughter, "is a prudent man." And she added under her breath, "Who is becoming a scaly scrub!"

Phoebe had inherited her grandmama's beauty and her father's innate kindness. She was a warm-hearted girl with a tendency to impulsiveness that years spent within the pristine corridors of a select Young Ladies' Seminary had not entirely subdued. Numerous visits to her grandmother, however, had borne fruit. Old Lady Ramsay had inculcated into her granddaughter a love of art and literature, an appreciation of the wonders of music, and a basic understanding of the finances involved in such things as running a great house, providing for governesses, schools, and University, and preparing for come outs. As a result, Phoebe could now sympathize with her sire's predicament. Belinda was only nine, and it would be several years before her presentation into Society need loom as a major expense. Julia, however, was not only fourteen, but already showing signs of becoming a real beauty. Two years, three at most, and she would have to be brought out. More urgently, Sinclair, surely the most unselfish and unassuming of brothers, was now reducing his tutor to despair because that worthy gentleman could barely keep up with his studious charge, much less teach him anything. At eighteen, Sinclair should already be at Oxford, and although he had never breathed a word of complaint, Phoebe was well aware that his brilliant mind must be clamouring for new fields to conquer. He was mad for archaeology, and it was his dream to study, travel,

4

and eventually teach that fascinating subject. She sighed again. Costly dreams.

Silent now, Lambert offered his arm. She rested her hand on it, and they began to stroll slowly back towards the house. The smell of blossoms hung heavily on the warm night air. The velvety darkness of the heavens was studded with the brilliance of countless stars, a half-moon was peeping over the horizon, and the music that drifted softly from the open windows of the ballroom was embellished by the trill of a nightingale. Surely, a night made for romance.

The Captain put his strong hand over Phoebe's dainty fingers and said pleadingly, "Am I *so* contemptible, fair one? The allowance my uncle makes me is far from being a pittance. My Aunt Ophelia has promised I'll be her heir, and she's a wealthy woman. Not," he added, "that I wish her to turn up her toes yet awhile."

Phoebe smiled up at him, and he halted and turned her to face him. "Sweeting, if I have angered you, 'tis only because I am so—so deep in love. I'd give you all the world was it in my power." Gazing down at her face, bewitchingly lovely in the moonlight, his clasp tightened and he said huskily, "Have you no hope to offer? Don't you really care at all?"

If the moonlight enhanced her fragile beauty, that same light on the Captain's aquiline features played havoc with her heart. Lambert was a handsome man, but in the glory of full dress Regimentals he was devastating. She reached up to touch his cheek and murmured, "You know I do." And as he took her hand and pressed kisses into the palm, she went on regretfully, "But since I left the Seminary, I have refused three wealthy and eligible suitors."

His head lifted. He said angrily, "Each one old enough to father you!"

"Yes," she sighed. "But if someone else *should* offer, Papa has every right to accept. And if it should be a younger man this time—and wealthy . . ."

"I'll blow the miserable swine's head clean off his shoulders!" snarled her fierce suitor.

The country seat of Sir George Ramsay was called Pineridge Park, although it could not really boast a park. Nor, in point of fact, could it claim pine trees; not, at least, in this year of 1746. Nonetheless, it was a charming estate, having elaborate pleasure gardens, a nice shrubbery, and a large wilderness area. The house, of red brick, was squarely conventional and had been built in 1589 as the Dower House of a much larger estate, now broken into parcels. The main pile, three storeys in height, was of no distinct architectural period, a fact that caused Lady Eloise Ramsay much distress. Her wistful pleas for the addition of Ionic columns having met with a seething "By Beelzebub—no!" from her life's companion, the house remained uncluttered by such impedimenta, the most recent addition, an adequately sized ballroom, having been built at the turn of the century to form the single-storey wing at the rear of the house.

Tonight, that wing was a blaze of light, for the Ramsay Summer Ball was a yearly tradition Sir George had been unable to bring himself to cancel. Not only were the Ramsay parties renowned for the quality of refreshments, but Sir George was well liked and admired as a bruising rider to hounds, his daughter had emerged from Seminary and a year of mourning to become an acknowledged Fair, and his wife was a charming lady whose occasional gaffes were thoroughly enjoyed by all, wherefore the County had turned out full force.

Phoebe and her captain re-entered the ballroom as a minuet was called. Lambet, who was obliged to return to duty, said his reluctant farewells, bowed over Phoebe's hand, and went off to say good night to his host and hostess.

At the far end of the large room several sofas and comfortable chairs were clustered about long windows that stood open to admit the cool outer air. Two ladies shared one of the sofas, and being unable to find Sir George, it was to them that the dashing Captain made his way. The older of the pair was a formidable dowager wearing a crimson brocade gown that drew the eye like a beacon. The Dowager Lady Ramsay was not a fleshy woman, but she had the square solidity of build that characterized her son, in addition to which she was unusually tall. She had been a statuesque beauty in her youth, and if her blue eyes were a little faded by age, they were as keen as ever and missed very little of what went on about her. The lady seated next to her was her opposite in every way. Small of stature and dainty of manner, Lady Eloise Ramsay at three and forty was distinguished only by her amiability, a tendency to speak her thoughts aloud, and a fine pair of green eyes. Those eyes were wistful as she watched Captain Lambert's approach. "Poor boy," she sighed. "Such a beautiful young man to lose his love."

The Dowager said nothing, and then Lambert was bowing

before them, expressing his sorrow at leaving a party "so blessed with dazzling beauties."

"Rascal!" said Lady Eloise. "Are you off so soon?"

"Alas, a cruel fate compels me, ma'am!"

She smiled up into his laughing eyes and went to the door with him, for he was one of her favourites. When she came back, Lady Martha said, "He seems cheerful enough. I fancy he's not given up hope yet."

Sitting down again, Lady Eloise said, "Do you think, Mama, that they will never marry?"

"I think George would likely give his consent, if Phoebe truly loved him."

Lady Eloise sighed. "I only pray that Phoebe is not denying him because she feels obliged. I could not bear to think of her going through life with a broken heart."

"She's much too sensible to be such a goose. If she has really given her heart, she will not become a burnt offering, even for her brother."

"Oh, Mama, how awful if Sinclair should do as he says! India! For a boy who is miserable in *England* in hot weather! 'Twould kill him! And only to try and bring us about!"

"Tcha! A fine high flight, and if you think George would let him go, you're witless! Sinclair is restive, merely; all nerves and youth and heroic imaginings, besides which he's frustrated because he yearns to be at University and is too mannerly to let us guess how much the waiting galls him. Had I the funds, he would have been off to Oxford a year since. I ain't—more's the pity!"

Eloise placed a consoling hand on the old lady's arm. "Do not blame yourself, dear Mama. We know you cannot help it."

"Thank you," snarled my lady.

Sinclair Ramsay was two years younger than his eldest sister, but he was not the kind to resent having to stand up with her for a dance. He was fond of all the members of his family, but between him and Phoebe was a rather special bond, deepened by the closeness of their ages and a quiet and mutual admiration. It was not flouted and never allowed to impinge upon or lessen their other filial relationships; still, it was there, and thus Phoebe was rather surprised that her brother was not waiting to scold her for being late for their minuet.

The cluster of admirers, who had been disconsolate when she

7

smilingly told them of her prior commitment, was beginning to re-form and, seeing from the corner of her eye an elderly and rather pompous pest bearing down on her, she directed her steps to the garden once more.

There was no sign of Sinclair, but as she wandered to the drivepath, a voice called with playful scolding, "Miss Phoebe . . . ? I saw you slip out here, you fascinating creature! Do not tease me, lovely goddess. Come out, come out, wherever you are . . . !"

Lord Olderwood had followed. She lifted her panniers to protect her skirt from dust, and retreated hastily into the shadow of the trees. And still the pest came! 'Drat the man!' she said under her breath, and ran farther into the elms that edged the east drivepath.

Peeping out, she saw Lord Olderwood search about hopefully, and at length return in a grumbling way to the house. It was unkind, she thought repentantly, but he would start on about his houses and his yacht, and his beloved sister (a waspish female at best) who would be so *very* glad would dear Miss Phoebe only consider his suit. And his corset would creak and his wrinkled hand pat hers (if she gave him the chance!) and tonight she simply was not able to—

"Oh . . . God . . . !"

The smothered moan came from close by. And the voice was that of her brother. Her heart gave a little jump of fright. Hurrying towards the sound, she called, "Sin . . . ? Is something wrong?"

A gasp. "No! Phoebe, go on back inside! Do not come—!"

But already she had found him, and she halted, frozen with shock.

He was kneeling, his neat wig dishevelled and untidy about his thin, sensitive face. But her full attention was on the sprawled figure of the man he supported, a man whose clothes hung in tattered shreds, whose bearded face was a mask of dirt and blood, and whose weak attempts to drag himself up as she approached ended in a groan and a helpless collapse into Sinclair's arms again.

"My heavens!" gasped Phoebe. And suddenly, many things fell into place. Her brother's frequent unexplained absences these past few months; the several occasions on which she had gone late to his bedchamber to chat, as they had done since childhood, only to find him not yet home, and his haggard look the following day, which he had excused to their parents as being the result of "studying too late." She had said nothing, suspecting with some amusement that Sinclair, handsome in his intense fashion, had entered early into the petticoat line. Now, her heart failed her as she cried, "A *rebel*! Oh, Sin! How *could* you? If he is found here, we—"

"Lord, d'you think I do not know it! I had no choice! He is far spent, and they were close on our heels when I managed to give them the slip."

It was typical of him that he made no attempt to deny his Jacobite involvement or to mitigate the danger. The thought of the brutal punishment that would be inflicted on him—on them all—if they were found to be shielding a fugitive made her blood run cold. She said, "What do you mean to do? If you hide him in the house—"

"No!" groaned the injured man feebly. "Ramsay—I'll not . . . bring death to—to your family!"

Phoebe's eyes were becoming accustomed to the gloom, and she saw that, under the dirt and blood, his straggling hair was fair. His eyes, a fine grey now clouded with pain, met hers in anguished remorse. "How came you to be so badly hurt, sir?" she asked gently. "You are a mass of cuts."

"Took a ball through my leg . . ." he gasped. "And—had to jump through a window. No—do not come too close, ma'am. I'd—I'd not sully your—lovely gown."

She felt suddenly ashamed of her 'lovely gown' and of her own fears. "You are not Scotch, I think. Are you a Catholic gentleman?"

He shook his head. "Just . . . admired Prince Ch-Charlie."

Phoebe looked at her brother. "Well, I suppose what's done is done. Those wounds must be treated. I realize we dare not call a physician, but perhaps we could hide him somewhere about the estate and if he is found, deny all knowledge. My father is known to be condemning of the Jacobite Cause, and—"

Sinclair intervened, "He must be brought to Salisbury as soon as may be."

"*Salisbury!* Are you mad? In his condition? How do you mean to convey him, pray? The troopers are searching all vehicles 'twixt here and the sea!"

A sudden flurry of nearby voices caused her to shrink. The fugitive struggled to sit up. "I—I must hasten," he muttered, but his face twisted with pain and he sagged weakly.

Phoebe thought, 'He is a human being, whatever his political persuasions, and is suffering horribly. How can I not help the poor soul?'

Reading her expression correctly, Sinclair said, "He is in no case to *crawl* tonight, much less hasten! I doubt he's eaten for days, and besides being exhausted, he's lost a deal of blood. It might serve if I could just get him down to the old basement. The troopers searched it last week, so he should be safe there for a day or so, until I can get some help to transport him to Salisbury."

"Yes," said Phoebe slowly, "and there is likely no one on that side of the house, for everybody is working at the ball! Can you lift him?"

He made a wry face. "No, blast it all! I tried, but he's too heavy."

"Perhaps I can help."

"No, no! Your gown must not be marked when you go back to the party! There is one chance, Phoebe. A risky one. Is a gentleman named Carruthers here?"

She frowned. "I—do not think so."

"Lascelles says he saw his team coming up the drivepath a short while ago, and—Oh, I'd forgot. Phoebe, this gentleman is Lieutenant Lance Lascelles. Lance, my elder sister, Phoebe."

A faint twinkle came into the strained eyes, "I'd say 'your servant, ma'am,' save that I—I fear I am more like to being your burden."

"Never mind that," she said kindly. "The important thing is to help you. Do you cry friends with this Mr. Carruthers?"

"Yes. He is a very old friend."

"A Jacobite, sir?"

He gave a faint croak of a laugh. "Lord, no! Merry despises the Stuart Cause. But—he's a loyal fellow, and . . . in the name of friendship might at least get me to . . . to Salisbury. He lives near there."

At least the name Merry was hopeful; he must be a good-natured person to rate such a nickname. Still, the risk was frightful.

Sinclair met her troubled gaze and said with a helpless shrug, "I fancy it our best hope. If he is a friend of Lascelles's, chances are he won't betray us, even if he refuses his help."

"Very well, I'll go and find him. How shall I know him, Lieutenant?"

"He's tall; a well-built chap. Nine and twenty, and—and you'll

10

likely spot him easily enough. He's very dark and . . . will not powder his hair.''

"Lud! He should stand out like a sore thumb. I'll be as quick as I can."

She started off at once, Lascelles's stammered thanks echoing in her ears. It was very possible that Lord Olderwood still lurked about the rear terrace, and she had no wish to spend long moments in polite evasion, besides which she was anxious to inspect her gown, for she had bent close to Lieutenant Lascelles, and the poor wretch was all blood. Sorry as she was for him, however, she was most fearful for her brother. If Sinclair was deeply involved with aiding the rebels, he stood in deadly peril. What a dreadful worry! And only moments ago her greatest concern had been whether she loved Brooks Lambert deeply enough to abandon her sense of family duty and tell Papa she wished to marry him!

She entered the house through the French doors to the darkened book room. Occasional wall sconces were lit in the hall, and she hurried along that deserted area, pausing before the elaborate gilt-framed mirror that hung over the Chinese chest. Peering anxiously at her reflection, she removed some leaves from her hair, then inspected her skirts. There was dirt on the hem of her gown, and leaves and twigs had adhered to her train, but having brushed away the former and detached the latter, she felt quite presentable, save that she was pale with nervousness. She pinched some colour into her cheeks and hurried to the ballroom.

Immediately, she was the centre of attention, and she laughed and flirted while her eyes sought desperately through the throng. She had not far to search. The gentleman was turned from her, presenting a view of a pair of broad shoulders encased in a beautifully tailored coat of grey velvet lavishly trimmed with silver embroidery. There could be no doubt who he was, for in a room where every head was either bewigged or powdered, he had bowed to neither affectation, his thick dark hair being tied neatly back with a silver riband.

Phoebe responded gaily to the pleas whispered in her ear by a dashing distant cousin, and wondered how to attract the attention of her quarry.

Her problem was solved. "There you are, puss!" exclaimed her father's resonant voice. "Come now, let her be, Monty. There's a gentleman fairly frantic to make her acquaintance."

Phoebe left her cousin groaning, and was led forward.

"Carruthers," called Sir George. "Here is my daughter!"

The dark head turned, and Phoebe all but gasped with shock. It was The Tyrant! She had first laid eyes on him at the Wyndhams' breakfast party in the spring. Since he'd been seated across the table from her, they had not spoken, and for some time he had not paid the least attention to her. She had peeped at him, fascinated by the scars that, like twin white lines, marred the left side of his face from hairline to chin, drawing up his eyebrow into a mocking slant that lent a devilish touch to his expression. A cold glance had been levelled at her from strange eyes that gleamed like pools of pale blue ice in the lean, tanned face. She had lowered her own eyes at once, and later had pointed out the gentleman to Cousin Wandsworth. That mincing dandy had said with a smirk, "Oh, that's old Meredith. Proper gruff and grim, ain't he? His brother calls him The Tyrant. Apt, what?" Noting again the heavy dark brows, the strong, thin nose, jutting chin, and uncompromising line of the mouth, she thought a dismayed '*Merry*, is it? Of all people! Why did that stupid Wandsworth not tell me his name was Meredith *Carruthers*?'

She was vaguely aware that her father had completed the introductions and that a particularly unpleasant sneer twisted The Tyrant's thin lips. She was staring again, as she had when first they met. He must judge her a very ill-mannered girl. She sank quickly into a curtsy. He bowed over her hand, and said drily, "Enchanted, ma'am," in a deep voice, the tone of which also said, 'you silly creature.'

Phoebe thought, 'Much help we shall get from this cold fish,' but she turned her most dazzling smile on him and said coquettishly, "My dear papa says you have been fairly frantic to make my acquaintance, Mr. Carruthers."

Sir George looked mildly discomfited.

Carruthers replied with slightly bored courtesy, "Who would not be, ma'am?"

"Flatterer." She retreated behind her fan. "Oh, dear! Here comes my lord Olderwood, and I am much too tired to dance again. Perhaps you will be so kind as to take me out onto the terrace, dear sir, so that we may chat in the cool air. It is so very excessive warm in here."

Carruthers looked stunned, but extended his arm dutifully, and she took it and pulled him gently towards the outer hall.

He said, "I had thought you wished to go onto the terrace, Miss Ramsay."

"Yes. But not that one. We shall be stopped by everybody, and I am—er, very weary of it all."

She knew that her father was positively goggling at her, for not only did she love a party, but she was renowned for her ability to dance the whole night away and never show a sign of weariness. She smiled warmly at Sir George, and started off.

Complying with her request, Carruthers led her into the main hall. She glanced up and saw that his lips were tight, and was not surprised when he observed with rather tactless bluntness, "If it is Lord Olderwood's dance, ma'am, you should grant it him. I had no intent to monopolize you."

"Perhaps not," she murmured, "but I mean to monopolize *you*, Mr. Carruthers."

She felt him start, and the pale blue eyes slanted down at her, a wary light dawning.

"I think I do not follow you, Miss Ramsay," he said, his steps slowing.

"No, but you must," she said, pulling at his arm without compunction and saying with low urgency, "I am desperately in need of your help. No, never look so aghast, I have no designs upon you, I promise. Only come. A friend of yours has arrived and wishes to see you. Now do not stand like a block! The servants are staring. Walk, sir! Left—right, left—right!"

He frowned, but a gleam of amusement crept into the pale eyes and he did as she asked. "I wonder why I have the unhappy premonition that I am about to be involved in something outrageous," he murmured. But when they came to the deserted east hall and Phoebe started down it, he halted, the smile in his eyes that she had thought oddly attractive dying away. "No, really, ma'am. This is insupportable. With all due respect, I must remind you of the construction that will be placed upon my taking you off like this."

"Oh, pox on what people will say!" She tugged at his arm. "*Do* come along!"

His hand closed over her own. He stood quite still, his face stern and unyielding. "Madam, I am not one for convention, but I think I will refuse to compromise a lady I have never before met. Not another step until you at least tell me the name of this—er, 'friend.' "

She could have shaken him, but, knowing he was justified, glanced around, then hissed, "It is—Lance."

"Good God!" he gasped, clearly astonished. "But why the secrecy, ma'am? Why does he not come—"

"He is—in trouble. Oh, *now* will you come?"

He made no response but accompanied her so briskly that she almost had to run to keep up with him. In only a few minutes they had escaped the house and were entering the trees.

Carruthers groaned, "If we were seen, you are properly in disgrace! And I also. This had best not be some poor joke, or—"

The words died away as they came out of the deeper darkness of the trees and into a little clearing. Lascelles now lay with his back propped against a tree, and Sinclair crouched beside him, holding a decanter of wine he had evidently appropriated from the house. Carruthers checked, and stood rigidly still.

With a twitching smile, Lascelles said weakly, "Now see . . . what I've done."

Two strides, and Carruthers was kneeling. Taking the trembling outstretched hand, he growled, "You blasted bentbrain! I might have known you'd get yourself into that miserable fiasco! Out with Charlie, were you?"

"Yes." A glitter of slow and painful tears came into Lascelles's eyes. "Until Culloden. Merry . . . if you'd *seen* that hell . . . !"

"I *did* see it! I was there. Only through the grace of God we did not face each other over our sabres! Damn you, Lance! I could break your stupid neck!"

"Well!" exclaimed Phoebe, indignant. "A fine way to talk to your friend! Can you not see the case he is in, sir? I'd think—"

He interpolated savagely, "Then I suggest you do so, madam! Do you look forward to seeing your father's head on a spike atop Temple Bar? Do you fancy they'd balk at meting out the same treatment to you? Or this young gallant who is, I take it, your brother?"

Bristling, Sinclair said, "I am Sinclair Ramsay, Mr. Carruthers. And I think there is not the need to take that tone to my sister. If anyone is to be blamed, it is me. I am now and always have been for the Stuart Cause, and—"

"Aye. You've a Scots name and Scottish forbears, I fancy. Catholic?"

"No. Many of the Englishmen who supported Charles were Protestants, and are—"

"Are dead, dying, racked, tortured, starving, hounded! Only look at *this* idiot!"

Lascelles muttered, "You need not—feel obliged to . . . to

help, Merry.'' But in spite of his brave effort, despair showed in the ravaged face.

Phoebe's lip curled. "My brother and I will help you, Lieutenant Lascelles. *We* are not afraid!"

"Lascelles?" snapped Carruthers, shooting a disgusted look at her.

The fugitive nodded wearily. "My fighting name."

"It is vital he get to Salisbury, Mr. Carruthers," Sinclair put in. "He said you live near there, so we thought—"

"Did you, indeed? Paint me the scenario if you please, young Quixote. Am I to carry this silly clod on my back, perhaps? Haul him off in my carriage, to be discovered by the first troop of dragoons we encounter? And they are thick on the highways, I do assure you. Is the reason I came late to your party! Shall I tell my coachman to kindly look the other way while we carry off a traitor whose presence would ensure the lifting of his head— if we were lucky enough to be spared questioning, first? Damme, what folly!"

"Yes," gritted Phoebe, yearning to claw him. "And folly you perpetuate! If you will not help your good friend as far as Salisbury, will you at least carry the Lieutenant to our basement so that I may tend his hurts? If it has escaped your notice while you worried for your coachman, he bleeds!"

Carruthers stared at Lascelles in silence, then said grimly, "If I take him inside your house, ma'am, I place every member of your family in jeopardy. Are you willing to bear so terrible a responsibility?"

A sick coldness clutched at Phoebe's middle. She knew that Sinclair's blue eyes were steady on her face and that he would abide by her decision. "He is a—a human being in need," she quavered.

"Lord!" grunted Carruthers scornfully. "A female Good Samaritan, no less!" But he peeled off his elegant coat and thrust it at her. "Hold this."

She took it, longing to wrap it around his throat, and he turned to Sinclair. "Now, give me yours."

At once shrugging out of his coat, Sinclair demurred, "But— I lack your physique. It is too small for you, sir."

Carruthers folded the coat inside out and tossed it across his shoulder. "You can go inside and find yourself other clothes. I cannot appear with bloodied garments, and I think it important I not simply disappear from your ball." In a less harsh voice, he said, "My regrets, Lance, but you're too tall for me to cradle

15

you. It's over my shoulder and bear it, old fellow. Up we go.''
He helped the fugitive to his feet, looked into the drawn face
searchingly for an instant, bent, and in a swift, powerful movement had thrown him across his shoulder.

Phoebe heard the faintest sound from Lascelles, then his tight
clenched hands were suddenly hanging limp. She gave a sympathetic little cry.

Carruthers said, "He's not feeling anything at the moment,
ma'am, but my back is, so be good enough to lead the way. The
sooner this is done with, the better!''

❧ *Chapter 2* ❧

The basement was cluttered, chill, and damp, but Phoebe had carried down a branch of candles from the book room, and a silver fruit bowl into which they had emptied a jug of water purloined from a table where provisions were being assembled for conveyance to the party. Sinclair had executed that tricky manoeuvre with considerable dash, waiting until a harassed footman had deposited his tray and departed, then making his raid and whipping out of sight before a heavily laden lackey came up. Phoebe ruthlessly appropriated the men's handkerchiefs, which she used as rags to wash the fugitive's face and bathe his countless cuts and abrasions.

These efforts restored Lascelles to consciousness, and Carruthers began to question him, pursuing his enquiries with ruthless persistence, even when his friend squirmed under Phoebe's ministrations. "Good gracious, sir," she cried, as Lascelles fought back a groan, "give the poor soul a chance! He has told you how he escaped after Culloden and managed to make his way this far, starved and hunted every step of the way. What more do you want? Oh dear, I'm afraid there is a piece of glass still in this cut, Lieutenant!"

"He has so far told me nothing I do not already know, ma'am," said Carruthers tersely. "Leave the leg wound, it is bound at least, and your brother can tend it. We've very little time, for I don't doubt but that we are missed by now. Lance, I want the truth, if I'm to help you get to Salisbury; though how in the deuce I'm to do so, the Lord only knows!"

Lascelles gasped threadily, "Sometimes, 'tis . . . best not to know . . . too much."

"Perhaps. But if I'm to lose my head in your devil's brew, I want to know more of it. First—is your sire aware of your Jacobite involvement?"

17

"My God—no! 'Twould kill him, I think! Merry"—the thin hand clawed out frantically, "you'll not tell him? Swear it!"

"I'll not tell him without your permission, naturally. But I think you underrate him."

Lascelles sighed with relief and lay back. "God bless the old fire-eater. Do you two go on any easier these days?"

"No. He hates my—er, insides. Just as he loathed my father. And do not try to change the subject. Why is it so 'vital' that you should get to Salisbury? You might better have laid low, I'd think, instead of running around in your condition."

At this point Phoebe succeeded in removing the glass fragment, and Lascelles closed his eyes and said nothing.

Carruthers grated, "I mean it, Lance. The truth—or no help from me."

"You are perfectly horrid," said Phoebe, desperately ignoring the blood on her hands and trying not to be sick. "I suppose *you* would be cool and composed with every dragoon in the country on your heels! What difference does it make if he panicked and ran?"

"It makes a deal of difference if my good friend here is the courier the soldiers hunt so eagerly."

Sinclair, who had remained silent during the interrogation, had reached for the decanter of wine, and Phoebe saw his hand jerk. His bewigged head turned swiftly to Carruthers, his obvious alarm frightening her.

"Courier?" she said. "What courier? What does he mean, Sin?"

Carruthers said grimly. "I've a friend in the military who told me that certain of the Jacobite fugitives carry part of a message. It has to do with the treasure that Prince Charles amassed to finance his regrettable Cause, but was unable to put to use before the end came. True, Lance?"

Lascelles hesitated, then gave a reluctant nod. "The Prince sent out a call for contributions. His followers were very generous. Jewels, plate . . . works of art, even, poured in. Now that . . . that our Cause is lost, the Committee who had—charge of storing the treasure, plans to restore it to—to the donors."

Carruthers shook his head. "Folly on folly! Is it truth that Charles Stuart was unable to get the treasure to France because of our blockade?"

"Yes. So, in desperation, he . . . had it sent down to England, hoping to ship it from—from here. But then—" He sighed drearily. "Culloden. And it was all . . . over."

18

"Jupiter! Do you say the valuables are in *England* now?"

"At three temporary locations, chosen in haste and—not very secure, unfortunately."

"And it is to be restored to the donors from each of the locations?"

Lascelles sighed, his head falling back against the old mattress on which they'd laid him.

Sinclair muttered, "Do not keep at him so, for heaven's sake. He's fairly exhausted. I'll tell you. The treasure is to be collected and shipped to some central destination. It's no use your asking me where, for no one knows save the Committee who sent out the ciphers."

"More than one, is there?"

"Yes. But how many I do not know. Only that each consists of a verse in which is hidden part of the message. Each courier is to deliver his portion to a secret destination. One man will decode them and know the location to which the treasure is to be delivered."

"But—how is it to be done?" asked Phoebe, gazing at her brother in fascination. "I mean—how are they planning to transport so vast a hoard?"

"I've no idea, thank goodness. My only function in all this is to try and help the poor devils get clear."

Lascelles said, "You must know how Jacobite sympathizers are treated, Merry. The families whose men followed Stuart have lost homes . . . land, every possession. They are quite literally starving to death. We must get their valuables back to them. I *must* . . . get my message de—delivered . . . I . . ." The words faded into silence and he appeared to sink into sleep.

Watching him sombrely, Carruthers muttered, "God help us all!"

Sinclair dragged an old trunk to swell the pile of bric-a-brac they had gathered to screen Lascelles, now covered with some moth-eaten but warm blankets they'd found. "You two had best get back to the ball," he said breathlessly. "I'll see to his leg. Here—take the candle. After you go, I'll uncover the half-window, and the moonlight will serve well enough."

Carruthers took the candle holder, cut off Lascelles's humble flow of gratitude by advising him he was a damned pest, then started across the cavernous chamber beside Phoebe. "Jove, what a witches' brew," he muttered. "You contrived to keep yourself neat, Miss Ramsay. I hope you may think of as neat a means to get the thimble-brain down to my country seat, for I certainly cannot."

Phoebe was relieved that he was willing to try, and said hopefully, "We could perhaps dress him as a groom or a footman, and—"

"And sit him on the box and watch him roll off and under the wheels within two minutes? Good God, ma'am! The gudgeon cannot stand up, much less walk! We'll be fortunate can we get him to the carriage before he lapses into a fever!"

She glared at him. "I realize you cannot help your natural tendencies, Mr. Carruthers, but *must* you always be so pessimistic?"

He leaned to her and murmured softly, "Were I to follow my 'natural tendencies' at this moment, I'd likely put you over my knee and spank you. *And* that silly chub of a brother of yours! He likely fancies himself a fine high-flown hero! Let him find himself faced with a disembowelling knife, and—"

Phoebe whirled on him, tears suddenly blurring her eyes. "How horrid! Do not! Do not!"

He grunted. "My apologies. But you must stop treating this as a jolly adventure and face cruel reality." Looking into her distressed face, he gave an impatient exclamation. "Enough! Lance ever had more pluck than good sense. I wish you were not involved, but you've courage, I give you that. Have you also a coach with a false bottom, perchance? Or a Trojan Horse?"

"A Trojan Horse . . ." she echoed, ignoring his reluctant compliment. She halted at the foot of the steps that led up to the hall door, and said excitedly, "Sir! If you were to invite us to visit your estate in Salisbury—"

"Near Salisbury," he corrected, balancing the candlestick on the end post of the stair railing.

"We could take a large trunk," she went on, "and—"

"And stuff poor Lance inside?" He chuckled. " 'Twould have to be a large one indeed. He's a longshanks."

"Oh, laugh then! All you can do is sneer. If you've a better scheme . . ."

Unexpectedly, a quirkish grin was slanted at her. "No. My apologies. You are perfectly right. And your idea is none so bad, except—our poor benighted fugitive cannot grace your ancestral pile for long, Miss Ramsay. Whatever we do must be done at once. I have but now made your acquaintance. On what possible pretext could I suddenly invite you and your brother on a sufficiently extended stay to warrant your taking such a monstrous amount of—''

A sharp click. A heavy hand was on the door latch. Phoebe gave a squeak of terror, the sound cut off as she was seized by iron hands, wrenched into a crushing embrace, and passionately kissed. Half-smothered, her ribs seeming to crack, torn between fright and outrage, she heard her father roar, ''Unhand my daughter, sir! You damned scoundrel! How *dare* you?''

Carruthers leapt back. ''Oh . . . Lord!'' he groaned, with realistic dismay.

Sir George Ramsay stood on the top step, his face mottled with fury. Lady Eloise, white and terror-stricken, peered from behind him, and a small crowd of guests and servants supplied a scandalized background for the dramatic tableau.

Shivering, Phoebe gulped, ''I—I can explain, P-Papa.''

''You can best let me do so, ma'am,'' said Carruthers. ''Sir George—''

''I will talk to *you* in my study, sir!'' rasped the enraged father. ''You will be lucky do I not employ a horsewhip! As for you, Miss Ramsay—get to your room!'' And as Phoebe stood, rooted in numb misery, he snarled, ''At once!''

She flew, the crowd parting before her, on each face a mixture of curiosity and condemnation. The entire horrid affair was too much for her already overwrought nerves, and tears streaked her face as she ran to the main stairs, trying not to see the gentlemen who grinned behind their hands, the ladies who whispered and shook their heads in delicious censure. Rushing along the first-floor hall, she saw her door swing open. Her abigail, Ada Banham, anxiety written large on her dark, pretty face, cried, ''Oh, Miss Phoebe! We been that frightened! We been looking and looking for you!''

Flinging herself into those cherishing arms, Phoebe wailed, ''I am ruined, Ada! Oh, but I am quite . . . r—ruined . . . !''

The whisper of her name disturbed Phoebe. For a moment she lay between sleep and waking, staring at the bed curtains. They were shaken agitatedly, and again her name was hissed. Sin's voice. With that awareness came the flood of memory, terrible and unrelenting, so that she threw open the curtains and saw by the light of the candle he held that her brother waited, elegant in a fresh coat of blue satin, the great cuffs and pocket flaps adorned with dark blue braid.

21

"At last," he grumbled, sitting on the side of the bed. "You women! Talk about insensate! How could you *sleep* after that miserable farce?"

"Oh, Sin," she cried imploringly, sitting up and clutching at his hand. "What has happened? I was sure Mama would come up, but *no* one has been near me. Not even Grandmama, and she usually forgives me before anyone else."

"Not your fault, old lady," he said gruffly, his thin, finely etched face solemn. "The fault is mine, and I wish to God I'd not involved you, but—if you *knew*, Phoebe! What that devil Cumberland has wrought in Scotland by way of reprisal is—well, beyond belief that any human being could be so—so bestial! And how the poor escaping Jacobites are hunted and—Oh, I won't go over it again. I'm only sorry you had to bear the brunt."

"Silly," she said, squeezing his hand fondly. "As if I would not be willing to share whatever scrape you get into—or that you would not help *me* in time of need! Only tell me what has happened. Did Papa challenge Mr. Carruthers?"

"Heaven forfend! The gentleman is an accomplished duellist. He's been out three times that I know of, and never been bested yet. But—Lord, what a rumpus! Mama was in hysterics, and Papa conducted poor Carruthers off to his study as though the headsman waited beyond the door!"

"Oh, dear! Whatever did Mr. Carruthers say?"

"Lord knows. I had it from my man that Papa did most of the talking, and that Carruthers came out stiff as a poker and his face as white as it had been red when he went in. Papa was all smiles, though."

Awed, she whispered, "Good gracious! How did Carruthers manage that?"

"I cannot imagine. He didn't impress me as being the diplomatist. The ball went on in high style, as you may guess. I doubt our guests can wait to regale their acquaintances with so juicy a scandal. All the old tabbies were fairly titillated."

Phoebe moaned and sank her face into her hands, then spread her fingers to peep through and ask, "Did you see Grandmama? Is she enraged?"

"Do you know," he said slowly, "I think she is not. She's a shrewd creature. Mayhap she thinks it was just a moment's foolishness."

She sighed, then said, "How selfish I am, to be asking only

of myself. What of your poor fugitive? If Carruthers has gone, how can we hope to—"

"Lascelles fell asleep trying to thank me, poor fellow. I felt guilty, leaving him in such miserable surroundings, but I fancy he's more comfortable than he's been since Culloden. And Carruthers ain't gone, love. He overnights." He saw her great eyes widen fearfully, and patted her hand. "I'd not tell you, save that you'd as well prepare yourself. Papa and Mama and Grandmama are to interview you and Carruthers at ten o'clock this morning."

Phoebe clapped a hand over her mouth to stifle her scream.

Surveying herself in the standing mirror, Phoebe moaned, "Lud, I'm so pale as any ghost. We shall have to use rouge today, Ada. I'll not have my family think I come before them crushed by guilt."

"What I don't understand, Miss Phoebe," said Ada Banham, her little face contorted as she struggled with the nine and twenty pearl buttons that closed the back of the cream muslin gown, "is why you went off with Mr. Carruthers the way you did, when your heart was give to Captain Lambert long ago. He's an attractive man and the ladies fairly sigh over him, but—"

"Attractive!" said Phoebe, defensively. "He is the most handsome man I ever saw!"

Ada pursed up her lips. "He had a beautiful form, I give him that. And I like the way his hair curls a bit, for all I think he should powder it, as do the other gents. But he's got a chin, and I'd not like to be the one to try his temper."

"Good heavens, girl! I was speaking of the Captain, not that horrid Meredith Carruthers!" She saw Ada cease her efforts to peer around at her in perplexity, and amended hurriedly, "He is a—er, passionate fellow, I grant you." And, remembering that sudden embrace, she had to admit it had been quick thinking, but—Lud, she'd as well be kissed by a bear! Very different to Brooks's tender caresses. Heaven help the girl Mr. Carruthers chose! She'd find she had wed a ruthless volcano. She was amused by the simile. Fire and ice . . . She realized that she was staring blankly at her reflection, and that Ada was watching her with such a silly grin that she yearned to box the girl's ears. "I wonder my mouth is not bruised," she said, inspecting it.

"Oooh!" squeaked Ada, hugging herself with vicarious enjoyment.

Restraining her irritation with an effort, Phoebe was overcome by a new wave of apprehension. "Oh, Ada, what will happen, do you think? If they send me up to Aunt Ormsby in Harrogate, I shall *die*! She is such a dragon!"

Ada, who was part gypsy and well seasoned with the lore of The Folk, said, "A big stripey spider runned 'crost me shadow. Afore breakfast! I crooked me fingers, but it was too late. 'Twill be a black day, miss, no doubting!"

"Oh, never say so! Ada—how did they know we had gone down to the basement?"

"One of the lackeys thought he saw you go down the hall, but no one never thought of looking in the basement till they'd searched everywhere else. It wasn't me, miss," she added in sudden anxiety. "I loves you dearly, I do, and would be trampled to death by bats 'fore I'd betray you to your doom."

"Phoebe!" Lady Eloise had thrown open the door to her daughter's bedchamber, and stood there, agitated. "Whatever keeps you, naughty creature? Hurry, do! Your dear papa has had such an upset tummy, and grows impatient!"

Running to seize her hand and cherish it to her cheek, Phoebe cried, "Oh, dear Mama, *pray* do not be angry. 'Twas but a misunderstanding, and—"

"Now come along, and *whatever* you do, you must not cry! Quick!" My lady hurried her into the hall and towards the stairs. Pausing at the landing to give her daughter's gown a tug here and a twitch there, she muttered, "Yes, you look charmingly, but I do not see why you keep that wretched girl to serve you. I vow she looks for all the world like a pert young witch! She would drive me distracted. Did I hear her speaking of bats? Ugh!"

"Yes." Half distracted herself, Phoebe asked inconsequently, "Mama, can bats trample people?"

"What a ghastly notion! I had supposed they only fly. Have they paws? Lud. I shall have to ask Sinclair. Here we are at last! Now, be *very* careful, child. I do not want Sir George any more upset than he is already."

Phoebe went, trembling, to face her sire.

Sir George stood by the withdrawing room fireplace, his square, weathered face enigmatic. Lady Martha was seated beside the open window that looked onto the terrace. Meredith Carruthers, looking grim but less intimidating in riding dress, bowed over Phoebe's hand and, straightening, shot her a molten glance holding a warning that made her knees wobble.

"At last," said Sir George, "we may get on with this unfortunate business." His stern gaze threw Phoebe deeper into an agony of dread, and imagination led her on a daunting tour of all the possible punishments for her depravity.

". . . have met before, I gather," her father was saying, looking at her expectantly.

'Met before . . . ?' Oh, he must mean that she had met The Tyrant before. She stammered, "Y—yes, sir. We met at the breakfast party the bats gave last spring."

"Good . . . God!" breathed Sir George, staring at his daughter.

"Wherever are your wits gone a'begging?" yelped Lady Eloise nervously. " 'Twas the *Wyndhams'* party!"

Praying the floor might open and swallow her, Phoebe gulped, "D—did I not say so?"

"You said 'twas the *bats'* party." My lady's voice faded. "And I really must discover whether they have paws, horrid creatures."

Carruthers looked from one to the other, astounded.

"What the deuce are you talking about, my lady?" rasped Sir George. "Here we are, faced with the scandal of the year, and you gibble-gabble about bats! Now, Phoebe, Mr. Carruthers has generously taken the blame for the disgraceful contretemps into which you have plunged us, between you. I'll tell you frankly, half the County went home chortling with glee, and I've no doubt the tale is already circulating through Town. You realize that there is but one way to mend the situation."

"You m—mean to . . . to send me off to Aunt Ormsby," she said miserably.

"Lord above, what nonsense!" cried Sir George, casting his eyes at the ceiling.

From the window-seat, Lady Martha put in, "Such a step would merely verify your shame, child. What your papa seeks to do is to coat it with at least a veneer of respectability."

"To which end," Sir George interposed, with a hard look at his formidable parent, "Mr. Carruthers has made a most attractive offer for your hand, Phoebe. And I have accepted."

It seemed to Phoebe that those words rang on the air with the lingering resonance of a great bell. She was so shocked that it was incredible to her that she did not faint. It was not possible! Married to *The Tyrant*? Only because she had tried to help a fellow human being, was she to suffer this most frightful fate?

25

She turned a white, stricken face to Carruthers and met eyes of grey ice and an expression that she thought positively Satanic.

Lady Eloise took her daughter's cold little hand and led her to Sir George, who in turn took her to Carruthers. "Sir," he said, "this is a havey-cavey business at best, and one you might have prevented by the use of a little—ah, gentlemanly restraint."

Carruthers's sneer became even more marked, but he drawled, "I was—overwhelmed by your daughter's beauty, sir. I'll not apologize for it."

Numb, Phoebe allowed her hand to be passed into his strong clasp.

He bowed and kissed her fingers, straightened, and said with a tight smile that did not reach his flinty eyes, "I shall strive to make you a good husband, ma'am."

She made no reply, staring at him as one in a trance. He squeezed her fingers so hard she almost cried out, but it reminded her that Death still hung over them. Somehow, she replied, "You do me great honour, sir," and sank into a curtsy from which she was not at all sure she would be able to rise.

Carruthers's hand was under her elbow. Lifting her, he said blandly, "I think this has been a surprise for your daughter, sir. Since we are now betrothed, I beg the indulgence of a moment alone with her."

Sir George frowned. "I'd have thought you'd enough 'moments' last night! We want no more lapses from polite behaviour, Carruthers."

Carruthers stiffened, his dark head drawing up and back; a look was levelled at the older man that appeared to have come from some Olympian height.

Before he could comment, however, Lady Martha inserted majestically, " 'Tis something tardy to be speaking of propriety, George. I think a stroll in the garden for a newly betrothed pair could scarce by construed an evil act. Especially since it is full daylight."

Carruthers darted a measuring glance at her. "Thank you, ma'am. By your leave, Miss Ramsay . . ." and he ushered his fiancée to the terrace.

Neither spoke until they were out of earshot of the house, then he muttered, "A fine mess you've got me into!"

"I!" she gasped, jerking her hand from his arm and glaring up at him, a surge of anger restoring her sagging spirits. "Was there *nothing* else you could think of to extricate us from this—this horrid predicament?"

26

With a lack of gallantry that was new to her experience, he retaliated, "Do you think I would have resorted to it had there been any other choice? Your papa saw that I had no way out, and lost no time in pressing his advantage!"

Phoebe gave a squeak of rage. "Do you fancy him desperate to fire me off? If you *must* know, my lord Tyrant, I've no least wish to be *Lady* Tyrant!"

She was appalled the moment her hasty tongue had uttered the scathing words. Carruthers became very pale, and she shrank before the savage anger in his eyes. "Perhaps," he said in a soft voice she found unutterably menacing, "you will be so good as to tell me why you chose *that*—particularly charming appellation."

'If I say it is what his brother calls him, we'll likely be burying the poor lad,' she thought, and said disdainfully, "Perchance because you always are so stern and cross."

The piercing eyes seemed to transfix her. "Whereas you admire foppish dandies with pretty wigs and lisps and mouths full of insincere flattery," he sneered. "How fortunate for you, ma'am, that I like this no better than you, and have no slightest desire to make you my bride!"

'Wretched, horrid beast!' she thought, and said, fluttering her fan, "Dear me! How *very* lacking in manners you are to say so!"

"A shared fault, apparently. At least there will be no hypocrisy between us. However"—he reclaimed her hand despite her angry efforts to pull it away, and dragged it ruthlessly to his lips—"do you not make at least an *appearance* of finding me somewhat less repellent than an earwig, we shall land ourselves, and your family, properly in the suds."

She blenched at the reminder and swayed to him gracefully. "I apologize. But you must make an effort too, sir, and try not to freeze me with your eyes! You obviously do not find me attractive either, but—"

"I didn't say I do not find you attractive. You are a very beautiful girl, which you know perfectly well."

How odd it was that he could say something nice and contrive to make it sound an insult. Seething, she said, "I was not fishing for compliments, Mr. Carruthers, but—"

"Then what were you fishing for?"

"I was trying to tell you," she said, gnashing her little white teeth as he led her along the path once more, "that I am—am promised to another gentleman."

He checked and stared down at her, his mouth twisting into that horrid quirkish grin she could learn to hate. "What— without the approval of your parents?" He clicked his tongue. "Never say I am about to be called out by some pretty young whelp?"

"He is *not* a pretty young whelp!"

His right eyebrow lifted to match the left one. "Ah, an ugly young whelp," he said, interested. "Well now, that's more promising."

"He is not a whelp of any kind, but a fine brave gentleman."

"Nonsense! No 'fine brave gentleman' would behave in so underhanded a fashion."

"Well, no matter what you think," she said crossly, "he *is* a gentleman, and—" A dread possibility dawned. "Oh, my! Are you very rich, Mr. Carruthers?"

"Would that make me more acceptable to you?" he sneered.

"It would make you acceptable to my family."

Amusement crept into his eyes which, oddly enough, suddenly seemed less grey than blue. "You're honest to a fault, ma'am. In the basket, are they?"

"Not deeply, but sufficient to put me in the position of—" She broke off, biting her lip.

"Aha! So your 'fine brave gentleman' has big empty pockets, eh? Has Lady Martha taken him in aversion, besides?"

The wretch had evidently realized that it was Grandmama who ruled the Ramsays. Phoebe murmured rather forlornly, "Everyone else likes him very much. And Grandmama has never *said* she does not approve. Only—I do not think it is just because he has no fortune, poor dear. He is excessively handsome, you see."

"Oh, egad! If your grandmama don't set much store by looks, I may well be doomed!"

Doomed, indeed! Refusing to respond to the teasing glint in his eyes, Phoebe agreed with a sigh, "Yes, for she holds that very handsome people are often vain and spoiled."

"I concur. Indeed, were I on the search for a bride, I would far rather settle for a kind plain girl with a well-informed mind than any Toast who is all looks and bosom and has not two thoughts in her head."

Phoebe shot an outraged glare at him and found him contemplating her low neckline. "You are a vulgar man, Mr. Carruthers," she declared, unequivocally. "The most important thing

28

is not how much we dislike each other, but how we are to get *out* of this horrid bog."

"To the contrary, Miss Ramsay," he declared, just as unequivocally. "Can you only stop thinking quite so much of yourself, you'll realize the most important thing is that we have now an excuse for you and your intrepid brother to visit my estate."

She flushed scarlet. "Oh! You mean to help poor Lieutenant Lascelles. You are perfectly right, of course. What have you in mind, sir?"

He said thoughtfully, "Your brother is bookish, I gather?"

"Yes. Quite brilliant. In fact"—a dimple flickered briefly beside her vivid mouth—"if we are so unfortunate as to be wed, you will likely have the expense of sending him to University. Another potential pitfall for you, sir."

"A pitfall I mean to avoid at all costs, I assure you, Miss Ramsay! Nonetheless, if we can find a large hamper, throw a shelf across the upper quarter and fill it with books, we may be able to slip our rebel into the lower section."

"But books weigh a ton!"

"And he weighs very little, poor devil. Now I've to go into Town and at least make a pretense of arranging a settlement and introducing your sire to my man of business. I've sent my valet posting back to the Hall with a brief letter of explanation for my mother and a warning to expect us tomorrow evening."

"You had brought a valet here?" she said, puzzled.

"I had been invited to overnight."

"I see. Are you, then, well acquainted with my papa, sir?"

He ran one long finger down the line of his jaw. "I know him slightly. I have met Lady Martha Ramsay a time or two. She invited me. All of which is beside the point. Can you and your brother manage while I'm gone, do you think?"

"We shall do our feeble best, but—oh dear! Here comes my mama. Mr. Carruthers, pray indulge my selfishness a little and tell me *how* we are to escape this betrothal?"

He took up her hand and again bowing his head over it, murmured, "I don't know. But by God, ma'am, if 'tis humanly possible to escape your toils, I'll do it, I promise you!"

She smiled on him and, as he bent lower, pinched the end of his nose. Hard.

He gave a gasp.

"Adieu, dear sir," she murmured. And whispered, "Let that be a lesson to you, Mr. Meredith Tyrant!"

"Adieu," he said, breathing erratically and his eyes rather watery. "Miss Phoebe Shrew!"

"Ah," cried Lady Eloise, coming up with them. "So you really *are* in love! How delicious!"

"Oh—Jupiter!" muttered Sinclair Ramsay, staring across the quiet book room at Carruthers. "Poor little Phoebe."

Carruthers bowed and said an ironic *"Merci bien!"*

"Oh! Your pardon, sir! I didn't mean—only—"

"Yes, I know. Your sister has other plans, she told me. However, I'm afraid we both are trapped and must make the best of it for the time. Meanwhile, what of Lascelles? Have you been able to provide him with food and water?"

"Yes." Sinclair glanced to the closed door and crossed to stand beside the window-seat onto which Carruthers had settled himself. "He goes along fairly well, save that he is so weak, and . . ."

"And?"

"I pray I may be wrong, but—I fancied he was feverish this morning."

"Damn! We do but need him to start raving in delirium! You've not been giving him wine?"

"Yes. It seems to strengthen him. Should I not?"

"I'm no physician, but I'd say discontinue it. Try barley water, rather. What about a hamper?"

"I've just the thing, and the beauty of it is that we've used it before to convey my books when we go down to Worthing in August. The lackeys are accustomed to its weight. I'll have it brought down from the attic to my bedchamber, smuggle Lascelles to my room tonight, and get him inside it in the morning before you come. You *will* be back tomorrow, sir?"

"Yes. If I leave within the hour. Your sire is protesting already at my haste, so I've had to invent that my brother is ailing. Oh—you will meet Jeff, incidentally, for he's down for the Long Vacation."

"A college man, is he?" Sinclair's face lit up. "We'll have plenty to discuss, then."

"I doubt it. Jeff is no scholar. More interested in muslin than leather bindings, unfortunately. Well, I must be off." He stood, adjusting the sword-belt about his lean middle. "Incidentally, Ramsay, I suggest it would be less trouble were you to have your hamper brought down here. You'd have not such a distance to haul Lance, and you could explain it away by saying you wished to take some of these books. I doubt any of your servants would find aught in that to quarrel with."

Sinclair agreed this was a better plan and they walked to the door together. Sinclair added diffidently, "Sir, you've been jolly good about all this. I'm most damnably sorry you were dragged into it."

To his surprise, Carruthers clapped him on the shoulder. "So am not I. Lance and I have cried friends since childhood. Did he lose that fine head through any neglect of mine, I'd never forgive myself. I should rather be thanking you, Ramsay. I told your sister you probably fancy yourself a fine high-flown hero, but—"

Sinclair gave a furious exclamation and jerked away.

"Perhaps I had better have said, an idealistic idiot," Carruthers amended with a twinkle. "Nonetheless, for such a sprig, you've done not too badly."

Sinclair met the strange pale eyes that were so at odds with the bronzed face, and sensed it was high praise from this blunt individual who appeared to pay little heed to the flowery speech and manners of fashion. Pleased, he flushed darkly, and said a shy "Thank you."

"One thing," murmured Carruthers, his hand on the latch, "Keep your sister clear, insofar as you are able. And—don't fret for her sake, Ramsay. I'll break this betrothal in some fashion, so that I may continue my blissful bachelorhood and she can wed her gallant Adonis."

His blue eyes glazed with shock and his handsome features suddenly pale and drawn, Brooks Lambert gasped, "*Meredith . . . Carruthers?* Of Meredith Hall in Wiltshire? No! My God— no! I don't *believe* it!"

The afternoon was warm and muggy, the silence of the birds warning of the storm that Ada Banham's bones had forecast earlier. The greenish light inside the graceful little summerhouse played softly upon Phoebe's pale green gown and deepened the hue of the great eyes that gazed anxiously at her stricken suitor. Poor dear Brooks. If only she could tell him. But, much as she loved him, he was first a soldier, second a lover, and she dared not confide so deadly a secret. "Are you—acquainted?" she asked.

"Acquainted?" He drew a hand across his eyes as though

trying to wipe away his confusion. *"Acquainted?"* He laughed harshly. "Oho, am I not!"

The following flood of profanity brought her to her feet, crying an appalled "*Brooks!* My mama allowed me to tell you, but I'll not listen to this!"

He checked abruptly. "Oh—Jove, I do apologize! It was just—I cannot credit—" He was silent a moment, then closed his eyes briefly and said in a controlled but quivering voice, "Phoebe—Meredith Carruthers is—is my *uncle*!"

She stared at him, her pretty mouth falling open slightly. "But—but he *cannot* be! Why, he must be only a few years older than you!"

"He is nine and twenty. Paul Carruthers had two daughters of his first marriage. His wife died when their eldest girl, Sylvia, was fifteen. Carruthers remarried, and Meredith was born. He was one year old when Sylvia eloped with George Lambert against Paul's wishes. I was born to them the following year. Paul cut my mama off, of course. Never spoke to her again, or left her a penny." He drove one fist into his palm. "Of all the scurvy tricks. *Him*—of all men!"

Phoebe, who had sunk down beside him again, tried to collect her scattered wits. "You told me once that you've an uncle who—who makes you an allowance. He—he is not . . . ?"

Again, that bitter travesty of a laugh rang out. "You have it, ma'am!"

She had never seen him so enraged, and, distressed, she said gently, "My poor dear, I know what a shock this is, but—he *is* your kinsman, and if he has been so generous as to—"

"Generous! If you could see him, lording it over his hapless tenants, wringing the last ounce out of the poor clods! As for his wretched brother, God help him! Jeff writhes under Meredith's heel!"

"Good gracious! I thought—that is, he seemed brusque, but a gentleman-like type of man, withal."

"Very," he responded scornfully. "Like his father before him, who drove his poor wife to—" He closed his lips over that improper utterance.

Dismayed, she peered up at him anxiously. "To—what?"

He stood and stamped off to stare blindly across the park. His shoulders sagged then. He said brokenly, "That was very bad of me. Forgive, I beg you, Phoebe, and forget what I said. It is not really so, and was most dishonourable in me to rail at him when he has been so good. Merry's a—a hard man, but a just one. Only—the thought of my perfect love . . . given into his keeping!" He swung around, revealing a ravaged countenance. "Phoebe, my darling girl, I am behaving like a proper fool. How much worse it must be for you!"

Phoebe lowered her eyes, wringing her hands in helpless misery. In a flash he was beside her and had dropped to one knee, his strong grip closing over her agitated hands. "I won't let it happen, dearest. I swear it! I'll take you off to the Border, before—"

"Elope?" she gasped, horrified. "Brooks! You cannot mean it!"

He said wildly, "It would be better than seeing you condemned to life with a man you do not love."

'It would, indeed,' she thought, but she put a quieting hand over his lips. "I should not say this, but—I think Carruthers is not—that is, there is a slight hope that he is—er, reluctant."

His eyes had narrowed. He searched her face. "Do you say he was pushed into it?" He frowned, then muttered, "Aye, Lucille would, at that."

"Lucille? Do you speak of his mama?"

He nodded. "A lovely little creature but has known precious little of happiness, poor soul. She is terrified of him."

"But—you said—"

"She can influence him. True. He tries to make amends. And, come to think of it, he never has been much in the petticoat line." Brightening, he returned to sit beside her once more. "This puts a different light on things. Love, why didn't you tell me at once, and I'd not have ranted so?"

She said ruefully, "I should not have told you at all and perhaps raised false hopes. Even now, Lamb, it will have to be handled very carefully. My family is—"

"Ecstatic, I do not doubt! Oh yes, I can quite see that!" He scowled, thinking rapidly. "When do you go to the Hall?"

"Tomorrow, if Mr. Carruthers gets back from London in time for us to make a start."

"I see. Look, Phoebe darling, I'm due a leave, for I haven't had one since I took that wound at Prestonpans. I'll talk to my colonel. I'm fairly sure he'll let me go, and I can be in Wiltshire within a day or two, at most."

Alarmed, she said, "Oh, Brooks, I wish you will rather give me time to try and work with Mr. Carruthers towards a solution. Besides, where would you stay? I believe his estate is rather isolated."

33

"It is, and I shall stay *there*, m'dear. Gad, but there's room enough for me! I'm a member of the family, don't forget, and Lucille is fond of me—deluded woman!" He grinned whimsically, then his fine eyes clouded. He asked, "Have you told Carruthers you love me?"

"I told him I was fond of another gentleman, but mentioned no names."

"Hmmn. As well. Better to wait a bit. And—what d'you mean 'fond'?" He took her in his arms and smiled lovingly down at her. "I will bring you out of this beastly coil and you'll marry me, if only out of gratitude, and never have to be so menaced again. Only think—this is bad enough, but next time it might be even worse. I heard your papa likes Olderwood. . . . Only say yes, beloved mine, and I'll protect you for so long as I live."

It was true; Papa and Olderwood were bosom bows. Phoebe shuddered. "Very well, Brooks. If we can break this betrothal, I'll tell my parents I wish to marry you."

"Allelulia!" he cried, and kissed her.

❧ *Chapter 3* ❧

Julia Ramsay, at fourteen a younger version of her beautiful sister, gazed at Phoebe with huge, awed green eyes, and said, "I thought we *never* would be allowed to speak to you in private. Is it true, Phoebe?"

"Did you really spend the whole evening alone with him in the basement?" asked nine-year-old Belinda, perched on Phoebe's bed, her eyes scarcely less wide than those of Julia. "What were you doing?"

"What do you think she was doing?" snapped Julia impatiently. "When a lady allows a gentleman to take her into a dark basement for hours and *hours*, he is trying to fix his attentions, and—"

"You mean he was kissing you and mauling you about?" said Belinda. "Ugh!"

This irritated Sinclair, who had been scanning the drivepath, and he exclaimed, "Oh, you two wretched girls! How do you know what goes on between a gentleman and his—er, chosen lady?" He glimpsed the militant gleam in Phoebe's eyes and added hurriedly, "And besides, why should you say 'ugh' in that silly way? Carruthers ain't a monster."

"He has been marked by the Devil!" declared Belinda. "Christina Rosewood says he is from an evil house!"

Phoebe protested angrily, "What a dreadful thing to say! For shame!"

"Of course the Rosewood chit says so," jeered Sinclair. "Carruthers went out with her brother, and—"

"And ran him through, and through . . . and through!" Belinda had seized Phoebe's new pink sunshade and lunged with it, duello-fashion. "Liver . . . lights . . . straight to the heart!"

"Revolting little ghoul!" said Julia. "If Martin Rosewood had been run through the heart he'd be dead, which he is not,

35

for he pulled my hair in church just last Sunday and pretended it an accident! Phoebe—how is it you have never mentioned Mr. Carruthers but kept the secret close-locked in your heart? Do you love him with a deathless passion?''

"No, I do not!" the newly betrothed maiden answered forcefully.

Julia gave a small dramatic screech. "You are *sacrificing* yourself, so that Sin will not go off and shrivel up in India!''

Phoebe threw a repentant glance at Sinclair's frowning face. "In the first place,'' she said, trying to mend her fences, "we were *not* in the basement for hours and hours, and Mr. Carruthers was not—er, mauling me about, as you so inelegantly phrase it, Belinda!''

Julia asked, puzzled, "Then what *were* you doing?''

"Lighting a fire, of course," explained Sinclair.

"A—fire? But . . . why?''

"Mr. Carruthers had a magic powder from his friend the Devil, and he threw it in the flames. It causes busybody little girls to turn into newts. You are getting gills on your neck already, Julia!''

His sisters subsided into giggles, and Phoebe asked, "Sin, why has Mr. Carruthers fought so many duels?''

He shrugged and said evasively, "He ain't, er, the most placid fellow I ever met."

"No more than any other volcano,'' Phoebe agreed drily.

Staring at her, Julia asked, "Is he very ugly? You are *so* beautiful, it doesn't seem right. And Brooks Lambert . . . oh *poor* young man! He will pine away."

"He will volunteer for a mission of deadly danger,'' whispered Belinda, "and be mortally wounded and lie and die in the dust with your name on his lips!'' Tears came into her eyes. She blinked, and said unsteadily, "Oh, I do hope he will not, for he is so very kind and handsome, and always gives me sugar plums."

Sinclair cried excitedly, "Here they come! Lord, but Carruthers must have rushed Papa along!''

They all ran to the window. Peeping through the lace curtains, Julia said, "Why, he's very good-look—Oh! I see. The other side of his face *is* scarred, isn't it? Still, it's not nearly as bad as I thought, and my, but he has fine long legs!''

"*Julia!*" exclaimed Phoebe, much shocked. And looking.

Belinda gave a shriek. "He *saw* me! Oooh! What diabolical

eyes! They pierced me to the gizzard!'' She flung herself backwards on the bed.

The door burst open and Ada ran in, her dark face a mask of tragedy. "He's *here*, Miss Phoebe!" she wailed. "He's *come!*"

"Oh my Lord!" snorted Sinclair. " 'By the pricking of my thumbs, something wicked this way comes.' "

Ada gasped, "Oh, Mr. Sinclair! You feel it, too!"

"Gammon!" He slanted a meaningful look at Phoebe. "Come along, old lady. The sooner we're out of this madhouse, the better! No, not you two brats! You'd best go and make yourselves presentable. I've no doubt Papa will wish to present you to Daemon Carruthers."

Julia and Belinda fled, squealing with excitement, and Phoebe walked with her brother to the stairs. "Sin," she whispered, "how will you get poor Lieutenant Lascelles into the hamper?"

"Already done. I smuggled him into the book room before dawn, and kept the maids out by telling them I was studying. I'd an idea Carruthers would light a fire under Papa, so I tucked Lascelles into the hamper half an hour ago."

"Poor soul! He looked dreadfully bad last night, and now this long journey will be so taxing. Sin, you do not think he will expire before ever we reach Meredith Hall?"

"After what he's been through, m'dear, I fancy this will be an easy ride for him." Despite the light words, his young face was grim. His fear was that the carriage might be stopped and searched. If that happened, there was but one course to follow; he would have to take full responsibility and be prepared to pay the hideous penalty. At least, he was not the head of his house and his family did not stand to lose everything; especially when he swore they had no knowledge of his Jacobite connections. On the other hand—he frowned, riddled with guilt—if Meredith Carruthers were caught, it would be a very different matter!

Sir George Ramsay had the sensation of having ridden a whirlwind. He had been rushed to London, where Carruthers's solicitor had received them despite the lateness of the hour. A report had been offered of the financial colour of the Carruthers holdings and investments. His future son-in-law had snapped out terse instructions for a most generous settlement. Dazed and delighted, Sir George was also considerably exhausted by the time he alighted from the dusty carriage.

That Carruthers meant to set off at once, hauling half his

prospective bride's family on an extended visit to his country seat, Sir George found baffling. He himself had prior commitments that made it impossible for him to accompany his daughter, as Eloise and Sinclair were to do. He rejoiced with his wife in private over their good fortune, and went down to wave goodbye. The little procession set forth: three carriages, and Carruthers riding Percent, Sinclair's favourite hack. Sir George and his three remaining ladies went back into the house. Sir George adjourned to the small saloon and took off his wig. He fell asleep blissfully recalling Meredith Carruthers's properties and fortune and, above all, that splendid settlement.

Not until they were well under way did Phoebe fully realize the enormity of their peril. Carruthers had warned that the roads were clogged with military; they were liable to be stopped and searched at any point of their long journey, and if the wounded fugitive was discovered, her beloved brother would certainly pay with his head, and very likely Carruthers would also. She and her mother could claim complete unawareness, and there was no doubt but that Sinclair and Carruthers would swear the ladies had had no knowledge of the presence of a traitor, but it would be small consolation to escape with her life if her brother were to lose his. She felt crushed by the threat of such a disaster, and it was all she could do to maintain the air of excited anticipation that was, she knew, expected of her.

My lady Eloise was not surprised that her son should choose to occupy the third carriage in solitary state, surrounded by his books. She did think it rather odd that so dashing a lover as Carruthers should elect to ride, rather than be in the coach with his beloved, but there was no doubt but that he was the athletic type of man. She also thought it peculiar that the large old coach which conveyed the servants and a good deal of the luggage should have the second spot rather than bringing up the rear, but she kept such thoughts to herself. She was not sorry of the opportunity to have a long talk with her naughty daughter, but Phoebe's rather astonishing lack of knowledge of the gentleman with whom she must certainly have been conducting a clandestine flirtation puzzled her. "Has he told you *nothing* of his family, or his estates, my love?" she asked with a lift of the eyebrows.

"He is—er, not much of a talker, Mama," said Phoebe, adding in desperation, "but he has a well-informed mind."

"Does he, so? Upon what subjects?"

'Good heavens!' thought Phoebe, and then remembered Carruthers telling Lieutenant Lascelles he had been at Culloden. "Military matters," she replied.

My lady stared at her. "He talks to you of . . . *military* matters?"

"Yes. For I was most interested to hear of—Cumberland, you see. And—and dogs, of course." (He would have dogs, surely?)

"How very . . . romantical," said her mother feebly, trying to equate such scintillating conversation with a man who had ruthlessly swept her daughter into a secluded basement for an hour.

Unhappily aware of her mother's bewilderment, Phoebe improvised, "And he is very—er, poetical."

My lady brightened. This was more promising. "Whom does he favour, love?"

'Whom, indeed?' thought the bedevilled Phoebe. If she named Shakespeare, it would be just like so contrary an individual to know not a single line when Mama asked him, as she most certainly would. "He—composes it himself," she declared.

"How splendid! I would never have guessed, for he looks so very much the strong, silent type of man. I vow, you can *never* judge by appearances!"

Phoebe seized this remark to turn the conversation to the appearance of one of her mama's most despised 'friends' and the creation she had worn to the ball. Since this had been a truly splendid garment, and the lady in question was endowed with an equally splendid bosom, most of which had been generously displayed, this launched my lady into such a long-winded discourse upon the lineage, disposition, miserable marriage, and obnoxious offspring of her 'dear friend' that Phoebe was able to indulge her private worries for several miles.

When they stopped for luncheon at a fine posting house near Hindhead, it was discovered that the second carriage had taken another route. Swinging from the saddle, Carruthers handed the ladies down the steps and into the inn, explaining that he had thought it as well to send the servants by another road. "Quicker," he said, with a charming smile, "but rather dull. I thought it might be nice if you were to find all your belongings neatly unpacked by the time you arrive at the Hall."

"How very thoughtful," said my lady, beaming at him.

He earned her further goodwill by having ridden ahead and

procured chambers so that the ladies could refresh themselves before partaking of the luncheon he had ordered. He was ushering them up the stairs when Lady Eloise glanced back and said, "My goodness, whatever has become of Sinclair? I will go and—"

"No, no, dear ma'am," he said. "He's likely fallen asleep over his books. I'll roust him out. Do you go and be comfortable."

"Do you know, my love," said Lady Eloise as they went along the narrow upstairs hall, "I was rather intimidated by Mr. Carruthers at first, and own I worried for your happiness, but I see I was mistaken. What a perfect gentleman. And such a lovely smile. I fancy you two will deal very well indeed."

Phoebe replied deviously, "I pray you are right, dear Mama."

The groom who was serving as coachman to Sinclair Ramsay was not at all upset to be ordered into the coffee room, and the ostlers had already unharnessed the team and taken them off when Carruthers flung open the door and jumped into the carriage. "How is he?" he asked with an anxious glance at the large hamper that took up most of one seat.

"Asleep, I think," said Sinclair. "Any sign of troopers, sir?"

"Yes, dammit! They're thick as thieves. I've detoured twice. I sent your servants ahead purely to get them out of the way. My coachman thinks I've run mad, I think, but if it looks as bad when we leave here, I may well have to tell him to detour again, and we're already late."

"But surely most of the troops detain north-south travellers?"

"Probably. But there's Bristol and the west coast to keep the military active. You go and join the ladies. Your sister will guess what we're about, but tell your mama that I mislike the competency of the ostlers so am staying out here. Eat your luncheon, then come, and I'll go in. We dare not leave our cargo." He raised his voice slightly. "Lance—are you awake, old fellow?"

A breathless, barely audible "Yes" answered him.

Carruthers slanted a grim look at Sinclair. "This is devilish hard on him. Did you raise the lid at all?"

"Twice. And let him stretch out his legs. And he has fruit and bread and water in there."

Carruthers nodded. "Easy with the water, Lance! Hang on, you madman. We'll get you through. Ramsay—I mean to reconnoitre carefully when we approach my home. If I see troops

I'll ride back and tell your coachman that one of his leaders looks to have picked up a stone. Do you hear, Lance? I'll choose a spot close to as good a hiding place as I can, and Ramsay will help you out of the coach as fast as may be. Lie low until we're away, then get to cover. Ramsay or I will come to you just as soon as possible. You understand?''

"I do. And . . . from the bottom of my heart—thank you both.''

Sinclair left the carriage and went into the dining room. Phoebe and his mother were at luncheon. Lady Eloise received his airy explanation of Carruthers's absence without question, remarking that Sir George liked a man who took care of his cattle before himself. Sinclair ate quickly, excused himself, and went back to the yard, thus enabling Carruthers to seek his luncheon.

Settling himself down, Sinclair took up a book. The door was wrenched open. He looked squarely into the belligerent features of a beefy dragoon, a straw between his teeth. "What you got in here?'' he demanded. "Family jewels, belike?''

Sinclair's heart jumped into his throat, and his mouth felt suddenly very dry, but this was not his first brush with death, and he managed to preserve a cool demeanour. "You might well think so,'' he said, raising the lid of the hamper and holding up a book. "My father's library, or some of it. First editions. Wherefore I am not allowed to stay for another tankard, but must stick out here with the fusty things!''

The trooper scrambled into the coach. "Let's have a look here.''

Sinclair, his palms wet, slouched back onto the seat. "Help yourself,'' he said, and knew he would fight for his life if necessary.

The trooper picked up a book and, holding it upside down, peered at the contents. "Can't see nothing valleyble 'bout this,'' he muttered.

"Well, as you see, it was published in Germany in 1480. Please have a care with the pages. My sire loves every one.''

"Ar. Then that's why I can't read it, eh? Writ in German.''

"True.''

The trooper tossed the book into the hamper and selected another. "And this'n?''

"Latin.''

The trooper said a comprehensive "Cor!'' and spat out his straw. "What's any good Englishman want wi' a book as is writ

41

in a foreign language? Proper foolish I call it!'' And much to Sinclair's relief, he jumped out and went off shaking his head over the stupidity of the Quality.

Sinclair leaned back his head. ''You awake, Lascelles?''

''No . . .'' said Lascelles feebly. ''I just died!''

Carruthers, meanwhile, had joined the ladies, voicing much anxiety as to their rate of progress, and begging their pardon if he ate hurriedly. Good manners forbade that Lady Eloise engage him in an involved conversation, but his hand jerked after one of her remarks and he slanted a stupefied glance at her. ''*Poetry*, ma'am?''

''It is no use to dissemble,'' she said with a little laugh. ''Your betrothed has betrayed you, sir. I shall be most eager to test your skill before we leave Meredith Hall.''

Carruthers turned, speechless, to his 'betrothed.'

Phoebe fluttered her fan at him. ''I had to brag of *some* of your accomplishments, sir,'' she told him, ''lest my mama think you have none.''

His answering smile was rather tight.

As he had feared, an hour after they resumed their journey, he was again obliged to detour, to the predictable indignation of his coachman, who scolded, ''If we takes that ugly north road, Mr. Meredith, sir, we'll be lucky do we get home 'fore dark!''

The 'ugliness' he referred to was the condition of the surface. Phoebe, suspecting what Carruthers was about, did her best to placate her mother, who was not only becoming tired, but vowed she was black and blue. Sunset was painting the North Downs with a mellow pink glow, but dark clouds edged the horizon when Carruthers announced that they were now on his lands. He rode off to scan the countryside ahead, then cantered Percent to the following carriage and warned Sinclair in a low voice, ''Trouble. Tell Lance to prepare to abandon ship at the curve of the road!''

He stopped the lead coach at the top of the next hill, and assisted the weary ladies to alight. Phoebe was aghast when she realized Sinclair's carriage did not follow, and her frightened eyes flew to Carruthers.

He said easily, ''I'm not surprised. Rather suspected the off leader had picked up a stone. I'll go back and see how the coachman is managing.''

Trying not to appear as scared as she felt, Phoebe put her arm about her wilting mother and walked with her to the rim of the hill. They looked over emerald valleys and darkly wooded slopes, with off to the east the roseate glitter of a large lake, reflecting the fiery skies. To the west rose the chimneys and Gothic church tower of a village, and here and there scattered cottages and farmhouses were shaded by venerable old trees and surrounded by tidy fields.

"Oh," Phoebe exclaimed, "but it really *is* lovely country, Mama."

Lady Eloise was thinking that it really was *not* very considerate of Mr. Carruthers to have subjected ladies to such an exhausting day. "I wonder how much longer we have to drive," she said, failing to keep the weariness from her voice.

Carruthers galloped up and dismounted. "The village you see is called Dewbury Prime," he offered. "There is another on the estate, some five miles north, called Dewbury Minor."

"It reminds me of Southwind," murmured Phoebe.

He glanced at her. The warm lamps of sunset illumined her face and brightened the red-gold ringlets that she had not powdered today. She looked nostalgic, and, curious, he asked, "A similar estate, ma'am?"

She gave a rather embarrassed laugh. "You will think me silly, but I once wrote a short story about a girl living on a country estate. This is almost exactly what I described. Does your home turn out to be a half-timbered Queen Anne with roses round the door, I shall be more than a little disconcerted, sir."

He did not reply, but the twinkle in his eyes was marked as he offered an arm to each lady.

Lady Eloise asked, "*Is* it a Queen Anne, Mr. Carruthers?"

"I mean to make you wait and see, ma'am," he said teasingly. The second coach came up, and he called, "Why do you not ride with your family now, Ramsay? You surely must have completed whatever you were trying to accomplish today."

Sinclair replied brightly, "I believe I have, and I think it will not hurt to let it rest for a few hours, at least."

Sublimely unaware of these double entendres, Lady Eloise reached out to him fondly. "Such a passion for books has my clever son, Mr. Carruthers. Oh, dear! Only look, there are some more of those wretched dragoons! I suppose we are to be stopped and searched and asked all manner of stupid questions!"

Leading them back to the waiting coach, Carruthers asked, "Do the dragoons alarm you, ma'am?"

"I do not like to think of what they're about, merely. What a nuisance this Rebellion has been, to be sure."

Above her head, Carruthers met Phoebe's eyes. He said drily, "Nuisance is a mild word, ma'am."

A few minutes later they were surrounded by redcoats. The young Ensign in command had a round face and a sneering insolence. Carruthers waited through his first bullying, then interrupted coldly, "Under whose command are you, sir?"

The Ensign was affronted and replied with curt resentment that his superior officer was Major Broadbent.

"A fine soldier," said Carruthers. "Hilary Broadbent and I served at Culloden together. You will please to tell him that Lieutenant Meredith Carruthers sends his compliments and he must come to the Hall and meet my betrothed." He frowned as a trooper engaged in a blasphemous dispute with the already irritated coachman. "You should keep your men more in hand, Ensign."

The Ensign stammered and flushed, roared commands at his men to be done, and waved the carriages on.

Sinclair chuckled, and said *sotto voce*, "Jolly well done, sir."

"An unpleasant young man," said Lady Eloise. "Only suppose we had been obliged to fear him!"

Phoebe asked uneasily, "In what way, Mama?"

My lady answered, "I could not help but think, you know, watching him, only suppose we were a Jacobite family, trying to smuggle one of our loved ones to safety—a son, perhaps, and brother, who had fought for the Scottish Prince. How terrifying it would have been, instead of merely a nuisance. For instance, what if we'd hidden a fugitive—say, in your hamper, Sin my love." She gave a shudder. "Just to think of it gives me chills! I cannot guess how people venture such deeds. It would not do for me. I declare I would die of fright!"

There was an instant of rather heavy silence as three culprits avoided each other's eyes. Then Carruthers was handing the ladies into the coach once more. "Just a little way, *mesdames*," he assured them. "When we top the next rise, you will have your first clear view of Meredith Hall."

They began to follow a well-maintained drivepath that wound between lush slopes and meadows begemmed with daisies and Queen Anne's lace. The air was heavy with the scent of flowers and quiet with the drowsy warmth of early evening.

"There is the Hall," said Carruthers. "Take it slowly now, Ferguson."

The carriage slowed. Phoebe peered ahead, and her eyes grew very round.

She looked upon a collection more nearly resembling a miniature town than a residence. It was as though succeeding generations of Carrutherses, dissatisfied with the achievements of their ancestors, had added their own mite to the ongoing expansion, in the shape of a wing here, a conservatory there; a court, to be later enclosed by yet another wing. And the whole, blithely disregarding conformity, incorporating turrets, spires, graceful bay windows, balconies, grim archways, and waterless fountains, was sadly run down. Windows were cracked, paint hung, peeling, steps sagged crookedly. No two sections of the structure were the same shade of paint, and here and there tiles that had fallen from the roofs lay shattered upon the bricked or cobbled pathways.

"Oh . . . my . . . !" murmured Phoebe.

Carruthers's lips tightened. He said curtly, "Had we been able to prepare for you, the gardens would have been weeded, of course."

Gazing upon lawns that more closely resembled abandoned hayfields, flower-beds in which weeds had long since claimed dominion, and hedges that rioted with wild abandon, Lady Ramsay whispered audibly, "What gardens?"

Phoebe battled the urge to giggle, and was rescued when Sinclair exclaimed with incomprehensible enthusiasm, "Oh, I say! What a fascinating place!"

Carruthers looked upon him with approval. "It—er, does need some renovations," he admitted, with a guarded glance at the solemn-faced girl.

A lady had come out onto a terrace at the middle of a gracefully curving central structure. Carruthers waved to her, and a warm smile illumined his face.

'How glad he is to be home,' thought Phoebe, and with an inward revulsion thought also how fortunate it was that, by no stretch of the imagination, would this monstrous collection of ruins ever become home to her.

✑ Chapter 4 ✑

As though determined that arriving guests should inspect each wing in turn, the drivepath first swung westward, then turned in a wide easterly loop around an enormous central lawn, in the middle of which a depressingly headless statue rose from a lopsided and dry fountain. Carruthers rode close to the carriage windows and with polite official-guide demeanour pointed out some features of each wing as they passed.

The Elizabethan, erected in 1601, two-storeyed and half-timbered, with large mullioned windows, contained the state apartments, the chapel, and the larger dining room. The Tudor addition, four storeys high, narrow, red brick and white stucco, with graceful gables and tall intricate chimneys, housed the buttery and the suites of the immediate family, besides quarters for whichever relations chanced (by dint of great persuasive powers on the part of their host, thought Phoebe) to visit the old place. From behind this wing, which had been built in 1490, one could catch glimpses of a building of even greater antiquity that lurked behind the semicircular two-storey central structure, which appeared to have been thrown up in an effort to hide it; the massive towers, battlements, and a flagpole rearing up defiantly at the rear.

Curious, Sinclair asked, "Why is it shut in, sir?"

"Haunted, I expect," Phoebe offered solemnly.

"Oh, yes, all the wings are haunted," Carruthers drawled, just as solemnly. "The old Keep, which is incidentally the original Castle Carruthers, was begun in 1249, and is rather falling away, unfortunately. It has not been occupied for two hundred years."

"But would it not have been simpler to tear it down?" asked my lady.

"My ancestors decided against it, ma'am, and built adjacent,

46

as you can see. The convex wing across the courtyard was originally designed to connect the newer structures directly, making it unnecessary to traverse the Keep. The wing beyond the Keep is Late Mediaeval, circa 1405, but since it was constructed during the period that the Lancasters ruled, we call it our Lancastrian wing."

Phoebe thought the old building quite charming, with its alternating courses of black-and-white flint and white stone. It housed, said Carruthers, the main ballroom and minstrels' gallery, and the famed Hall of Mirrors, plus the servants' quarters. The last of the structures Phoebe thought the most bizarre. Built of grey stone, it was comparatively modern, having been put up in 1659, yet it was remarkable for an abundance of griffins, gargoyles, eagles, and small elaborate towers. A large projecting bay, with decrepit latticed windows, appeared rather forlorn and out of place amid such Italianate extravagances, but Carruthers informed them that their most distinguished guests were invariably quartered there, and that he hoped they would find it comfortable.

Each structure had its own entrance, but the carriage halted before the two great studded doors in the convex central wing, and Carruthers dismounted to assist the ladies to alight.

Decidedly stunned, Lady Eloise murmured as he handed her down, "I fancy you must do a great deal of entertaining, sir."

"Oh, no. Very little," he said in his brusque way. "Well, Mama, I have brought you some splendid company."

Lucille Carruthers came to the edge of the steps to meet them, the great skirts of her beige brocade Watteau gown swaying gracefully. Tiny and frail, she could scarcely wait for her son's introductions before embracing first Lady Eloise and then Phoebe. She was, she proclaimed in a high-pitched, nervous little voice, "so *thrilled*! So surprised. Had no least notion! Oh, how *very* lovely the child is! How*ever* did you win her, Meredith? And so this is your son, ma'am? How charming! So *good* of you to come! No, not in the *least* trouble, we are only delighted!"

Phoebe thought her bewitchingly lovely, with her great wistful blue eyes, delicate features, and the luxuriant hair, high-piled and powdered, that was, she guessed, several shades lighter than that of her dark son.

The butler, whose name was Conditt, was made known to them. He was tall and emaciated-looking, with a gloomy expression and a magnificent carriage, and he ushered them into a wide hall that stretched off to left and right until it was concealed by the inward curve of the wing. Through the windows on the opposite wall, the courtyard of the great Keep could be seen, and the enormous room appeared to be a sort of weaponry, containing many finely preserved suits of armour, some so arranged as to hold great lances, and one splendid fellow in twelfth-century regalia brandishing a mighty two-edged sword. Axes, crossbows, maces, and other mediaeval weapons adorned the walls. Trailing behind her mother and Mrs. Lucille, who were chattering like old friends, Phoebe was brought up short by the sight of a knight on a rather moth-eaten-looking horse, mounted on a dais, and with a large black cat snoozing on his lap. Stunned, she halted to stare, and Carruthers murmured, "This is the Armour Hall, ma'am. We use it only to intimidate guests and are seldom in here, I assure you. The breathing addition to the exhibit is named Satan, and rightly so."

Hurrying to them, Sinclair exclaimed, "Jove, sir! What a place! I could spend a week in this room alone."

"Oh, no, you could not," said Carruthers softly. "Unless I mistake it, my mama will have made many plans, and somehow we've to move our fugitive into the Cut."

Phoebe waited until they passed an apparently petrified lackey, then whispered, " 'The Cut'? What is that?"

"Some of the land hereabouts is very uneven. To the north is a great gorge we call the Quarry, and leading from it for several miles is a fissure known as the Cut. Providentially, there is a small cave in the wall that will provide temporary shelter, at least."

"I'd think it would be the first place the army would search," said Sinclair worriedly. "Poor Lascelles was in a bad way when I got him out of the hamper. I had to all but carry him to the little hollow he told me of, and could not have managed that had you not distracted the coachman, sir."

"A hollow, merely?" Phoebe put in, dismayed. "But Mr. Carruthers, he cannot be left there for long. Did you notice those big clouds? If we have rain, it will likely—"

"Madam," he interrupted, with an impatient toss of the head, "I can but do as I see fit."

"Fit! What is fit about a hollow, and a clammy cave for a man who is half dead already? What about that great crumbly Keep of yours? There surely must be a secret room, or a priest's hole? Almost all old houses have—"

Lucille Carruthers called, "Do come along, Meredith. Poor

Miss Ramsay must be sadly in need of a quiet rest before dinner.'' They hurried to catch up with her, and she went on in gentle chiding, ''Why ever did you bring them by the north road? It really was rather thoughtless.''

Carruthers said, ''Miss Ramsay is much taken with our Armour Hall, Mama. And speaking of thoughtlessness—where is my brother?''

All the animation left Lucille's lovely face. She clasped her hands, regarding her tall son anxiously. ''He was tired of waiting, so took Justice for a walk. I—I am sure he will return directly.''

''One can but hope,'' he muttered.

His mother bit her lip, then hurried off with Lady Eloise.

Phoebe thought in astonishment, 'Brooks was right. The poor little creature is terrified of her own son! How disgraceful!'

They reached the end of the Armour Hall at last, and a liveried footman swept open a connecting door. This, thought Phoebe, must be the Lancastrian wing.

They entered an interminable hall, the occasional double doors on either side suggesting that the rooms were extremely large. Occasional side halls with recessed windows provided the only light, and it was a dim place, having an air of disuse. When they were safely alone, Carruthers said in a low and implacable voice, ''I'll not have a Jacobite traitor under my roof, Miss Ramsay, however good a friend he may be. Not unless there is no possible alternative.''

Phoebe halted. ''We had him in *our* house, and he was not even our friend.''

He looked down at her coldly. ''That was your decision. It is not mine.''

Sinclair said, ''I am most grateful to Carruthers for what he has done, Phoebe. Only look at the pickle I have run him into.''

''Him!'' she flared with righteous indignation and, sticking her pretty nose into the air, she stalked into the vast Great Hall of the new wing, from the centre of which rose the majestic sweep of a mahogany staircase.

''Thank the Lord,'' muttered Carruthers, ''for the carefree life of a bachelor!''

He was, Phoebe told herself, gritting her teeth, an innocent victim. But it was all she could do not to retaliate with a fervent 'Long may you enjoy it!'

* * *

Ada was waiting in the overpowering suite assigned them, and lost no time in informing her employer that she 'could *feel* the ghostes!' her manner implying that Meredith Hall fairly thronged with such apparitions. Phoebe laughed at her. She washed, changed into a wrapper, and enjoyed the tea and biscuits that were sent up. Her efforts to rest were useless, however, and she rang for Ada only half an hour after her handmaiden had departed, and was dressed for the evening, her hair restyled and powdered. She had chosen a new green taffeta gown with the flattened panniers now fashionable. Little lace frills were layered down the front opening of the skirt and repeated in a double line about the swooping neckline. Her only jewellery was the strand of pearls that had been her gift from Papa on the occasion of her come-out. She knew she looked well and, ignoring Ada's horrified wails, ventured forth to explore a little before she went to find her mama and Sinclair.

The passage stretched on and on. The glow from the lighted branches of candles or the wall sconces seemed to peter out ahead, and the air grew chill. Phoebe hesitated, but although Meredith Hall was a perfectly hideous collection of decrepitudes, she could not deny that she found it interesting, and eventually she went on again.

After a few more minutes, however, she had to admit she was properly lost. Wherever she was now, the hallway was becoming wider, the ceiling buttressed by beautifully carved beams. She came to a railed balcony running around a squared well. Below was a huge, dimly seen apartment that must be the ballroom Carruthers had spoken of. At eye level, a gigantic inverted mushroom was suspended from the ceiling high above her. The chandelier protected by that holland cover must be vast. She could envision minstrels playing up here, and below, gentlemen in doublets and hose dancing sedate measures with ladies in huge farthingales. She smiled dreamily. Not fearsome ghosts, as Ada had sensed, but—

She felt rather than heard a stealthy movement just behind her. Trying not to be silly, she waited for someone to speak, but the silence was heavy and undisturbed. The air seemed suddenly much colder and she *was* frightened! She gave a yelp of terror as something icy cold slid into the palm of her hand, and she whirled around, to be confronted by great doleful eyes and an ample sufficiency of wrinkles. She leaned against the railing for a moment, regaining her breath. The rail creaked ominously, and her hand flew instead to the head of her unexpected companion.

The bloodhound wagged his tail shyly and uttered a tentative 'wuff.'

"How do you do?" replied Phoebe, grateful for his presence. "You must be Justice. Perhaps you can guide me to your master, sir." The tail continued to wag, the dog regarding her with patient friendliness. "Find Carruthers!" she ordered sternly. He sat down and repeated his previous remark. It was unchanged through every command Phoebe could think of until she hit on the lucky "Would you like a walk?" whereupon he at once sprang up and began to pad back the way she had come, glancing over his shoulder from time to time, to ensure that she did not draw back from their bargain.

He turned to the left at the first side hall and went down some dim-seen stairs. Phoebe slowed. The hound could see more clearly than she was able to do, besides which he was in familiar territory. By the time she had groped her way to the ground floor, he was out of sight once more. The draperies were drawn across the windows, and with the approach of evening the hall was hushed and shadowy. The dog did not respond to her calls, and there was not a servant in sight. Phoebe suspected she must still be in the Lancastrian wing, and turned to the right. She entered the first room she came to, a shabby saloon bathed in the fading glow of sunset. Here the draperies had not been closed, and she hurried to the window to see if the ominous dark clouds she had noticed earlier were still coming this way.

She had arrived at the rear of the house and looked out onto gardens and lawn with a drivepath beyond. Carruthers, rather impressively clad in evening dress, although his thick dark hair was still unpowdered, stood on a flagged path, hands on hips, in an attitude of vexation. She began to wonder if he was ever cheerful. The casement opened easily enough, and she started to call to him, only to pause when he growled "So you have deigned to appear at long last! Where the devil have you been? I'd think you could manage to be here to welcome my prospective bride and her family!"

Phoebe looked curiously at the young man who strode to meet him. She was as agreeably surprised in him as she had been in his mama. As fair as Meredith was dark, Jeffery was a little taller and of slighter frame. His features were more finely chiselled, and about him clung an air of careless impudence far removed from his brother's stern manner. Phoebe already knew

51

he was eight years the younger, but she would never have supposed them to be brothers; in fact, the only resemblance she could find was that Jeffery's handsome head was as innocent of powder or wig as was Meredith's.

"I do apologize, Merry," he said in a pleasant, repentant voice. " 'Fraid the time eluded me. I know you'll not approve, but truth to tell, I was sallying to the rescue of one sore-afflicted, who—"

Meredith's hands dropped. He said in a near snarl, "*Rescue*, is it? By God, Jeff, if you've allowed yourself to become involved with some damnable Jacobite . . . !"

Phoebe's eyes widened.

"Oh, for Lord's sake," exclaimed Jeffery. "As if I would do such a bog-brained thing! You know how I feel about their idiotic Cause! No, a far more pleasant rescue. I chanced upon the sweetest little creature, trying to climb down a tree whilst carrying a baby bird she had seen fall from its nest."

"Whereupon you played the knight-errant, eh?"

"Did you fancy I'd neglect so fine an opportunity? A luscious morsel, Merry. I've not seen her since I went off to Cambridge, and—"

"You amaze me, brother, considering you're more often out of that seat of learning than in it! Who is this 'luscious morsel'? Do I know the chit?"

" *Assurement!* She has changed in so delightful a way—*many* ways, in fact—that I did not recognize her. And not until old Lockwood came galumphing up, complaining we were on his lands—"

"Were you? *Dammit!* You *know* I'm already at odds with the old curmudgeon!"

"Well, I suppose we were. But Rosalie managed to charm him out of his bad humour."

Meredith said thunderously, "*Rosalie?* Do you refer to Rosalie Smith?"

"Yes. And do not come the ugly, aged mentor. You've had an eye in that direction yourself, from all I hear!"

"She is one of my village people, and I'll not have her pestered!"

"She don't talk like a villager. Nor behave like one. And as for her being pestered—have you *exclusive* pestering rights, perchance?" Jeffery's amiable demeanour had undergone a subtle change; he was standing very straight, resentment in every line of him.

Meredith seized his arm. In a voice harsh with anger, he ground out, "My relationship with Rosalie need not concern you, bantling! Suffice it to say that if you annoy her, you'll answer to me!"

Jeffery wrenched free. " 'Tis my understanding you've brought your future bride here. Do not be a hog, Merry!" He grinned, in a sudden disarming shift of mood. "No, really, old fellow, I am most enthralled by this bombshell you've hurled. To think that 'neath that formidable exterior lurks a yearning heart!"

"Yearning, is it? Say rather that I yielded to Mama's importunities."

"Oh, Gad! Your affianced is a dragon, with tombstone teeth, a squint, and a figure like a blob!"

"Oh!" gasped Phoebe.

Meredith drawled with a grin, "But of course. Did you fancy I would offer for a beauty?"

"I cannot feature you offering at all. I thought you irretrievably shackle-shy. How did you manage it, old lad? Were you the gallant, dropping to one knee to plead your suit? Did she yield her lips with a tremulous sigh, or—"

"Scatter wit! As I recall, she said something about—bats."

Amused, Phoebe saw Jeffery's look of disbelief.

"Bats?" he gasped.

"Bats. And her mama made some remark about their feet."

"Good God! Have they feet, then?"

"Well, of course they have feet! How d'you suppose they go on when they come to earth?"

"Well, I don't think they stroll about much. They hang upside down in caves. By their tails."

"Tails!" They began to walk away side by side, Meredith saying scornfully, "For Lord's sake, Fidget, did you learn nothing in Nature Studies?"

"Never mind about Nature Studies," Jeffery argued, his voice fading. "It sounds to me, Merry, as if you've offered for a proper widgeon. Best get out of it, old lad. I don't want no addle-pated nephews. . . ."

Closing the window without a vestige of guilt for having been so dishonourable as to eavesdrop, Phoebe murmured, "Nor are you likely to have any, Mr. Jeffery Carruthers! Your grump of a brother will probably remain a bachelor to the end of his miserable days. Unless he marries your luscious Rosalie!"

Sinclair was not in his room, but when Phoebe returned to her suite she found her brother sprawled in one of the overstuffed chairs, deep in a book.

He glanced up idly when she entered, then closed the book, staring. "Jove, but you look nice in that green thing."

It was a rare compliment, for although she knew he was proud of her, he seldom deemed it necessary to remark upon his own sister's good looks.

"Thank you, kind sir. But it is not green. According to the milliner who sold me the material, it is *menthe poivrée glacée.*"

"Well, it's jolly pretty, but were I you, old lady, I'd think twice before pitching my peppermint at Carruthers."

"Pitching . . . my . . ." she gasped. "*Oh!* Why ever would I do such a thing?"

"Do not try to throw dust in *my* peepers! He ruffled your feathers when he did not melt at your feet the way all the other fellows do. I saw you fire up."

"To put it mildly." She crossed to perch carefully against the end of the great tester bed. "Now, Sin, you cannot really think I would be interested in such a creature?"

"Because of those scars? I don't think he's so bad-look—"

"Of course not because of the scars. What rubbish! Because of his disposition, rather. He bullies his brother, terrifies his mother, is brusque and lacks polish, and if you say the least little thing that displeases, he fairly freezes you."

"Yes, but don't forget it is thanks to him that we—"

"Oh, pish! Lascelles is his best friend, yet he begrudges every least thing he does for the poor soul! Sin—whatever are you going to do?"

"I'd a word with Carruthers whilst you and Mama were resting. We're to slip out tonight and move Lascelles to this Cut he told us of."

"And that's another thing! How can he be so heartless as to refuse to bring his friend into the Keep? Lascelles would be a deal more comfortable. He is terribly weak and ill, Sin. That wound in his leg must be properly dressed, and he needs food and water, much Carruthers cares!"

Rather surprised by this outburst, Sinclair came to sit beside her. "Not like you to be so unfair, m'dear. Carruthers is head of his house, and as such is directly responsible for the well-being of both his brother and his mama. It is very obvious he dotes on her, and—"

"*Dotes* on her? Why, he frightens the poor lady half to death! Did you notice how scared she became when he started growling about Jeffery? Oh, that reminds me! Sin, I have seen his brother, and we must be very cautious, dearest. Jeffery is a fine-looking young gentleman, a very different article to Meredith. But oh, so contemptuous of the Jacobites." She giggled suddenly. "Meredith flew out at him because he suspected he'd been helping a rebel. I wondered he could keep his countenance, considering what *he* has been about!"

Sinclair's lip curled. "I've heard rumours about Jeff Carruthers. He makes a practice of being rusticated, silly block. Here he is so fortunate as to be able to go to University, and—" He bit off the sentence hastily. "Why did Carruthers think he'd been helping a fugitive?"

"Jeffery said he'd come to someone's rescue, but it turned out to be only some village belle. And when Carruthers railed at him for it, Jeffery told him to his head it was known he himself has eyes for the girl." She sighed heavily. "A fine rake I'm to take to husband."

They chuckled together. Sinclair said, "You little witch! Carruthers is no rake, and you'd never be able to get him to the altar, so don't fret."

"*Get* him! Why, you horrid! I'll wager I could have Sir Grimly at my feet in a month!" She saw her brother's troubled look, and hugged him. "Silly! I am only puffing off my allure!"

He did not look wholly reassured. "You are altogether too alluring in that gown for my liking. And did you see how Mrs. Lucille fairly floated when we arrived? She was in *alt*! It would be unkind in the extreme did you tease Carruthers. He is really in a desperate situation."

"Well, I shall not tease, never fear. At all events, he dislikes me. And why his mama should be in alt only because her son has contracted a far from brilliant marriage, I cannot fathom. He is a fine figure of a man, and were it not for those scars would be quite handsome. He is vastly rich, I gather, and for all this place is such a ruin, I fancy he could bring it up to style without being in the slightest purse-pinched. All in all, I wonder he's stayed a bachelor so long, but I suppose his manner frightens the ladies away, no?"

"No," he said baldly. "His mama's reputation."

Astonished, Phoebe gasped, "His *mama's*? You cannot mean it! Tell me!"

He was not one to gossip, and looked uncomfortable. "I don't really know, save that years ago there was some sort of lurid scandal."

"My heavens! And *this* is the family Papa was so happy to marry me into!"

The blue saloon was fairly well preserved, the couches faded but not uncomfortable, fine old rugs upon the polished boards, and some beautiful paintings and prints adorning the walls. Phoebe noted these details only in a remote fashion, however, for she was appalled to see scarlet coats among the dozen or so people who turned expectantly as Conditt opened the door and announced them. It was natural enough, of course. Carruthers was a former army officer, and likely had many friends among the military. His reluctance to bring the fugitive into his home took on another dimension.

Mrs. Lucille ran to them with a glad little cry. "Here you are! Now I mean to introduce you, my lady; Jeffery will take your son under his wing, and—Meredith! Come here and do your duty!" But as a murmur of admiring comments was heard, and her sons came forward dutifully, she murmured behind her fan, "Meredith is very cross with me, because I arranged this little welcome party for you. He says you are too tired, but you are not tired, are you, Lady Ramsay?"

Phoebe was of the opinion her affianced was correct for once, for she was sure her mama was very tired indeed. Ever courteous, Lady Eloise murmured that she thought it a charming gesture, and was borne off by her triumphant hostess.

Meredith, looking very well in his dark blue coat and paler blue unmentionables, offered Phoebe his arm. "I'm sorry about this," he muttered. "But I collect we're properly in for it."

"For a short while," she amended.

"One hopes," he said gruffly, and waved forward the handsome young man Phoebe already knew to be his brother.

Jeffery had changed into a dull-gold velvet coat and a waistcoat of rich gold brocade. He lacked his brother's breadth of shoulder, but he was graceful, and the colour of his dress emphasized his light hazel eyes. He had powdered his fair hair, and on one slender hand a great topaz sparkled. He came up to be presented, threw Phoebe an elaborate bow and was clearly awed. Despite this, he said with a twinkle that she had his deepest sympathy, and shook hands with Sinclair, then went off with him.

Chuckling, Phoebe said, "What a nice boy."

"Yes. He's a good fellow." Carruthers took up her hand and startled her by pressing a surreptitious kiss into the palm. "Try to look smitten, for God's sake," he murmured. "I'm believed to have swept you off your feet, remember?"

She smiled at him adoringly. "So long as you confine such onerous duties to my hands, we may go along without open warfare, sir."

"We had better, ma'am! Be very careful not to snipe at me tonight. Both the officers who dine with us are extremely shrewd."

One of those officers called, "Come on, Merry! You cannot keep her all to yourself, you graceless dog!" and Carruthers gave a commendably reluctant grin and began the business of presenting his affianced to his friends.

The officer was Major Hilary Broadbent, a slight, fair-complected young man with freckles that spoke of hair to match his sandy brows, and long eyes of an even lighter shade of hazel than those of Jeffery Carruthers. His easy manner betrayed a deep friendship with his host. "You don't deserve such a glorious Fair," he declared, bowing over Phoebe's hand. "I shall make it my business to see you accused of some heinous crime, so as to steal her away."

Phoebe laughed. Carruthers pointed out that he had already fought several duels and one more would be child's play, and they moved on.

The second military gentleman was a drawling, dandified type with a languid manner and penetrating dark eyes. Phoebe judged him dangerous and treated him with polite cordiality. The other guests were, by and large, a likeable group of people, all eager to congratulate Carruthers and to be pleased by his lovely and pretty-mannered prospective bride.

Dinner was served in a large and rather depressing chamber, which Carruthers said was "the small dining room." Both before and during the excellent meal, he was the butt of considerable teasing because of his having so completely hidden his *tendre* for the fair Miss Ramsay. He took it in good part until the second hour, when his chin began to tilt upward. Lucille stood earlier than Phoebe had expected and led the ladies to the withdrawing room.

Phoebe now became the recipient of the good-natured teasing, and she found it tiresome indeed, partly because it was all a sham, partly because she did not know the proper answer to some of the questions, and partly because she could hear a light rain pattering at the windows, and she was full of anxiety for their fugitive. She wondered uneasily how Carruthers and Sinclair could hope to get away from all this company so as to take Lascelles food and some protection from the weather. She was further troubled by a fear that her brother, an idealist who was inclined to expect too much of people, had set Jeffery down as a silly dandy. Sinclair had a fine and sometimes devilish vocabulary, and she could only hope he would not antagonize the younger Carruthers.

By the time the gentlemen joined them, Phoebe was not only ready to drop from weariness, but was concerned for her mother, whose kind eyes looked positively hollow with fatigue, but who would, she knew, fall to the floor sooner than disappoint her hostess by pleading exhaustion.

Meredith came at once to Phoebe's side, as befitted a sorely smitten suitor. Bowing to her ear, he imparted that her brother was a fiend with the tongue of an asp, and that she looked properly hagged.

She leaned back in her chair and smiled up at him. "How *very* un-charming you are, dear sir," she said very softly.

"Oh, yes," he said just as softly, "I lack all the social graces, praise God! Allow me to demonstrate." He stood and raised his voice. "My friends, you will forgive do we go early to bed tonight. My betrothed and her family have been travelling since early morning, and are fairly exhausted."

Such blunt dismissal of guests was new to Phoebe's experience, and she stared at him in astonishment, aware that her mother's mouth was all but hanging open.

Major Broadbent rose to his feet at once. "You are perfectly right, Merry. I'll be off, and thank you for your hospitality." He kissed the hand of his hostess, bowed to my lady and Sinclair and, voicing the hope he would meet Phoebe again very soon, went out.

Lucille was plainly distressed and implored her friends not to run away, saying that although Lady Eloise and Miss Ramsay certainly must be fatigued, there was no need for everyone to leave.

Carruthers maintained a cool but implacable silence and, taking the hint, the other guests made their polite farewells and departed.

When they had gone, Phoebe retreated to the stairs with her mama, Carruthers leading the way, and proffering their candles.

My lady bade him a rather disjointed good night and started up the stairs on Sinclair's arm.

Phoebe accepted her candle and gave her affianced a searching look. "Good gracious, sir," she said. "I appreciate your concern, but in truth I wonder you've a friend to your name."

"Concern be hanged! I had to get rid of that lot if your brother and I are to tend to our—encumbrance."

She stared at him, not quite knowing whether to be amused or stern.

While she was thinking about it, Carruthers swooped down and planted a kiss on her cheek.

She jumped back, saying indignantly, "I thought it was agreed there was to be none of that!"

He shook his head at her. "You'd make a poor spy, Miss Ramsay. You seem quite incapable of understanding that this is a most deadly predicament you have got me into."

"Of course I understand, but—"

"It is of vital import that we keep up the pretence if we are to come out of this alive."

She glanced around. "Certainly. But there is no one here to—"

"One of the first things I learned in my military career," he said gravely, "was that one does not fail to post sentries merely because there is no sign of the enemy."

Phoebe regarded him suspiciously, then started up the stairs. She halted on the third step and looked back. He stood there, watching her. She fancied to detect a quickly suppressed grin, but then he said, "I believe we have taken sufficient precautions for tonight, ma'am. Mustn't overdo it."

The insolence of the creature! She announced with regal hauteur, "I was merely going to enquire as to when you mean to attend the—er, encumbrance. My brother is very tired."

"Then he'll be a touch more so. I've to present my head for combing, first." And with a short bow, he strode back towards the drawing room.

She remained there for a moment, looking after him. How straight was his walk, yet with the faintest suggestion of a cavalry swagger. Would his mama really comb him out? At dinner there had been an unmistakable hint of Lucille's holding a partiality for Jeffery, who was certainly the more charming and agreeable of her offspring. Still, Phoebe went to her suite troubled by the knowledge that because he had helped them, Carruthers must now attempt to pacify an incensed parent.

Snuggling into bed, she sent Ada off for the night. She yearned to go to sleep at once, but as soon as she was alone she sat up again and began to read one of the marble-covered novels her papa so deplored, knowing that if Sinclair saw a light under her door, he would come in for a moment. Despite her efforts, she had fallen asleep sitting up when she felt the book gently slipped from her hands and found her brother bending over her.

"Oh, Sin," she said, stretching sleepily. "Thank goodness. Dearest, you will take care and let me know what happens?"

He sat on the side of the bed and yawned, stretching his legs out. "It has happened," he said.

Phoebe snatched the little clock from her bedside table. "Heavens! Twenty minutes until three o'clock! Sin, how is Lascelles? Were you able to move him?"

He gave her a weary smile. "One at a time, old lady. When Carruthers and his mama—Lord, you should have heard her scold him! One might think him the world's worst ogre to have heard her lamentations!"

"What—with *you* in the room?" she gasped.

"In the adjoining room. But she made such a to-do, she must have known I could hear. That pretty brother of his had tried to bring her out of her pet whilst Carruthers was giving you your candle, but he soon lost all patience with her and went stamping off to bed. I'll own I could scarce blame him. But when Carruthers came back, she properly flew out at him."

"She is braver than I! I fancy he gave her one of his icy set downs. Or did he rail at her? I'd not put it past him."

"He was meek as a lamb. Agreed with everything she said."

"Oh! Is there anything more horrid! One is left with nothing to say! Poor lady. Well, never mind that, tell me of our rebel."

"We found him well enough. Had to walk, though, because Carruthers did not dare risk waking the grooms."

"Poor Sin. How very tired you must be. Is it very far?"

"Seemed seven leagues to me, but Carruthers made nothing of it. I think the man is solid steel and don't know such a word as 'tired.' At all events, between us we helped Lascelles to a little sort of hollow in the wall of this famous Cut. It's devilish country, Phoebe. I'd never be able to find it again."

"Were you able to leave him in any kind of comfort?"

60

"Not much, but he was grateful, poor fellow, and said it was better than many a hole he's slept in. He told us he had spent most of one night up to his neck in water, when they'd set dogs on his trail."

"Oh, poor man! How ghastly this is! One might think the war was not over at all. Do you think he will be safe there?"

Sinclair gazed drowsily at his muddied boots. "Carruthers says he'll likely be all right for a few days. As soon as Lascelles is able, he means to deliver his cipher. He's half crazed with anxiety to be done with it."

"Yes, he would be. He struck me as the steadfast type of man. Well, thank heaven he is not still in Surrey!"

Sinclair nodded, and stood, but Phoebe called him back at the door to beg that he not take Jeffery Carruthers in violent aversion.

"Can't very well, since he's my host," he said. But he stuck his head around the door to add with a grin, "But he *is* a block, you know! Oh, by the bye, Carruthers means to take us on a ride about the estate in the morning. Early. Best get into your habit first thing."

"But it's morning *now*," wailed Phoebe.

"Then be so kind as to let me to my bed, m'dear," said her brother, and went away, muttering, "Gad, but I hope that dainty Jeffery don't mean to ride with us. . . ."

✑ Chapter 5 ✑

Sinclair's aversion to Jeffery Carruthers had been heartily reciprocated. Jeffery had not the least intention of accompanying the riding party next morning, nor did he mean to endure a jeremiad from his brother, and thus was up and out at an hour that astonished his valet almost as much as it would have astonished Carruthers.

The rain of the previous night had stopped. The sky was a clear blue, the air pure and cool. Jeffery found the head groom in the stables and ordered up his favourite horse.

Leading out the rangy grey, the groom, a large young man with pleasant features and light curly hair, said slyly, "Poor Mouser is properly betwattled, sir. Bean't used to waking at this hour."

"Never mind your impudence, Henry Baker," said Jeffery, straightening the frill of his jabot, and wondering if he should have worn the blue riding coat instead of the bottle-green.

"Were I being imperdent, sir?" Baker slapped a saddle on the grey. "Now fancy that. And I didn't think as I'd said a word on Rosalie Smith."

"No, you rascal," Jeffery responded, colouring up. "And you'd best not, or *I* might mention a bright-eyed little lass by name of—er, Ada something-or-other."

It was Baker's turn to redden. Jeffery grinned at him. "You great clunch, I saw you staring at her last evening when you was helping unload the coach. You'd best be careful, Baker. She's got a saucy way with her eyes, that one."

"Aye, sir," mumbled the big man shyly. "But they do be awful pretty eyes. And what am I to say if Mr. Meredith asks for ye?"

"Only the truth, my lad," said Jeffery, swinging easily to the saddle. "You've no least notion where I went."

Watching him ride out, Baker shook his curly head worriedly. "I got a *very* good notion where ye be going, Master Jeff," he muttered. "And if ye ride round *that* paddock, Mr. Meredith'll have your ears, so he will!"

Had Jeffery been aware of this sombre prediction, he would have shrugged it off and gone on his way, but perhaps with a shadow thrown over his plans. As it was, he proceeded blithe and untroubled through the brilliant morning, and was rewarded on approaching the village by a sight of the very maiden he had hoped to find. His pulse quickening, he leapt from the saddle, and called, "Good morning, Miss Rosalie."

She turned, a pleased sparkle dawning in her wide hazel eyes.

Perhaps because he himself was fair, he had never much cared for fair girls, but he was dazzled now by the gleam of the sunshine on her golden curls and the perfection of her dainty features. "What a glorious morning," he went on, "especially with you to brighten it."

"What a nice thing to say." The soft, cultured tones were a legacy from her mother, who had been well, if not nobly, born, and was said to have married beneath her station in life. If that was so, Grace Smith had never appeared to regret her decision. She had educated her daughter with the encouragement and support of Lucille Carruthers, whom she had once served as companion. As a result, Rosalie was accustomed to speaking with those her tempestuous grandfather said were her 'betters,' and she betrayed no timidity now, as Jeffery appropriated the basket she carried. "You are early about," she teased. "You have changed, Jeff. I remember when we were children how Merry used to fret because he and Lance had to wait for you to be dragged out of bed."

"I am a reformed man," he grinned. "My tutor holds out great hopes of my making him famous someday."

"Only listen to the humility of it! Pray tell in which subject you mean to excel. Politics? Or perhaps"—she dimpled mischievously—"the study of the female of the species?"

He laughed. "The latter, certainly. Would that one might make a decent living at it."

They began to walk on together, and she asked in sudden anxiety, "You're not in financial distress, I hope?"

"Lord, no," he said, touched by her solicitude. "The dibs are more or less in tune. I'll own it will be grand when I come into my inheritance at the end of the year, and don't have to go grovelling to my brother for every farthing."

She frowned a little. "Is he very hard on you? I'd always thought you were good friends."

"We are, really. But—well, you know how Merry is at times. He can be so curst cutting." His handsome face darkened. He said broodingly, "He's furious because I was rusticated again, and has warned that—" He broke off. "What a fellow I am to be prosing on about such dull matters. Let me see now, you had asked . . . ? Oh, yes. Well, I think I mean to be a great ornithologist. What d'you say to that?"

She chuckled. "Any particular species, Learned Professor? Or do you only say it to please me?"

"No such thing! Why should I wish to—" The words trailed off. She was smiling up at him, and he felt a quite unfamiliar depth of affection for the pretty creature. With a great effort he reminded himself that she was one of their own people. Merry was very fond of her grandfather besides, and would really be in a rage if the old fellow was upset. 'Slow and easy, my lad,' he told himself, and finished, "—wish to please such a *lovely* expert on the feathered little varmints? Speaking of which, Rosalie, how came you to have so deep an interest in 'em?"

She was not deceived, and knew very well how close she had come to being kissed. She had always been fond of this tall boy, but she remembered him more as a harum-scarum playmate than as the handsome aristocrat he had become. A little disconcerted, she replied, "My father loved to watch them, and the books your dear mama allows me to read have helped me to learn a good deal, though I've not as much time for reading since Papa died and I have to help in the bakery. Not that I mind that, of course. Mrs. Johnson comes in at ten and all day Tuesdays, but Grandfather is much too old to be working. I am very glad to be of use to him."

Jeffery thought it a crime that so delicious a girl should have to slave over dough and hot ovens, but he said, "Yes, of course. But I'm glad you have some time left for reading, and that you are able to use our books. If—" Struck by a sudden thought, he interrupted himself. "I say, do you know anything about bats?"

"A little. Why?"

"Have they paws? Or—well, some sort of feet?"

She laughed hilariously. "Of course they have . . . whatever did you think?"

"Never really thought about 'em at all," he admitted. "I know they hang by their tails, though—"

Again, that ripple of laughter rang out. "They hang by their *feet* and their thumbs."

He stared at her. "You're bamming me. What bird ever had thumbs?"

"Ah, but they are not birds, Professor Carruthers."

He chuckled. "Very well, you've teased me properly, little rascal. I knew you were bamming."

"Indeed I am not," she protested, still half-laughing at him. "They are mammals, you see. And the most fascinating little creatures. I'm sure Merry has some books that will tell you more about them if you are *really* interested."

He assured her that he was, and received a warning that the next time they met she would quiz him to see how much he had learned of the subject.

He escorted her as far as the village green, and watched her go on her way, her walk as graceful and unaffected as her manner. 'What a little darling of a girl,' he thought. And, turning for home, was so lost in reverie that he failed to see the malevolent glare that was levelled at him by the large villager who leaned from a cottage window. Nor did he see Ben Hessell spit contemptuously into the weedy garden as he passed.

"Mammals, by Jove," he murmured, and hastened his stride. He must find the books Rosalie had spoken of and learn as much as he might so that he could present himself without delay for the quiz.

Despite the early hour and her interrupted night, Phoebe went downstairs humming softly. The morning was bright, and she knew the brown habit with the big gold buttons became her. In the hall, a maid with dust mop in hand bobbed a curtsy. Phoebe bade her good morning, wandered to an elaborate gilt mirror, and took one last careful glance. Her broad-brimmed straw hat with the great orange feather curling down could be set, she decided, just a trifle more to one side, and she adjusted it carefully. The mirror reflected another face crowned by a flowing periwig. She turned and crossed to the far wall and the portrait that hung there, somewhat overshadowed by the tall armoire chest beside it.

The gentleman wore a magnificent blue velvet coat with snowy lace at his throat and wrists. His mouth was shapely but disdainful, his features lean, and a half-moon patch on one cheekbone enhanced the beauty of a pair of thickly lashed grey eyes.

Phoebe stared, fascinated by that arrestingly handsome face. The chin was sharper than Meredith's, there was a difference about the mouth, also, and his son had not inherited such a perfectly chiselled nose, yet the likeness between the two, especially about the eyes, was marked. She was so intent that she failed to hear a step behind her, and gave a little shriek as the hat she had so carefully arranged was knocked forward over her eye.

Spinning around, she found Carruthers behind her, looking amused. "What a miserable trick!" she exclaimed. "You've an odd sense of humour, sir."

The quirkish grin dawned and he reached upward. "You give me credit for a deal more courage than I possess, ma'am. Wretched beast, will you never mend your manners?"

The last remark was addressed to the large black cat that he lifted down from the top of the chest.

"So this is Satan," Phoebe said admiringly. "What a beautiful creature."

"And, like most beautiful creatures, spoiled, vain, and ill-mannered." He met her level stare and drawled mockingly, "Dear me! Did you fancy I referred to you, Miss Ramsay?"

Fuming, she stroked the cat, which had draped itself lazily over his arm. "Not unless you judge me beautiful."

"I am hoist by my own petard," he sighed. "Horns of a dilemma! Allow me to escape by presenting another of my—encumbrances. Wicked hat-whacker, pay your respects."

He lifted the cat until it looked directly into Phoebe's face, and it blinked great amber eyes at her, purring. She ruffled up the dense fur about its neck and it emitted an amiable trill and began to knead the air with big paws.

Justice padded up and sniffed enquiringly. Satan became a hissing porcupine, jumped down, and streaked away; the hound in hot, if rather ungainly, pursuit.

"Will Justice catch him?" asked Phoebe anxiously.

"For his sake, I sincerely hope not. Satan would make mincemeat out of him."

She said, smiling, "I did not mean to be ill-mannered. I apologize for assuming you had knocked off my hat."

He bowed gravely. "I have no need to remove it. At present."

There seemed to be some hidden meaning to the words. She could not guess what, and deemed it safer not to enquire, so returned her attention to the portrait.

"I see you have discovered my father," he said.

"Yes. A splendid gentleman." He made no comment and, watching him from under her lashes, she added, "It seems rather an odd place for him."

His eyes were fixed on a point below the level of the frame. "Does it? I'll admit I can think of a better one."

"You are very like him," she persisted.

The cool stare lifted to her. "I presume you intend that as a compliment." His mouth curved into that twisted smile, but his eyes were bleak. "At least, I shall give you the benefit of the doubt."

She was unutterably shocked that a man could speak thus of his father, and asked with a lift of the brows, "Where would you prefer to hang his picture? In your portrait gallery?"

"Oh, no. I had thought rather the place of honour atop a large bonfire." The ice in his eyes melted, and laughter crept into them. "Poor Miss Ramsay. How I do destroy your faith in human nature. Never mind, your fine handsome lover—ah, friend, will soon be able to reclaim you. Meanwhile, pray forgive, but some of my people are waiting to consult with me. Your brother is already out at the stables, and if you would not mind riding slowly, I'll contrive to come up with you just as soon as I can." He bowed and strode off.

Phoebe stared after him, then turned to gaze up again at the likeness of Paul Carruthers. One might suppose that any family would have been proud to hang the portrait of so splendid a gentleman where it must instantly impress any visitor to their home. Yet here it was, hidden away in a corner, as though displayed more from a reluctant sense of obligation than from affection or pride. 'What an odd lot they are,' she thought, and walked slowly to the stableyard, puzzling at it.

"You have to admit it is beautiful country," said Sinclair, as he and his sister walked their horses slowly to the top of the broad hilltop.

Scanning sunlit, rolling woodland, verdant meadows dotted with fat cattle, and the distant charm of Dewbury Prime, Phoebe agreed. "And the Hall, so inspiring." She had spoken in jest and was taken aback when her brother endorsed the remark with enthusiasm.

Sinclair was less enthusiastic as the minutes lengthened into a quarter of an hour. Percent was fidgeting with impatience, and Sinclair said at last that he could wait no longer, but would explore the estate alone. "As well to leave you two love-birds together," he added, and galloped off, laughing at the indignant comment Phoebe sent after him.

She watched him out of sight, her eyes fond, very aware that, despite his teasing, he blamed himself bitterly for having pulled her into such a fiasco. That it *was* a fiasco, she could not deny, but she would have endured many such fiascos rather than have him changed by one iota. Besides, she had no real fear that she and Carruthers would be forced into matrimony, since he wanted it no more than did she.

Rapid hoofbeats announced the approach of Carruthers, and she turned about to see him coming full tilt across the meadow, mounted on a tall black horse. The meandering stream with the low wall just beyond it was a treacherous jump, but horse and man cleared it in a style that drew an admiring exclamation from Phoebe. 'My goodness,' she thought, 'but he can ride! Small wonder he was a cavalryman,' and her smile was genuine as he cantered to join her. "I'd say he was a beautiful creature," she said, twinkling at him, "save that I've found it to be a dangerous remark."

He had expected recriminations and, pleased by both the lack of them and her admiration of his mount, he patted the arched neck of the black and responded, "I'd have to agree with you, but alas, part of my qualification still applies. He is excessive vain and inclined to be ill-mannered."

"How is he called?"

"Rogue." He reined the stallion away as Phoebe leaned to stroke him. "Careful, ma'am. He tends to live up to his name."

"Is that why you named him so?"

"No. I named him for a friend."

They started off, side by side, and Phoebe said, "So you have rogues for friends, have you?"

"Don't we all? But the nice thing about this particular friend is that there's no doubting his reprehensible qualities. He makes no bones of the fact that he's a rascal, which simplifies matters. You'll likely meet him sooner or later, for Roland usually stays at the Hall, is he in the vicinity. Has your brother decided against riding today?"

She replied demurely, "Say rather, he decided against waiting today."

At once his chin lifted. "My apologies to him. I'm not usually so beset, but I was away, as you know, and there were a few things—"

"A *few*! Good heavens, sir, I'd have said the entire village waited for you! I never saw such a mob. Whatever have you done to cause such an outpouring of woes?"

His glance darted to her, the pale eyes flashing. "They're a worthless lot," he gritted. "Expect all the luxuries. Roofs, paint, glass in windows, chimneys that draw! There's no end to their demands!"

Phoebe stared, her eyes very round, but despite his grim scowl she glimpsed a furtive twitch beside his mouth and could not restrain a laugh. "Horrid man! No, but the village looked lovely from what I could see. Why do they pester you so?"

"Race you to the hill," he said, and was away with a thunder of hoofs and a creak of saddle leather.

"Oh!" she cried indignantly and followed. She came up with him halfway across the meadow and went past with a triumphant shout, the orange feather fluttering, the air rushing at her face, her blood exhilarated. But when Carruthers came galloping to the hilltop, she frowned at him. "I do not care to be *allowed* to win, Mr. Carruthers."

"Then you would ever lose against this fellow," he grinned. "There's no horse in the south country can equal him, save Roly Otton's Rumpelstiltskin."

"Never mind about your roguish friend," she said sternly. "I shall not be fobbed off so easily, sir. Tell me about your villagers."

He gazed down to where Dewbury Prime spread in tranquil loveliness under the cool morning sunlight. "We'll go down," he murmured, "and you can have a closer look. We've done a lot these four years. I've a fine steward, whose help is invaluable, but if you'd seen the state it had come to when I inherited!" His lips tightened and the dreamy look vanished from the light eyes.

"Was it mostly a matter of roads and roofs, and suchlike?"

"It was a matter of twenty years of neglect! Not one roof that did not leak; scarce a window not boarded; no paint left; wood rotten; chimneys that could not draw; fields and farms gone to rack and ruin!"

She looked down at the well-kept road, the sturdy roofs, bright paint, and gleaming windows. "Then you have certainly worked miracles. But—surely you need more help. Could not your brother—"

He took up the reins and started down the hill, saying with some impatience, "Jeff's away at school."

"I hear," she murmured tentatively, "he is often rusticated."

"Do you?"

"Perhaps," she persisted, "he doesn't care for school. Perhaps he would prefer to be helping you here; learning about the estates, and—"

"And the local belles," he said with a brittle laugh. "No, he's no interest in business or management, I'm afraid."

"Have you given him a choice?"

He frowned and said grimly, "I mean to do so. He may choose between some steady application at University next term, a pair of colours, or a sojourn on our plantation in Jamaica!" Phoebe gave him a shocked look, and he went on jeeringly, "You are thinking me the Tyrant, I see. But he'll not ruin himself as so many of these young bucks do today, can I help it! One more—" He caught himself up, flushing. "Gad, but I should not talk so."

"To the contrary. I think you should talk more often, Mr. Carruthers. To Jeffery. If he understood your concerns, he might—"

"Judge me a proper grim and gloom, as he does already." His eyes narrowed suddenly. "Observe—and see how right he is!" He drove home his spurs. Rogue was away like a black streak to the picturesque hump-backed bridge whereon two villagers argued beside a heavily laden cart.

Phoebe took the hill in more sedate style and came up in time to hear Carruthers snarl, ". . . see some more work done, or I shall cease to rent you a cottage of any description and you'll be obliged to leave the Prime!"

The big man he addressed so scathingly stood with dark head bowed, his gaze fixed on the shabby hat he wrung between powerful hands. "I know we've not pleased yer, sir," he said humbly, "though we've tried, Mary and me. If ye'd just give us a bit more time, Mr. Meredith."

"I gave you time, Hessell! I've instructed Mr. Boles to look into the matter of the supplies. I shall await his report. Until then, do not be piling a double load onto the cart only to save yourself an extra trip!"

The big man began to plead in a hushed, broken voice. Uncomfortable, Phoebe guided her horse over to the ancient little man who held Rogue's reins. As she came closer, he snatched off his straw hat, threw her a quick, bright-eyed glance, and returned his attention to the two men.

Having no wish for a further demonstration of Meredith Carruthers's harsh disposition, Phoebe said pleasantly, "Good morning."

"Sssh!" hissed the ancient, his eyes glued to the fray. "Nor Oi doan't mean no disrespec', marm," he went on in a hoarse whisper. "But—d'ye hear that? Oh, j'y! Oh, bliss!" He hugged himself ecstatically and did a small tottery dance in the one spot.

Amused, Phoebe turned in time to see the big man walk away with dragging step and shoulders slumped. 'Poor thing,' she thought, and viewed her betrothed without delight.

Carruthers gave her his satyr half-grin, pressed a coin into the old man's hand, and swung into the saddle.

The villager tugged at his booted leg imperatively.

Carruthers leaned down. In a very different voice, he asked, "What now, Joseph?"

One arm waved, the sleeve of the smock flapping about its frailty. "Oi doan't want this here, Mr. Meredith," he piped, holding up the shilling. "No, no. Oi'll not take payment when Oi were treated to a foine show like that 'un." He cackled and slapped his fragile knee. "Oi been a'watching Ben Hessell fer years an' years, ever since he come down from Lun'on Town and married silly Mary Wells. Watching and waiting and praying as how some'un would give he a smash in the face." His own gnarled old face radiant, he exulted, "Ye done it, Mr. Meredith! By goles, but ye did!"

"You're a rascal. I laid no hand on the man, and well you know it."

"Not a hand, p'raps, but ye tongue-lashed him good and proper, so ye did. 'Oi'll cease renting ye a cottage,' says you. Hee, hee, hee! Look how he goes yonder. Stamping and so surly as any bear, he do be. And a grizzling bear, at that. And they be the surliest of all. Oi knows a lot about bears, Oi do. Oh, but this be a j'yful day. Proper j'yful!"

Carruthers frowned. "Has Hessell been intimidating you?"

The radiance died from the wrinkled features. Drawing himself up to his full fifty-five inches, Joseph said proudly, "Oi? 'Timidated? Ye'd oughta know better nor that, Mr. Carruthers. Ain't no man living can 'timidate the loikes o' Joseph Smith!"

Phoebe held her breath, dreading another display of the Carruthers temper, but he only said, "No. I certainly should have known better."

"Ar, so ye should." But the old man unbent sufficiently to add, "Now, me granddarter be another matter. So pretty as any pitcher be my Rosalie, bean't she? Oi'll never ferget when my

John and his Grace, God rest 'em, brung her from Lun'on Town. So wee, she was. Best s'prise o' me life, it were. An' look how sweet she growed. So sweet as any flower. Many's the foine young chap do have come smiling an' smirking arter her." His seamed face took on a crafty look. "Oi doan't need ter tell *ye* that, now do Oi, sir?"

Phoebe thought, 'Rosalie, again. So that's why Carruthers looks so cross.'

Joseph was saying, "And my Rosalie wasn't born to be no rich gent's toy, and so I tell 'ee! 'Sides, she be too young, and her pretty head all full o' they books as yer mama loans her. Reads 'em ter me every night, so clever. Not," he added hastily, "as Oi cannot read me own self, but 'tis me eyes. Not just as young as Oi used t'be."

"You go on remarkably well, even so," Carruthers said. "Now, tell me what Hessell has been about."

Joseph hesitated. "Oi doan't like the way he looks at her."

"She's a lovely sight, Joseph. There's small harm in a look."

"Maybe not. But Oi got me blunderbuss loaded, Mr. Meredith! Were Oi in me prime, now, Oi'd take that Ben Hessell by the ear and throw 'un clear over the smithy, and then Oi'd go and jump on his weskit till he were all one with the mud, so Oi would." Having uttered which fearful threat, he nodded reinforcingly and took his frail self off, weaving unsteadily up the picturesque bridge and into the serenity of the village known as Dewbury Prime.

They came at the gallop to the top of the rise, with no talk between them as there had been none since they left the village half an hour ago.

Carruthers reined up and turned Rogue so as to face Phoebe. Almost knee to knee with her, he enquired, "Do you mean to sulk all day, or will you get it said before we go back?"

"I am not sulking," she denied loftily. "Faith, but I've no interest in the way you handle your people, or your properties, Mr. Carruthers."

"So I should hope. It would be most improper, under the circumstances. Still, I would prefer not to return to the Hall while you behave like an outraged virgin I've attempted to seduce."

She gave a shocked gasp. His leering grin taunted her.

"What is it, ma'am? Do you fancy me to have been playing a little slap and tickle with a pure village maid?"

She said through her teeth, "You may play at whatever you choose with—with your *vicar's* wife, for all I care!"

"How generous in you. I shall tell him I've your permission. She's a shapely woman, for all her thirteen stone!"

"If you are quite done with your crudities," she said, nose very high held, "I expect you will be anxious to check on poor Lieutenant Lascelles."

"I am not done with my crudities, and 'poor Lieutenant Lascelles' will be the better for not having a constant stream of visitors drawing attention to his hiding place. Now, if you're consumed with jealousy because Rosalie and I are—"

"*Jealousy!* Oh, now really! That is too much!"

"I agree most emphatically. You have a fine handsome lover, so why should not I have—"

"I think I did not say anything so crass as to imply that I have taken a lover, sir," she said glacially. "What kind of girl you fancy me to be I cannot guess, but I assure you the closest *I* have ever been to bringing down scandal upon my family was when you . . ." And she stopped because his face was suddenly dead-white, his eyes a savage blaze of steel.

"Yes, ma'am?" he rasped. "Go on. Pray do not cease your ugly little insinuations on my account!"

For a moment her own rather bewildering rage was checked. What on earth did he mean—'ugly little insinuations'? Good heavens! Did he imagine she had referred to the scandal that had involved his mother? Her breath checked briefly from the shock of it. Then her shining white teeth fairly snapped together. She took up her reins and leaned forward in the saddle to glare into his suddenly remorseful eyes.

"How—*dare* you believe I would say so spiteful a thing?" she hissed furiously. "Were I a man, sir, I would—I would call you out for—for even—"

He grasped her reins. "Phoebe, I did not—"

"Liar!" she raged, and brought her riding crop down with all her strength across his hand.

He flinched, drawing away instinctively, and Phoebe, driven by a fury such as she had never before experienced, kicked home her heels and sent the fine roan mare racing down the rise and across the lush green meadow. Almost at once she heard the black start in pursuit. Her rage was such that she lashed the mare to greater efforts. They fairly flew across the meadow and

Phoebe crouched, preparing the mare for the upcoming hedge and taking it at a speed that mildly astonished her. She heard Carruthers shout at her to stop, and with a little snort of contempt, she rode on. They were coming to another hedge, with beyond, she supposed, either another field or a lane, but it was high, and she eyed it dubiously.

A thunder of hoofs. Carruthers was alongside. His arm flashed out. His gauntleted hand closed on her reins again, and the roan was drawn to a plunging halt.

Breathless and defiant, Phoebe turned on him. "Brute! You hurt her mouth!"

"No. You did. I told you to stop."

"And I stop when it pleases me to do so, sir!"

"Do you indeed? And would it please you to join Sir Malcolm under his carriage, or on his roof?"

Through a break in the hedge she could now glimpse a lane and a luxurious coach. A florid-faced, powerful-looking gentleman of middle years was advancing through the break, waving his cane at them. Flushing, she said a rather feeble "Oh."

"Just so," drawled Carruthers. "Can you find your way back to the Hall from here, ma'am?"

She thought, 'He does not want me to meet this gentleman.' And she responded perversely, "No."

"Pity," he murmured, and dismounted.

The newcomer stamped across the grass to confront him. "Glad I found you, Carruthers," he observed in a growl of a voice. "Saves me a journey."

"By all means, join us," Carruthers invited.

"Devil take you, sir! I do not—"

Carruthers lifted his hand. "Allow me first to present my betrothed. Miss Phoebe Ramsay—Sir Malcolm Lockwood."

The hard dark eyes flashed to Phoebe and widened a trifle. Sensing the dislike between the two men, she smiled warmly and bent to hold out her hand. "How do you do, Sir Malcolm?"

He stamped over, perforce, touched her fingers, and swung back to Carruthers. "You had the colossal impudence to complain because my hunt dared to cross a corner of your land last week."

"To trample a broad swath through my south cornfield. Yes, I complained."

"And I told you to—" Lockwood champed his jaws, glaring furiously at Phoebe, and reworded, "I said it had been unavoidable."

"To which I responded—rubbish! Have you now come to apologize, sir?"

"Damme, I've not!" Sir Malcolm flourished his cane angrily. "What I *should* have done, and would have done had I known I'd find you, was to bring my horsewhip! Any man who would take his revenge on another man's dogs, sir, is—"

"What the devil are you talking about?"

"I'm talking about my best pack, sir! Damn near wiped out, sir! Poisoned, sir! *That's* what I'm talking about!"

"Good God!" Not looking at Phoebe, Carruthers thrust his reins at her. "Hold him, if you please." He strode closer to Lockwood's fury. "Do you say they all are killed?"

"Not yet! Thanks only to my kennelman. I tell you, sir, 'twas the most dastardly—"

Hands on hips, Carruthers voiced a soft but deadly interruption. "And you accuse *me* of having done this? Take care how you answer, I warn you!"

"*Warn* me? Why, damn your eyes—of *course* you did it!" The baronet groped stabbingly in his pocket and drew forth a gauntlet of black leather, the letters 'MBC' picked out in gold on the deep cuff. "Deny that is yours," he snarled.

Carruthers took the glove and frowned down at it. "No. I'll not deny it. This was found near your kennels, I take it?"

"It was. And within the hour my dogs were near death! Now tell me why I should not call you out for such unmitigated savagery."

Still scowling at the gauntlet he held, Carruthers said slowly, "I can think of no reason why you should not call me out, Lockwood. Indeed, few things would please me more than to meet you at any place, at any time. But not for this."

Thrusting his impassioned face at the younger man, Lockwood grated, "Will you give me your solemn oath you did not interfere with my hounds?"

Carruthers's dark head came up. His eyes met and held the baronet's black glare. "I pledge you my word of honour I did not, nor ever will, interfere with your hounds." And he added, "If truth be told, I am the one should call *you* out for having the confounded gall to suspect me of such a damnable act!"

"If you ever find *my* glove in your kennels, in like circumstances," fumed Lockwood, "you'll likely think yourself well justified."

They glared at each other, for all the world, thought Phoebe, like two dogs bristling to attack. She said, "What a perfectly dreadful thing, Sir Malcolm."

Neither man would have admitted it, but both were relieved by the interruption her gentle voice provided. The baronet returned to look up into her beautiful and concerned face. Removing his tricorne, he said, "It was touch and go, Miss Ramsay, I can tell you that."

"My papa hunts a fine pack, and I can guess how he would feel. Is your huntsman hopeful of complete recovery, sir?"

"He is, I thank you, ma'am."

Carruthers said with cool courtesy, "If we can be of any assistance, Lockwood . . ."

Sir Malcolm grunted, "Perhaps I was too hasty. But—that glove of yours did make it look as if . . ."

"Yes," said Carruthers, thoughtfully. "I'd give a deal to know how it came there."

"I must accept your word as a gentleman. Good day to you. Happy to have made your acquaintance, ma'am. You're to be congratulated, Carruthers."

"Good gracious," murmured Phoebe, watching the baronet stalk back through the break in the hedge. "Why ever should he suspect you of such infamy?"

"Because he's aware of my 'manifold sins and wickedness,' of course," he sneered. Phoebe looked at him levelly. His mocking gaze fell away. He said with an impatient shrug, "Gad, madam, I'd think you might guess that had he really believed it, he would have come with a blunderbuss and not stopped to argue." He took the reins from her. "He has no love for me, I'll grant you. Partly because I cry friends with his son."

She watched his lithe swing into the saddle and asked, "Why should he object to that? You grew up together, I expect."

He reined around and walked Rogue along beside her. "The Squire and my father did not see eye to eye. They quarrelled violently, in fact."

"But your papa has been dead for some years—no?"

"Four, to be precise. The Squire has a long memory. He has never forgiven us. But his son is as gentle and kindly a fellow as the old boy is fierce."

By mutual consent they urged the horses to a trot.

Phoebe asked, "Does Mr. Lockwood reside with his father?"

He seemed lost in thought, then answered, "He went to Town about six months ago after a—er, family squabble and seldom comes down any more. The Squire holds that against me, too. Thinks I influenced his son away from him—though, Lord knows, I was in the army at the time."

"I suppose you were. What was your rank, sir?"

"Lieutenant. And never likely to go higher, I pray. I sold out after Culloden."

"Then you have not been long home."

"Nor long gone. It was an exercise in futility."

"Cumberland?" And when he looked at her measuringly, she set him a small test, wondering how his score would compare to that of Brooks—not that it mattered at all. "I have heard other officers say they could not tolerate his reprisals, and my dear grandmama is quite militant on the subject. Was it truly as dreadful as we hear?"

He was briefly silent, a bleakness creeping into his eyes that she had not seen before, even when he had been so angry with her earlier. He said in a low, bitter voice, "A thousand times more dreadful than you could ever imagine, I hope. Cumberland sought to pacify our panicked government, but—" He was silent for a moment, then, in a strained fashion, he said, "Miss Phoebe, I know we neither of us wish this silly betrothal, but—so long as we've to play-act—Oh, I don't mean that! Lord, I'm a clumsy fellow! Ma'am—will you forgive? I—should have known you'd not make such a—a—"

"Horrid, cruel, and improper insinuation," she finished for him.

His head bowed. He said with uncharacteristic humility, "Yes."

"I think I shall not let you off that easily, sir. What do you offer by way of inducement?"

He looked at her from under his lashes and suddenly his eyes held a blue sparkle. "Name it."

"That you will go and see about our fugitive."

He ran a finger along the line of his jaw in the way she had noted before. "Done."

"Then I forgive you," she said with a smile.

"Good. I'll give you a handicap and perhaps you can beat me back to the Hall. You can see it yonder, so should not get lost."

"How much of a handicap?" she asked, eyeing the restive stallion dubiously.

"Halfway across the meadow."

She considered it, shot him a laughing glance, and was away.

She looked back when she passed the marker they had set and saw Rogue swoop down the slope after her. Her heartbeat quickening, she bent lower in the saddle, joying in this contest. The trees seemed to fly to meet her, then she was in them, following the winding drivepath, the roan racing at blinding speed. She could hear Rogue's hoofbeats now, and gave a squeak of excitement to see him coming up at incredible speed with Carruthers crouched low over the pommel. Phoebe urged the roan to greater effort, but starting across the park she could see from the corner of her eye that he was almost level. He passed her well before they came to the house, his grin a white flash in his bronzed face, and was waiting to lift her down when she came up, a stable-boy grinning beside him.

She leaned to him, laughing and breathless. "Wretch! Even then, I think you held him back!"

"It grieves me to mortify a lady."

The boy chuckled and led the horses around to the back of the house.

Phoebe asked, low-voiced, "And—you *will* go to see the Lieutenant, soon?"

"No. I think not."

She stiffened. "But—you promised!"

He threw up one hand, cowering in exaggerated terror, "Do not strike me again, I beg!"

She bit her lip, already ashamed of that angry blow.

Carruthers murmured, "I saw Lance before you were awake, ma'am. He's going along quite well, and has plenty of water and food."

"Oh!" she exclaimed. "Wicked creature! Why did you so deceive me?"

His mouth took on the cynical twist. He drawled, "Because, sweet shrew, you are so captivated by my tyranny."

Yearning to give him the set-down he deserved, Phoebe could think of nothing to say, and thus proceeded as regally as possible into the house.

❦ Chapter 6 ❧

"Only look at your hands," exclaimed Rosalie Smith, shaking her head over the mud on Sinclair's well-manicured fingers. "It was indeed kind in you to help me gather herbs, Mr. Ramsay, but I do hope those marks will come out of your cuffs."

It was, he thought, a small price to pay for having spent an hour with this enchanting little creature. He had found her with her basket in the copse, and one glimpse of her fair, trusting face had set his vulnerable heart pounding like a hammer. He had taken his time at first, content to watch her graceful movements and listen to the quaint old folksong she had sung as she gathered her herbs. His quietly uttered request for directions to Meredith Hall had served as an introduction, and within five minutes he had been gathering whatever she pointed out, while she held the basket and chattered unaffectedly, delightfully, with him.

"Never give it a thought," he said. "My man is a magician with stains."

"And will likely spend hours labouring because I neglected to warn you to roll up your ruffles."

"If he does, 'twill be the first time he's laboured at such length in my behalf. No, really—he's a dreadful fellow, and so strict with me, one would think him my tutor rather than by valet."

She laughed at him and, having taken note of his fine-boned, intelligent face, the white tie-wig that became him very well, the rather too sensitive mouth, stubborn chin, and intense blue eyes, she decided that in his own way he was almost as attractive as Jeffery. She pointed to some wild mint and said rather wistfully, "Your sister is betrothed to Meredith, I hear. They say she is very beautiful."

Avoiding some nettles while he cautiously gathered the mint, he verified this. "Do you live nearby, Miss Smith?"

"In the village." And responding to his swift look, she added with a smile, "My grandfather owns the bakery next to The Meredyth Arms."

He thought, 'Good Lord!' and said easily, "I shall have to pay it a visit."

"You are surprised because of the way I speak," she said with grave dignity. "My mama was well-born, you see, but I am not of the Quality, Mr. Ramsay."

Embarrassed by this forthright speech, he gave no hint of it. "Well, that's a relief," he said brightly. "Do your parents live in the village, then?"

"Alas, no. Mama died three years ago, and my papa followed her six months later. They were very happy together; certainly, she never repented having married beneath her—which everyone insisted she had done."

"She must have been a wonderful lady." He noticed that she was staring at his hand and glanced down to discover he was pulling the leaves from the mint, one at a time. Scarlet, he stammered, "What I mean is—you would *have* to have grown up in a happy home. It is writ in your face."

He was obviously much embarrassed. With a relaxing of the faint apprehension that had begun to be instinctive of late, Rosalie thought, 'He has not been much around girls. How nice he is.' She said, "Thank you. Good gracious, but your hands are in a state. There is a stream just over here, if you would like to wash."

They went, side by side, through the trees, and while Sinclair strove to repair some of the damage, they chatted with ever increasing ease about the villages and the Carruthers estate, emerging at last, laughing, because of Rosalie's description of the atrocities perpetrated upon Justice by Meredith's cat.

"So there you are."

Jeffery Carruthers, astride his fine grey Thoroughbred, Mouser, scowled at them.

Rosalie called blithely, "Good morning, Jeffery. Mr. Ramsay was helping me gather my herbs."

His chin very high and his eyelids drooping disdainfully, Jeffery's gaze flickered to Sinclair. "Really?" he drawled.

For the first time, Sinclair thought that this man did, after all, bear a marked resemblance to his brother.

"Why, Meredith," said Lucille, looking up from the letter she was reading as the two young people came into the breakfast parlour, "how very light-hearted you look this morning. Had you a nice ride?"

"Very nice, thank you." He pulled out a chair for Phoebe and then went to drop a kiss on his mother's upturned cheek. "Miss Ramsay has a splendid seat, and hands light as a feather."

" 'Tis seldom one hears such an endorsement from him, my dear," exclaimed Lucille. "You really have made an impression!"

Glancing at her betrothed, Phoebe found a smile in his eyes that was rather appealing. "Thank you, ma'am," she replied. "Do you like to ride?"

"In a nicely sprung coach," said Meredith, quizzing his mother. "Preferably on a journey of no longer than thirty minutes' duration, and one enlivened by a companion with whom she can enjoy a comfortable cose; which is to say a—er, critique of all their dearest friends."

"Villain!" Lucille tossed several letters to him. "Here is your correspondence, sir, and 'twill serve you right are they all duns! Now—we will pay him no heed, my dear. You must be fairly famished after your ride. Conditt, be very sure to offer Miss Ramsay some of those mushrooms, they are really superior this morning." She prattled on and Phoebe responded politely, Meredith saying little until his mother asked, "Did you meet anyone on your long ride?"

"Oh, I saw Ben Hessell," he replied idly. "And had a word with old Joseph Smith."

"One of our local oddities, Miss Ramsay," observed Lucille. "But a very dear old man."

"Indeed, he seemed so," Phoebe agreed. "Though very bloodthirsty. He was fairly beside himself with joy because Mr. Carruthers was cross with Hessell." She was amused by the recollection of the quaint little dance Joseph had essayed, but glancing to her betrothed, met a flashing look of irritation.

Lucille sighed. "You are very hard on the Hessells, Meredith. I really think you might be more lenient; poor Mary does her best, and Hessell has always been most respectful."

"Of course, for he's a toad-eater," he said in his gruff way. "And is a lazy rascal—to say the least of the matter."

Lucille looked flustered, and Phoebe intervened hurriedly, "And I also met your neighbour, the Squire, ma'am."

Carruthers's hand tightened on the napkin he had just laid beside his plate.

Lucille's anxious gaze flew to him. "Were you on Sir Malcolm's preserves, then?"

"No. He was on ours." He leaned over to cover her little white hand with his long tanned one, and said in a gentle voice that was new to Phoebe, "Now never look so troubled, love. We parted most amicably." He slanted a meaningful glance at Phoebe. "Is that not so, Miss Ramsay?"

It was very obvious he did not want anything said about the poisoning of the dogs, and Phoebe at once confirmed his remark.

Lucille gave her a tragic look and clung to Meredith's hand. "But—*why* was he on our land?" she asked, her voice trembling. "He did not call at the house, or—Oh, my! What a nasty welt! How ever did you come by it?"

He whipped his hand away, but not before Phoebe had seen the lurid swelling that was already darkening to a bruise. She looked at him repentantly.

"Miss Ramsay did it," he said easily. "Only because I will not wear a silly wig."

Phoebe, who had opened her mouth to protest, closed it again.

Lucille said with a tremulous smile, "I'd not blame her a bit. Now, Meredith, do be truthful. Did you come to blows with Sir Malcolm?"

"Lord, no. I promise you it was only a foolish—Oh, hello, Jeff."

His brother hurried in and went at once to kiss his mother and wish everyone a good morning. He had gone for an early ride, he said, this drawing an incredulous stare from his brother. He asked Phoebe what she had thought of the estate, warned that she must take a strong hand with Meredith from the start, and made Lucille laugh by telling her a vignette about the vicar's wife. He was cheerful and light-hearted, and Phoebe began to realize that Sinclair was right; he was the apple of his mother's eye. In no time Lucille was chattering happily with him, her previous anxieties quite forgotten. Phoebe was swept along by their conversation, but Meredith fell silent and surreptitiously broke the seal on a letter and began to read it.

"Now, Mama," said Jeffery, taking his third piece of toast, "what have you planned for today?"

"I shall ask you to show Mr. Ramsay about the district," she answered, and turned to Phoebe, thus missing the dismay that came into his eyes. "And as soon as she is ready, I mean to take Miss Ramsay through the gardens. After lunch—"

"After lunch," Meredith interposed, not looking up, "I am driving her over to Dewbury Minor."

His mother's mouth drooped into the little pout Phoebe was soon to associate with the lady. "Oh. Well, I suppose it is natural enough that you would wish to do so. Then I shall take Lady Eloise for a drive."

"I think she will love that, ma'am," said Phoebe. "Your lands are so very beautiful."

Jeffery was keeping a wary eye on his brother, but asked, "And what of your famous tea-party, Mama? Is it all arranged?"

"Yes, dearest. It is to be on the third of August. Only five more days, Miss Ramsay, before you will be meeting all our friends and neighbours! I would have scheduled it sooner, but I knew Meredith would wish you to have a period of quiet and be more settled here before I subjected you to such a large party."

Phoebe thought, 'Five more days here?' But, after all, Lambert would soon arrive and then they could start to find the way out of this pickle, so it might not be too bad. She said with warm insincerity, "How very kind of you, ma'am. Shall you need help with the invitations?"

"No, no. Thank you, my dear, but they are all done."

Meredith said, "So soon?" He addressed his mother, but for an instant his gaze had gone to Jeffery. Phoebe intercepted both that look of steel and his brother's fading smile, and could all but feel the rising tension in the room.

"Oh, yes, am I not efficient?" trilled Lucille, pouring Jeffery another cup of tea. She gave a little-girl giggle. "I must be truthful. Rosalie came up from the village to help. She has such a fine hand and is always so willing, sweet child."

Jeffery's preoccupation with his brother was abandoned. He said eagerly, "Rosalie Smith? Jove, how surprised I was to find her all grown up! A childhood friend, Miss Ramsay, grown into a charming girl! She tells me you have kindly loaned her some of our books, Mama. Did you know she has an interest in birds?"

Eyeing him uneasily, Lucille agreed, "Yes, a very great interest."

"One supposes your fascination with bats will increase," said Meredith drily. "In the meantime, I'd like a private word with you." He stood. "You will excuse us, ladies?"

Lucille turned pale. "You may run along, Meredith," she quavered, "but you are not to take Miss Ramsay away, and I

83

want Jeffery to tell me about this new interest in—did you say bats, dearest?''

Meredith bowed expressionlessly, and left them. Phoebe waited a few minutes, but sensing that Lucille wished to speak to her son alone, made her excuses and started off on the long trek to her bedchamber to put off her riding habit. She encountered Meredith in the cavernous Great Hall, conversing with a pleasant-looking man whom he left when he caught her eye. Going to her, he asked, "Assistance required, ma'am?"

She hesitated, then, as they walked slowly towards the stairs, said, "I think you are angry again."

"Not with you, Miss Ramsay. Did you really find my lands beautiful?"

It was a warning to stay clear. She accepted his right not to discuss whatever had so enraged him that he fairly vibrated with it, but ignored his question. "Mr. Carruthers, why was your glove left in Sir Malcolm's kennels? Did someone deliberately seek to throw suspicion on you?"

"Or perhaps merely throw my glove at the Squire's dogs," he said lightly.

Halting, she said, "You must realize it is a serious matter. If you have an enemy who would do so dreadful a thing and try to implicate you—"

"If I do, I can think of no possible reason why you should be troubled by it, ma'am. I am only sorry we had to meet that old curmudgeon."

"Perhaps he is curmudgeonly because he misses his son."

"Are you always so kind as to make excuses for bad temper?" He smiled faintly. "If so, you may even begin to think more kindly of me."

She laughed. "Ah, but you have no sons to vex you, sir." She regretted the words the instant they were spoken, and he reacted just as she feared he might.

"Only a fribble of a brother," he muttered, his brow darkening again.

In an attempt to pull his thoughts from Jeffery, she asked, "Shall you see Sir Malcolm's son? Perhaps you could help them to reconcile. What is his name, by the way?"

"Sir Malcolm Lockwood."

Starting up the stairs, she said, "Well, I know that, foolish man. I mean his *son*."

Again, that brief hesitation. Then he replied quietly, "Lancelot."

Phoebe stumbled on the second step and clung to the railing. Turning back to look down at him, she gasped, *"Lancelot?"* Surely—My *heavens*! He is not *Lascelles*?"

He nodded. "Yes, ma'am. He changed his name, as did so many, in an attempt to protect his family."

"But . . . but . . . Oh! You must *tell* him! Poor man! To think that his son is so badly hurt and only a little distance away! You should have told him when—"

A footman passed, glancing at them curiously.

Carruthers interposed a curt and low-voiced "Pray moderate your tone, Miss Ramsay. And I should have done nothing of the sort."

Indignant, she cried, "I cannot *credit* that you could be so—so unfeeling! The Squire is not a casual acquaintance—he is the Lieutenant's *father*!"

His lip curled. "Do your powers of recollection cease at that point? Certainly, you heard Lance beg me to say nothing. I gave my word I would not. A gentleman don't break his word and, despite my many failings, I hope I am still a gentleman!"

He turned on his heel and left her, his spurs jingling as he returned to the man who still waited at the far side of the hall.

Phoebe went upstairs, vexed by his ill manners and stupid stubbornness, and dismayed by the awareness that her little chat with him had done nothing to improve his dark mood.

Ada greeted her with a glowing look. "What a lovely day, miss."

"It would be, were we away from this horrid place," said Phoebe crossly.

"Oh, I dunno. It's got a lot to—er, recommend it."

Allowing her blouse to be removed, Phoebe glared at her. "I suppose that coy look means you have captivated some poor helpless male."

"Has Mr. Carruthers upset you, miss?" evaded Ada demurely. "A bit of a tartar, ain't he? But his people think the world of him. And I must say as I likes them devilish eyes. They make me come over all jellyfish-like."

"Vulgar baggage!" snapped Phoebe, turning on her in a flame. "He is a stubborn, arrogant, foul-tempered—"

Ada's mouth hung open. "But—*miss*! If you hate Mr. Carruthers, why ever did you agree to wed him?"

Close to tears, which was as infuriating as it was inexplicable, Phoebe cried, "*Wed* him? La, I'd sooner wed a coal scuttle! If ever there was a—" Ada's stupefied expression restored her to reality and the perils of her situation. She drew a deep breath and turned away. "Oh, pay me no heed," she muttered.

"Dear Miss Phoebe." Ada patted her shoulder consolingly. "A lover's quarrel, right enough. 'Tis what adds spice to the pudding, so me ma used to say."

It was, thought Phoebe broodingly, a singularly revolting expression. But she wondered, as Ada hummed happily while removing her riding habit, why she felt so very miserable.

Meredith Carruthers's temper, sorely tried by the obtuseness of Miss Phoebe Ramsay, was not improved by the subsequent interview with his steward, nor by the long wait for his brother. It was another half-hour before Jeffery was able to leave the breakfast table. He arrived in the stable area to find Meredith in the large barn looking like a thunder-cloud and the steward obviously relieved by the interruption. Boles, a man of middle years, ample girth, and excellent humour, had been in the service of the family since boyhood. He was that rare commodity, a contented man, enjoying his cheerful wife, his six lively children, and, now that Mr. Paul was gone, his work. He beamed at Jeffery, whom he considered a right slap-up young gentleman and, in response to a jerk of the head from his employer, made his excuses and slipped away, taking with him the groom who had been currying a fine bay mare.

It was warm in the fragrant barn, and Meredith's coat was slung over his shoulder. Noting his expression, Jeffery attempted to head off disaster and attacked first. "This fellow Ramsay," he said. "I take it you're aware he is annoying Rosalie Smith?"

Meredith frowned. "I was not aware they'd met. Do you say he has behaved towards her in an ungentlemanly way?"

"Well, not—er, that, perhaps. But there's not much doubt what he intends. It is not always necessary that a man see a lovely girl more than once to—er, that is—well, I saw him—"

"Indeed? You were present during this—ah, orgy?"

Clenching his fists, Jeffery growled, "I chanced to see him pawing her."

Stiffening, Meredith said sharply, "Did you, by God! I'll own myself surprised, for I'd not have thought him the type to take advantage of one of our people whilst he was a guest in my house. I'll put a stop to it, you may be sure." He added slowly, "As I would did *any* man maul her."

"Deuce take it," exclaimed Jeffery, burdened with the guilty awareness that he'd not only carried tales, a trait he despised, but that he'd actually had very little justification. "If you mean me!"

"Should I? It will not do, Jeff."

"I should like to know just what you mean by that!"

"Nonsense. You know perfectly well what I mean by it. If you plan to enter the petticoat line, my lad, you must look farther afield."

"To leave the field clear for *you*—is that it?"

Meredith's jaw set ominously. "You forget, I think, that I am betrothed. As you conveniently forget other things."

Before the lash of tone and look, Jeffery felt suddenly very small and stupid, which did not help his temper. "For instance?"

"I have just learned that you were rusticated at the beginning of *May*! One collects you enjoyed a jolly sojourn in Town."

Jeffery paled, but said with defiance, "You may think whatsoever you please. Be damned if I'll allow you to dictate—"

Meredith flung his coat aside. "I shall dictate to you for so long as you are under my guardianship. You young fool, d'you think I do not know what you were about? You were with Glendenning again."

"What if I was? I—I suppose you'll not dare to say that *he's* beneath my touch? Tio is—"

"Horatio Glendenning is a fine fellow. He's also a *man* who has been on the Town several years, and—"

"And *I*," interposed Jeffery, smarting at the implication, "am a silly stripling, is that it? Well, you may as well know that I *was* with Tio. I like him, and I like his brother, and be damned if I can see why you object."

"I object not to him, or Michael, but to the company they keep, and the beliefs Tio holds. You know he runs with de Villars and that crew."

"And from that you deduce that Glendenning is a Jacobite? Stuff! I've heard nothing to substantiate it. Besides, *you* sold out because of Cunningham, so you must—"

"To have sold out because I was revolted by needless brutality is one thing. To bring down a military surveillance on this house is quite another! And apart from that indiscretion, I should like to be apprised of the reason you were rusticated—this time."

"Some snivelling sneak wrote to you, I gather."

"It would appear to be a courtesy that my friends write me, since *you* choose not to be above-board."

Jeffery's eyes fell. Very red in the face, he muttered, "It is only until next term, for Lord's sake."

"I did not ask till when. I asked why." A pause, then Carruthers said in a kinder voice, "What the devil ails you, Jeff? If you hate Cambridge, only say so and I'll haul you out and buy you a pair of colours, or—"

"I don't hate it." Jeffery stole a glance at him and said with a sheepish smile, "But thank you for the escape route." The frown returned to his brother's eyes, seeing which he frowned also and, with a typically swift change of mood, added irritably, "Deuce take it, were *you* never rusticated? No, I suppose not. You're so damned sober and industrious! One might think that since *you* take after Papa, whereas—"

In sudden white-faced fury, Meredith gritted, "Do not *ever* say so, or by God—" He shut off the savage words, then added harshly, "For Lord's sake, do not push me into an action I've no wish to take. Tell me why you were rusticated."

Jeffery hesitated, started to speak, tightened his lips, and turned away. "No. It was a personal matter."

"A petticoat, I suppose. Dammit, Jeff, you offer me little choice but to—"

"To do what?" flared Jeffery. "Have me flogged and thrown into the oubliette? I am a *man* now! For the love of heaven, leave me be!"

Meredith caught his wrist as he started away. "I'll not leave you be while you ruin yourself and bring danger on this house!"

Striving in vain to free himself, Jeffery shouted, "I'll not endanger your precious estate, blast it all!"

"There are *people* dwelling on this 'precious estate' you turn up your silly nose at. Or does Mama's well-being matter a jot to you?"

It was the last straw. Torn between remorse and a secret sense of valiant justification, Jeffery's temper burst its bounds. He wrenched free, thus also tearing the shoulder of his new coat. With a cry of rage, he lashed out.

Meredith dodged the blow and retaliated as hotly. It was not the first time they had engaged in fisticuffs in the heat of a quarrel, and for a few minutes the action was fast and furious. Jeffery was eight years younger, and although slenderly built, was fast and well-taught. Meredith, however, was solidly powerful and in perfect condition from long days spent in the saddle or toiling with his men on the land. His own wrath soon evaporating, he contented himself with blocking Jeffery's furious attacks but making no attempt to strike back. Unable to break through that strong defence, Jeffery's rage was fanned to the boiling point. Meredith evaded a flying fist by the simple expedient of a supple sway to the side, and said with a grin, "Oh, enough, bantling." He lowered his fists and stepped clear.

Blinded with wrath, Jeffery jumped in and struck hard and true. Hurt at last, Meredith reacted instinctively. Jeffery was smashed backwards and went down to lie with arms wide tossed and crimson streaking down his chin.

"*Do* come, Sin," urged Phoebe, critically viewing the pale primrose gown and the matching hat Ada had set over the dainty cap atop her curls. "It is such a lovely day, and Mrs. Lucille is eager to show me the gardens."

Lounging on the bed, her brother grinned at her reflected image. "Much you care about the gardens unless Lambert's in 'em. When does he arrive?"

Phoebe sighed and turned to face him, pulling on her mittens. "I don't know. Oh, *what* a pickle it is! I have no wish to upset Mrs. Lucille when she has so kindly accepted me for her daughter-in-law. She's such a dear."

"A dear widgeon," he said without rancour. "Lord, Phoebe, did you ever see such single-mindedness? One might think Jeffery walked on water."

"Well, he *is* a nice boy. A trifle rackety yet, perhaps, but that is only youth."

Amused, he asked, "Is that how you think of me, dear dowager? I'm much of an age with him."

"Yes, but you were born wise. Besides, Meredith handles him in the worst possible way."

"Alas, poor Meredith! He's the one most truly caught in our trap, and Jove, I wish he were not, for I like the man. Only—" He shrugged. "What matter? You'd best run now. Does Mama go with you?"

"No. She is a little fatigued from the journey, I think."

He crossed to open the door for her, but on the threshold she paused, looking up at him. "You accused me of having taken Mr. Carruthers in aversion, which is not true. But you, I think, really dislike his brother. May I ask why?"

He regarded her in his serious, unsmiling way for an instant, then gave her a broad grin. "Jealousy. I met the most choice little village lass. It appears he also is enchanted, and when he saw me with her was so enraged he—"

"So there you are, Miss Ramsay. And how charmingly you look!" Lucille came along the hall with a swish of draperies, herself so lovely in lilac cotton over a white eyelet underdress that Sinclair was moved to compliment her.

"Such a delightful boy," murmured Lucille, accompanying Phoebe down the stairs. " 'Tis easy to see why the girls so admire him."

Phoebe slanted a sharp glance at her. "Sinclair has never been in the petticoat line, ma'am, if that is what you mean."

"Good gracious! How forthright you young people are today!"

"Oh—your pardon. I only meant—"

"No, no. I admire loyalty. Especially between family members. It is just that—Jeffery chanced to mention your brother was much struck by one of our local beauties. And I—er . . ."

"A word of warning?" Phoebe smiled as they crossed the Great Hall and walked towards the back door. "Never say she is a designing woman, ma'am?"

"Indeed not! The dearest child imaginable. Only . . ." Mrs. Lucille murmured almost to herself, "I cannot like to see Jeffery so . . ."

"Infatuated? Surely, he is a handsome fellow, and will have many conquests before he meets his own lady."

"True. If only it were not Rosalie. It would never do. . . . And—and Meredith, you know, is excessive protective of her."

A lackey had followed at a discreet distance and now hurried ahead to throw open the back door for them. Lucille smiled at him, then put up her parasol as they stepped into the bright sunlight and walked toward the drive. "Do not misunderstand," she went on. "My sons are devoted, as you have seen. Meredith is a trifle severe with Jeffery at times, but they are deeply attached, and—What on earth . . . ?"

A small crowd of grooms and stable-boys were gathered around the open doors of the barn, watching what was, to judge by the sounds, a lively scuffle.

"How disgraceful," said Lucille, hurrying forward. "I *do* apologize that our servants indulge in such crude behaviour."

One of the boys glanced around, saw them, and in a flash the doorway was cleared. Determined to put a stop to the brawl, Lucille hastened into the dim interior, Phoebe close behind her.

They arrived in the same instant that Meredith declared a halt to the fight. Phoebe gave a gasp of indignation as Jeffery attacked after his brother had lowered his hands. Her shock was smothered by Lucille's shrill scream as Jeffery went down.

Meredith spun around. In his shirt-sleeves, his hair disordered, his lean body poised for action, he looked like some young buccaneer, Phoebe thought, and had a brief image of him clinging to the rigging of his great galleon, a cutlass brandished in one hand as he prepared to board an enemy vessel.

Lucille experienced no such delusions. She flew to sink to her knees beside Jeffery. "My darling boy," she sobbed, dabbing a dainty square of lace-edged cambric at his split lip. "Oh, my dearest child!" Tears spilled over. She glared up at Meredith and demanded brokenly, "Why? *Why* must you be forever so—so churlish and harsh? I know you cannot help it, but—is there *none* of the Bainbridge gentleness in your blood?"

He said nothing, standing motionless, watching her.

Dazed, but hearing her angry denunciation, Jeffery said feebly, "No, no, Mama. My . . . fault. Not—Merry's."

"Not Merry's!" she exclaimed, wiping his mouth tenderly. "As if I had not seen him strike you down so brutally!"

Meredith picked up his coat and stalked out, not so much as casting a glance at Phoebe.

Seized by the belated awareness that she might have spoiled the match she had so eagerly welcomed, Lucille turned a dismayed glance to the silent girl. She encountered a shocked look and said falteringly, "My—my apologies, Miss Ramsay. My sons . . . a small disagreement only, you understand."

"Yes, ma'am," said Phoebe quietly. "I have a brother myself. Will you pray excuse me?" And without waiting for a response, she hurried into the yard.

She was seething with indignation when she entered the house. It seemed imperative that she come up with Meredith at once, but there was no sign of him in the rear hall. She went outside again and hurried around to the front. The man she met was not her quarry, but the perspiring steward, who had been mopping his close-cropped head, and now clapped on his wig in embarrassment.

"You are Mr. Boles, I believe," said Phoebe. "Did Mr. Meredith come this way?"

"No, miss." He eyed her curiously. "Nothing wrong, I trust?"

She hesitated, but his broad countenance radiated kindliness.

"I'm afraid he and his brother had a—er, slight disagreement," she told him.

"Turn-up, eh? Well, if I may be so bold, miss, it's nought to be in a pucker over. They come to cuffs from time to time, being two very different articles, as you might say. But—Lord help any outsider as dares cause trouble with either one. The other's after him like a shot!"

"I guessed as much. Only—well, Mrs. Carruthers chanced to see Meredith level his brother rather neatly."

"Lordy, Lord! Then the fox is in with the chicks, and no mistake. The missus gave Mr. Meredith a raking down, I'll warrant."

"Yes. Do you know where he went?"

He ran a thoughtful gaze over her. A lovely little creature and no denying, he thought. But she'd a mind of her own, and unless he mistook the matter, that mind wasn't exactly soppy with love for her future husband.

Aware that she was being summed up, Phoebe turned her dimpling smile on the steward and, with a sigh, he capitulated. "He's likely gone to the old abbey, miss." He indicated a wooded hilltop. "If you follow the track there, going up the side of the hill, you'll come to it."

❦ *Chapter 7* ❦

The path was fairly steep and seemed even steeper in the heat of the day, and it was some minutes before Phoebe reached the pleasant shade of the trees. She could see no sign of a building, but walked on. After a while, the woods grew oddly hushed. The sun still slanted in a delicate tracery through the branches, the breeze moved the upper leaves idly, but lower down the air was very still, even the bird-songs seeming muted. She saw a structure ahead and hurried forward. There was not much left of the abbey to which Mr. Boles had referred: one soaring, crumbling wall, part of the aperture wherein had been a high Gothic window, and a tumbled heap of large stone slabs. The light wavered, the sunlight dancing through the leaves to draw sparkles from a little stream that chattered busily past the ruins.

Carruthers was sitting on a massive slab, head and shoulders resting against the wall, one knee drawn up and his arm propped across it. She walked slowly towards him. He looked up, frowned in irritation, but came to his feet.

Stopping before him, Phoebe found herself talking very softly, almost as though it were required here. "How lovely this place is. Like a chapel."

He drawled a cynical "Have you come to pray for my depraved and despotic soul?"

She knew a moment of intense impatience, then thought, 'He must be hurt and angry. And he knows I witnessed that disgraceful little scene.' "I do not believe you to be depraved, Mr. Carruthers," she said.

"Only despotic, eh? Well, I take leave to tell you, ma'am, I did not drag you here by your hair!"

She sighed. "You are all consideration, but I will take leave to tell you something, also. Namely, that if I thought 'twould serve to free us from our—unhappy entanglement, I'd gladly allow you to drag me back to Pineridge in such fashion.''

"Would you? Well, I can sympathize with your feelings. If ever there was such a *damnable* coil!''

She gave a shocked gasp and threw one hand to her heart.

Carruthers scowled down at her. "If my language offends, I apologize. I've not a silver tongue at the best of times.''

Phoebe, who had been present at several lively exchanges between her sire and his outspoken mama, folded her hands in saintly fashion and declared that she could endure it. "For they are only words, after all, and I expect it is merely a matter of—what a lady is accustomed to.''

His eyes narrowed. "To judge by the conversation of most ladies these days, you must be accustomed to nonsense.''

'Brute!' she thought, and responded meekly, "Oh, yes. For it is, you know, what the gentlemen like to hear.''

He threw back his head and gave an unexpected shout of laughter. "*Touché!* Do you always come up fighting?''

"Only when excessively provoked.''

"Is rare in a woman. Usually, they tend to—'' He bit his lip.

"Dear sir, you must not deny yourself on my account.''

"Be grateful, ma'am,'' he warned, amused. "I restrained a most unkind comment.''

"Tell me, Mr. Carruthers, have you a flag? A family banner, perchance?''

"Of course. Why?''

"May I suggest you hoist it at once to the top of your flagpole? Truly, this is a very special occasion!''

He chuckled and took her by the shoulders, shaking her gently. "Little shrew!''

"Large Tyrant,'' she returned equably, but marvelling at the change laughter wrought in him.

"Miss Phoebe,'' he said, the smile lingering in his eyes, "might we, do you think, cry friends?''

Such an overture was completely unexpected. Her cheeks flamed and her heart began to flutter in so silly a way that she could hardly command her voice, but she managed, "That would probably be advisable, Mr. Carruthers, since we plot our treason together.''

"I have another name, you know,'' he pointed out gently.

"Yes. Well—Mr. Meredith, then.'' She started to pull back, but his grip tightened. Phoebe looked up at him questioningly.

94

The hushed silence, the dim arboreal light enfolded them. Carruthers drew her close, and kissed her.

It was a kiss that bore no resemblance to those that Brooks Lambert had shared with her. Carruthers's hands were like iron; his mouth was hard and fierce and hungry. She felt crushed and half smothered, and something else; something powerful and primitive, so that, frightened, she drew back. He released her at once, and she stood staring up at him. The eyes she had thought grey and icy were lit as with a clear blue fire. The lean planes of his face were pale beneath his tan, and the mouth that had taken hers so demandingly curved to a smile at once tender and confident.

Muddled, she asked inconsequently, "What is this place?"

"It is called *Abbaye Enfoncée*."

"Why? It is not submerged, but on a hilltop."

He glanced with proprietary fondness around the little glade. "Yes. But the monks who built here were very taken with the peace and stillness." He added with the shyness of a man fearing ridicule, "It—er, does have rather an atmosphere of being under water, do not you think?"

"That is exactly it," she murmured. "An enchanted undersea hilltop."

Distantly, someone was calling. She started. "Good gracious! You kissed me, Mr. Carruthers!"

"Merely exercising my rights."

"But—we—"

"We *are* officially betrothed, you know."

He was still holding her hands. He was, in fact, pulling her back to him. She wondered in a remote way if her ribs would survive another of his hugs. The blue blaze was in his eyes again; he was leaning to her, lips parted, that incredible tenderness in his face that made her breath hasten and her resolution disappear altogether. Resistless, she swayed closer. . . .

"Phoebe . . . ? Where in the duece *are* you?"

"Sin!" And he sounded impatient. Phoebe drew back. She felt positively twittery, and said in a hurrying rush, "I must go."

This time he did not release her, but said huskily, "He'll find you. Let him wait a minute."

"No. I should not— *We* must not— Oh, you are a *dreadful* man!"

She ran quickly from the little glade, hearing his low chuckle sound behind her.

Sinclair came toiling up the hill. "So there you are! Lord, Phoebe, there's the deuce to pay!"

"My heavens! Not Lascelles?"

"No, no. *Lambert* is come, which is going to make it so dashed difficult. Why is your face so red? Oh—because your love is here, I suppose."

It was ridiculous to feel such a crushing sense of guilt. She was not actually betrothed to Lamb. In point of fact, Carruthers had more right to—She thought, 'Lord, but I must be a shocking flirt!' and asked quickly, "Why should it make things difficult for Carruthers? You knew we meant to try and break the betrothal."

"I didn't mean just Carruthers. I hadn't stopped to think that with Brooks staying right in the Hall, and hungry for promotion—and you know how he despises the Jacobites! Blasted sticky."

She gave a gasp. "Oh dear! Well, thank heaven it's such an enormous, rambling place. Hopefully, you and Carruthers can slip in and out and scarcely be noticed."

He grunted. "Hopefully. Oh, and the reason I came seeking you is that Mama wants to see you. She's properly up in the boughs because Lambert has appeared."

Phoebe moaned, and hurried into the house.

Lady Eloise awaited her with an aggrieved air and a firm lecture. Kneeling beside her parlour chair and looking up at her pleadingly, Phoebe pointed out, "But Brooks often comes here. He is Carruthers's nephew, Mama."

"Which is ridiculous on the face of it," her mother argued. "You might just as well say his cousin, Duncan Tiele, is also Carruthers's nephew. Which, in the very silly involvements that so often result from second marriages, I suppose he is. You may be sure I shall say nothing to Lucille Carruthers about your— er, about Captain Lambert's hopes with regard to yourself, and you had best caution *him* not to do so."

"Yes, ma'am. But I am sure Mrs. Carruthers will make nothing of his coming here on his leave."

"Probably not," said my lady, the frown still evident in her green eyes. "But *I* make something of it, Phoebe. And so will your papa! And when the old lady comes . . . Oh, frightful!"

Phoebe stared at her. "You mean—Grandmama is coming . . . here?"

"Yes. She did not like to come at once, you know, but she

told me she means to come as soon as she can get away from that bazaar for the orphanage.''

"How—lovely," said Phoebe rather hollowly, and having promised her mother that she would do nothing to displease Mr. Carruthers insofar as Brooks Lambert was concerned, she went off in search of the Captain.

She had not far to search, for when she stopped in her bed-chamber to take off her hat, Ada told her that Captain Lambert had sent up a note. It was brief and to the point:

P.
Must see you. Will wait in the Elizabethan garden.
Urgent.

L.

Phoebe glanced uneasily at the clock. Quarter to twelve. Mrs. Lucille had not yet taken her through the gardens, and after lunch she was to go for a drive with Meredith. Still, if she hurried, there should be time. She went downstairs and out to the back of the house. The air was hot and rather lifeless now, with a few clouds creeping into view to the east. Across the drivepath were lawns and a belt of dense trees, beyond which lay the stables, barns, coach-houses, and tack-rooms. She made her way to the left, following a rock pathway that was extremely uneven. It wound along the rear of the 'new' wing and continued past the Lancastrian building, where it was shaded by a depressed-looking and sagging trellis covered by wilting vines. At the end of the pathway was an arched gate, and, opening this, Phoebe found herself in the great courtyard, with to her right the glooming bulk of Castle Carruthers.

It was of the broad, massy-walled variety, rather than the tall proud type that she preferred, and put her in mind of the central keep at Arundel. Surveying its crumbling walls, broken steps, cracked dry moat, and the gaps in the battlements, she thought it had a melancholy, lonely look, and felt a pang of sympathy for the poor old thing. It was part of the heritage of this land and should not, she thought, be allowed to moulder away until no one would ever remember the sieges it had withstood, or the invincible face it must once have presented to the foreign invader. She realized she was dawdling, and hurried her steps. The courtyard was very wide, the cobbles even more irregular than the pathway had been, and her feet in their light slippers began to be sore. She was relieved when the gate leading to the garden of the Tudor addition came into view. This was where the family dwelt. There was a path in a better state of preservation than the others had been, but she walked on the lawn this time, grateful for the many old trees that provided shade and, hopefully, concealment from the windows. The garden was well tended, and she could see a distant gleam of ornamental water and intricate flower-beds that she would like to investigate when she had more time. At last she came around the corner where the Elizabethan addition commenced. This garden had seen very little care of recent years, by the look of it, but there was what must once have been a charming rose arbour and a drooping summer-house in which a man waited, who rose as she approached and came down the steps.

Lambert held out both hands as he strode to join her, his enchanting smile warming her heart. "At last," he exclaimed, bowing his handsome head over her fingers and pressing kisses upon them. "Gad, how I yearn to kiss you properly, my adored girl, but I'd best not, just in case."

"No. But do let us get in out of the sun."

He ushered her inside, and seized her hand again. "Phoebe, you're lovelier each time I see you. Tell me what has been going forward. Have you told him that I am the third side of the eternal triangle?"

"No, because you asked that I wait. I am so glad you were able to get leave."

He made a wry face. "I was—with reservations. It seems there's some miserable hound of a rebel lurking about, and the whole area from here to the coast is to be beaten. I am ordered to join the search if I'm called on. And knowing the Colonel in command down here, I'll likely be called on!" He peered at her uneasily. "Are you all right, love? You're frightfully pale."

Phoebe was in the grip of cold terror. She managed somehow to reply that she was a little troubled by the muggy heat. "I shall be so glad when this is over, Lamb. However are we to go about it, do you think?"

He sighed. "With difficulty. The announcement of your betrothal appeared in *The Gazette* this morning."

"Oh, my heavens! But—but I thought—Oh, Lamb! There will be *no* getting out of it, then."

He slipped an arm about her. "Cheer up, dearest. We'll come about." Having first cast a furtive glance about the weedy gardens, he dropped a kiss on her brow, and asked, "You are quite

98

sure Carruthers is willing to give you up? I'd think the man who agreed to let *you* escape him must be properly rabbit-brained."

Firmly denying the memory of a dark, ardent face and the kiss that must surely have bruised her lips, she said, "Carruthers is not in love with me. How could he be, for we had never before met to speak of?"

"Well, that's a point in our favour, but"—he tilted her face upwards—"I cannot like to see your lovely eyes so worried. Chase away your fears, dear heart. I shall go at once to speak with Carruthers, and—"

She caught at his hand. "No, Brooks! You must wait!" He stared at her and she went on hastily, "He was—er, in a black rage earlier, and—"

"Say no more!" He shuddered. "I know Merry's black rages. Like father, like son. Mayhap his mood will improve by this evening. I'll approach him after dinner. It's as well you said nothing; better I confront him with it."

She stood. "You will be careful not to let anyone hear? Mrs. Lucille is very pleased by our betrothal, and I would not wish to hurt her."

"Nor I." Having also come to his feet, he said, "Poor little thing, she has much to bear, one way and another. Must you go so soon, dearest? I've had very little of your time, and there is so much I want to ask you."

She hesitated, but he regarded her so wistfully that she relented and sat down again. "Just a few minutes, though, and I've a question for you, first. Brooks, you must know Meredith well. Has he enemies?"

"Lord, yes!" He grinned. "The only type of man who can go through life without 'em must be an insipid kind of fellow, and whatever else one might say of my uncle, he's not insipid. Why d'you ask?"

She told him about Sir Malcolm Lockwood and the poisoning of his dogs. Lambert whistled softly. "Zounds, but I mislike the sound of that. What did Merry say?"

"Very little, but it was clear he doesn't want his mama worried by it, so please do not mention it when she is by."

"No, I won't. But I'll keep my eyes open and see if I can find out anything. And now for my much more important enquiries."

"For instance?"

"For instance," he said rather hesitantly, "has my rich uncle replaced me in your affections?"

The question annoyed her. She said, "I scarcely know Mr. Carruthers, but from what you have told me I could not fail to be grateful to him, if only because he has been good to you."

"And that properly set me down. As I deserved, for being so crass. Faith, I'll be lucky do I not drive you right into his arms with my jealousy."

"Small chance of that," she assured him, albeit with another guilty pang because she had already been wrapped in Carruthers's arms. "I rather gather your uncle is very much enamoured of another lady." He looked at her curiously, and she said with proper nonchalance, "Rosalie somebody or other."

"What—Rosalie Smith?" he chuckled. "No competition to you, dear heart, though I could wish otherwise. She's pretty as any picture, but at best would only be a—er—"

"You mean she is his mistress."

He looked miserable. "I did not say that, Phoebe."

"You did not have to. It is very clear, and of no interest to me. But I am sufficiently unsophisticated, Brooks, that I would very much like to wed a gentleman who, at least for a while, would be content with—just me."

He swept her into his arms. "My God! Who could possibly look elsewhere once he had seen *your* radiance? Have no fears, my darling, you are all *I* could ever want!"

The blue eyes gazing at her adoringly were a so much deeper blue than those other eyes, and full of adoration; not a blaze that threatened to consume her. He was so loyal to Carruthers; so faithful in his love; such a gallant young man. She really was most fortunate to have found him. She allowed him one quick kiss, and was left with neither crushed ribs nor bruised lips.

Lady Eloise was taken by Mrs. Carruthers for a stroll through the several gardens and returned full of praise for the beauty of the ornamental water and fountains. It was very clear the two women thoroughly enjoyed each other's company, and when they all were gathered in the small dining room for luncheon, Phoebe thought Mrs. Carruthers fairly glowed with happiness. If there was still animosity between the brothers, neither showed it, and if Lambert noted the swelling beside Jeffery's mouth and the welt along Meredith's jaw, he made no comment. The worst moment for Phoebe was when Meredith presented her to Lambert as his 'betrothed.' She did not know where to look, but Lambert responded easily, "Miss Ramsay and I are acquainted,

Merry, and you've my heartiest congratulations, you lucky dog."
He proceeded to tease Carruthers in so good-natured a way that
Phoebe was astounded by his acting ability. He did not manage
nearly so well a short while later, his jaw dropping and stark
disbelief coming into his eyes when my lady said, "Now, Mr.
Carruthers, do, I beg you, favour us with one of your poetical
pieces."

"Lud!" gasped Lucille, turning an amazed stare on her eldest
son.

Meredith, who had been in the act of cornering some green
peas, was so jolted that the peas sprayed the table. He flushed
scarlet, his eyes positively glazing with shock.

Jeffery gave a muffled snort and disappeared into his napkin.

Carruthers shot a stunned glance at Phoebe, who smiled at
him benignly, while fighting to smother a bubble of mirth.

Making a recover, Lambert said wickedly, "Oh, yes, *pray*
do, Meredith. It would be so diverting."

"I—could not do so without . . . seeming to brag," said
Meredith. "Miss Ramsay must recite them, rather."

"Alas, but I've not a copy with me," she mourned. "But you
must recall the ode you writ to my eyes, Mr. Carruthers. I shall
jog your memory. The first line, as I recollect, went: 'Those
great and sparkling emerald eyes . . .' " She rested those eyes
on his desperation with demure encouragement.

"Oh, *do* complete it, Merry," gasped Jeffery, apparently
troubled by something in his own eye.

His back to the wall, Carruthers directed a swift and vengeful
glance at Phoebe, then stammered, "Ah—Those great and—
and sparkling—er, emerald eyes . . . Ah, Whose beauty—er,
fairly petrifies . . ." He mopped his brow, but struggled on,
"petrifies . . . My-self who—is, er, am—not very wise."

Lady Eloise stared at him. "Oh," she said blankly.

Phoebe's eyes sparkled indeed, as Jeffery succumbed to a
great shout of laughter.

Lucille looked from Lambert's muffled hilarity to Jeffery's
tears, and said indignantly, "Well, I think it is really quite remarkable!" She smiled consolingly at the sweating Meredith.
"And you two boys are behaving disgracefully."

"For which," growled Meredith, "there will be a moment
of reckoning."

He had not spoken with real animosity, but Jeffery's mirth
was wiped away. One hand lifted involuntarily to his damaged
mouth, and for the balance of the meal he was subdued. Guess-

ing that he was miserable and repentant, Phoebe felt sorry for him.

When they left the dining room, Meredith asked very softly, "Would you prefer to ride to your execution, Miss Ramsay? Or to drive?"

She stifled a giggle, and replied that since it was rather muggy, she really would prefer to ride.

Coming level with them in time to hear this, Lambert asked good-humouredly, "Are we allowed to accompany you?"

"Certainly not," Meredith answered. "Find your own lady! I'll not have you dazzling Miss Ramsay with your glorious scarlet coat and making me look a drab fellow by comparison!"

Lambert said nothing, but stood very still for an instant, his smile rather fixed.

Jeffery succeeded in detaining his brother in the Great Hall and offered a humble apology for his unsportsmanlike behaviour. "I explained to Mama that I had struck a foul," he said, "and I know she feels very sorry for what she said to you."

Meredith walked up the stairs with him. "It takes two to make a quarrel. I'm a deal short on tact, I fear. No, do not go on with your humility, for the love of heaven. I'm glad to see your sparring improves!"

Jeffery glanced at him shyly, met a wide grin, and gripped his shoulder in silent gratitude.

When they reached the first-floor landing, Meredith paused. "Do you care to ride with us to the Minor?"

"Thank you, no. I've another—appointment."

They strolled on, and after a minute Jeffery voiced the thought that was in both their minds. "Mama did not mean it. You know that. She—she is deeply attached to you, Merry."

"Yes."

"It is only . . . Oh, damme, I know you do not care to hear it, but—sometimes you *do* look so blasted well like him."

"Whereas you had the good sense to resemble the Bainbridges." Meredith cuffed him gently. "I know that, too."

When they parted, Meredith said, "I shall not ask with whom is your appointment. I ask only that you do nothing that may cause Mama distress."

Jeffery grinned. "I'd not dare! You carry an invisible sledgehammer in your dashed fists!"

102

The afternoon had become sultry and still, a line of clouds darkening the eastern horizon. Phoebe was a little surprised, on going down to the ground floor, to find Sinclair waiting alone, a set expression on his face. "Your beau has gone stamping off to the stables," he imparted tersely. "It seems he don't care to be kept waiting."

"Oh, does he not! Surely I am not very late?"

"Course not. What's half an hour to you ladies?" But his anger was almost palpable, and Phoebe linked her arm through his as they walked to the back door. "He has really put you out of curl. What is it? Something to do with our fugitive?"

"No. He—he properly warned me off, is all. And—I've done *nothing*, that is what rankles."

"Oh, dear. The little village girl? I rather gather that she is—er, his."

He pulled away and said vehemently, "That is not so! She's the loveliest, purest, most innocent of creatures! I'd like to know what gives him the right—" He checked, scowling darkly.

"Just so, love. If *you* owned the villages—"

"I'd not think it gave me the power of life and death over the folks who dwell in 'em! The man is so set up in his own conceit, one might think him a—a veritable deity!"

"Good gracious! What did he say to you?"

He shrugged, and muttered sullenly, "No straight-out accusations. Just some aimless chatter that brought things around to her, and then a remark that she is so lovely he's already had to warn some of the local bucks that she is one of 'his people' and he'll not have her annoyed. 'Annoyed,' indeed!"

"Is that all? It sounds to me as if he was most—"

"Well, he was not! Those damnable icicles he has for eyes fairly stuck right through me and half a yard out of my back! Damned puritanical busybody!"

She fought a smile. "Are you being quite fair, Sin? If he has some reason for supposing—"

"*If* he has, then it's his mealy-mouthed brother has put the notion in his head."

"Perhaps you'd best not ride with us, dear."

He flung open the door and waved her through. "I wish I might not, but however top-lofty he is, we *are* indebted to him. I wish to heaven we weren't! And I can well guess how much you wish it, poor girl."

"Mmmn," said Phoebe.

In the stableyard, Carruthers was chatting with a groom who held a fine dapple-grey horse.

"Oh, but he's splendid," Phoebe cried enthusiastically.

Carruthers bent to receive her foot and throw her into the saddle. "He is called Showers, and is one of my sweetest goers." A spirited roan gelding was led out, and Carruthers went on, "Ramsay, this fellow is yours. You shall have to watch him. He's a tendency to run away."

Sinclair concealed his admiration of the fine animal, and murmured a cool acknowledgment.

Carruthers gave him a grave look, and whistled. A magnificent bay mare with three white stockings trotted from the stables to dance around and halt beside her master.

Sinclair quite forgot his anger. "I *say*, but she's a beautiful animal! How is she called?"

"Spring. And she's a handful, as she means to prove, I'm afraid."

He was right. Spring was full of fun and went in dancing circles, Carruthers making no attempt to restrain her. Sinclair recalled belatedly that he had been dealt an unwarranted insult, and was haughtily silent. The clouds that had fringed the horizon were sliding up the sky, and a hot, fitful wind began to stir the tree-tops. Phoebe felt the tightness in her head that the presence of lightning always brought, yet she was exhilarated by the beauties about her and scarcely noticed her brother's withdrawal.

They followed the estate road at first, passing several neat cottages which Carruthers said were the homes of retired servants. They rode past softly swaying fields of young corn, leaving the road about a half-mile past the cottages and turning north through open land where fat black cattle grazed contentedly. Uphill, gradually, and a low slate wall blocked their way, stretching off to right and left. Carruthers asked with a twitch of the lips, "Do you fancy you can negotiate this, ma'am?"

Before Phoebe could give him the set-down he deserved, Sinclair interpolated heatedly, "My sister can take a sight higher obstacle than that stepping-stone!"

"Indeed?" drawled Carruthers. "I shall have to find you some worthwhile jumps, ma'am."

He leaned forward in the saddle, spoke softly to Spring, and the mare cantered along and sailed over, as light as thistle-down. Showers was only a head behind, clearing the wall neatly. Sinclair, angry, set the roan at the wall very fast. The big gelding soared high into the air, landed much too close to Spring, drawing a startled shout from Carruthers, and was away at a thundering gallop, Sinclair's roared "Whoa's" echoing behind him.

"Damned young fool," fumed Carruthers. I *told* him the brute tends to run away! Why in the devil did he take that little wall as though it had been ten feet high?"

"Because he is the smarting victim of unjust calumny," she replied.

He snorted impatiently. "Don't like to be forewarned, eh? And here I'd fancied I was treading lightly."

"My brother is more interested in books than petticoats. But he is growing up, of course." Watching him from under her eyelashes, she added, "I think he is really smitten. Your village lass must be a rare charmer to have won so many admirers."

At once his dark brows twitched into a frown, "Many? I know of only one other. Shall we get along, ma'am? Those clouds look rather threatening, and I'd not have you soaked to—"

"No. First I must talk to you." She glanced around and then felt silly. As if anyone could overhear, and yet how pervasive was the threat, even now. "I was chatting with Captain Lambert, and—"

"You know him well?"

It seemed an idle question, but again she paused. What an ideal opportunity to tell him that she was promised to his nephew; but Brooks clearly wished to handle the matter. Carruthers turned to her with an enquiring expression, and she replied quickly, "We have had his acquaintance for some years. And I have been so anxious to tell you that he says the whole countryside from here to the coast is to be beaten. Will Lascelles be safe where he is?"

He reined up. "Devil take it! No, he will not. Did Lambert say when this search is to begin?"

"No. Only that he is subject to recall if needed to participate in the hunt. I rather gather it is imminent."

He swore under his breath. "Then we must move Lance tonight. Certainly we cannot do anything by daylight, so we'd as well have our ride, if—Oh, blast!"

Following his irked gaze, Phoebe saw Justice coming up, limping painfully, his tongue lolling, and in a state of near exhaustion. Carruthers dismounted and dropped to one knee beside the dog. "You confounded old fool," he scolded.

"Poor fellow," said Phoebe, sliding from the saddle. "Is he ill?"

"Not as young as he used to be—like Joseph." He lifted the right front paw to inspect it narrowly. "I *told* my man not to let him out, for I knew he'd follow. He hurt this article recently and it was near healed." He tugged a handkerchief from his pocket and began to wrap it around the torn pad while the big dog sprawled helplessly and tried to lick his hand.

Phoebe asked, "Can he walk all the way home?"

"I suppose he could, but I'd prefer he not do so." He stood, glancing around. "If I carry Justice to that stand of oaks at the foot of the hill, would you object to waiting with him while I ride on to my farm? It's quite close by and should not take above a quarter of an hour. I'll bring one of the lads with a cart, and he can convey the old fellow back to the Hall." He glanced eastward and added uneasily, "Those clouds are really blowing, in; we may not be able to get to the village after all. I'm dashed sorry, but he really shouldn't walk on that paw, so if you don't mind—"

"Oh, do stop talking such fustian, Meredith! Of course I don't mind."

Carruthers grinned at her, and gathered the dog into his arms. She had wondered how he meant to accomplish this, for Justice was a big animal and she fancied he might be alarmed and struggle against being lifted. Carruthers managed it quite easily. Justice's paws rested on his master's shoulders, and Carruthers supported his hind quarters. The dog's soulful eyes regarded Phoebe with calm placidity, as though he thought, 'What did you expect?'

"Jove, but I'm a thimblewit," groaned Carruthers. "I should have helped you mount up first, but it's not very far. Can you bring Showers, ma'am? Never worry about Spring—she'll follow me."

The mare was grazing and apparently paying no attention to them, but they had gone a very little way before her muzzle was at Carruthers's neck, and she stayed close beside him until he had set the dog down in the shelter of the trees. "I'll be as quick as I can," he promised. "This is miserable for you, but—"

Phoebe jabbed a finger in the direction of the waiting horse, and Carruthers chuckled, said, "Aye, aye, ma'am," and threw her a brisk salute. The wind moaned and the branches swayed agitatedly. "Are you cold?" he asked, and began to shrug out of his coat.

"I am not cold. I am perfectly well. I think I will not perish of hunger or thirst whilst you are gone, and I fancy Justice will protect me from any lurking brigands," she replied, twinkling at him. "Be off with you, sir!"

He mounted up, said firmly, "Justice—*stay!*" and with a flourish of his tricorne was away at the gallop.

Watching horse and rider streak across the meadow, Phoebe found that she was still smiling. Meredith Carruthers was a stern gentleman with a daunting manner, but he was very obviously obsessed by a need to protect any creature for whom he felt responsible. It was, she reflected, rather an endearing quality.

After a few minutes she started to wander about a little, but Justice immediately began to struggle to his feet, so she went instead to sit beside him. He lolled against her companionably, and she fondled his head, pulling the great folds of loose skin into ripples around his face and then telling him how silly he looked. He thumped his tail to show that he did not at all object, but cringed as thunder rattled distantly. The moments drifted past; the wind seemed to rise a little, and the dark clouds slid ever nearer. Justice gave a faint moan as lightning flashed, and Phoebe ducked her head against him as the following thunder boomed out. "A fine pair of cravens we are," she said, then jumped up eagerly. It did not seem as if fifteen minutes had gone by, but a rider was approaching. A moment later, she saw a familiar bay mare and the erect figure of Brooks Lambert, and she waved and called to him.

He turned his mare to the trees. "Phoebe! What the deuce are you about?"

Justice gave a deep bay and wagged his tail in welcome. Lambert swung down, tethered his mare loosely, and hurried to take Phoebe's hands.

She explained rapidly, then asked, "Were you looking for us?"

"Yes. I'm recalled, curse it! That confounded Colonel has roped me in, and I've to report at once. I'll be damned if I will leave you here without I've told Carruthers how matters stand, so came to find him and lay our cards on the table."

She said uneasily, "Brooks, I wish you would let me tell him."

"Why should you have to do it? The only reason I delayed was that I hope to catch him in a good mood and enlist his aid. I've no wish to antagonize him, nor," he added with a grin, "to lose the allowance he makes me."

"I see that, of course," she said rather dubiously. "Although I own—"

A shout interrupted her, and Carruthers rode up at the gallop. He dismounted, looped the reins around the pommel, and turned Spring loose. Justice limped eagerly to meet him, and he patted the hound while glancing curiously at Lambert.

Her heart beginning to leap about with nervousness, Phoebe said, "Captain Lambert came seeking us."

"So I see. One of my people is bringing a cart to take this silly rascal back to the Hall. We'll be fortunate are we not rained on before we reach home. Now, what's to do, Brooks?" With a faint smile, he said teasingly, "I think I do not like to find you alone here with my lady."

Lambert said, "Well, that's the point, you see. Phoebe is *my* lady."

It was said. Phoebe thought numbly, '*I* could have handled it more diplomatically than that!' and felt utterly wretched.

Carruthers stood motionless, staring at Lambert's wry smile in silence.

Thunder growled, closer this time.

Lambert asked anxiously, "You don't object, do you, Merry? Phoebe said neither of you wanted this betrothal."

"*You* . . . ?" said Carruthers in a very soft voice. "*You* are her—fine brave gentleman?"

"Well—er, yes," answered Lambert, flushing slightly.

The pale eyes darted to Phoebe, and she was reminded of Sinclair's remark about being transfixed. "Truth?" he demanded.

Her voice cracking in a ridiculous way, she said, "Brooks and—er, I—"

"Yes, it is truth," interpolated Lambert, irked. "Do you think I—"

"Be silent!" The words were flung at him, and he stared uneasily.

"Miss Ramsay," Carruthers grated, "I am at a loss to understand why you saw fit to conceal this—attachment. Perhaps you will be so good as to explain."

"Don't take that tone with her," protested Lambert. "She—"

"I asked . . . *her!*"

"The devil," said Lambert, bristling. "There's no—"

Phoebe interposed desperately, "I told you, Mr. Carruthers, that my family has not given their approval."

"That don't explain why you'd have failed to mention that your admirer was my nephew." He turned a smouldering gaze on Lambert. "You instructed her to keep silent, is that it?"

"Yes. Had I known about it beforehand, you may believe I'd have come to you at once. As it was already a *fait accompli*, I thought it better to wait until I could come down and explain things, and ask your help."

Carruthers echoed rather incredulously, "My—*help*?"

"Well, after all, old fellow, *you* don't want to wed Miss Ramsay, and *she* don't want to wed you. On the other hand, *I* want very much to wed her."

At this point a cart came rattling into view, a tanned youth driving the sturdy cob. Carruthers lifted Justice once more and carried the dog to the rear of the cart, the youth jumping down to lower the back.

Lambert muttered, "He's in a flame. Dammitall, I might've known he'd take one look at you, and—"

"No, no, Lamb! 'Tis only that he is cross because I did not tell him at once. I wish I had!"

"I didn't want you to have to tell him. He has such a ferocious temper, there's never any knowing—" He broke off as Carruthers instructed the youth to "take it carefully," waved the cart off, and returned to them.

"Well," he said briskly. "Let's try and come at the straight of this. You want me to draw back, I take it."

Relieved because the steely look had eased, Phoebe nodded. "You said you were willing to do so."

"No, ma'am. I said if it was humanly possible to escape this—ah, contretemps, I would do so. I begin to think it may not be possible."

"What?" shouted Lambert furiously.

"Why?" demanded Phoebe.

"Firstly, ma'am, although neither you nor I want to wed, both our families are delighted by our betrothal."

"Yes, but you knew when we were obliged to—" She bit her lip as his eyes flashed a warning.

He went on, "Secondly, since I cannot jilt you without ruining you, the only way out that I can see is for you to jilt me."

"Yes, of course," said Lambert.

"Oh . . . *dear!*" gasped Phoebe, genuinely dismayed. "Is there no other way?"

"If there is, I wish you may tell me of it. And since there has already been a touch of scandal in my family, for my mama's sake I'd as soon not add to our reputation. Even so, I'd allow you to jilt me were there a possibility you and Brooks could wed. But—"

Lambert interrupted angrily, "But you have begun to think you'd not be averse to take Phoebe for your bride, eh?"

Carruthers looked at him steadily. "I begin to see that to get out of this is going to result in pain to a number of people, and disgrace for me."

"But, dammitall, she—don't *want* you!"

"True," said Carruthers agreeably. "But the chances of her being able to marry *you* are remote, and I find myself unwilling to face ostracism and censure in so uncertain a cause."

"I'll win 'em over!" Lambert declared. "I'll *find* a way! I'll go to your grandmama at Pineridge, Phoebe. On my *knees*, if I must!"

"Grandmama is coming *here*," she said.

"Excelsior! Only let me *try*, Merry! You know you've always maintained you mean to remain a bachelor. If I can win the old lady over, Sir George will not dispute it, and your mama likes me, doesn't she, Phoebe?"

"Yes. You know she does."

"There must be *some* way to get into Lady Martha's good graces," said Lambert. "If you would only help us, Merry."

Carruthers regarded Phoebe speculatively. "On a condition— perhaps. Miss Ramsay, if you are forbidden to wed Lambert, you will be obliged to marry someone, no?"

She nodded.

"In that unhappy event, would it be repugnant to you to become my wife? No—do not answer quickly, out of courtesy. I want the truth. I know I am not a handsome fellow and inclined to be quick-tempered. You must not hesitate to be honest if marriage to me would repel you."

Firing up again, Lambert cried, "Now, see here!"

"Well, of course it would not!" exclaimed Phoebe.

She looked so indignant that Carruthers's lips quirked into his sideways grin. "Then I think I will not allow you to jilt me; at least for a while. However, before you explode, Lambert, let me say that I appreciate your predicament, and mean to do my best for you. If you can win Lady Martha Ramsay over within a month, I will find some pretext and withdraw my offer. If not—the spurious betrothal will become a genuine one."

Phoebe searched his face, but his expression was unreadable.

"A month!" Brooks cried, triumphantly. "I'll think of *something*, Phoebe, I swear it! Surely, between the three of us, we should be able to find a way out! Merry, you're a dashed good fellow. I know how difficult it will be for you. Thank you!"

Carruthers said, "Save your thanks till the twenty-ninth of August, Brooks."

The lightning flash was brilliant, and the thunder spoke an instant response. Lambert's mare shied skittishly, and he said, "Jove, I must go, or my fiendish Colonel will have me facing a firing squad. Merry—you'll see that Phoebe gets back safely?"

"Marplot! Here I had thought to toss her into the Quarry for her betrayal of me." Carruthers threw Phoebe up into her saddle. "Shall you return tonight, Brooks?"

"I hope so, but I rather doubt it. Fotheringay's a stern taskmaster!"

Carruthers jerked around. "*Fotheringay?* Major Mariner Fotheringay?"

"Lieutenant Colonel now, dear boy. You know him?"

"I do. He's a tartar. Have a care. If you are demoted your chances will lessen, you know."

Lambert groaned, waved, and rode off through the spattering rain.

Phoebe murmured, "If only I could tell him how we entrapped you into this, Mr. Carr—"

"Meredith." He stripped off his coat and handed it up to her. "No, do not argue. As you can see by this brown face of mine, I'm accustomed to being out in the weather."

She pulled it around her shoulders. It was still warm, and smelled of him: soap and leather, and the faintest hint of a clean, masculine fragrance. She felt snug and, oddly, secure.

Carruthers was grinning at her. "What became of your arms?"

She waved one.

"That will not do, ma'am. We're in for a downpour, and you must put it all the way on." He mounted up, leaned over and helped her slip her arms into the sleeves and fold back the great cuffs. "There, that's better."

She put her hand on his wrist, then shrank as the lightning flared garishly and the thunder cracked, seemingly just above the tree-tops. Carruthers's hand turned to claim hers and hold it strongly. "Don't be scared, but I think we'd best get out from under these trees."

"Oh! Look at the rain! Meredith, you will be soaked!"

"Yes. Only think what a pest you are."

She smiled, and they started off, side by side.

He said, "I fancy you are wishing me at Jericho for not immediately falling in with your plans. The thing is, I'd not realized our betrothal would so delight my mama. And—well, she has known a deal of grief. I'd prefer she not suffer any more, on my account."

So that was why he had struck the bargain with Lambert. She said, "Then we must see that she is not injured by this horrid mess."

He was briefly silent, then asked, "Do you notice how short is the distance you can see clearly?"

She blinked through the downpour, then cried eagerly, "You mean to go to Lieutenant Lascelles!"

"Mariner Fotheringay is an excellent officer, and very determined to become a full colonel, I've no doubt. To capture Lance would turn the trick for him. I wish your brother had not disappeared, but—never mind." He paused of necessity as another peal battered them. "I'll take you as far as the drivepath, Miss Phoebe, and you can explain to my mama that I turned aside to free a sheep that was drowning, or some such thing. If you find your brother, tell him to head north to try and come up with me."

She looked at him uneasily. His white shirt was already clinging wetly to his muscular frame. "Oh, you are soaked," she cried, and drew Showers to a halt. "And north is in the opposite direction!"

"Yes. Do come along, ma'am. We waste time."

"No!" She reined about. "I will come with you and help. We must be halfway there."

"If you suppose for one minute that I would—"

Phoebe kicked home her heels and Showers galloped off.

Swearing in exasperation, Carruthers followed.

Phoebe trod cautiously along the littered floor of the Cut, Carruthers holding her arm and guiding her around puddles, rocks, and other obstacles. They had left the horses tethered under a clump of stunted trees, and seemed to have been clambering amongst undergrowth and boulders for an inordinate length of time. Phoebe tripped over her wet skirt, and Carruthers's grip tightened.

"If you would just have stayed with the horses, as I told you to do!"

"No. You might need me. Besides, I mean to be sure—"

"Hell and the devil!"

His firm clasp was withdrawn and he was running. Peering

113

through the grey curtain of the rain, Phoebe saw him leap a fallen tree branch, then go to his knees. Her heart leapt into her throat. She plucked up her skirts and stumbled on as rapidly as possible. "Are you all right?" she gasped, coming up with him.

"Yes. But this stupid gudgeon is not!"

She saw then that he was lifting Lascelles, who looked dead, and was sprawled in full view of anyone who might have come past.

"I'll have to haul him again," grumbled Carruthers. "Do you go on ahead, ma'am. I'll direct you. And have a care, this loose shale is tricky."

He pulled Lascelles across his shoulder, then struggled to his feet. Slipping past, Phoebe set off, his softly called instructions guiding her to a dense growth of vines and shrubs. She pulled these aside, revealing a shallow indentation in the rocky wall. Carruthers carried Lascelles inside and laid him on the blankets that had been smuggled here the night before.

"I'll have to tie that wound again," he said roughly. "Do see if you can find the brandy. We brought a flask. And tear me some bandages from that old sheet, if you please."

She obeyed, flinching as she watched his crude surgery, yet noticing that, despite his begrudging manner, his hands were very gentle. When he was done, he wrapped the injured man in one of the blankets, and Phoebe used another piece of the sheet to dry Lascelles's wet hair. Carruthers, his own dark locks dripping, propped his friend's head and shoulders, and Phoebe contrived to get a little of the potent liquor through Lascelles's teeth. For a moment there was no change, then he coughed weakly, groaned, and blinked up at them.

"Merry . . . ?" he faltered. "What—the deuce . . . ?"

"What, indeed? Are you quite out of your senses? Why did you venture out?"

Lascelles frowned, then said fretfully, "Must get . . . cipher delivered. Late now. Gave—gave solemn . . . word. Must get—*away* from here!"

"Now listen, you confounded idiot, the military are thick, searching for you! I'd tie you if I thought it would serve, but it won't. So I must move you into my Keep."

Phoebe looked at him sharply.

Lascelles started up, frantic. "No! Merry—you cannot! Think of your mama . . . and Jeff . . ."

"Damn you! Do you think I've *not* thought of them? Phoebe, will you stay with him while I bring the horses up?"

"No," she said, and ran out of the little shelter and into the rain.

Carruthers was after her in a flash. "Ma'am, when I ask you to *stay*—"

"Yes, but I am not Justice. And—no, Merry! If the Lieutenant became agitated and delirious, I could not control—"

His hand clamped across her mouth. Listening intently, he whispered, "Someone's coming!" and dragged her back into the cave.

With a swoop, he gathered up Lascelles's discarded rags and the brandy flask. Phoebe flew to pile the bag of food, bottles, and bandages on the heap Carruthers had made. Turning, she cried an aghast "Merry!"

Lascelles, muttering incoherently, was on his feet and hobbling painfully to the opening. Carruthers sprinted after him, spun him around and struck once, then caught him as he fell, dumped him unceremoniously with the piled articles, and threw the grey blanket over the whole.

Phoebe, torn with sympathy, protested, "*Had* you to strike him?"

"No time to write a letter!"

She was swept up and laid down. "My apologies to your Fine Handsome," he muttered, swooping down beside her. Before she could gather her shocked senses she was snatched into a crushing embrace and relentlessly kissed.

A sudden brightness; a stifled laugh. Phoebe tore free and jerked her scarlet face to the opening. A captain stood there; not, as she had hoped, one of the young officers who had been guests in the Hall last evening, but a man of sturdier build. She made a swift assessment of a jutting chin below a small mouth, just now pursed with contempt; hard blue eyes, and a person neat, despite the rain. He said on a note of disgust, "So it's you, Carruthers. My apologies for the—intrusion."

Two grinning troopers peered from the entrance. Carruthers sprang up and helped Phoebe to her feet. She turned away, instinctively straightening her hair. She shook her wet skirts and stood where she could hide as much as possible of the blanket-covered pile, sick with dread that Lascelles might at any second recover consciousness.

Carruthers said with a rather embarrassed laugh, "Jacob Holt, isn't it? My affianced and I were caught in the rain and—er" —he winked confidingly—"took shelter. Might I enquire what you're about?"

115

"We're hunting a damned rebel, and when we catch the bounder it will go hard on him, I can tell you. Take care, Carruthers. He's a desperate rogue and not likely to stop at murder would it help him escape the axe."

"And you think he is on my lands?"

"If he is—we'll find him! Good day to you. Ma'am."

With a short salute, he marched out. They heard the diminishing sounds of the search party, and Carruthers slipped outside.

Phoebe, shaking, uncovered Lascelles and propped his head on a rolled-up coat. Carruthers came back, and she asked, "Have they gone?"

"Yes. Towards the Quarry. We'll go the other way."

She was aghast. "You never mean to move him *now*?"

"No choice, ma'am. He's too far gone to know what he's doing and would run himself into capture did we leave him another hour. I'll haul the silly fellow, but can you manage the rest of this paraphernalia? We daren't leave any evidence."

"I think you are raving mad," she told him. But she gathered all the articles into the blanket, rolled it as well as she could manage, and followed him into the dank and deadly afternoon.

No sooner had Phoebe sent Ada away than a scratch at her door was followed by the appearance of her brother, who crept in, pulled up a chair, and eyed her with a mixture of anxiety and amusement.

"Oh, Sin . . . !" she gulped, reaching out to him.

He moved the chair closer to the bed and squeezed her hand. "You look a properly drowned rat. What the deuce happened? Mrs. Lucille is beside herself, and Mama says you came back soaked to the skin and with your teeth chattering like castanets, and 'twill be a miracle do you not catch the pneumonia."

"I know. I am under strict orders to keep to my bed. Have you spoken with Carruthers?"

"I've not had the chance. When last heard from, he was spinning some nonsensical tale about your horse running off because it was scared by lightning, and him having to chase it for five miles. On *that* mare? Fustian!"

"Yes. Sin—we moved Lascelles into the Keep!"

Sinclair turned white, then red. Springing to his feet, he thundered, "You—*what*?"

"Ssshh!" she hissed, throwing a terrified look to the door.

116

"Do you tell me that wild man dragged *you* into such a mad start? In broad daylight?"

"*Will* you be quiet? Sin, he had little choice."

"He could have sent you to find *me*! To think he'd be so daft as to—"

"He wanted me to leave him. I would not."

He stared at her for a moment, then sat down again. "I know that look! You crazy madcap, do you *know* what you risked? Oh, never mind. Tell me."

So she did, and he sat there listening, lips compressed and eyes angry. "Holt!" he exclaimed. "I know *him*! He nigh had Johnny Boothe last month! Go on, old lady. How did you bring Lascelles here?"

"Slung across Carruthers's saddle, poor man. And Carruthers vowing to spank me because I kept with him. We saw no one, thank God. When we came to the back of the Keep, he told me he would knock me down, as he had poor Lascelles, unless I swore to stay in the trees with the horses. And—do you know, I really believe he would! He carried Lascelles inside, then came back for the blanket roll, and ten minutes later came out, and we circled around and rid in together."

"God!" exclaimed her brother, rising and striding up and down. "To think of him taking such a chance! He is all about in his head!"

Phoebe said quietly, "And—rather splendid . . ." He stared at her. She went on, "He fears this Colonel Fotheringay, and I believe his attachment to Lieutenant Lascelles is a very deep one, for all he grumbles so."

He came closer to the bed and said slowly, "Yes. He is a man who acts rather than one who is all talk."

"As are you, my dear. You did what you thought best in this dreadful war. You sought to help those who are hunted and hurt, and desperate."

He smiled. "Thank you for that, old lady. 'Dreadful war' is the name for it. Brother against brother, families divided, Britons hacking off the heads of Britons! And all for an ideal that a hundred years from now will have been forgotten."

"Well, at least Lascelles is safe, for the time."

"Aye. Carruthers doing *my* work, and my dear sister at risk, while I was off . . ." He hung his head and was silent.

Phoebe sat up. "Sinclair Ramsay! You have been with that village girl again!"

He slanted a guilty glance at her. "Yes. And worse, I'm afraid."

"Sin! You didn't—I mean, she did not let you . . ."

"Lord, no!" he said, with humility forgotten. "She is not Haymarket ware!"

She thought with dismay of how awful it would be if he had formed a lasting attachment for Miss Smith. "Carruthers does not know you were with her?"

"Which one?"

"Oh, heavens! Jeffery saw you?"

"He caught us together, in a rather compromising pose. I'd my arm about her. I came along when some hulking lout of a villager was accosting her. The poor little soul was fairly terrified. I think I'd not have been so angry had he been some love-sick swain, but the man must be forty, at least. One of those revolutionary types with sly eyes and a sneering mouth and an unwashed smell. To think of him pawing that dainty little angel fairly made me see red, I don't mind telling you. I told him to be off, and he took up a stout cudgel. For a minute I thought I'd a fight on my hands, but Rosalie said he'd best not harm one of Mr. Carruthers's guests, and the horrid fellow went slouching off, fairly snarling his hatred."

"He sounds a beast. Shall you tell Meredith?"

"No need. Jeffery came up and in the ensuing—ah, discussion, Rosalie told him what had happened. He was mad as fire, and when she'd gone into her cottage, he rid back here with me. Silly fellow started making veiled hints about Rosalie being an innocent, so I told him I'd already been taken to task for having interfered with her—which I had *not* done!—thanks to him running to his big brother with his tales."

"Oh, Sin! You never did?"

"You may believe me. Lord, but he was red in the face. He said they had a perfect right to protect their people. And I asked who protects their people against *them*, and he all but called me out!"

He grinned broadly, but Phoebe cried an alarmed "Sin! You'll not *fight*?"

"No, silly chit. I told him to go and stick his head under the pump, and gave his horse a cut with my whip, and he went flying off, shouting all kinds of ferocities." He chuckled. "What a blockhead!"

"Oh, dear! Thank heaven I am not obliged to come downstairs for dinner! Sin, *please*, do not provoke him any more."

"I'll try." He started for the door, then turned back. "What about you and Lambert? Do you think Carruthers will really help? It don't seem likely to me."

"Oh—I think he will. He said once that he could conceive of no worse fate than to be tied to a reluctant bride."

He eyed her, wondering if she knew how very beautiful she was.

That long, speculative look made her nervous. She babbled, "Besides, he says I saved his life."

"Does he, by Jove? How?"

"By being with him when Captain Holt and the dragoons found us in that horrid cave. Carruthers said that he'd never have been able to think of anything near as convincing as to make it seem we were—er, lovers."

He said with a slow grin. "It seems to me his mind works very rapidly indeed. What was it like, being kissed by him, old lady?"

"Like nothing so much as being embraced by a polar bear," she said, somehow achieving a creditably derogatory sniff. "I vow I pity the lady he weds. My ribs were already fairly crushed from the first time he—" She checked, biting her lip.

"From the *first* time?" Intrigued, Sinclair trod nearer. "Why, you little flirt! You let him kiss you before today!"

"*Let* him! I had as well try to stop a charging bull elephant!"

"Hum," he said, his eyes dancing. "Must I call him out? No, I suppose I cannot very well do so since you are betrothed. Really, Phoebe, I do not quite see how you can forbid him. Under the circumstances. You had best tell Brooks, and see what he advises."

"An excellent notion," said Phoebe rather stiffly, and knew both that her face was very red, and that she certainly would not tell Lambert.

Phoebe had not expected to sleep at so early an hour, but the crowded events of the day had left her more worn out than she realized and she fell asleep soon after her dinner tray had been removed. As a result, she awoke with the dawn and, after staring at the canopy of her tester bed for what seemed hours, her various worries so wrought upon her that she got up. She was reluctant to disturb Ada at five o'clock in the morning, so washed in cold water and attired herself in the new dusty-green habit with the jade buttons that had been delivered only a week before her sudden betrothal.

It was a bright morning, with the promise of a beautiful day, and she found herself looking forward to the early ride. She went downstairs hoping to be offered a cup of coffee, but the house was still wrapped in a dense hush; the servants were not yet abroad. She was not altogether alone, however. A ripple of air stirred her curls as she passed a display cabinet in the Great Hall, and she looked up to discover Satan blinking at her, a front leg still outstretched. He made no response to her scold, but suddenly became a sphinx, hips wiggling and whiskers sticking out ferociously.

Phoebe glanced around as Justice came padding up, wagged his tail at her but went on past. Almost, she warned him, but it really seemed unsportsmanlike. Satan launched through the air, skidded across the bloodhound's back, causing him to leap away with a shocked yelp, and, landing beside him, stood on his hind legs, waving both front paws at the startled dog and hissing like a nest of vipers. Enough was enough. Justice growled and charged. Satan was off, ears back, tail fluffed out and held sideways. In hot pursuit, Justice sent rugs flying, causing Phoebe to think repentantly of his hurt pad. She called softly but unavailingly and hurried in the wake of the rout.

There was no sign of them for the length of the corridor leading across the Lancastrian building, but she heard a muffled crash and hurried past the enormous silence of the ballroom until she arrived at the Armour Hall. She was just in time to see Justice standing peering about in a baffled way. Satan darted out from under the trappings of the horse on the dais, dealt Justice a sanguinary swipe, and shot into the family wing.

"Justice!" hissed Phoebe, but the hound ignored her, continuing in determined pursuit of his tormentor. Following, Phoebe heard stealthy footsteps and she halted, belatedly aware that it was not proper for her to venture into this wing unaccompanied.

Others were apparently less concerned with propriety.

A girl's voice said low and urgently, "I know I should not have come, but I've been fairly distracted. Dearest—I am so grateful—"

Meredith's deep tones interrupted, "Don't be such a thimble-wit, Rosie."

Phoebe stood very still, her eyes wide and unblinking. They were tiptoeing down the spiral staircase that wound from the upper floor. She saw the girl's long cloak, and Meredith's high riding boots.

At the foot of the stairs, he said, "Here."

She waved his hand away. "No, no. You have been too generous. You spoil me, my dear, and it is not necessary."

He smiled and tilted up her face. "You cannot live on love, little one."

A beam of sunlight touched the girl's head as her hood fell back and illumined high-piled golden curls and a dainty profile.

"Yes, I can," she said intently and, cherishing his hand to her cheek, murmured, "How can I ever tell you what I feel? Merry—my dearest, you'll find a way for us to be wed. I know it."

He held her shoulders, looking searchingly down at her. "You're willing to wait till I can find a way out of this? To trust me?"

"With my life. You are the bravest, the most gallant and honourable man I—"

"Huh!" snorted Phoebe, then drew farther into the shadows as Meredith turned swiftly.

"I think the servants must be getting up. You must go, love. You have the key?"

"Yes."

"Go, then. And if you come again by daylight, be very, very careful."

"I will. God bless you, my very dear."

He stooped to kiss her, then opened the door that led to the courtyard.

Phoebe seized her opportunity and sped across the Armour Hall and the two adjacent wings until she came, breathless, to the stairs.

She reached her room undetected, and raging. The *wretch*! The miserable, conniving *snake*! How *dare* he bring his lightskirt here while his affianced bride was 'neath the same roof! *And* her family! 'My heaven!' she thought, pacing furiously to and fro, 'I have heard of gauche behaviour, but this bears off the palm!' He would 'find a way' for them, would he? This villain, who had first told Lambert he meant to remain a bachelor all his days, then promised that immoral little village creature he meant to wed her. Only yesterday that 'most honourable man' had declared his intention to honour Miss Phoebe Ramsay with his noble name—if only to 'spare his dear mama' any further grief! The *beast*! To so deceive the poor trusting country

121

innocent—though, come to think on it, she was not very innocent! Nor had she spoken with a country accent, but more like a lady of quality. Phoebe's lip curled. The well-bred lightskirt! And to think that she herself had come near to being taken in by the monster! His brutish cave-man-style kisses should have told her. A depraved lecher was what he was! A faithless, heartless libertine, masquerading behind that air of cold indifference; unexpectedly flaunting the so-different smile, and allowing that clear blue light to come into his eyes that was so very . . . She thrust the memory away. She knew him now for what he was! Poor Brooks was quite taken in; *and* her mama, who obviously thought him a perfect gentleman. Well, he'd not have to give up his carefree bachelor life for her sake! Miss Phoebe Ramsay would remain a spinster all her days sooner than bear the revolting name of Carruthers!

❧ *Chapter 9* ❧

"See here." Jeffery reached around Rosalie to turn the page of the book of woodcuts he had found in the library. "It distinctly says that the newborns hang on to the mother's breast with their teeth—little varmints!"

Blushing furiously, Rosalie pulled clear of his encircling arm. "Mr. Carruthers!"

"Oh, the deuce!" he cried, dismayed. "But—but it *does* say it—only look. I didn't mean no disrespect, save that it sounded so dashed uncomfortable, their little fangs having hooks on 'em, and—"

Rosalie could not restrain a giggle, and he gave a sigh of relief.

She had been astounded when, only an hour after she had arrived, late, he had bent his fair head to enter the fragrant little bakery, and, although she had much to do, she had succumbed to the temptation to look at the beautiful old volume he'd brought. "I must get on with my work now," she said. "But I am very pleased that you find the bats so fascinating, sir."

"Must admit they're interesting articles," he murmured, gazing at the flour on her rounded white arms. "It don't tell you much, though. I shall see if my brother has any more books about 'em. Wouldn't at all mind doing some reading in that line when I go back up to Cambridge."

Rosalie had carried several more bowls to the table behind the counter, and he wandered around to investigate. "What're you going to do now? Jupiter, but that smells delicious!"

She slapped his hand, but already he had snared a finger-full and sampled it. "Almond icing! For a cake?"

"A bride cake. No! Keep your hands out of my icing, sir!"

He grinned, watching as she beat briskly at the icing. She caught the bowl closer, her efforts causing her shapely figure to be jostled in a way he thought most delightful. She glanced up, blowing a wisp of hair from her heated forehead, and caught his eye. Reddening, he said hurriedly, "Here, let me have a crack at it."

She pursed her lips, but stood back. "Be careful, then. If you drop it I will very likely chase you out of our shop with a hatchet!"

"Well, if ye doan't, Rosie, Oi reckon as how Oi might!"

Jeffery gave a gasp as Joseph Smith staggered into the shop, the sunlight streaming through the open door to make a halo of his white hair. "I was just helping your granddaughter, Mr. Smith."

" 'Pears to me, Mr. Carruthers, more like as ye's hindering her." The old man wavered to the counter. "Bringing books to take up her time, when she be a'trying and a'trying to get her baking done 'fore it do get too hot fer the poor lass. 'Sides, Oi've read that'n and could tell it to Rosie, word fer word, Oi could." His rheumy brown eyes met Jeffery's hazel ones defiantly.

Rosalie's hand, reaching for the bowl, was arrested. Her grandfather's inability to read was a closely guarded secret and one that Carruthers could easily expose.

Jeffery said earnestly, "It's about mammals, sir."

"Ar. Big woolly things they be," agreed Joseph.

Without the flicker of an eye, Jeffery said, "Quite so, but I don't know much about them. It's the bats I was interested in."

Joseph peered at him. "Why ever would ye be interested in they, Master Jeff? Horrid ugly things they do be. Oi could tell'ee lots about 'em, that Oi could."

Jeffery pulled up a chair for the old man and with a small sigh of relief Rosalie began to stir again. 'Master Jeff' was a vast improvement over 'Mr. Carruthers,' and thank heaven Jeffery was being so tactful. She glanced at his intent comely face, and felt a deepening affection for him.

"Lotsa bats Oi seen in me time," expounded Joseph, settling comfortably onto the chair. "Why, even Oi were in His Majesty's Navy, our ship would sometimes come on flocks of 'em so thick Cap'n couldn't see the sun, and he'd steer us round in circles with they bats flocking all over us. Many's the time we've come right back where we begun, an' the sails full o' nests from the dratted things."

"Nests . . . ?" gasped Jeffery. "In—in the *sails*, sir?"

"Ar," confirmed Joseph fiercely. "Doan't ye know nothing,

Master Jeff? Ain't ye never heared o' sailors climbing up ter the bat's nest?''

"But—I er, I thought it was called the '*crow's* nest,' Mr. Smith.''

Joseph blinked, but made a quick recover. "Aye, 'cause some fool tar didn't know a crow from a bat! Did ye ever see the crow as could build a nest a man could stand in—comfortable-like?''

With really heroic gravity, Jeffery managed, "You mean—*bats* build such . . . nests, sir?''

"That they do, young man. Ye likely think they're all *little* birds, and there's yer mistake. Why, Oi seen bats so big as any pig! And with wings stretching so wide as my Rosie is tall!''

"Now, Granfer,'' said Rosalie in mild scolding. "You're exaggerating, and will—''

"No, Oi bean't,'' he snapped. "You jest pay heed to yer old granfer, Rosalie Smith! If more folks would listen to what Oi says we'd have a sight less trouble round Dewbury Prime! Take that there soldier chap, now. Willyum Lemmon and Sam Goodall and ugly Ben Hessell, they all said as he was gone fer good. But Oi told and told 'em he weren't nobody's fool, fer all he might look it, and as he'd be back soon or late.''

Jeffery said with a smile, "Oh, Captain Lambert comes to the Hall fairly often, sir. Nothing to be in the boughs about. He's related to us, y'know.''

"Oi doan't mean him—though a very fine officer *he* do be, Oi'll own. Oi mean t'other un. That there Major Foggy something or t'other. Only they gone and made him a colonel now. Not a proper colonel, mind. Only a lieutenant colonel, which is about half-past major.''

The amusement chased from his eyes, Jeffery asked, "Do you mean Fotheringay, sir? Has *he* come back here?''

"Ar, that be the one. His sergeant told me he'd been arter that there promotion fer years, an' now he got it 'cause he went an' caught some special sort o' rebel what was made ter tell a lot 'fore they took his head orf and stuck it on Temple Bar.''

Jeffery frowned, but said loyally, "So end all the King's enemies!''

"I rose early, especially to discover how you went on, dear Miss Ramsay,'' said Lucille Carruthers, looking anxiously across the breakfast table at Phoebe.

"If every lady looked as well as does Miss Ramsay after being half drowned in a storm," said Carruthers, walking in booted and spurred, with Sinclair beside him, "storms would bring crowds out by the hundreds."

Phoebe watched him without delight.

"Oh, prettily said, Meredith," said his mother, blinking at him in mild astonishment.

"Very skilful," agreed Phoebe drily. She was aware he would have every right (in his mama's eyes at least) to drop a kiss on her brow, and when he rested one hand lightly on her shoulder as he passed behind her chair, she jerked quickly away from that contaminating touch.

Mrs. Carruthers saw the movement, and anxiety came into her big blue eyes. Meredith kissed her and told her she looked charmingly in the negligee of royal blue and the dainty matching cap heavily trimmed with ecru lace. She thanked him absently, her troubled gaze on his affianced.

Meredith glanced at Phoebe and pulled out a chair. "I think *you* must have slept well, ma'am."

She answered a short, "Passably, thank you," and turned a brilliant smile on Sinclair as he sat beside her. "Good morning, dear," she said.

"A very good morning," he said, his eyes holding a reproof. "Carruthers took me through the Keep. It's a most interesting old place."

They must have gone to check on poor Lieutenant Lascelles. Phoebe stared at her plate. How horrid it was that she *must* continue to feel indebted to the Lecher. But, on the other hand, why should she care how low he was, or worry for that village trollop? The silly chit had brought it on herself, goodness knows. And how funny that Sinclair was angry because she'd put Carruthers in his place, not dreaming of the cause of her vexation. He'd have a different notion of the man did he know how Carruthers had seduced and betrayed the girl he himself so admired. With an effort, she managed to sound less glacial. "You must show me this famous Keep, Mr. Carruthers."

Lucille said, "Oh, you must be careful over there. It is very, very old, you know, and quite falling down in places."

"I suppose it sounds silly," said Phoebe, "but when I look at it, I think it is grieving. Poor old place. What a pity it has been allowed to fall to rack and ruin."

Carruthers's lips tightened, and Sinclair said hurriedly, "Mr. Carruthers says he may restore it."

"To an extent, at least," qualified Carruthers, watching Phoebe thoughtfully.

"How nice," she said.

"Should you care to have another try at seeing Dewbury Minor, ma'am?" he enquired.

"I am invited to ride with you," Sinclair put in. "But I do not mean to play pest-in-residence, so if you'd prefer to be alone, please say so."

She laughed at him. "Don't be so silly."

"One of the reasons I chose your sister," drawled Carruthers, his colour a little heightened, "is that she is so sensible and does not indulge the silly romantical notions that clog the brains of most females."

Sinclair grinned at this hit, but Lucille looked at Phoebe uncertainly. "I suppose you modern misses *are* more practical-minded than my generation."

"Perhaps we are, ma'am," said Phoebe sweetly. "It is, after all, better to face reality than to indulge silly romantical notions and later be disillusioned."

Carruthers met her eyes steadily for a moment, then asked his mother what were her plans for the day. She was, she said, taking Lady Eloise to meet the curate and visit the dear old church in Dewbury Prime. "She is so interested in antiquities."

Phoebe said with a warm smile, "You and my mama are enjoying each other, I think, ma'am?"

"Oh, yes, my dear. It is lovely to find a friend with whom one can discuss all one's concerns. Such a delightful creature. How fortunate I am, for I have gained both a daughter *and* a new friend."

Phoebe's heart sank, and she dared not look at Meredith.

He said briskly, "Fortunate, indeed, Mama. Where is Jeffery, by the bye?"

With the assurance that her news would please, Lucille replied, "He is off with the military, dear. He volunteered to help search for this dreadful rebel."

"Surely, sir," said Sinclair, as they rode side by side through the bright morning, "you will now be obliged to tell your brother?"

"Only as a very last resort," said Carruthers.

Astonished, Phoebe expostulated, "But Jeffery *must* know

about your hidden room in the Keep. What if he comes upon the Lieutenant?''

Carruthers gave a faint smile. "If he does, the chances are he'll be as eager as are we to protect him. You must remember, ma'am, that Lance and Jeff and I grew up together.''

"And Miss Smith,'' she murmured.

His eyes narrowed. "Most decidedly Miss Smith. Though she was just a little sprat of a girl then.''

"She has grown past that stage,'' said Sinclair. Carruthers's gaze shifted to him, and he said with fine innocence, "Speaking of beautiful sights . . .''

They had come to the crest of a hill. About half a mile distant, thatched cottages clustered around a small village green with a pond in the centre. Ducks bustled about busily, chestnut trees swayed with the gentle breeze, and faintly could be heard the sound of singing.

Sinclair exclaimed, "How Mama would love to sketch . . .'' He paused, tilting his head, listening.

They burst like a red tide over a slope, the 'pink' coats bright against the turf, the hounds baying in excitement as they streaked after the small, terrified fox, the horses racing in pursuit.

Carruthers drove home his spurs. He had ridden Rogue today, and the big black fairly shot into a gallop and was down the hill in a flash.

"This is the jolliest place,'' cried Sinclair. "Never a dull moment! Come on, Phoebe!''

She was already urging her mare forward, apprehensive because the large man in the forefront of the hunt could only be Sir Malcolm Lockwood.

They passed the village at great speed, people running out of cottages to stare as they swept past, and two dogs trying, with much frenzied barking, to keep up.

Far ahead, Carruthers's black soared over a hedge at undiminished speed. Sinclair was hard on his heels, but Phoebe detoured to a lower spot which her mare took in fine style. She saw then that a pleasant farmhouse lay ahead, well-tended fields of vegetables and young corn surrounding it. And the hunt was charging right across the first of those neat fields.

Following a narrow path through the corn, Carruthers raced towards the fence at the far side, shouting, "Shut the gate! Quick!''

A labourer, toiling near the fence, jerked up his head, saw

128

the hunt approaching, and sprinted. The fox shot through, and
Carruthers came up just after the high barred gate swung shut.

Phoebe's heart contracted. Surely he was not going to attempt
that gate? But horse and rider soared into the air and disappeared
on the far side. Her heart in her mouth, she kicked home her
heels and the mare flew.

She heard a shout, then a shot, and wondered in anguish if
Rogue had broken a leg. There was pandemonium now; an outburst of furious shouts and cursing, of horses whinnying, dogs
baying, and Sinclair, who had climbed onto the gate, laughing
hilariously.

Flinging herself from the saddle, Phoebe ran to the gate and
peered through at a crazy confusion of milling hounds, flailing
huntsmen, plunging horses. She was in time to see Carruthers
standing very straight amid the chaos, a smoking pistol in one
hand, and Sir Malcolm Lockwood, enraged, stamping forward
to slash his riding gloves across Carruthers's face and back again.

"I wish you will stop laughing, Sin," Phoebe said severely.
"There is nothing funny about a duel."

They had ridden away from the farm and were now in the hills
above the rural beauty of Dewbury Minor, where much of the
hunt had adjourned to rage over its spoiled sport in the tap of
The Jolly Countryman.

"If you had but—seen it," gasped Sinclair unrepentantly.
"Damn near lynched you, sir!"

Phoebe whitened, her scared gaze flashing to Carruthers's
grave countenance. "Dear God! What for? Oh—you never really *shot* someone?"

"By Jove, but he did," chortled Sinclair.

"Six of the idiots with one bullet," Carruthers jeered. "Jolly
good, eh?"

"Oh, for heaven's sake," she said crossly.

"He shot a chicken," said Sinclair.

"A . . . *chicken* . . . ?"

His mouth trembling to a grin, Carruthers murmured, "The
hounds evidently decided there was—er, 'some soul of goodness
in things evil.' "

Sinclair gave a whoop. "In other words, Phoebe, they forgot
about the fox and settled for the victim readily available. Old
Lockwood was fairly gibbering with wrath—his hunt with him!
And this gentleman standing there, laughing at 'em. Oh, what

a sight! And that quotation was from *The Merchant of Venice*—no?"

"No."

"Here you are with a duel facing you and you argue about a quotation," cried Phoebe in exasperation. "I hope you may find it as laughable does Sir Malcolm choose pistols."

"Not his choice, ma'am. And of course I don't mean to shoot the half-wit. Can't very well"—his crooked grin slanted at her—"his son is my closest friend."

Sinclair stared at him. "How can you get out of it, sir? They all saw him strike you."

"And they all know I'll not accept his challenge—and why. Never fear, I'll not be ostracized as a craven. I've been out sufficient times, heaven knows."

Her nerves still quivering, Phoebe said irritably, "What heaven has to do with two grown men ready to shoot one another only because a silly hunt was upset is beyond my ken."

"Do not let Papa hear you say that," cautioned Sinclair. "Dashed unsporting would be his verdict, I'm afraid. Although, come to think on it, our huntsman would likely faint were he instructed to prepare for sport during the growing season. Why the deuce does the Squire do such a thing? I wonder any respond to his invitation."

"He's sporting-mad," said Carruthers. "And I've a notion he is pretty much crippled from rheumatism during the cold weather. It's unorthodox, I grant you, but since most of the land hereabouts is owned either by him or by me, he usually has only me to deal with. This was one thing that was not a bone of contention between the Squire and my father. He did not object. I do."

"I have it!" exclaimed Sinclair. *Richard the Second!*

"Wrong again."

"Deuce take it! What, then?"

"I think I will not tell you. You shall have to wade through all Mr. Shakespeare's works. Wager you a guinea you do not have it by dinner-time!"

"Done!" Sinclair wheeled his mount. "I'll have it by the time you reach the Hall!" And he was away at a canter, soon disappearing from sight.

They were alone again. Carruthers rode in silence. Phoebe's earlier fury had been tempered by time, and she persuaded herself that how this man conducted his *affaires de coeur* held not the slightest interest for her. She was genuinely interested in

Meredith Hall, however, and when the buildings came into view across the valley and Carruthers suggested they allow the horses to rest for a few minutes, she let him lift her down, then strolled to gaze out at the distant buildings.

Joining her, he said, "Is it possible that my home, at least, no longer disgusts you?"

There was a note to the deep voice that warned her. She did not look at him, nor rise to the bait, but answered, "It does not. But it is an unfortunate jumble, isn't it?"

" 'Truth, where is thy sting?' " he sighed.

"That should be 'death,' " she pointed out.

"My own version. At all events, I'm not ready to die merely because you find my home unfortunate."

She did look at him then, and the gleam of laughter in his eyes prompted a reluctant smile. At once he said, "Will you tell me why you were so angry?"

She lowered her lashes. "No. I—really, it was not my right, and—"

He took her hand. "Phoebe, I would prefer that we be honest with each other."

Honest! As he was being honest with Rosalie Smith? Rage blazed through her again, and she had to fight to remind herself that it was none of her business. She touched the heavy gold ring on his tanned hand. "I saw that device over the mantel in the withdrawing room. A sword and a rose."

"Yes. I fancy you've seen it in many places beside. It is probably reproduced somewhere in every room of the house."

"I apologize for my lack of observance, Mr. Carruthers."

He sighed. "Which means I've been clumsy again. I warned you I've not a silver tongue. I suppose I should rather have complimented you upon your perspicacity."

"Do you fancy I cannot live without empty compliments?"

"Yes. I mean—no! I mean—Oh, God, I don't know. D'you want to hear about it or not?"

She could not hold back a laugh. "If you please, kind historian. I take it the design is part of your coat of arms."

"The best part, I think. Although you will also find griffins and eagles lurking about here and there, especially around the exterior of the new wing."

"Ah, yes. I have seen them. Tell me about the sword and the rose—unless it is sad, in which case I don't want to hear it."

He led her to some nearby boulders, dusted one, and when she was settled more or less comfortably, he sat on the grass at

131

her feet and began, "It's a rather lovely old legend. It began when one of my ancestors, Peter, fought in the Third Crusade with Richard Coeur de Lion. He met a beautiful Saracen lady who had inherited the colouring of her English mother, who had been stolen and sold as a slave, poor creature. But her daughter was a real beauty with—" He checked. Phoebe glanced at him sharply, but his gaze was fixed on the loom of the great house, his eyes remote and dreaming.

"It was that doubtful commodity," he went on, "love at first sight. They were hopelessly forbidden, of course, but during the Siege of Acre he risked death many times to meet her. On the night before the great battle, she made him promise to wear her talisman next day, and she gave him a fine red rose. During the battle he fell, grievously wounded. While he lay helpless, a Saracen knight came up to finish him. At the last moment the Saracen saw the red rose. His sword was swung aside. Peter was taken prisoner instead, and nursed back to health. His attacker had been brother to his lady."

"Oh," whispered Phoebe, entranced. "What happened? Were they able to marry?"

"Yes, believe it or not. With her help he was able to escape, and together they fled back to England. Our climate, alas, did not suit her, and she died in his arms soon after the birth of their son. With her last breath she is said to have vowed that their love was immortal and that down through the ages they would meet again. He was quite inconsolable. He built a shrine to her memory and was found there one day, dead, but with the first smile on his face that anyone had seen since he lost her. His death was attributed to a broken heart."

"Wretch!" she exclaimed, her own tender heart touched. "I asked you not to tell me if it was sad!"

He said absently, "Did you think it so? I find it beautiful rather, but there is more. The next instance we know of took place two hundred years later. The Carrutherses had for decades engaged in a fierce feud with the neighbouring Meredyth family. Thanks to the machinations of their enemies, the eldest Carruthers son, Anthony, was accused of being in league with the Devil, and was dragged off to be burned at the stake. The neighbour's daughter, Lady Clemency Meredyth, was arranging flowers for the church altar. She heard the uproar and ran out. (She left a journal, incidentally, in which she wrote that the instant she saw Anthony Carruthers, she knew he was her love.) She tried to intercede with the mob, but her pleas were ignored and

Anthony was tied to the stake. When the torches were lit, Lady Clemency ran onto the pyre and declared she would burn with him. She still held in her hand one of the flowers from the church. A red rose. Not even the insanity of the mob could prevail against such devotion, and Anthony was spared. Lady Clemency's father, who had coveted the Carruthers estates, realized he could acquire them without bloodshed. The lovers were married, the estates joined, and the feud ended."

Watching him, Phoebe saw the dreaming look vanish. He glanced up, went very red in the face, and said gruffly, "So much nonsense, probably. There are said to have been other instances, but I fancy the tales have been much romanticized. Still . . . that's the legend. A sword and a rose, and the gentler object prevailing."

Phoebe's gaze drifted to the far hill whereon stood the ruins of *Abbaye Enfoncée*. "And was it Anthony Carruthers who had the abbey built?"

"Yes. On the site of the twelfth-century shrine. Their wedding was delayed, in fact, until the *Abbaye* could be completed. It became a family tradition for weddings to be held there."

Phoebe turned to him. He was looking at the great house, but she was sure he had been watching her. She wondered if he resembled that earlier Carruthers, and decided that as soon as they returned, she would ask him to take her to the portrait gallery.

When they walked into the cool dimness of the Great Hall, however, her request was forgotten. A new arrival stood talking to Conditt; a tall, slender gentleman with a fine pair of shoulders. His back was to them, and when he turned, Phoebe was mildly shocked. She had thought never to see a man with finer features than Lambert's, but this individual, although rather wan-looking, was almost indecently handsome. He was clad in a superb black riding coat and black breeches, and a large carven onyx was set in his neat stock. Thick waving hair, immaculately powdered, was tied back with a black velvet riband. His eyes, long-lashed, brilliant, and near black, were set under heavy, slightly flaring brows, his nose was straight and classically slim, his cheekbones high, his chin resolute, the well-shaped lips above it curving now to an impudent grin.

"Roly!" cried Meredith, obviously delighted, and strode forward, hand outstretched.

Removing his admiring gaze from Phoebe, the newcomer returned the handshake, his dark eyes alight with affection.

133

"Hello, you old war horse." He flicked a finger at Carruthers's damaged mouth. "Brawling again?"

"Stumbled onto a glove. Speaking of which, you look awful! Have you been ill?"

"Stumbled onto a sword-point." The laughing gaze turned to Phoebe once more.

"My apologies, ma'am," exclaimed Carruthers. "Allow me to present Captain Roland—er, Otton. Roly, my betrothed, Miss Phoebe Ramsay."

Phoebe curtseyed and Captain Otton swept her an impressive bow. "Can I believe this?" he said, his eyes twinkling at her. "However came you to be so taken in, ma'am? Or have you performed some great and noble deed, Merry, to win yourself so fair a flower?"

Phoebe blushed, and thought, 'What a saucy rascal!'

"Never you mind what I've done," Carruthers retaliated. "You see what I meant when I told you I had named my black truly, Miss Ramsay!"

Otton extended his arm, she slipped her hand onto it, and he led her across the hall to the stairs. "Never listen to him," he whispered. "He's terrified for fear I might win you away from him."

"Be off, varlet," said Carruthers, stepping between them. "But—not too soon, I hope. You do stay with us, Roly?"

With a hand on his heart, Otton said, "Nothing could drive me away!"

Amused by such outrageous flirting, Phoebe excused herself and went up to her chamber to change for luncheon. Ada found her mistress unusually quiet, and having made a few attempts at conversation, she lapsed into silence.

Phoebe's thoughts drifted from the legend of the lady with the rose to Meredith's plans to renovate the old house and the castle. He loved his home. Pride for it shone in his eyes, and his voice held a caressing note when he spoke of it. Not that she could blame him. It was a monstrosity at the moment and could never be made into a conventional dwelling, but it had its own unique charm and, with a good architect and a great deal of money, could be vastly improved. There was no doubt but that Carruthers had the wherewithal, and what fun it would be to engage in such a large undertaking. . . .

Her reverie was interrupted when Sinclair scratched at the door and entered to say contemptuously, "Who is that jack-at-warts downstairs with Carruthers?"

"Jack . . . at-warts?" gasped Phoebe. "You *cannot* mean Captain Otton?"

"Well, he's a counter-coxcomb if ever I saw one. Did you mark the blacks?" He sprawled in the armchair. "Effective, I'll own, in a sinister sort of way."

"No, really," she cried, much diverted. "He is quite the most handsome gentleman I ever saw, and a very good friend to Meredith Carruthers."

"And something of a dandy, eh?"

"A dangerous dandy, Mr. Sinclair," Ada put in, "if that there colleychemardey is to be believed."

All attention, Sinclair said, "Colichemarde? Are you sure?"

She nodded. "Me first lady was wed to a fencing master. I knows all the swords, I do. And that nasty murdering thing in especial. My lady's husband was used to say as it was designed by Count Königsmark, and the man as carried one meant to kill."

Sinclair put up his brows. Phoebe looked at him curiously. "Is that truth, Sin?"

"An exaggeration, but there's no denying it's a fine duelling sword. I'll be dashed! So our—" He checked, springing to his feet as Lucille Carruthers peeped around the door.

"Do I interrupt?" she asked timidly.

"Of course you do not, dear ma'am," said Phoebe, standing to welcome her. "My brother just stopped to chat for a minute."

"And must go and change for luncheon, is he not to starve," declared Sinclair, and with a smile and a little bow, departed.

"I hope I did not chase him away," said Mrs. Carruthers. "But—I am most anxious to have a tiny cose with you, Miss Ramsay."

❧ *Chapter 10* ❧

Ada had closed the door quietly behind her. Mrs. Carruthers was neatly disposed upon the love-seat, and Phoebe waited expectantly.

Lucille fluttered her fan, smiled, and said shrilly, "How—how lovely you are in that blue gown, my dear."

"You are very kind, ma'am. But—forgive . . . are you also rather troubled about something?"

Lucille closed her fan, gripped it between both little hands, and stared down at it. "Not that—exactly," She peeped up at this beautiful creature she so very much wanted for her daughter-in-law, and quavered, "Frightened, perhaps."

Phoebe crossed to sit beside her. "Is it—I mean, has Meredith—"

Lucille sighed, rose, and walked to the window. Gazing blindly into the sunny gardens, she said in a voice that shook, "It is of my son that I—I wish to speak, yes. There are—things you should know, since you are to be part of our family."

Horrified by the deepening tangle of this deception, Phoebe sprang up. "Oh, no, ma'am! Please do not—"

Lucille turned a pale, stricken face. "You *are* still betrothed? You have not drawn back? His—his temper and brusque ways have not—"

'Oh, heavens!' thought Phoebe, and said helplessly that the betrothal was unbroken.

Lucille's hand went to her throat. "Thank goodness!" She sat in the window-seat, but when Phoebe made as if to join her, she said quickly, "No—pray do not. What I have to say is—painful in the extreme, and—"

"Then I *beg* you will not so distress yourself. There is not the need."

"You mean, I expect, that you have heard of my—disgrace."

136

Lucille bowed her head. "Then—my dear child, you *must* let me tell you the truth of it, for I fear you will have heard a rather—garbled version, at best."

'Poor little creature,' thought Phoebe. 'She is telling me this because she thinks I am going to marry her immoral son, and how dreadful she will feel when she finds it is all a sham after all!' And because Lucille must not suffer such an embarrassment, she said boldly, "Mrs. Carruthers, I have no wish to pry, and—and surely all families have secrets, or things they are not perhaps quite proud of, and—"

"But I *am* proud!" declared Lucille, her head coming up. "I loved once, with all my heart. I shall never feel any shame for that. I want to tell you my story because I fear you may be cross with my son. And that my—manner also may have caused you to think—Oh, *please*, let me explain, as best I may."

And so Phoebe listened perforce, cringing with shame.

The story was a familiar one. The lovely but timid girl, fresh from the schoolroom, the older man, already widowed, handsome, assured, much courted, so that Lucille had readily consented to become his bride, though he was more than twice her age. The idyllic happiness of the first few months; Carruthers's eagerness to show her his great country estate, an estate that proved to be sadly neglected and that he left as soon as he tired of the youthful innocent he had wed. He had visited her from time to time, and when she presented him with the heir his first wife had failed to provide, he had begun to warm to her again. But then—and this Phoebe had not known—had come the accident.

Paul Carruthers had become a devotee of the favourite sport of an Indian friend: a dangerous sport, unknown in England, called polo. It appeared to consist of two teams of horsemen in competition for a small ball which they pursued with vigour and long-handled mallets. Paul had enlisted some friends to try the sport. A reckless player, however, he had inevitably come to grief. He was struck in the eye by a flying mallet and rendered unconscious. Recovering, he seemed to have suffered no major ill effects, but from that day his slightly autocratic nature began to deteriorate. Occasional flashes of temper became more numerous and ever more violent. Whispers spread through the *ton* of scandalous *affaires*, yet his behaviour towards his lonely and neglected young wife was increasingly unkind. He became obsessed with the mastery of weapons, which was as well, since his quarrelsome disposition led to several duels, all of which he won. Lucille, who had looked forward to his visits, began to dread them, because now, if she displeased him, he struck her.

Despite her isolation, she was so beautiful that she attracted attention, and Paul returned one spring to find she had set up a small court of admirers. Enraged, he bullied one quite innocent, middle-aged gentleman into a duel and crippled him. The scandal plunged Lucille into isolation once more, the gentlemen staying clear of so dangerous a diversion. Paul, triumphant, went back to Town, and for several years Lucille was left to her child and her solitary life, only occasionally interrupted by visits from her husband.

And then she had met Edvard Hoagland, a soft-spoken, fair man of Norwegian ancestry. He had gazed at the sad-eyed beauty and given her his heart, and she, hungry for affection, had found at last a gentleman who adored her and could not seem to do enough to make her happy.

"I had seven years," Lucille murmured. "Seven years of such happiness as I had never known. And then . . ." Her voice was almost suspended; she said threadily, "Paul found out."

"My heavens!" said Phoebe. "How awful."

"I expect—you may have heard . . . that Paul went to Town and challenged Edvard. But—first, he . . . he came after me." She drew a trembling hand across her eyes. "He'd not been here for almost a year. I can see it, as if it was yesterday. I was in the drawing room, arranging some roses in a tall crystal vase. The sunlight was so bright, slanting through the windows. The house was quiet and peaceful. And then—*he* came in. Like a crazed savage. He began to scream at me—the most ghastly denunciations. I think I had always known that, sooner or later, it must come, but I was so terribly frightened, I could not say a word. I just stood there, unable to move, unable to cry out. Paul tore the vase from my hands and smashed it against the hearth. I ran then, but—he caught me and—and dragged me back by my hair. He snatched up what was left of the stem of the vase, and he said . . . he would so disfigure me that—that no man would ever look at me again!" She gave a muffled sob and jerked her head away.

Stunned, Phoebe stared at her, then, with a little cry of pity, ran to gather her into her arms. "You poor little thing! How ghastly!"

Clinging to Phoebe, shaking, Lucille went on, "I screamed. And—Meredith came."

Phoebe was very still. "Ah . . ." she breathed.

Lucille nodded. "He was home for the Long Vacation, and he heard me. The servants were too afraid, but he got between us, somehow. He was only fourteen, but he was strong and he managed to force Paul's hand from my hair. I ran, terrified. And then—" She buried her face in her hands. "My husband was *mad* . . . quite out of his mind! He—turned on the boy! Oh, my God! I shall never forget. Never! Poor Meredith's face . . . !"

Her own eyes blurred with tears, Phoebe said huskily, "It was not your fault. How horribly lonely you must have been. And it would be a—a poor son who did not try to prevent so frightful a thing! I am very sure that Meredith has never blamed you."

"No. Never. The servants came then, and Paul stormed out of the house. He went straight to Town and challenged Edvard." She looked haggard, suddenly, her eyes turned into the past with a grief so deep that Phoebe dared not say a word.

"He killed him," said Lucille. "That gentle, kind, wonderful human being. He destroyed that dear life. When I heard . . . I thought I would die, too. I wanted to be dead."

Phoebe hugged her tight and gently dried her tears. "There," she said, her smile quivering, "it is all said and we can forget about it. Only . . . I am so very sorry."

Shyly, Lucille kissed her cheek. "How kind you are. But— the dreadful thing—the *most* dreadful thing, Miss Ramsay, is that—in spite of what he did, in spite of the fact that I know how very much he loves me . . . sometimes, I can scarcely endure to look at Meredith."

A pang pierced Phoebe's heart. "Because of those scars? I suppose they must remind you of it all."

"Yes. But more than that . . . I feared and hated Paul. I despise his—his very memory. And—it makes me so ashamed, but you see, Meredith is—is so very like him. The eyes, you know. The way they have of seeming grey when he is angered, and blue when he is happy. He is not like Paul, of course. He is strong, but kind too, and honourable. And, underneath that fierce way of his, he is very shy and tender. I *know* all that. Yet . . . oh, how dreadful it is!"

Phoebe was silent. So much had fallen into place. She thought, 'He knows how he repels her, so he has built a wall of coldness to protect himself. I suppose that is why he meant never to wed, for fear of having someone else turn from him in fear and revulsion. Poor soul. How dreadful . . .'

Lucille was watching her anxiously. "My dear, if you despise me, I shall quite understand. But—if anything has occurred here to—to lessen your regard—Miss Ramsay . . . you *do* care for him, still?''

How pleading the blue eyes. Phoebe could hear Carruthers saying 'My mama has known a deal of grief. I'd prefer she not suffer any more on my account.' She felt the trap closing around her, but—surely this was not the moment to break free? And so, she said gently, ''I do care, ma'am. Your son is a very fine gentleman.''

''You are a very fine idiot!'' Having delivered himself of this encomium, Roland Otton leaned back in his favourite chair of the pleasant library and regarded his scowling friend with amusement. ''You know the chit for ten minutes and *offer*?'' He sat straight again and wagged a censorious finger. ''I'll tell you what it is. You've chose her because—''

''She is a beautiful girl,'' said Carruthers hastily. ''And my mama—''

''—Because she has red hair,'' Otton overrode ruthlessly. ''She fits your hallowed legend.''

''Nonsense!'' Carruthers carried his tankard over to the window and stared at Satan, who lay atop the terrace wall with his legs hanging down each side. ''As if I'd do such a bird-brained thing. What a romantic you are, Roly.''

Otton laughed softly. He was a man of few friends, for he had learned very early in life that to offer either love or trust was to invite pain and disappointment. Carruthers had dealt out neither commodity, and was one of the less than half dozen men for whom he held a deep respect. Resting his chin on one long-fingered hand, he murmured, ''Yet yours is the scarlet phiz.''

When he felt the heat of his countenance subsiding, Carruthers moved to occupy a chair. ''If it is,'' he said coolly, ''it's because I offered before—''

''Offered! You were manoeuvred into it, I'll warrant! Oh, never glare, old fellow. When I saw you in May, you'd no more intent to become a benedick than a tailor. Less, by Jove!''

''A lot can happen in two months.''

Otton touched his chest and said ruefully, ''I'll own that! I suppose you'd have me believe you took one look at each other and tumbled deep into love! The Ramsays are short of the ready, I heard. Not under the hatches precisely, but—the jolly old Carruthers fortune would not be viewed with disdain.''

Carruthers growled, "Which would explain why she wants to cry off."

Otton's amused grin faded. "Does she now. Why?"

"As I started to say before I was given the benefit of your ignorance, the poor girl was as trapped—well, what I mean is, I was unaware that she had already plighted her troth."

"Without the knowledge of her family? Naughty girl! Then why publish the notice? Ah—did her eager papa wait on the flagway until *The Gazette* opened its doors in the dawn so as to get the announcement in print before you could draw back . . . ?"

"Do try not to be so vulgar, Mathieson."

"Otton."

Carruthers fixed him with a scornful look.

Otton grinned. "Your icy shards are wasted on me, dear boy. I've no shame. But speaking from the loathly depths which I inhabit, I will advise you. She's a very choice morsel, I grant. But if she loves another, cry off. Loud and fast!"

"And ruin the girl."

"Would you sooner she ruin *you*? Have some sense, Sir Knight! You offered in all sincerity. She accepted with extreme *in*sincerity! For Lord's sake, what is your alternative? Wed her and leave the side door open for her lover on your wedding night?"

Carruthers said angrily, "Of course not, but it must be handled with care. My mother is pleased. *Her* family is pleased. And Miss Ramsay is a lady. I—"

Otton groaned and covered his eyes. "And you're the type wants one woman for eternity—from which may the good Lord deliver me! Merry, Merry—listen to the voice of experience! They're *all* ladies. Or fancy they are. I wish I'd a sovereign for every such 'lady' to be had for the price of a well-turned phrase, a few trinkets, a way with a kiss. And not one of 'em worth five minutes of regret! I guarantee you I could win your pretty filly from her lover in a week. Aye, and—By the way, who *is* her lover? Anyone we know?"

Carruthers glared at him, but said with reluctance, "Brooks Lambert."

For a moment Otton's face was a mask of astonishment, then he shouted with laughter. "Your famous *nephew*? Heavenly heresy! What a treacle pot! Are you not very careful, my poor clod, you'll either wind up being jilted and as a result cut by every man in Town, or married to a chit who yearns for your nephew!

141

Be damned if I know which would be worse. I know what *I'd* do in the matter, but I'm a dedicated villain."

Carruthers, who had been considerably less than honest with his friend, said, "I hope you're wrong, and that we'll somehow contrive to come through with no scandal. Besides—you're not a villain, Roly. You only think you are."

For a rare moment the arrogantly handsome face was grave. Otton said slowly, "Oh, but I am, old lad. Did you know the depths to which I have sunk . . . some of the things I have done . . ." He broke off, and the twinkle returned to the velvety eyes. He finished blithely, "You would most assuredly forbid me to ever again set foot across your threshold."

"What rubbish you mouth. Desist, and tell me of yourself. Were you really bested in a duel?"

"I was, but it's too long a tale to bore you with. Nor would you admire my part in it. Suffice it to say I lost. This time."

"The tale is not told, then? The prize must be sizeable if you've bled for it."

"Sizeable!" Otton leaned forward, glanced to the door, and said in a voice of suppressed excitement, "It is *vast*! No less than the treasure the Jacobites gathered to finance their cause."

For a moment, Carruthers's stare was fixed, then he drained his tankard and set it down. "I've heard rumours. There are ciphers, one gathers, and every scoundrel in the three kingdoms after the poor devils who carry them."

"Speak not harshly of me and my brethren."

"Lord, Roly," said Carruthers, shaking his head at him. "Is it worth it? The price you pay in your lusting for ill-gotten gains."

"Not ill-gotten if *I* gain 'em. And blood has been shed for gold since time immemorial."

"Why not achieve something of your own efforts and abilities? I'd think 'twould be more gratifying than the dangerous pursuit of quick riches."

"But riches are so delightfully—*rich*, my Meredith. And as for my own efforts and abilities—huh! Much they won me! I soldiered for a pittance and spent three months on my back in a verminous Flanders hovel for a bonus! I was a bully for hire, an assassin—"

Carruthers frowned. "Not that last, surely?"

"Faith, but I must not shatter your illusions. You've sufficient to plague you, poor fellow. Even so"—the dark eyes glinted— "I'll get my hands on that treasure or die trying, I assure you!"

Regretfully, Carruthers believed him.

They had planned to play *paille-maille* on the lawn that afternoon, but although the weather continued bright and sunny, the grass was still very wet from yesterday's storm. As an alternative, Carruthers conducted his guests on a tour of the various wings. Otton, who knew the Hall well, accompanied the little party. He was a great favourite with Mrs. Carruthers, and his dry wit added much to their enjoyment of the tour. His main target, however, was Phoebe, and before they had progressed through the first floor of the Lancastrian structure, he had managed in a deft and casual fashion to detach her from the side of her betrothed.

"Have you noted the fine quality of the woodworms in here, ma'am?" he asked. "Most hardy type."

Carruthers called warningly, "Roly, behave yourself!"

Otton laughed and manoeuvred Phoebe around the small group as they paused to gaze from the railed balcony into the great ballroom below. "The gallery is far more interesting. Come."

Phoebe threw a startled glance to Carruthers. That this charming man was dangerous she had no doubt, and she was not sure she cared to be alone with him. Her mama, however, was asking with a great deal of interest about the emblem of the sword and the rose. Otton's mouth trembled on a smile, his hand attempted nothing more wicked than to support her arm, and somehow, she was being shepherded along the corridor towards the convex central wing. "I expect," said Otton, "that Merry told you some fustian about each of these ridiculous buildings, but did you know why the Tudor wing was built on the far side of the courtyard? It was because the head of the house at that time took his son's wife in such aversion, he built their dwelling as far from his own as was possible and warned them never to darken his door again."

She laughed. "I believe you made that up."

"No, dear lady. It's perfectly true. And now, allow me to conduct you through the gallery of the infamous."

The graceful curve of the hall was hung with the portraits of endless Carrutherses, the dark faces seeming to eye her with either curiosity or disdain as she passed. They were, she thought, a singularly comely lot who, if their apparel and jewels were any indication, had all enjoyed great prosperity. She saw traces of Meredith in several of the paintings and came to a halt before one of obvious antiquity. The frame was magnificently carven, the canvas lovingly preserved, and the portrait retaining a richness and depth remarkable in view of its age. She gazed up at an unsmiling face: a young man clad in a dark blue tunic emblazoned with richly embroidered heraldry. He wore a small, neatly trimmed beard, but aside from that and the absence of the disfiguring scars, the fine face above her might have been that of her betrothed. There was the same faint hauteur in the set of the mouth, the same proud tilt to the dark head. She looked at the eyes and was enthralled; they were wide, darkly lashed, and of a rich blue, and in them she saw a lurking smile—the smile of a happy man.

"Miss Ramsay?"

Phoebe started. "Oh—your pardon. You said . . . ?"

"That he is said to resemble Merry. Much better-looking, though, don't you agree?"

"No!" she said, indignant. "As a matter of fact, I—" She broke off, blushing and confused, and horribly aware of Otton's broad grin. "He is—very impressive," she said with as much dignity as she could muster. "What a lovely frame." And, idly, "Who was he?"

"His name was Anthony, and he is connected with the legend that is continued"—he led her towards the centre of this fine sweeping hall—"in the *pièce de résistance.*"

The room broadened into a deep bay that jutted out into the courtyard. The walls here were bare, with only some old chests on which were crystal bowls holding tastefully arranged sprays of white blossoms and fern. In the middle of the bay was a single large painting. Phoebe drifted towards it almost fearfully. The girl depicted in the life-size portrait was about eighteen. She wore a fitted white gown, the broad square neck edged with a band of pink embroidery, the same band repeated across the line of the hips, from which the skirt fell in a rich fullness. She stood leaning forward slightly, as though looking from the frame, her lips parted and an expression of eager enquiry upon her face. Her features were pleasant, but not remarkable, and yet there was an inner glow to the heart-shaped face, a purity in the gaze, a warmth in the expectant half-smile that created a rare appeal. Her eyes were blue, and her crowning glory was her hair, which the artist had shown as falling in a shining red-gold cloud, past her shoulders and continuing to hip level. And in her right hand she held a great red rose.

Phoebe trod closer. The plate proclaimed, 'Clemency, Ladye

Meredyth-Carruthers.' She knew, after a timeless moment, that Carruthers was close by, and turned to find him watching her, his face enigmatic. She was conscious of a panicked bewilderment, and said hurriedly, "She is lovely. You didn't tell me that—that she had red hair."

Otton teased, "Merry's fatal weakness."

"Since you are so adept at conducting house tours, Roly," said Carruthers, somewhat flushed, "I mean to make you work for your supper. Ladies and gentlemen, Captain Otton has asked to be your guide. I am going to keep a promise by showing my betrothed through the castle."

Otton murmured *sotto voce*, "And I think *I* am a villain!"

Outside, the wind was rising, whipping about the weeds that sprang from between the cobblestones. Justice bayed happily and came limping over to join them. Carruthers bent to inspect his paw.

"What is worrying you?" asked Phoebe.

"Oh, the old fool won't keep the bandage on, but it's much improved."

"I didn't mean that. You are disturbed about something."

"I—er dread you will disapprove of my ancestral Keep and—"

"Mr. Carruthers," she interpolated sternly, "you asked me a short while ago if we could be friends."

"Yes, and you said we could, but almost at once took me in violent aversion."

"For which I apologized. If I truly were your betrothed, sir, or your—your wife, you would have the right to protect me, but since we are no more than friends, nor ever likely to be—"

"Anyone who dwells on my lands, or is a guest in my house, is entitled to my protection, Miss Phoebe, and— Great gadzooks, what a demoniacal glare! I beg you will stop frightening me so. Will you be as domineering when we are married?"

"I will very likely take an axe to you," she said through her teeth.

He chuckled. "I'll lend you one when we reach the Keep. If you can hoist it, I'll be much surprised. Now be a good girl and come along. My mama keeps country hours, as you know, and you will want to change that pretty gown before dinner, I expect." He proffered his arm.

Phoebe ignored it, and marched on with her head very high.

"Justice," sighed Carruthers, one hand on the dog's furrowed brow, "your name denies you a place in this procession."

Phoebe's lips twitched, but she walked on briskly, Carruthers and the hound following. When they had crossed the drawbridge and reached the steps leading to the massive front doors, however, Carruthers took her elbow. "Be careful of what you say in here," he warned softly. "There are ghosts everywhere."

Ignoring this frivolity, she whispered, "We *are* going to see the Lieutenant?"

"He was in such a turmoil about that blasted cipher, I don't trust him. He's half out of his head, and there wasn't much in it to begin with."

She gave him an indignant look, and he added, "Your axe awaits; *entrez, s'il vous plait, mademoiselle.*"

The door opened easily and Phoebe went inside. She stood in a narrow hall that led off to either side. Faintly lit by slotted windows in the deep outer walls, it was a gloomy place and the air was chill and dank. She reached instinctively for Carruthers's hand, and found instead cold steel. She glanced around swiftly. He held a gigantic war axe, the handle of which he had put into her grasp. "Ready to decapitate?" he asked.

She eyed the weapon with some dubiety. "All right. Let go."

He rested the point of the great curving blade on the stone floor and stood back. "Swing away," he said, holding aside his cravat and tilting his head obligingly towards her.

Phoebe swung up the axe. About half an inch. "Oh, my!" she gasped.

"Do not torture me," he complained. "This waiting for death is agony."

"Wretch!" She gripped the haft with both hands, settled her feet and heaved. The axe lifted. Phoebe gave a squeal. Carruthers grabbed the weapon in time to prevent its amputating her toes. "Would you object to employing the method of the Borgias instead?" he enquired. "I think this little dealer in death is more like to put an end to you than to me."

She laughed breathlessly and relinquished her grip. Carruthers grinned and replaced the weapon in sturdy brackets beside the doors.

"Is this the Great Hall?" asked Phoebe, looking about disparagingly. "It's awfully narrow. And what is that hole in the ceiling?"

"It is not the Great Hall, doubting Thomasina, but the outer death-trap. That hole up there was kept closed until the enemy was fairly inside, at which point boiling pitch was poured on them."

"Ugh."

"It is the origin of the phrase 'a warm reception.' "

She looked at him. His face was innocent, but one long bronzed finger was tracing the outline of his jaw. She knew the gesture by now. "You're fibbing."

He started to guide her to a flight of steps and a crumbling arched opening. "You don't know that."

"Oh yes, I do."

"How?"

She smiled mischievously. "I think I will not tell you. It gives me an advantage."

He said obliquely. "You already have too many of those, Miss Ramsay."

Phoebe decided it was best to avoid his eyes. "Oh, now this is *really* a Great Hall," she exclaimed as they went up the steps and passed through the arch. "My heavens! You could entertain all London in here!"

Her voice echoed through the enormous chamber. It was not nearly as decrepit as she had expected, and although the walls were fallen away in places, there was no debris on the flagged floor. Larger windows admitted the daylight, revealing lofty vaulted ceilings and, directly across from where they stood, a vast fireplace. Phoebe went to inspect the large carving above the mantel. "Your crest," she said, turning to him.

He nodded. "Rather nice, isn't it?"

She reached up, her fingers tracing the deep indentations. "A griffin, an eagle, a sword and a rose. What does the Latin mean?"

"Gentle be my strength."

"Oh, I like that! And I like this old place. Meredith, do you really mean to restore it?" She turned to face him. "It would be such a pity not to. It is part of the history of our land, and heritage is so terribly important, do not you think?"

"I do." He gazed down at her. His expression was very far from being fierce and, even by the muted light, she saw that the blue flame again lit his eyes. He stepped closer. His fingertips touched her cheek, sending sparks through her veins. "Would it please you were I to restore it?"

She said faintly, "It is . . . none of my business, of course. I . . . should not have . . ."

His arm slipped around her. She lifted her face, and he kissed her. Gently this time, but with a soft, heightening passion that made her head spin and her knees tremble. Desperate, she

147

groped for the memory of him kissing Rosalie, and pulled away. "You—take shameful advantage of . . . of the situation," she gasped.

"Of course." He still held her hand and pulled her back towards him.

She wrenched clear. "Where is Lieutenant—Lascelles? In the dungeons, I suppose." She started to walk to a crumbling downward spiral of stairs at the side of the hall.

Carruthers drew a deep breath. "No. This way."

He took her to another arch that led into a long corridor, but before they went through, he paused, glanced keenly around, then pressed on two of the stone slabs simultaneously. A crack appeared in the wall. Carruthers pushed, and gradually the wall swung inward until a narrow opening, large enough for a man to squeeze through, was revealed. He motioned Phoebe inside and she entered a tiny chamber. Lascelles, fully dressed save for his coat, was sitting on a crude wooden bed. He struggled to his feet, stammering a welcome.

"Pray sit down, Lieutenant," she said. "You should be in bed."

"And I knew you would not be, you dolt," growled Carruthers, shoving the little door closed again.

Lascelles's haggard face was flushed. He smiled and said cheerily, "Must try to get my strength back. Never—never get well, lying about all day. It *is* day?"

Phoebe touched his forehead gently. "Poor soul. Yes, it is afternoon, and—Oh, Merry! He is so hot!"

Carruthers came at once and the feel of the burning, dry skin brought a vexed "What have you been about? You were in better case this morning. You've been trying to walk, and worked yourself into a fever, you dimwit!" He forced his friend to lie down.

Lascelles struggled against the strong hands and, failing, began to pluck fretfully at the blanket Phoebe pulled over him. "You do not understand," he muttered. "I *must* deliver the cipher! Gave my word . . . of honour. Must get it through . . . must . . ." He sighed wearily and his eyes closed.

"Damn!" muttered Carruthers, frowning down at him. "Here we've brought him safe through a veritable sea of dragoons; I've a house fairly crawling with military, and now, for a bonus, have a hungry bounty hunter under my roof; and all the block can think of is that curst stupid cipher!"

Phoebe said, "So that is what worried you. Your friend Otton is a bounty—"

"Otton?" Lascelles's eyes were wide and frantic. He struggled up, tossing the blanket aside. "Murdering swine! You'll not take me!" He hurled himself at Carruthers, striking out furiously.

"Lance!" Carruthers blocked one blow and seized the flailing arm. "Lance, you madman—it's me—Merry! Give over, damn you!"

Running to seize his other arm, Phoebe cried, "Lieutenant, it's all right! He's not here. It's all right!"

The light of reason came back into the hollowed eyes. Lascelles breathed, "Merry? Jove, but—it is. Sorry . . . dear old boy. Thought you was that—that devil . . . Otton."

Carruthers directed a warning glance at Phoebe and, together, they guided the fugitive back onto his bed. "We just chanced to mention his name, Lance. Never fear, you're well hidden."

Lascelles held his hand in desperation. "Leave me your pistol . . . I beg you, Merry. I'll kill myself sooner than . . . public dismemberment and—disembowelling knife. M'father . . . 'twould kill him. You won't tell . . . promise, Merry . . . for old times' sake. Y'won't . . . tell . . ." The pleading words faded into an incoherent mumbling.

Phoebe said, "The poor soul. How ill he is. Those dressings must be changed. I'll—"

"You will do no such thing. I'll attend to it. I cannot have you looking at another man's legs, Phoebe. I mean—Miss Ramsay."

His eyes twinkled at her. She said sternly, "See that you remember it, Mr. Carruthers. And I think there is no call to use such—terms."

He laughed softly. "You mean 'tis all right for you to dress the wound in his—er, limb. But not all right to use the word."

"I mean," she said, "that I will stay and help you. After all, a woman is better—"

"Better thought of does she do as she's told," he interrupted, seizing her arm and propelling her firmly to the door.

She opened her mouth to protest.

"Sssh!" he warned, and cautiously tugged the door open.

All was quiet. He nudged Phoebe into the Great Hall.

"Odious Tyrant!" she hissed.

"Little shrew!" he riposted.

Turning from this exchange of compliments, they both were smiling.

∞ *Chapter 11* ∞

The sunlight slanted benignly through the lofty windows of the crimson saloon. Two of the panes were broken and had been boarded, but by and large the dilapidations in this irregularly shaped chamber were minor, and if the furnishings were far from new, they were, at least, comfortable. The company did much to compensate for the shabby surroundings. Captain Otton was dashing in a dull-red coat lavishly trimmed with gold lace, his powdered hair constrained by a red riband; Sinclair presented a neat, if shy, appearance in a tie-wig and a coat of bottle-green that was beginning to show signs of being outgrown across the shoulders, and Meredith was elegant in a peerlessly tailored coat of dark brown velvet over a waistcoat of brown-and-cream brocade and cream small clothes. Lucille Carruthers wore a violet-blue *robe à la française* with violets in her high-coiffed and powdered hair, and when Phoebe's pomona-green sarsenet-and-Alençon lace, and her mother's dove-grey satin were added to the rest, the room was a rainbow of colours.

Otton was in rare form and soon had them all laughing. Mrs. Carruthers seemed happy on this warm summer evening, but confided to Phoebe that she was afraid Meredith would be angry because Jeffery had not yet returned.

"I doubt he will be cross," said Phoebe. "After all, your son is helping in the search for rebels, and—"

"But he is not, Miss Ramsay. Hilary Broadbent dropped in whilst you were changing your dress, and complained to Meredith that Jeffery only put in a token appearance, and then wandered off somewhere. Broadbent felt we should be doing more to help the military."

'Oh, dear!' thought Phoebe.

Jeffery arrived just in time for dinner and hurried into the saloon, shooting the lace at his wrists, his fair hair gleaming here and there through powder that had obviously been hastily applied. He slanted a guilty glance at his brother's face, and watching Meredith's grim expression, Phoebe thought it would be an appropriate time for the lady with the rose to make an appearance. Between his worries for his rebel friend, his rebellious brother, the Squire's poisoned hounds, and his soon-to-be-terminated betrothal, he stood in dire need of *some* moral support.

"He's tough as steel, you know," murmured an amused voice at her side. "And surely it cannot be as bad as you think."

Otton was offering a glass of ratafia. She accepted the glass but did not return his smile, looking at him steadily as she said, "It is very bad, Captain Otton." She was about to request the favour of a few words in private with him when she saw that his lazily mocking gaze had already left her.

"Jove," he said. "See what you mean!"

A hush had fallen over the group. Apprehension seized Phoebe in a vise as the same Captain of dragoons who had found them in the cave marched purposefully across the room, an agitated Conditt hovering behind him, and two troopers waiting in the doorway.

His tricorne under one arm, the Captain said, "My regrets for the intrusion, Carruthers."

Lucille uttered a little cry of fright. Jeffery stood very straight beside her chair. Sinclair's face was the colour of chalk.

Meredith said in frigid accents, "I fancy my butler must have explained that we entertain guests. Do you wish to speak to me, Holt, I would suggest—"

"I cannot stand on ceremony in this matter. I must tell you that my men are even now searching this—er, your various buildings."

Both Lady Eloise and Mrs. Carruthers sprang up. Sinclair moved at once to his mother's side. Lucille clung, shaking, to Jeffery. Otton, swinging a gold-chased quizzing glass, regarded them all with covert amusement.

"For what?" exclaimed Carruthers, his brows gathering into a black scowl. "There are no rebels in this house, Captain."

"Then you will have no objection do we—" Holt's cold gaze had slid to Jeffery, but at this point suddenly encompassed Otton. His jaw dropped. He looked almost ludicrously astonished.

Otton stood and bowed, grinning. *"Encore nous nous rencontrons, mon ami."*

"Ah—ha . . ." breathed Holt, staring wide-eyed.

151

"I am a fairly frequent visitor, you know," Otton pointed out mildly. "Carruthers is that rare commodity—my friend."

Obviously making an effort to recover, Holt said, "I fail to see why you should object to a search, Carruthers. All loyal subjects are expected to cooperate in apprehending rebels. Especially," he added, his voice hardening, "reserve officers." And he marched out, his troopers following him briskly.

Meredith gestured, and Condit hurried to him. "I am so sorry, sir. He would not permit that I announce him. And there are so many of them."

"How many?" interjected Otton casually.

Wringing his bony hands, Condit said, "Oh, Captain, I do not know. Twenty, at least! They're—they're *everywhere*, Mr. Meredith!"

"Are they, by God!" growled Carruthers.

"Lay you odds half of 'em never find their way out," Otton murmured; and added, his keen eyes fixed on Sinclair, "be funny if they found something, would it not?"

Jeffery looked at Otton curiously. Placing a different interpretation on his remark, Lucille moaned for the safety of the T'ang Dynasty flask, the Cellini bowl, the Meredyth ruby.

Carruthers demanded, "Condit?"

"A member of the staff goes with each one of them, sir."

"That was well done." An approving grin lit the dark face, and Condit gave an audible sigh of relief. Carruthers went on, "Still, it would behoove me to stay with our zealous Captain. You will forgive, Mama?"

"Yes. Do go, dear."

He bowed, gave an almost imperceptible jerk of the head to Otton, and started away.

"Alas," sighed Otton, regarding Phoebe tragically. "I am summoned. Ever the faithful sycophant." And he wandered off, Lucille's anxious "Why *ever* did they come here again . . . ?" following him.

In the hall, Carruthers waited. "You know Holt?" he demanded as soon as the door closed.

"We have had some . . . encounters. A dangerous man, friend. And a very ambitious one. Have a care."

"Why should he have been so shocked to see you?"

Otton shrugged, watching the quizzing glass that swung gently from his long white hand. "I fancy he is surprised to discover I have a friend. He knows me well." The cynical dark eyes lifted to meet Meredith's keen ones levelly. "And he follows the same lure as do I."

"The devil! Do you think this poor fugitive they hound to a firing squad really *is* on my lands?"

"If he was and I knew of it, can you suppose I'd not have warned you?"

For an instant Carruthers watched him, unsmiling. A glint crept into his eyes. He said, "I think you would throw me to the dogs if it was a case of my life or the treasure."

Otton spread his hands in a faintly French gesture. "But, of course."

Carruthers murmured onë word. Otton shuddered and covered his ears. But as Carruthers started on his way, he called softly, "I sometimes wonder, Merry, why—knowing me so well—you still name me friend."

Over his shoulder, Carruthers called, "Because I know you better than you do. I hope."

Otton shook his head and went back into the crimson saloon.

It was almost dark by the time the soldiers had concluded their search, and they were tired and hot and frustrated. It had been thirsty work, and as Captain Holt marched across the Armour Hall, he slanted an oblique look at Carruthers's set face. "My fellows would be the better for a tankard."

"And you too, I fancy. There is a decent tavern in Dewbury Prime. It is called—"

"I am aware of what it is called." Holt stamped across the terrace and down the steps. "Thank you for your hospitality," he said ironically, taking the reins a trooper handed him.

"The only possible return for your courtesy," replied Carruthers with equal irony.

Holt reddened, swung into the saddle, and went clattering away at the head of his troop. Carruthers watched them disappear into the dimness of the night and returned to the house.

He was able to allay his mother's fears and to assure her that all estates were being subjected to the same treatment, since the hunted man was known to be an aristocrat. His brother looked troubled. Carruthers fixed him with a brief but meaningful stare, and the boy nodded a weary acknowledgement of an impending interview.

Walking in to dinner on the arm of her betrothed, Phoebe

whispered, "What crimes has your poor brother committed, Sir Implacability?"

"Two. One is that he persists in crying friends with a man highly suspected of Jacobite leanings. I believe that is what prompted this evening's invasion."

"Then you must *tell* him, Merry! If he knew—"

"If he knew he'd be as guilty as am I. No, ma'am. Not while I can possibly prevent his involvement!"

"But how can you force him to obey you?"

"By exercising my tyranny, m'dear. And, by God, if I failed to act for his first offence, I most certainly would do so for the second!"

Irritated, Phoebe thought, 'The second being the irresistible Miss Smith,' and said no more.

Despite the long delay, the food was still excellent and the meal went off well enough, although there was a good deal of anxious speculation from Mrs. Carruthers as to the possibility of desperate fugitives lurking about the area. It was almost ten o'clock by the time the ladies withdrew and, because of the lateness of the hour, the gentlemen soon joined them. Lady Eloise, who was musical, agreed to go to the harpsichord and played a selection of operatic airs by Herr Gluck, who had arrived in London the previous year. His new opera was not held in high esteem, and to judge from Meredith's expression, he shared the views of the critics. Sinclair was quiet and preoccupied, Jeffery looked miserable, and Lucille showed a tendency to doze off. Phoebe was relieved when the tea-tray was carried in, and very soon afterwards Lucille announced her intention to retire. Sinclair accompanied his ladies, and Meredith escorted them to the stairs, handed them their candles, and wished them a good night. From the corner of her eye, Phoebe saw Otton, a thin cheroot in his hand, strolling across to the withdrawing room where were French windows open to the garden.

As they started up the stairs, Sinclair murmured, "Jupiter, but that was a close one! You bore it very well, old lady, but I hope I never see you turn so pale!"

"Thank God it was no worse! How frightful it *could* have been!" She started to tell him about Lascelles, but he interrupted, saying that Carruthers had already told him that he meant to arrange for someone to stay with Lascelles for as much of the time as was possible lest the man do something disastrous while in the throes of delirium. Wondering how Carruthers meant to accomplish this, Phoebe entered her parlour.

Ada was dozing in the chair, and Phoebe sent her to bed, claiming that she had come to get a shawl and meant to sit out on the terrace for a little while, to escape the heat inside the house. Ada was not an admirer of night air. It was, as she lost no time in advising her young mistress, dangerous to the health, containing many noxious fumes from plants and flowers that "turn poisonous" after the sun goes down. Besides which, it was well known that germs, spiders, and all creatures that bite and sting are abroad at night in search of the unwary.

Braving these perils, Phoebe at length was able to creep down the stairs, across the Lancastrian wing and into the Armour Hall of the connecting wing. A sleepy lackey sprang to open the front door and she repeated her small excuse of the heat in her room. This provoked another lecture, the well-meaning man urging that if she meant to walk in the grounds, she not go too far. "Not with them murdering Jackeybites skulking about, miss." Thanking him for his concern, she escaped.

Meredith Carruthers was a confusing blend of the stern and the tender, besides which he was an immoral man, but his mother's tale had touched her heart. She could no longer deny an admiration for him, and the poisoning of the Squire's dogs continued to trouble her. She was not of the opinion that there would be a duel, but if there was any chance that Roland Otton could throw some light on why Carruthers's gauntlet had been found at Lockwood's kennels, she meant to beg him to do so.

It was cooler outside. There was no moon, the stars hanging like brilliant jewels against the velvety blackness of the heavens. Phoebe peered about without success for Otton's tall figure. She walked the length of the terrace, turned back, crossed the gardens to the new wing, and was relieved to find that the drawing room windows still stood wide and that from across the hall a glow of light shone from the study. She thought, sympathetically, 'Poor Jeffery!' and went towards the rear of the house, moving with caution so as not to trip in her high-heeled slippers.

She could discover no sign of Otton and was about to give up and return to the house when she caught a whiff of smoke. Relieved, she started to call to him, but with the windows wide open, Carruthers might hear, and she had no wish to attract his attention. She crept to the drivepath, straining her eyes, and halting, surprised, when she heard low voices near at hand.

". . . not dreamed my arrival was so fortuitous. Do tell me, coz, have we our cipher-bearer comfortably trapped?"

It was Roland Otton's low, sardonic drawl. Phoebe stood rigid. *Coz?* The response caused her an even greater shock.

"Were he comfortably trapped," muttered Captain Holt, "I'd not be compelled to order my men to rake through every damnable inch of your freeze-me-dead friend's damned decaying monstrosity! And furthermore, Roly, I find it a devilish strain on coincidence for you to have 'chanced' to arrive here just as we have cornered one of the couriers. You're hot on the trail of that treasure—admit it."

"Dear my Jacob, why this resort to redundancy? You know I mean to have it."

"Even if the finding of it costs Meredith Carruthers his head?"

A pause. Holding her breath, Phoebe could all but see Otton's shoulders go up in his graceful shrug. "All's fair in love and war. I think he is not involved, but if he is—winner take all! Now tell me, Jacob, what have you?"

"A rebel cur who calls himself Lascelles. Twice we've had our hands on him and he's gulled us. He's wounded and has been on foot this last seventy miles, and running, with dogs after him part of the way. Threw himself through a window to escape Mariner Fotheringay, and was properly cut up by the look of things. He must be all in. We lost him near Guildford, but have reason to believe he'll head this way. See here, Roly, if you spot him, *I* want him!"

"For a stupid promotion? If you help me snabble the treasure, you'll be a deal better off! Besides, without the other stanzas of the poem, what good would one be to those Whitehall maggotwits?"

"There must be some clue, else you'd not seek it either. Certainly, it contains part of the message, which might be all we'd need to come at it. If I can but get my hands on Lascelles . . ."

After a short silence, Otton asked, "What makes you think Carruthers is involved? He fought with *you* fellows, not for Bonnie Charlie."

"He became squeamish after Culloden."

"But you did not, eh, Jacob?"

Holt snapped, "I follow orders. War is no game for children."

"Precisely. Nor for innocent women and babes."

"You'd do well to guard your tongue, cousin. And your friend would do well to tighten his rein on his scatter-wit of a brother."

"Jeffery? No fear there, dear boy. He despises the Jacobites."

"Yet cries friends with Horatio Glendenning, who cries

156

friends with Trevelyan de Villars, both up to their ears in aiding rebels, I'll go bail. And both of whom will be lucky to have their heads when we see the end of this."

A soft whistle sounded, then Otton said, "I still think you're in the wrong of it. However, it opens an interesting door. Rest assured, coz, I'll watch here, and if anything . . ."

They were moving towards her. Shivering despite the heat of the night, Phoebe fled.

The same lackey swung the front door open as she hurried across the terrace and he again disregarded protocol by murmuring in a friendly way that he had been a touch worried about her. "Another minute or two and I'd have fetched the master," he said with a fatherly smile.

"Thank you. Is Mr. Meredith still about, or has he retired?"

The lackey conveying the information that the master was still in his study, she proceeded to the new wing and turned down the hall. She paused when she heard Jeffery's voice, sharp with resentment, ". . . perfectly well I've *never* been in sympathy with Charles Stuart! And as for Rosalie . . ."

Phoebe retreated. She had no intention of interrupting so emotional a quarrel, nor could she bear the thought that at any moment she might be confronted by the treacherous Roland Otton. She quickened her steps and went directly to her bedchamber.

Upon opening the casements next morning, Ada announced that it was a beautiful Sunday and she was glad to find Miss had not been ravished and garrotted by some murdering rebel fugitive during the dark hours. Phoebe advised her ghoulish handmaiden that there were worse creatures in the world than rebel fugitives. She refused to elaborate, however, asking instead that Ada be as quick as possible in completing her toilette.

Walking slowly downstairs, Phoebe thought that as soon as her brother was about she would tell him what she had overheard last evening, and let him break the news to Meredith. That it would come as a blow was beyond doubting. It was clear that his friendship with Otton was—

"Step lively there!"

Her head shot up and, with it, her spirits. In the lower hall, dazzling in scarlet uniform and furred pelisse, one hand carelessly resting on the hilt of his sabre, stood Brooks Lambert.

With a squeak of joy and relief she flew down the remaining

stairs. "Brooks! Thank *heaven* you are come! I am in the most dreadful dilemma!"

The two lackeys who were by chance loitering nearby obligingly looked the other way. Greatly daring, Lambert pressed a salute on her brow. She drew back in alarm and whispered, "Oh, Brooks, you should not!"

He checkled. " 'Tis what makes it the more delicious. Now tell me, love—what has been occurring?"

They repaired to a quiet bench in the shade of a cluster of birch trees at the end of the terrace. Lambert listened intently to her account of their meeting with the Squire, and the accusation he had hurled at Carruthers. When she finished he made no comment, but sat staring into space.

"Do you think it could possibly be a coincidence that Carruthers's glove was found there?" she asked anxiously.

He frowned. "I think it more likely that someone seeks to increase the bad feeling between them. Perhaps somebody has a grievance against Lockwood and hopes Merry will put a period to him." They were both silent, then Lambert asked, "How do Merry and Jeff go on these days? Any—er, uproars whilst you've been here?"

"Heavens! Brooks—you cannot think Jeffery would—"

"So here you are." The deep voice cut off Phoebe's words. Carruthers had come up, Justice beside him.

"Good morning, old sportsman," said Lambert amiably. "I've been given back my leave, or a portion of it at least, so hurried here to accompany you to church and also discuss a way to put our plan into action."

"Did you?"

"How?" asked Phoebe, inwardly amused by Carruthers's lack of enthusiasm.

"Well," said Lambert, "it's not a brilliant scheme, perhaps, but—suppose when your grandmama arrives tomorrow, Phoebe, we were all to go for a jaunt. And suppose . . ."

Phoebe's hope to tell Sinclair of Otton's duplicity was thwarted when he was late in joining the group assembling to journey to Dewbury Prime, and then rode, rather than travelling in the carriage. The village was serene and picturesque; the ancient church with its lovely old windows and mellow woodwork was a delight, and the curate's sermon delivered with a blessedly light hand. Phoebe and her family were made much of after the service, and Lucille said happily that her prospective daughter-in-law was a credit to them all.

They returned to the Hall for a late luncheon, after which they were to make one more attempt to see Dewbury Minor. Both Lady Eloise and Lucille were to join the party, although they meant to occupy a carriage. My lady was not pleased to find that Lambert was again present. The handsome young soldier betrayed no resentment of her daughter's betrothal, however, and was so solicitous for her own well-being that she could not for long remain out of temper with him. He settled her into the carriage, brought an extra cushion for her back, and asked anxiously if she was comfortable. She was unhappily aware that she had caught a cold, but assured him she was feeling quite well enough to enjoy an afternoon drive, and was especially eager to see the smaller village which Sinclair had said was so very charming.

Carruthers rode up, Justice limping at his stirrup. "This old fool wants to go along," he said. "Would you ladies object was he to ride with you?"

Both dog lovers, the ladies said they would not at all object, and Sinclair nobly volunteered to ride inside with them and control the hound if he became rambunctious. Justice, looking more a judge than a criminal, was duly ensconced, having been sped upon his way by a swipe from Satan, who had lurked under the coach. Brooks tossed Phoebe into the saddle, then mounted up himself, and they were off.

It was a pleasant afternoon, the wind preventing the temperature from becoming too warm. The three riders led the way, Phoebe in the middle, Carruthers to her left, Brooks to her right. For a while they chatted of commonplace matters, then the conversation turned to the hunt for the fugitive Jacobite, which was being pursued with much vigour and enthusiasm by soldiers and citizenry, said Lambert, but without appreciable results. "It sounds to me," he remarked, "as though you've had more excitement here, Merry. What's all this about old Lockwood holding you to blame for poisoning his hounds?"

Carruthers directed an irked look at Phoebe.

"Yes, I'm the one who blabbed," she admitted.

"I wish you will not mention it to anyone else, Brooks," he muttered. "You know the Squire's disposition. All show and no go."

"That doesn't explain your gauntlet having been found at the scene."

"No, and I cannot explain it, either. Possibly one of the hounds simply came upon it and appropriated it. Who knows? Now, ma'am, as to this daring rescue Lambert has suggested for tomorrow's entertainment, the more I think on it, the less I like the scheme. What if your mount should *really* panic and bolt, could you control her?"

"Her? Which of your mounts do you mean to put me up on, sir?"

"Not the one you ride today, I do assure you. Showers is too full of spirit. Did *he* ever decide to run away, you'd have a tussle to control him, and I'll not take any unnecessary risks."

"My papa taught me to ride, sir," she defended indignantly, "I am accounted a very fine horsewoman, moreover. Besides, if you put me up on a slug, it will scarcely look as if the animal is bolting without I lash it for ten minutes, which might lack conviction."

"There are no slugs in my stables, madam," Carruthers informed her.

"Besides, Merry is quite right," said Lambert. "How ever I may hope to please your grandmother, your life is much too precious for us to take any undue risks."

"Oh, fiddle! You are a magnificent rider, Lamb, and will be able to 'rescue' me so deedily that my grandmama cannot fail to be impressed. Where are we to stage this gallant deed, Mr. Carruthers? Hereabouts?"

"Heaven forbid! The Quarry is less than a mile to the northeast. If anything went amiss and your mount ran in that direction, Brooks would have his work cut out to reach you in time." He glanced to the carriage and Justice, who was baying at something on the wooded slope to their left. Rogue danced about nervously.

Carruthers frowned and reined sharply in the direction of the slope. In the same instant, the vicious roar of a flintlock shattered the morning stillness. Birds soared, squawking, into the air. Meredith felt a sharp tug at his left cuff even as Rogue shied, screaming his fright. Phoebe's plunging mount, seared across the back as though by a hot iron, leapt forward with a shrill neigh of pain and terror, and was off like the wind. Shocked and bewildered, Phoebe flung a terrified glance at Carruthers. Showers jumped a gorse bush, then reared in added panic as a large hare fled in a tan streak for safety. Almost thrown, Phoebe lost her grip on the reins and made an instinctive grab for the grey's mane. He took the bit between his teeth and bolted in earnest. Straight to the northeast.

"Go on, Brooks!" shouted Carruthers.

Lambert was battling his beautiful bay mare who, no less startled by these events, had apparently decided to travel backwards on her tail.

Carruthers crouched, tightening his grip on the reins.

Lambert fought his mare down, despite the unhelpful shrieks from the carriage, drove home his spurs, and was after the runaway.

Carruthers followed. Showers was heading straight for the Quarry and he dared not take the chance that Lambert might fail. At the back of his mind was rage at whoever had shot at them, but that matter must wait until Phoebe was safe.

"Spring 'em!" howled Sinclair, as the coachman sat gawking in astonishment after the three rapidly disappearing riders. "Dammitall! *Spring* 'em, you great gaby!"

Reassured by this familiar form of address, the coachman whipped up his horses, and the carriage swayed and rattled in pursuit of the riders, the frightened ladies clinging desperately to the straps, Justice baying deafeningly, and Sinclair hanging half out of the window.

Screened by the trees, another and quite unsuspected rider had wheeled his tall chestnut horse and was riding at reckless speed through the copse in the direction whence had come the shot. Checking his mount, he could hear the crashing sounds of someone rushing frenziedly through the undergrowth, and he spurred forward. It was an uneven chase. In only a moment the horseman had raced ahead of the would-be assassin. Sobbing for breath and desperate with fear, Ben Hessell burst through the trees and into a clearing, only to meet Nemesis in the form of a dashing gentleman who aimed a long-barreled pistol with a hand steady as a rock.

Petrified and reeling, Hessell dropped to his knees. "Don't shoot, guv," he gasped out. "Accident! Poaching I was . . . I'll be honest, but—"

"Verminous animal," said Roland Otton, his voice soft, his smile most unpleasant, "your lie is as rank as your odour. If you wish to live—just a little while longer—you will do exactly as I say."

Whining, Hessell shrank lower.

Just as frightened, though for a different cause, Phoebe clung to Showers's mane. Carruthers had warned against riding northeast, and she was horribly sure that was exactly the direction in which this miserable horse was going. All her efforts to break his pounding stride were in vain. Maddened with fear, he fled with the blind stubbornness of his kind, and nothing would stop him until he ran out of wind, or crashed into some obstruction. All she could do was fight to keep from being thrown.

She managed to look behind and saw with a gasp of relief that Brooks was coming up fast, Carruthers close behind him, riding like a centaur. Vastly comforted, she turned back again and gave a squeal of terror.

The lush turf was thinning, with slabs of rock and slate thrusting up through the pebbly soil, and ahead, boulders and loose shale. No country to gallop in. And then she saw the ultimate horror and her blood seemed to freeze. Distantly, stark rocky walls thrust upward, but before them was an emptiness that widened with every flying hoofbeat. She was hurtling at the Quarry—and certain death.

She risked another backward glance. Lambert was very close, looking grim and competent. She would not have to resort to flinging herself from the saddle which, at this rate and with the ground littered with boulders, might result in as sure death as if she went over the edge. And then her strained eyes dilated. Lambert's bay stumbled and went down, Lambert thrown clear, but rolling helplessly.

Phoebe gave a horrified sob. She was doomed, then. That terrifying chasm was less than a quarter mile distant. Her only hope was to jump. She kicked her boot from the stirrup.

"Hold on! Phoebe! *Hold on!*"

She jerked her head around again. Carruthers had come up with incredible swiftness. She watched the distance shorten as the great black horse thundered closer and closer. But the chasm was coming closer also. The straining nostrils of the stallion were level with the grey's tail . . . with the stirrup. Carruthers's face was set and pale, his dark hair blowing wildly. Showers's reins hung straight down between his pounding forelegs. Leaning perilously from the saddle, Carruthers grabbed for the flying mane, caught a handful and hauled back desperately. Showers swerved, but pounded on madly. The gorge was too close, thought Phoebe, despairing. They would both go over unless Meredith drew back.

At the brink of the gorge was a wide strip of clear grass. Gauging the distance, Carruthers forced Rogue into the grey; riding a little ahead now. With Rogue's hoofs practically treading the edge, he crowded Showers into a wide right turn. And just as Phoebe felt that frantic stride break, the big grey's plunging head collided violently with that of Rogue, and they were down in a crazy tumble of flying hoofs, shrill neighing, and shock that drove the breath from Phoebe's lungs. She had seen Meredith hurtle towards the edge and, sure he had fallen to his death, a terrible desolation crushed her.

She lay unmoving, uncaring. And then someone was gasping out her name. Through down-drooping, tear-drenched lashes, she saw boots stagger up, then Meredith had fallen to his knees beside her.

"Phoebe! My God! Phoebe! Do not be hurt . . . please do not!"

She felt bathed in joy and relief, but her foolish lips would not speak. His hands were running over her; taking the most awful liberties. Oh—he was looking for broken bones, of course. In a detached and shocking way, she hoped he would be very thorough before abandoning his efforts. She did not hurt in one particular place, really. She just could not seem to catch her breath, and was powerless to move. Meredith was whispering in a frantic way that was very touching; she really must try to ease his anxiety. She opened her eyes. At once, hands and words were stilled. His gaze searched her face with anguished desperation. He asked hoarsely, "Are you hurt? Can you move?"

She blinked up at him. "Oh dear . . . you have cut your head."

He brushed an impatient hand at the graze across his temple. "Never mind about that. Is anything broken, do you think?"

She experimented by moving cautiously. How white he was. "No, I don't think so, thank you. Are you all right?"

With a muffled groan, he snatched her up and crushed her to him. She really had no objection except that it seemed only sensible to retain one or two ribs. She murmured, "Nothing *was* broken . . ."

He put her from him. His eyes were suspiciously bright, but he said roughly, "*Now* do you see what might have happened had we attempted Brooks's stupid scenario?"

"I see," she contradicted, "that—that someone wants your death, sir."

He laid her down again very gently. "Stay there," he commanded. "I'd best find out how my nephew goes on."

"My heavens!" said Phoebe, and was at a loss to understand how Brooks could have slipped from her mind.

163

ᨄ *Chapter 12* ᨂ

Having sought Carruthers out in the stables, Otton walked back across the yard with him, arguing frowningly, "Young Ramsay said you fell almost at the brink, Merry, and that your arm, in fact, went over the edge."

"It was a trifle close, I'll admit. I would have told her to jump, but the ground was too rough, and when it was safer"—he shrugged—"there was no time left."

"Hmmmn. It would seem, my tulip, that you've a determined enemy."

After an introspective moment, Carruthers said slowly, "Every man has enemies, Roly. Unless he's a jelly-backed mealy-mouth."

"Not every man has enemies who resort to murder. Would to heaven I'd been with you. I'd have tracked the dirty blackguard."

Carruthers cuffed his shoulder. "And perchance got that pretty head blown off your shoulders, had the fellow an extra gun to hand."

Otton shrugged. "Quick and clean. There are worse ways. What d'you intend to do?"

"Do? What the devil can I do?"

They had reached the back door to the new wing and, exasperated, Otton drew his friend to a halt. "You know damned well it was one of Lockwood's people."

"No, no. You're quite out there. Lockwood is hot at hand, but he's one of the most sporting men I know. To shoot from ambush would be utterly repugnant to him, and he'd have the liver out of any of his people who'd dare try such a thing!"

Otton said grudgingly, "I suppose it *could* have been accidental. A poacher so intent on his game he didn't notice your party coming. I give you my word if *I* decided to have a shot at

164

you, I'd not miss. And there's no one else unaccounted for, except—" He broke off suddenly, and finished with rather forced heartiness, "You're right, it *must* have been a poacher."

Carruthers eyed him steadily. "It was not Jeff, Roly."

"Of course not. Didn't mean to imply—"

"We've had our differences, but he'd never wish me harm, much less attempt it."

"I could scarce wait to tell you," said Jeffery, carrying Rosalie Smith's basket as they walked side by side through the golden afternoon. "I'd have brought the volume to show you, save that—" He paused, his lips tightening. "Well, my brother was in the library and I'd no desire to endure another lecture from him."

Rosalie dropped some wild thyme into the basket and slanted a glance at him. "Why? Is Merry cross with you?"

He rolled his eyes heavenwards. "A massive understatement! I'm given my choice between Jamaica and a pair of colours!"

She halted, staring at him. "Good heavens! Why?"

"Two unforgivable crimes. One: I refuse to stop seeing you, and—"

"Oh, Jeff! You should not be here, then!"

He dropped the basket and seized her hands. "I'll own I'd not expected to find you so close to the Hall, but I'd have come to the village to find you at all events. I shall see you as often as I please!"

She pulled free. "What is the second reason he is so angry?"

"Oh, it's nonsensical! It chances that—I've a friend named Horatio Glendenning, and there are rumours he's sympathetic to the Stuart Cause."

She whitened. "*Is* he a Jacobite, do you think?"

"I very much doubt it. Tio's the best fellow and has been kind enough to teach me—" He broke off, a flood of colour darkening his fair face.

"Teach you—what?"

He said shyly, "Well, you know Merry's such a tartar, but he's a good fellow, for all that. Only, I can never come up to what he expects of me. I—I'm not clever at Latin or Greek; I've no bent for debates, or interest in politics; I've no ambition to become a general, or to command some great flagship. Only—I am rather keen on . . . on architecture."

"Jeff!" she cried enthusiastically. "How splendid! Only

165

think—Merry longs to start work on renovating the Hall. Why don't you tell him of your—"

"Lord—no! Not yet. He'd think I was only saying it to persuade him to give me more time, or he'd put me with some horrid tutor who'd look down his nose and make fun, and tell Merry I'm a hopeless case. Anyway, Glendenning's very clever at it, and he's been so kind as to help."

"Jeff, you *must* tell Merry! If he knew why you'd been seeing Lord Glendenning, he—" She interrupted herself. "Is the viscount a Catholic?"

"Well, yes, as a matter of fact, but—Oh, now you look just like Merry! He *will* have my friendship with Tio was the cause for a crowd of dragoons to search the Hall last evening, and—oh—Jove!" He leapt to support the girl, who swayed dizzily, her face paper-white. "Whatever is it? Are you ill? Look here! You've hurt yourself!"

She looked swiftly at the stain on her sleeve. "No, it was my—my grandfather cut himself while shaving, and I helped him. Jeff—did the soldiers really go through the Hall? What did Merry say?"

"Oh, he was mad as fire, but I still don't think it was my—Rosalie! Now why are you weeping?"

"Nothing. Nothing! It is only—these are such frightening times, and poor Merry has—"

A new voice demanded irately, "What the deuce is the matter?"

Rosalie stepped back. Relinquishing his delightful armful, Jeffery scowled to see Sinclair Ramsay, a large volume under his arm, hurrying across the woodland glade that had, until this moment, been so peaceful. "Devil take the fellow," he muttered.

Rosalie dried her eyes and managed a tremulous smile. "Good afternoon, Mr. Ramsay."

Sinclair had every intention to tell Jeffery of the riding accident, but the sight of Rosalie's woebegone little face drove all rational thought from his mind. "What have you done to her?" he snarled. "How has he made you weep, ma'am?"

"Oh, no, really. Mr. Carruthers did not—"

"What the blazes d'you imply, Ramsay? And whatever I've done is no concern of yours!"

"Damn you, you have caused her to cry!"

"No, sir. Truly, he was trying instead to comfort me. Pray tell me what is the book you have brought, Mr. Ramsay."

Jeffery interposed scornfully, "It is the book I was telling you of, Miss Rosalie. There was no cause for *you* to bring it, Ramsay. I've already told her about it."

Ignoring him, Sinclair stepped closer to the girl and opened the book. "See here, ma'am. It tells of some very large bats who are—"

"Every bit as big as your grandpapa was talking about, Rosalie," put in Jeffery, also moving closer and fixing Sinclair with a grim look of warning.

"Indeed?" Rosalie's eyes began to twinkle, as a girl's will when two young men quarrel over her. "Thank you for bringing the book to show me, Mr. Ramsay." She took the volume and looked curiously at the page he had marked.

"They are, in fact—" began Sinclair, taking another pace, his eyes flashing.

"Carnivorous," Jeffery snarled, looking extremely carnivorous himself as he edged closer to Sinclair, his chin jutting.

"And," went on Sinclair with stubborn determination, "they are from—"

"South America—damn your eyes!"

Rosalie looked up. Her two swains had quite forgotten her and stood only inches apart, their impassioned faces thrusting at one another. She shook her head, took up her basket and, leaving the book, went on gathering her herbs. She left also angry voices that grew in volume until Sinclair gave a crow of triumph and roared, "The flying fox bat! And you did *not* know, so don't pretend you did!"

"It was *my* subject to share with her. Who asked you to come sticking your long nose in? You knew no more than I, at all events!"

"To the contrary, *I* have known about bats since I was in leading strings!"

"Probably used to ride on one!" Jeffery's chortle was interrupted as Sinclair planted a flush hit on his nose.

"Oh, dear!" Rosalie sighed.

Carruthers rode into the yard and dismounted stiffly. Bobby was first to reach him, and pocketed the groat with a whoop of triumph as he led Spring away.

Boles, who had been waiting, scolded, "You spoil the boys, Mr. Meredith. Ain't no need of your giving 'em a tip for doing what they're paid for." And eyeing the drawn face anxiously, he added, "You been looking like you wasn't getting your sleep o' late, Mr. Meredith. Did you find anything?"

"Only that there were two of the bastards. One mounted, one afoot. And they went off together, seemingly in the direction of the Cut, where the tracks are lost, of course." Absently flexing a bruised shoulder, he saw his steward's concerned frown, and stopped at once. "Now do not maudle over me, Fred. I feel perfectly fit."

"Aye. You look fit. Fit for your bed! Now, Mr. Meredith, you've been in the saddle for hours. Wouldn't do you a speck of harm to have a bit of a kip before dinner."

With a sigh for the bullying of old retainers, Carruthers said he'd likely do that very thing, and added, "Do you know how Miss Ramsay goes on?"

They started to walk to the house together. Stifling a grin, Boles replied, "I hear she's been asleep since you last asked after her, sir, but her woman said she'll come downstairs for dinner. A right spunky lady, if I may say so. Sir—I was thinking, we could send the men out to search along the Cut as far as the village. We might come up with something."

"Some more bruises and scrapes for the horses, not much else, I doubt. Whoever it was is well away by this time."

Boles grunted. "And you still think it was poachers, sir?"

"Yes. Which is likely why they ran."

Boles scowled but said no more, and they parted at the back door, the steward going off towards his own cottage and Carruthers walking into the house, only to check, turn about, and leave again by the front doors. The prospect of a rest in his room held small allure. He was in no mood to have Howell fussing over him as that devoted fellow would undoubtedly feel obliged to do. He started off to his sure haven, but stopped as Lambert strode around the corner of the house, the handsome features reflecting a thwarted fury. Glancing up, Lambert halted and said bitterly, "I properly failed her, didn't I? You won that round."

Carruthers said coolly, "I'm sorry if you are embarrassed, but her life is too valuable to risk."

"Dammitall! Do you think I don't *know* that?" His face twisting, Lambert turned away, then, apparently regaining control, faced about again. "I'm behaving like a proper fool. I should be thanking you from the bottom of my heart. Had you not followed . . . Lord, it don't bear thinking about!"

"No. It doesn't. And you took a nasty fall. How are you feeling?"

Lambert's smile was rueful. "As if my Company had rid over me."

"Lucky you didn't break your neck. Is your mare—"

Lambert swore. "Curst stupid hack! I'd as soon shoot her!"

Carruthers stared at him. "It's deuced rough country. I scarce think—"

"Oh, pay me no heed! I'm just so damned furious that I let Phoebe down! Sorry, old fellow. Just at this moment I'm devilish poor company."

He stalked off towards the stables and Carruthers went on his way, deep in gloomy thought.

Jeffery Carruthers eased the back door open, stuck in his battered head, and peered up and down the Armour Hall. "Clear, thank the Lord," he whispered. "Come on, Sin."

His bruised face apprehensive, Sinclair crept in. "Can we get upstairs without being seen? I must discover how my poor sister goes on."

"We'll try the back way. I fancy Miss Phoebe is laid down upon her bed, and likely to remain so today. At all events, you cannot let her see you in your condition. Hurry now."

The two tattered warriors trod softly along the lengthy halls, ducking into empty rooms when they heard servants approaching, and managing somehow to reach Jeffery's bedchamber without detection. "Safe!" he exclaimed, with a sigh of relief.

"Welcome home," said Meredith drily, from the armchair.

"Oh . . . Egad!" groaned Sinclair.

Meredith stood. He looked slightly haggard, but, scanning the cuts and bruises of the combatants, smothered an understanding smile and asked mildly, "Might one enquire how large a mob attacked you?"

Recovering his wits, Jeffery said, "If you are not the most complete hand, Merry! From what Ramsay's been telling me, you've been rescuing damsels in distress. Are you all right?"

"Perfectly all right, thank you. And never look so anxious, Ramsay. Your sister is, I am told, sleeping peacefully and will likely be none the worse for her fall by tomorrow. As for being a hand, Jeff, I must admit I think it rather ill-mannered in you to give a guest the back of yours."

"It wasn't his fault, sir," Sinclair put in earnestly. "Well, that is to say, it was, but—"

"He gave as good as I sent," interrupted Jeffery.

"So I see. And what of your search, Ramsay? Have you discovered the source of my quotation as yet?"

"At long last, sir. Henry the Fifth. But, dashitall, too late to win the wager."

"Well, you found it, at all events. You'd best hasten now. We have already delayed dinner by half an hour."

Groaning, Sinclair departed.

Carruthers turned to his brother. Guessing that now they were alone he was in for a scold, Jeffery tensed. "I suppose you want to know what we were fighting about."

Meredith strolled to the mantel and looked up at the portrait of his mother that hung there. He had a very good idea of what had provoked the fisticuffs, and was, if anything, relieved that their verbal sniping had resolved itself into a scuffle. It had cleared the air, and there was already a marked difference in their attitude to one another. He said slowly, "I suspect it was for a different reason than the dispute which caused you to be rusticated."

Taking off his muddied coat and starting for the wash-stand, Jeffery checked and stared at his brother in astonishment. "You—*knew* it was for fighting?"

"I have had a letter brought from Lady Martha, confirming that she will arrive tomorrow. She also mentioned you had broke young Price-Wintersby's jaw, but he would not tell the reason. I know the Price-Wintersbys, and I can guess the reason."

Jeffery felt as if a great weight had been lifted from his shoulders. He said with a shy smile, "I couldn't tell you. I wanted to, but—I know how you feel about Mama, and I—well, I thought you might . . ."

"Rush up to Town and call his father to account? No. It's rather late in the day, but it finally dawned on me that my duelling but added fuel to the fire."

Jeffery had started to pour water into the bowl, but he set the pitcher down with a clatter and spun around. "My God! You never mean *that* was the reason for all your duels? Then—is it . . . *truth*?"

Meredith ran a finger down the line of his jaw. "Perhaps you should tell me what he said."

"Lord—he was ugly drunk, and he—he said my mother had—er, taken a fellow named Hoagland for her lover, and that Papa killed him." He read confirmation in his brother's steady gaze, and exploded wrathfully, "Well, if that is not damned detestable! To keep it from me all these years, I mean! And now I've

170

gone and broke Price-Wintersby's jaw for nothing! I hope you may be satisfied. For the love of God—*when* will you give me credit for having reached an age when I may be trusted?''

Meredith glanced again at the portrait. ''Mama asked that I not tell you. I think—she dreaded you might . . . condemn her.''

''*Condemn* her! Dear little soul! When I think of the life Papa led her!''

''Just so. Besides, Price-Wintersby was most unchivalrous to speak of the matter. You likely taught him a well-deserved lesson.''

Stripping off his shirt, Jeffery grinned. ''By Jove, perhaps you're in the right of it. Now, since we're talking man-to-man, as it were—what's all this that Ramsay was telling me? You cannot *really* think a poacher shot at you?''

''I might,'' said Meredith, reluctantly complying with the dictates of a certain young lady. ''Save that there have been a couple of other instances.''

Jeffery lost all his colour and, with the towel thrown over his shoulder, strode to face his brother. ''What—the devil? You never mean . . .''

'' 'Fraid I do, old lad. Someone seems to think the world would go on better without Meredith Carruthers.''

''Oh . . . now—now deuce take me . . . !'' gasped Jeffery.

Phoebe awoke, stretched, and uttered a small shriek.

Bending above her, bathed in the brightness of the morning sunlight, Ada said sympathetically, ''My poor dearie! My sweet lamb! So stiff as any board you be. Didn't I tell ye as this was a evil house?''

''Non—sense,'' gasped Phoebe, gritting her teeth and contriving to sit up. ''Had it not been for Mr. Carruthers, you'd likely by laying me in—my coffin! Now, Ada, pray do not weep all over me. What o'clock is it? Lud, but I never meant to sleep so long. You must help me get up at once.''

Ada sniffed and turned to fetch the breakfast tray she had carried upstairs. ''It's ten minutes past ten, Miss Phoebe, and the family already ate, so there's no need for you to be fretting yourself. Here you go. Now, let me make your pillows more comfy.''

She arranged Phoebe's bed with her usual solicitude and in response to an eager enquiry conveyed the information that Mr. Meredith had indeed come down to breakfast. ''Though it was

171

long before his mama," she went on, pouring Phoebe a cup of tea. "Such a fine man. Saved your life, miss. No doubting. Best master he ever had, says Henery Baker, and—"

"Who is Henry Baker?" asked Phoebe, accepting the cup of tea.

"Mr. Meredith's head groom. And mightily taken with hisself."

"You little hussy. I expect you've been driving the poor fellow distracted. Is Captain Lambert all right?"

"Proper doom-struck he is, poor chap, but if he's hurt he's not making no fuss and feathers. My, but he's a lovely gent, isn't he? Poor Miss Phoebe! Do you think you'll be able to wed him in spite of—"

"And where is Mr. Carruthers?" Phoebe intervened hastily. "Has he been here?"

"Twice, miss. So anxious. What a shame you can't marry both of—"

"I must find him. Take down the cream silk with the blue broidery, Ada. And I'll not wear my hair powdered this morning. Do hurry!"

An hour later, Phoebe limped into the shade of the trees near the abbey and was at once enfolded in the hush of this lovely place. She paused to catch her breath, for with all her aches and pains it had not been an easy climb. Continuing after a minute, she came to the little clearing and saw that her guess had been correct. Carruthers was seated in the same place as before. She watched the strong profile for a space. Boles had said he came here when he was troubled, but he did not look so much troubled as angry, and— She gave a startled cry.

Carruthers had moved so fast that he seemed to blur before her eyes. In one instant he was sprawling lazily on the fallen slab; in the next, he was facing her, slightly crouching, a small but deadly-looking pistol glinting in his hand and aimed straight at her.

She said threadily, "The axe . . . or n-nothing, sir."

He had already straightened. The hammer was eased back, the weapon slipped into his pocket, and he was at her side. "My poor girl, I am so sorry." His arm went about her in a supporting way, and he guided her to his impromptu chair as though she were fashioned of sheerest glass. She yielded to this proprietary assertiveness gratefully, but wondered also what he had been thinking when she first arrived, and whether he suspected that his friend was disloyal. "Who did you think I was?" she murmured as he lowered her gently to his rocky perch. "A one-eyed Cyclops?"

He looked down at her unsmilingly, then sat at her feet. "I think you are a very brave lady, but you should not have walked all this way after suffering such a shock."

"I had to find you and thank you for saving my life. Which I should have done at once, instead of behaving in so foolish a way."

"Nonsense. Most ladies would have been quite in the vapours, and your mama was justified in having you put to bed. As to thanking me, you'd as well blame me! You are a guest on my estate. Under my protection." His eyes twinkled at her in a most disconcerting way. "Temporarily, at least. And for anything to happen to you would be insupportable."

"Something nearly happened to *you*. Sir, that was a musket shot. And you came very near to being hit." She bent forward, searching his face. "Who wants you dead, Meredith?"

The quirkish grin flickered. "Likely dozens of people, but I fancy it was nothing more calculated than some lads poaching."

"*Poaching?* In broad daylight? I think my brother would say you're bamming, sir."

"Perhaps he would. But *you* should not say it, you know. And, speaking of your brother—"

"We were not. Although I'll own you change a subject very deftly."

"Not deftly enough, evidently. You're a determined woman, Miss Phoebe."

"And you a most evasive gentleman, Mr. Meredith."

He said with sudden gravity, "I've no least wish to be evasive with you, m'dear."

Phoebe's breath began to flutter. It was this place! There was an enchantment about the old ruins—oh, but definitely, there was! Off-stride, she said the first thing that came to mind. "Your gallantry in saving me has properly won my mama's heart."

He was leaning back, hands clasped about one drawn-up knee. "I am honoured. But Lambert feels very bad, poor fellow. It had as well been Rogue who went down, you know."

She said in light scolding, "I believe you held back, which was, I do not scruple to say—"

"*Stupid!*" he said, ducking his head and adding in a scourged voice, "It was damnably, *unforgivably* stupid! That I could have been so *careless* as to risk your life—in such a cause!"

Her attempt at teasing had gone awry. Contrite, she leaned to touch the thick, unruly hair, and when he at once looked up, she shifted her touch to his forehead, driven by a need to smooth away the tormented frown. "No, no," she said soothingly. "I spoke in jest only. You were superb, else I'd not be sitting here now." He gazed at her speechlessly, and she drew back, alarmed, and asked, "Are the horses all right?"

"What . . . ? Oh—er, Rogue has a few bruises, and Showers's knees are cut, unfortunately."

"Not too badly? *Pray* do not say he must be destroyed."

"No, no. My farrier's an excellent man and assures me there is nothing worse than the—the bad shaking he received."

"Which is not what you were about to say."

He put back his head, laughing. "*What* an inquisition! I beg you will believe all the horses will recover, Lambert is well, and I am undamaged, so the only one we've to fret for is—your lovely self."

He looked rather incredibly attractive, sitting there, smiling up at her, and she wondered how she could ever have believed him to be harsh and unfeeling. With an effort she remembered what she had really come for, and said quietly, "No, sir. I believe we have something else to worry about."

"Poor Lascelles—of course. But—"

"Hush!"

He folded his hands and closed his lips, looking up at her from under his brows with such uncharacteristic meekness that it was all she could do not to laugh at him. She managed to keep her countenance, and said, "Tell me about your friend Captain Otton."

His expression changed subtly. "Roly? He's a dashing rascal, isn't he? You likely think it odd that he should cry friends with a dull dog like me."

"Do *you* think that you are a dull dog, sir?"

He reddened, but answered, "Oh, naturally not. I find myself a fascinating fellow of enormous accomplishments. But Roly tells me I'm a dull dog and I fear he may view me with less bias."

At this, she did laugh. "Out upon him! He has all the privilege of a bosom bow, I see. How long have you known him?"

"We were at school together."

"I see. Long-standing. So he should be—loyal to you."

He glanced at her sharply. The morning sun slanted a sly ray through the branches, bathing her in a golden light, and causing her unpowdered hair to glow about the perfection of her features, like a halo. He became aware that he was staring and replied hastily, "Oh, yes. I would trust Roland with my life." She looked disturbed, and he moved to sit beside her. "What is it, ma'am? Never say that rascal has dared offend you?"

She bit her lip. "You have so much on your shoulders, I dread to add to it."

He took her hand, and held it. "Tell me."

And so she did, omitting nothing from the drab little recital of betrayal, nor removing her hand from his warm clasp.

Carruthers listened in silence. When she finished, he muttered, "Roly does not always say what is in his heart. Indeed, I think he seldom does. He *is* a mercenary, however, and if it was our well-being or his confounded lusting after that Jacobite gold . . ." He thought of Lance, weak and helpless, and his jaw hardened.

Phoebe said, "I have brought you ill news, I'm afraid. I am so sorry."

"And I, most grateful. But don't be worrying unduly. Roly thinks himself a very bad man, but if it came to a test, he would never betray me."

Anger blazed through her. She thought, 'Trusting fool! You judge him by your own high standards!' She jerked her hand away and stood.

He at once followed suit. "I'll talk to him, but I will not tell him that you were the one overheard. Ma'am, I wish you will not be so concerned. I—"

"Then your wishes will go ungranted, Mr. Meredith," she interposed crossly, "for I *am* concerned." She knew at once that she should not have said it, for the tall shape of him became tense and he was gazing down at her with that dreadful blue light in his eyes. Her knees started to dissolve again. She gasped, "Now, I must . . . go. . . ." But she made no move to leave.

Carruthers stepped very close. She concentrated on a dandelion, but despite all her resolution not to do so, she peeped up at him. He was so near, so manly-looking and strong. And his eyes . . . ! His arm had managed to slip unnoticed about her waist and was drawing her to him. His heartbeat was speaking to hers, and hers, wretched thing, was answering.

"Phoebe," he murmured. "Is it at all possible—"

Terror overwhelmed her. With a muffled and incoherent apology, she fled, leaving him standing alone in the enchanted glade.

ᕫ Chapter 13 ᕤ

Phoebe left confusion to find more confusion. A familiar carriage was drawn up on the drivepath, and servants hurried to and fro, unloading bandboxes and valises, while others loaded in more of the same. In the Great Hall, a distracted Hampden rushed past, carrying Lady Eloise's jewel case, and divulged that Lady Martha Ramsay had arrived and that Miss Belinda had contracted whooping cough and was in a proper state, calling for her mama.

Phoebe went quickly to her mother's suite. Despite her cold, Lady Eloise was cheerful, for it was, she admitted, lovely to be going home, how ever much she had enjoyed her visit. "Your grandmama will stay with you, my love," she said hoarsely. "I had hoped Sinclair might escort me, but he is nowhere to be found, and Papa has sent my own footman and two grooms beside Alfred Coachman, so I shall go along well enough. Still, I wish the naughty boy was going with me. Well, never mind. Belinda is doubtless counting the seconds, so I must be off. You know how she frets if I am not there when she is poorly."

Lady Martha came in, and was duly embraced by her granddaughter. She was full of instructions on how to care for the sick child, and assurances that Eloise was not to worry about Phoebe, for they would be very comfortable.

They all trooped downstairs to see my lady off, Phoebe embracing her mama fondly, and sending her love to her ailing sister; Lady Martha adding a caution against allowing Belinda to get up the moment she felt better; and Mrs. Carruthers tearful because she was losing her new friend.

Waving, as the carriage rumbled along the drivepath, Lady Martha said for Phoebe's ear alone, "What a wretched shame that aggravating grandson of mine could not have been here! Your mama has been telling me of his infatuation for that village minx, and I would like of all things to have had an excuse for packing him off home!''

Fond as she was of her brother, in a way Phoebe agreed with these sentiments. But Sin would not have left, of course; certainly he'd not leave them to solve their traitorous problems alone. And how shocked Grandmama would be did she only know that there was more to threaten him at Meredith Hall than the presence of a beautiful but ineligible damsel.

Roland Otton sat in the window-seat of his bedchamber contemplating the peaceful gardens. ''If you must know,'' he said at last, ''his mother was half-sister to mine.''

''I see.'' Carruthers leaned against the bedpost, arms folded, and said coldly, ''So our estimable dragoon *is* your cousin, and set you here to watch us.''

Otton's impenitent grin was a white gleam. ''Come now, dear boy. I do my own watching, and I am never 'put' anywhere. At least, not without a considerable fee. And my cousin Jacob is almost as short of the ready as am I.'' Carruthers fixed him with a hard look, and Otton protested aggrievedly, ''Zounds, but I've visited you often enough before and you've not accused me of—''

''Suppose I told you that you were overheard talking with your ambitious cousin and that you promised him you would spy on us?''

Indignant, Otton responded, ''I'd say that's dashed unfair! You must play the game by *your* rules. *I'm* the one so base as to eavesdrop on private conversations!''

Meredith's lips tightened. He shoved his shoulders from the bedpost and stood straight.

Otton chuckled and held up both hands. ''I am an invalid, Merry! Recuperating from a horrid wound. You would not strike a sick man?''

''*Would* you betray us for that damnable gold?''

''There is something to betray?'' Otton's eyes sharpened; he said eagerly, ''You mean you *have* given sanctuary to the fool? My dear chap, all I ask is the cipher. Do as you wish with the wretch. A copy only, and I'll be gone, nor ever breathe a word, upon my honour!''

Carruthers frowned, and said cautiously, ''Then the tales of ciphers are true?''

''Deliciously. They are concealed in four stanzas of a poem,

177

each containing part of the destination to which the treasure is to be conveyed. Lascelles is one of those carrying a stanza.''

"You've ferreted out a lot. My felicitations. Do you know to whom the stanzas are to be delivered?''

"Would that I did!'' Otton's manner was brisk now, his affectation fallen away like a discarded cloak. Rising, he asked, "Merry, have I your hand on this?''

Carruthers laughed at him. "Use your wits, man! I've all I can do at the moment to keep my guests entertained and to introduce Miss Ramsay to my friends and tenants. It is quite possible that we may not be able to break this betrothal. Can you really suppose I'd endanger my betrothed, my family, my estates by hiding some wretched Jacobite? I hold no brief for the Stuarts; never have. And I've more to do with my time than go hunting this Lascelles fellow.''

Briefly, the black eyes glared frustration. Otton tossed himself into a chair. "Well, I've time aplenty,'' he muttered. "If he's hereabouts, I'll get to him before the army does, damn his eyes!''

Carruthers looked at him thoughtfully. "Have you no pity for the poor devil?''

"None. Nor understanding of what drives 'em. I'll tell you this—they're a rare breed. It never ceases to amaze me that a man like Quentin Chandler, for instance, with everything to live for, would be willing to endure wounds, starvation, torture, and even face the horrors of the block—all for an ideal. Oh yes, a rare breed.''

"If you think that, I wonder you can bring yourself to hunt them down so mercilessly.''

Otton shrugged. "It is because the good Lord spared me the paths of the honourable. Too painful a road by far for a comfortable hedonist.''

"How very pleased your grandfather would be,'' Carruthers said deliberately, "that you have so fully lived down to his expectations.''

There was a faint hiss of indrawn breath; one long hand clenched hard, and for an instant Otton was very still. When he lifted his gaze, his eyes were more than usually brilliant. "One can try, dear Meredith.'' He sighed. "One can but try.''

"He *offered*?'' echoed Phoebe, staring in astonishment at her handmaiden's pink cheeks. "But—we've not yet been here a week!''

Fastening the pearls about Phoebe's throat, Ada said, "Henery came to Pineridge once with Mr. Meredith. 'Sides, it don't take a week. Not when the right man puts his arms round you. When I first see my Henery, I thought he was a bit of all right, 'cause I always like a big, manly chap. And when we came down here, I noticed how kind he was. Always respectful to the females, and a bit on the shy side. Not the Fancy Dan what always knows how to say the right clever things. I looked up one day while I was popping a bit of pig's trotter in me mouth, and he was watching me—with such a *look* on his face!" Smiling nostalgically, she broke off, horrified. "Oh, miss! I never meant to go and make you sad. I won't say another blessed word!"

"No," said Phoebe rather huskily. "I'm very interested. Please go on."

If talking would help, thought Ada, she'd talk all night. Miss Phoebe wasn't happy, that was plain, and never had she served so gentle and uncomplaining a lady, nor one so little given to puff off her consequence. "Well," she said, "when I got over me choking fit (the pig's trotter went down the wrong way, account of the Look) I give Henery a grin. And he give me a grin back. And after supper, he whispers to me from the side hall, so out I goes. And we walked and didn't say much, but then he held me hand."

"What did you feel when he did that? Tingly?"

"Oooh, yes! But nothing like when he—begging your pardon, miss—when he kissed me! On the cheek, it was. And I felt like as if I was floating off. And when I turned round, he grabbed me and give me such a buss! I wonder I got any teeth left! And I got all over quivery-like. And that's when I knew Henery was my man. And he knew too, 'cause he—popped the question, as you might say."

"How wonderful." Ignoring the inevitable ramifications of this unexpected betrothal, Phoebe persisted, "And—and did you ever feel that—that *sure* with any other man?"

Ada shook her head. "Not in the same way, I didn't. Course, it don't come all at once, like a voice from heaven, or something. It sorta grows and you don't hardly notice. And then, one day, something happens, and—bang! You got no more doubts. With me, it was the pig's trotter."

Phoebe smiled rather wanly, and then sighed.

The poor little thing was proper heart-broke, thought Ada, and no wonder. Forced into marriage with Mr. Carruthers, when her heart belonged to that handsome Captain Lambert. Always so friendly and bright was the Captain. And Mr. Meredith was a good young man, but not much of a one for larking about and smiling all the time and saying saucy things. Ada's warm heart was wrung, and she had to turn away.

Walking to her grandmother's suite, Phoebe was deep in thought. Surely, if she cared for them equally, she must love neither? Or perhaps her moment of revelation had yet to come.

Knowing that her grandmama's health was not as robust as that grande dame would have people believe, Phoebe had deemed it wiser not to apprise her of the accident until she was comfortably settled. Upon reaching the suite allocated to Lady Martha, however, she found the old lady in a great state of indignation. Sinclair had put in an appearance and one look at his battered countenance had thrown Lady Martha into a rage. "It was bad enough," she told Phoebe, "that he was in the toils of this village gel, but to think he would be so rag-mannered as to fight—to *fight* with the son of his hostess . . . ! Lud, what is the world coming to!"

Phoebe set herself to calm her, but had spent very few minutes at that task before Lady Martha interrupted to send her abigail away. "Phoebe Ramsay," she said grimly, when her devoted Swedish minion had left them, "there is more amiss here than your brother's shocking misconduct. Be so good as to tell me and not wrap it in clean linen!"

Very few people had ever succeeded in pulling the wool over those shrewd old eyes, and Phoebe knew better than to attempt it. She spoke of the accident in as light a manner as she could muster, but my lady paled. She did not interrupt, however, only at the finish expressing her fervent gratitude to Meredith Carruthers, and announcing her intention to properly thank him. "Now," she commanded, having kissed her granddaughter, and snorted her indignation because neither Eloise nor Lucille Carruthers had seen fit to break the news of the runaway, "now— tell me the rest of it. What has been going on with you and Carruthers? And why is Brooks Lambert here?"

And so it went. My lady questioned, and Phoebe answered. The Dowager watched her narrowly, reading more from hastily averted eyes, a tremor in the soft voice, a sudden rush of colour to the smooth cheeks than her granddaughter would have dreamed. Phoebe, she thought, was properly in the boughs.

180

Several possible reasons for this occurred to her, and she determined to have a long chat with Meredith Carruthers.

She was thwarted in this resolution at luncheon because, of the gentlemen, only Jeffery was present. Meredith, suspecting rightly that he would be the object of the old lady's gratitude, had persuaded Roland Otton to accompany him to the village. Sinclair, already in disgrace with his formidable grandparent, made himself least-in-sight, and Brooks Lambert also decided it behooved him to be occupied elsewhere.

Lucille chattered happily, breaking the news that a 'small dinner party' had been planned for the evening, whereupon Lady Martha zestfully joined with her in an involved discussion of the lineage and relations of some of the prospective guests.

When the meal was over Lady Martha expressed an interest in the famed Hall of Mirrors and Lucille was pleased to conduct her guests to view not only that chamber, but several others that caught my lady's eye along the way. The afternoon was drawing in by the time Phoebe returned to her chamber, and she was quite willing to allow Ada to loosen her stays and put her to bed for a short nap. A deep dread of facing her two suitors plagued her however, and she was unable to sleep. If she begged to be excused from going down to dinner because of the after-effects of the fall, there would, she knew, be no questions asked. She also knew that such an action would merely increase her fears. Besides, the dinner party had been arranged so as to present her to some of Meredith's friends, and she was reluctant to disappoint either her 'fiancé' or his mama by failing to put in an appearance. She therefore rang for Ada earlier than intended, and instructed her handmaiden to pay particular attention to the dressing and powdering of her hair. This having been accomplished to her satisfaction, she chose a very wide-hooped gown of palest orange, the deep scallops trimmed with Brussels lace. A fine topaz and seed-pearl pendant constituted her only jewellery, and Ada having helped her to don her gloves and handed her a dainty fan, Phoebe went along the hall to collect her grandmama, her knees trembly, but her head high.

Meredith awaited his ladies at the foot of the staircase. He had bowed to custom for once and had allowed Howell to powder his hair and arrange it in a less severe style. Phoebe thought the loose curls exceedingly attractive and the blue of his faultless coat found an echo in the blue that shone from his intent eyes, setting her heart to beating faster.

Lady Martha threw her arms about the startled gentleman and

conveyed her gratitude with words, hugs, and kisses that left him scarlet with embarrassment. She had him to thank, she told him, for her granddaughter's continued existence, and there was no cause to shrivel up because she felt obliged to buss him.

Meredith grinned, mopped his brow, and took Phoebe's hand. He gave it a quick, reassuring squeeze and winked at her, but said nothing to cause her the least qualm, so that her tight nerves were able to relax somewhat.

Many elegant people were gathered in the drawing room, obviously agog to meet the bride-to-be. Carruthers had taken the precaution of warning them of her mishap, so that to their admiration of her looks and grace was added an appreciation of her courage. So many compliments came her way that she could not but glow. Her grandmama beamed, and Lambert was obviously hard put to it to tear his eyes from her. He was also the life of the party, winning the ladies with his charm and good looks and amusing the gentlemen with small anecdotes of military life. Otton had also set himself to be pleasant and, curbing his natural instincts, he concentrated upon the more mature ladies present, much to their delight.

It was, after all, a pleasant meal. Phoebe chatted easily with the retired diplomatist seated to her right, and managed to address a few fairly sensible remarks to Carruthers who, with commendable nicety, divided his time between the Dowager Lady Ramsay and her granddaughter. Several discreetly modulated conversations were under way. Phoebe caught snatches of talk—mostly scornful—about the Duke of Cumberland; of the probability of war with France; of the wildness of Prince Frederick; and of the Tory alliance with the Jacobites. She was not sorry when Mrs. Carruthers at last rose to lead the ladies to the withdrawing room. The gentlemen stood, of course, and it was Lambert who bowed them from the room, his gaze resting yearningly on Phoebe's smile as she passed.

She remembered that gaze as she lay in bed soon afterwards, for she had yielded to the insistence of Lady Martha that she should go early to her chamber. Almost at once, however, her thoughts turned to Meredith. She had caught his eyes upon her several times during the evening. On each occasion he had looked quickly away, but when she had left the table, his had been the hands to pull back her chair, and it had seemed to her that he bowed so low above her that his lips brushed her hair. Even to recall that instant caused her to tremble. Dozing off, she thought, 'And I did not see him again. . . .'

What awoke her she could not tell, but she sprang up, gasping for breath, her heart hammering wildly. Save for the faint light from the oil lamp beside her bed, the room was dark, and the house wrapped in a silence so deep it seemed to beat against her ears. She listened intently, one hand pressed to her bosom as she tried to breathe more evenly. That effort was abandoned as the door suddenly burst open. She gave a little squeal of terror as a man staggered into the room, gasping, "Do not be . . . scared. It's . . . only me."

She was out of bed in a flash and turning up the lamp, as he swung the door shut and leaned, panting, against it.

Through lips suddenly icy-cold and stiff with fear, she whispered, "Meredith!"

He was clutching his right arm, and as he pushed himself away from the door and lurched forward, she saw with a dizzying pang that blood dripped from the ends of his fingers.

"Dragoons . . ." he gasped. "After me. Tried to—to get cipher . . . through."

She ran to support him. "Oh, my dear God! Here—sit down. I'll—"

He shook his head, blinking at her. "Not too bad, but—you must . . . you must warn . . ." And with a small sigh, he crumpled and lay in a dead faint at her feet.

Even as she dropped to her knees beside him, there came an urgent knock and the door was again flung wide. Helpless, she crouched lower over Carruthers, gazing at the newcomer with great, terrified eyes.

Jeffery halted on the threshold, staring at the dramatic tableau. His jaw dropped; he became almost as white as his brother, and stood frozen with shock.

Finding her voice somehow, Phoebe croaked, "Shut the door!"

He did so, then knelt beside her. "Merry! My God! What on earth . . . ?"

Folding back the great cuff of Meredith's sleeve, she countered, "How did you know he was in here?"

He wrenched his gaze from his brother's still face, and stammered, "There's blood all—all along the hall, and down the side st-stairs. I thought—"

Shaking, she said, "You'd as well know that my brother and I were hiding a fugitive gentleman. Merry tried to help him and got caught."

"He—*what*?" he gasped, his face a study in rage and bewilderment. "But—but *he* was the very one who— He said—"

"No time for that. If you care for his safety and are willing to risk—"

He pulled himself together. "Devil take it! D'you think I'd let them find him? But—hell and damnation, the roads are alive with troopers! They've only to see the trail he left . . ."

Her trembling hands striving, Phoebe cried, "Then take some towels—anything. Clean it up. Afterwards, if you can, send my brother to me. Oh, heavens! He's bleeding terribly!"

"Here—let me get his coat off."

"No, no! I'll cut the shirt-sleeve. Go! Hurry!"

He jumped to his feet, whipped a towel from the rack, gave her a numb look, and ran.

Phoebe ran also; to her dressing table. She snatched up her scissors, wrenched off the pillowcase, and knelt again. Meredith lay as one dead. She tried to slice through the cuff of his shirt, but the little scissors would not penetrate the thickness. Biting her lip and trying not to shake so, she inserted the blades into the bloody rent the ball had made, cut through the sodden linen to a point midway between elbow and shoulder, then cut around and slid the sleeve down over his limp hand. She forced herself to look directly at the wound, whimpered, and, for a sick instant, closed her eyes. He must have been holding his arm level when he was hit, for the ball had scored a deep groove from above his wrist to the elbow, where it had angled into his forearm. Whispering prayers for strength, she lifted his arm and found the jagged wound where the ball had exited. It was pulsing blood, but she could only know relief that the bullet would not have to be dug out, a procedure she had dreaded.

The wound should be bathed and sewn up, then treated with basillicum powder, but he had said the troopers were after him. She made some cuts in the pillowcase, tore some strips, then made a pad and was binding it over the higher wound when she felt his arm jerk, and looked up to find him watching her.

He was haggard and deathly pale, but muttered, "What a fool to . . . to go off like that and frighten you. Have . . . they come?"

"No. Merry, whatever happened?"

"Thought I was clear. Came out of the trees and . . . a whole troop was right behind me. I was—firing back . . . just to slow them a bit. Someone shot straight. Just—my arm. Luckily."

184

She bit her lip as he winced from her hand. "Oh, I am so sorry. It's very nasty. You must have a surgeon."

His smile was wan. "That would put the hare in with the hounds. Bind it as tight as you can . . . little shrew. And I'll get out of your room. Can you warn your brother?"

"Jeffery has gone for him."

At once his frown evidenced. "*What?* How did Jeff—"

She nerved herself and pulled the bandage as tight as she could, and his words were cut off abruptly. She stifled a sob when she heard his faint gasp and, blinking through scalding tears, quavered, "Jeff came in just after you fell. It's no use fretting. I had to tell him. Can you put a finger on this knot for me?"

He looked dazed and his pallor seemed intensified, but he did as she asked, finding the knot gropingly, but pressing down on it without faltering.

Phoebe secured the knot, dashed away tears, and began to bind the long gash tightly. Not a sound escaped him, but when she glanced up again, his head was turned away, his eyes closed.

He jerked to his left elbow when the door swung open and Sinclair ran in, pale and distraught. "What *damnable* luck! Sir, I am so—"

"No time," muttered Carruthers threadily. "Get me up, Sin. I cannot seem to—to manage."

Phoebe said, "Wait!" She secured the last knot with Sinclair's help, then, between them, they got Carruthers to his feet. He swayed, and mumbled something inaudible.

"Can we get him all that way to his room?" asked Phoebe.

"No!" gasped Carruthers. "Brandy, Sin." He peered downward. "Am I a bloody mess?"

"Very," Sinclair answered. "What the devil happened?"

"Later. Run—bring clean clothes and—and decanter from my—credenza. Quick!"

Jeffery rushed in as Sinclair ran out. The towel he had taken was gruesome. He panted, "I daren't leave this anywhere. Damn you, Merry! When I think—"

Phoebe snatched the towel and thrust it under her mattress.

Carruthers said weakly, "Yes, I am sure you—yearn to pummel me. I'll let you . . . when I'm more the—the thing. Help me walk—will you please?"

Phoebe cried, "Oh, do take care! It's a horrid wound. Jeff, he says the troopers are after him."

His arm about his brother, Jeffery groaned, "Dammit, they

are! I could hear them shouting about the grounds. Ma'am, I don't pretend to understand any of this. Where is your fugitive?''

"Secret room. Keep," said Carruthers, his voice a little stronger as Jeffery supported his halting steps. "It's—Lance."

"*Wha-at?* Oh, Lord alive! One might guess that stupid—"

Phoebe interpolated desperately, "Whatever shall we do if they *come* here? He is in no condition to—"

"I shall manage," Carruthers interrupted doggedly. "Got my . . . second wind." He smiled. It was a ghastly effort.

Phoebe wiped sweat from his forehead. "Jeff, you'll *have* to handle them and get rid of them somehow."

"No use," argued Carruthers. "If Holt's with 'em, he'll demand to see me, and I—I don't think I could negotiate the stairs alone. Better to—to be already down when they come."

She turned to Jeffery in desperation. "He looks like death! He can hardly stand. Oh, *do* let him rest for a minute!"

Jeffery eased his brother onto the bed, and Carruthers sat there, head down, gripping his arm painfully.

Very strained-looking, Jeffery said quite steadily, "You'd best wash your hands, Miss Phoebe, and put on a wrapper, or something."

She looked down at herself and blushed scarlet. In the exigency of the moment she'd not so much as thought that she wore only the revealing nightdress. She ran to the washbowl, poured in some water and rinsed her hands quickly, then wet a small towel and ran to give it to Jeffery. "Bathe his face. He looks ready to collapse."

Jeffery obeyed and Carruthers gasped out thanks.

Sinclair returned, panting heavily, his arms full of clothing and a decanter clutched in one hand.

"Let me have a swig of that, Sin," muttered Carruthers. He drank, coughed, and swore under his breath, but when next he spoke, his voice was stronger and there was a little more colour in his face. "Ma'am, if you'll go into the hall and keep watch, I'll get changed."

She flung her dressing gown around her, slipped quietly into the hall, and tiptoed along to the top of the stairs. 'Thank God,' she thought, 'it's all quiet. They must not have seen him after all.' But even if the troopers did not come, Otton was in the house, and Lambert, and Meredith's military friends could drop in at any time. How on earth were they to— She jumped then, as from the foot of the stairs Justice began to bay a warning.

Almost at once, a thunderous tattoo sounded from the main entrance. Outside, she heard a man shout, "Are troopers posted at all the doors?" She felt faint, and ran back to the bedchamber.

Meredith was already walking out, his left arm across his brother's shoulders.

"Hurry! Oh, hurry!" she cried. "They're here!"

Carruthers called softly, "Phoebe, run downstairs and light some candles in the library. Be sure the draperies are drawn first."

She flew. When she reached the ground floor, the front door shuddered to a barrage and, distantly, she heard more pounding. They were at all the doors, not much doubt of that! Running into the library, she said a quick prayer of gratitude because the draperies were tightly shut. She remembered that the tinder-box was kept beside the fireplace, groped her way there, and bent, fumbling blindly. A blow thudded between her shoulder blades. She almost fainted from shock, waiting for the dread words, "In the King's name!" Then, small feet raced across her back. "Satan!" she sobbed. "You—perfect *beast*!"

With shaking hands, she found the tinder-box and managed to light a candle. As she carried it to six others in a heavy silver candelabrum, she heard angry voices from the Armour Hall, then Sinclair and Jeffery rushed in, Meredith staggering drunkenly between them.

Phoebe snatched a book from the shelf and, as he sank into an armchair, thrust it into his hand. "Can you hold it?" she hissed, bending over him. His eyes were glazed, but he nodded. She wiped streaks of perspiration from his face and pinched his white cheeks; hard.

"Ow!" he exclaimed, and she was amazed to see a flicker of his grin as he muttered, "Second . . . time, you wretch!"

She had to fight tears again, then stamping footsteps were approaching. Jeffery had gone somewhere, and Sinclair dragged her out of the library and along the corridor. They ran, and reached the foot of the stairs just as a footman, looking haughty despite his lack of a wig and the lurid dressing-gown he had tied over his night-shirt, opened the front door of the new wing.

Captain Holt, pale, tired, and very obviously angry, pushed his way inside.

Sinclair said with cool dignity, "What in the *deuce* is going on now?"

Holt snarled, "Where is Jeffery Carruthers?"

"In bed, I should think," said Sinclair. "Though he's likely on his way down after all that uproar."

"We'll see that," said Holt grimly. "Two of you men guard the stairs. Don't alarm the ladies if you can help it. The rest of you—this way."

Sinclair said meaningfully, "Stay close beside me, Phoebe."

Holt threw him a withering look and marched toward the line of light that shone from the open door to the library.

Phoebe took Sinclair's hand and half-ran along, praying.

Holt stamped into the lighted room. Peeping around the soldiers, Phoebe could have laughed aloud. Meredith was sprawled in the chair, apparently dozing, his chin propped on his left hand, his right hand loosely clasping the book on his knees, and Satan curled up on top of it. As the dragoons entered, Meredith started, his elbow slipping from the chair arm realistically. He blinked up into Holt's fierce countenance. "What . . . the . . . ?" he muttered, and yawned.

Unafraid, Satan sat up and inspected the new arrivals disapprovingly.

"We shot a rebel," snapped Holt. "Damn sure he rode this way. Where's your brother?"

"Just behind you, Captain," said Jeffery, in an irked manner. "And I'd be in my bed had you not raised such a fuss."

"Your bay mare has been rid hard," snapped Holt, addressing Carruthers but fixing Jeffery with a piercing stare.

Meredith scowled. "Did you take Spring? Where the *devil* have you been?"

Jeffery drew himself up. "If you must know, I went to that cockfight in the village."

"Damn you, Jeff!" Meredith leaned forward slightly. "I *told* you—"

"I'll remind you, brother, that I am past one and twenty," snarled Jeffery.

Marvelling, Phoebe thought, 'How can they do it? How can Meredith look so cross when he must be in frightful pain?' She saw his eyes slant to her and realized in the nick of time that he must stand. She sank quickly onto a nearby chair as he snapped, "Your extreme age don't give you the right to take my mare out, and— But we'll discuss this in private. What do you want of us, Holt? I promise you there are no wounded rebels in this house."

Holt grinned broadly. "Not even you, eh?" He fetched Jeffery a clap on the back that made him stagger, and watched him narrowly.

"Devil take you! I'm no lover of Charles Stuart," declared Jeffery angrily.

Voices were raised in the Armour Hall. Meredith got to his feet, Satan scrambling onto the chair arm. "If you've upset my mother, Holt," he gritted, "I'll register a protest with Fotheringay, by God, but I will! This is becoming damn ridiculous!"

Otton came strolling in, his dark hair free of powder and much disarrayed, his eyes heavy with sleep. "What's to do?" he drawled.

"As a former army officer," said Holt, "I ask you, on your honour, sir, if any injured man has sought sanctuary in this house tonight?"

Otton stared at him. "You may be sure the dog would have woke us all, had that happened."

Holt's lip curled. Looking at Jeffery, he said, "Unless the fugitive was known to him."

To her horror, Phoebe saw that Meredith was leaning precariously. He half-sat, half-fell into the chair, not perceiving that Satan had claimed it, and the cat made a frantic last-minute dart for life. A grimace of pain twisted Meredith's face, but he had turned away so that the lapse went unnoticed by all save Phoebe, who flinched with sympathy. "Jeff," he said wearily, "to reassure poor Holt, would you please submit to an examination?"

"Be damned if I will," flared Jeffery, glaring at Holt.

"He seems to think you are stoically concealing a mortal wound," said Sinclair with a sly grin. "Poor chap likely won't sleep a wink do you not humour him."

Jeffery said disgustedly, "Fella's lushy drunk, was you to ask me."

"We shall all humour him," Otton laughed. "Clothes off, everyone! Inspection time!"

Phoebe's heart lurched. She gave a little scream.

Otton glanced at her. "Whoops! As you were, men!"

"Very amusing, I'm sure," snapped Holt, red-faced.

"No, really, Jacob," purred Otton. "Enough is enough."

A trooper ran to the door. "Captain!" he called breathlessly. "They got the chap cornered over to Birch Hill!"

Holt brightened. "No surprise there!" He clicked his heels. "Apologies, Carruthers. Duty is duty."

"So they tell me," said Carruthers drily.

The soldiers marched off with a stamp of boots and a jingling of spurs.

Sinclair said, "Come along, Phoebe. Bed for you, my girl."

She stood at once. "Yes. Oh, how dreadful this is!"

Otton glanced curiously at Meredith. "You keep late hours, old fellow. And you look like the devil."

"I stayed up to have a word with my—brother," said Meredith, catching his breath for an instant as Satan sprang onto his lap once more. "And I'm afraid I may have caught Lady Eloise's cold. Jeff—stay here, if you please. Good night, Miss Ramsay," he added, managing to stand up. "Don't worry about this nonsense."

Phoebe smiled and went out, trembling in every limb, Sinclair gripping her arm tightly. She heard Otton drawl, "From the frying pan to the fire, Jeff. My prayers will be with you! *Bonne nuit.*"

As they approached the stairs, Phoebe glanced back. Otton was sauntering lazily towards the Armour Hall. She whispered frantically, "Sin, he suspects! Did you see how he stared at Meredith?"

He muttered, "I'm only glad Mrs. Carruthers did not waken—or Lambert! The fat would really have been in the fire!" He glanced over his shoulder. "He's gone. I don't think he will give Carruthers away, whatever he may suspect. He's only out for himself. I'm going back to give Jeff a hand, and how ever tired poor Meredith is, we've to make some plans. No—not *you*, my girl! You've done enough. Go to bed, and stay there!"

She clutched at his arm. "You *will* come? Or Jeff? I'll be worried to death."

"I'll come, then. Bless you, old lady. You're a dashed good sport."

The 'dashed good sport' went to her room, where she burst into tears. Weeping, she gathered together Meredith's bloodstained clothing. The men had shoved it all under the bed, but if the troopers had again searched the house, they would have been discovered. She wrapped all the telltale articles in the butchered pillowcase and stuffed it under the mattress. She felt drained and very tired, but she dried her tears, poured some of the brandy into her water glass, and sipped it. She made a face, but she could feel the liquid fire igniting her interior regions, and she soon felt much restored.

Half an hour later, a soft scratch on the door preceded Sinclair's appearance. He crept in, looked at the glass in his sister's hand, and lifted one eyebrow. "Is there another glass?"

"You'll have to use the decanter. Sin—how is he?"

Sinclair took a healthy swallow, and blinked rapidly. Taking the bedside chair, he replied, "Not about to turn up his toes, but the poor fellow's in a deal of pain, though he won't own it." He shook his head. "He's not wanting for pluck, your betrothed. Hey—have you been piping your eye?"

"I fear I rather disintegrated. Oh, what*ever* are we to do? Meredith *must* have a doctor, and soon! He is sure to be worse tomorrow. He'll never be able to hide it!" Her eyes closed briefly. "I keep thinking . . . suppose Holt had clapped *Merry* on the back, as he did Jeffery . . . !"

They looked at each other soberly.

Sinclair muttered, "We'd all be on our way to the Tower. Carruthers says he has the cipher well-hid and will try to explain away his appearance by claiming that 'cold' has worsened. We shall have to think of something better, but the poor devil was all in. It was as much as he could do not to give way, I think, but there was not a murmur of complaint because I dragged him into this mess. I only hope . . . it don't end with his head on a spike!"

Phoebe sank her face into her hands. Sinclair was at her side at once and slipped his arm around her. "Sorry, m'dear. You've become rather fond of him, I think."

"How could I help it?" she said brokenly. "Sin—we *must* find a way out of this, for his sake."

He nodded glumly. "I wish I could think of one."

"I think I may have," she said, and as he turned to her eagerly, she went on, "It's a desperate chance, and so much will depend on Meredith. If he should be delirious in the morning, or too weak to function normally . . . I do not dare to think what— But never mind that. We must pray very hard tonight. Sin—go and fetch Jeffery, and I'll tell you my scheme. Perhaps he may have already thought of something better, but if not—it just may serve."

ᕉ *Chapter 14* ᕎ

Standing motionless in Birch Hill's sunny morning room, Sir Malcolm Lockwood turned a white, stricken face from Phoebe to Jeffery Carruthers.

Jeffery said kindly, "Perhaps you should sit down, sir. I'm afraid we broke it rather bluntly. The thing is, we're rather pressed for time."

Lockwood groped blindly for the sofa and huddled on it. Phoebe walked quickly to sit beside him. "I am so sorry, Sir Malcolm. I expect it is a sad blow to you."

"Do you say," he muttered, dazedly, "that—that all the time I thought my son was a confounded Bond Street saunterer, he was instead fighting with Charles Stuart?"

"I'm afraid so, sir."

"By . . . God!" whispered Sir Malcolm. He drew a hand across his eyes and sat straighter. "My apologies to you both. It was the shock. And Carruthers has shielded the boy, you say? Is—is Lance very badly hurt?"

Jeffery perched on the arm of a red brocade chair. "He is very weak, sir, and has a leg wound, and the troopers gave him the deuce of a run down from Scotland. You might as well know, he's—" He hesitated, glancing uneasily to Phoebe.

She said, "He is the fugitive everyone's hunting. The one who carries the poem the Duke of Cumberland values so highly."

The Squire sprang up, a flush coming into his pale cheeks and his eyes kindling. "Now is he, by Jupiter! And to think I called out poor Meredith! Why the deuce did he not *tell* me? Did he fancy I'd be anything but proud of my boy?"

Phoebe and Jeffery exchanged surprised glances. "Lance feared you would be far from proud," said Jeffery. "He swore my brother to secrecy."

"Then your brother's a blasted fool for heeding him! He should have told me anyway!"

"You are exactly right, sir," agreed Phoebe. "But Mr. Carruthers has a ridiculous habit of keeping his word."

Lockwood smiled. "Does he know you came to me, my dear?"

"No, sir. He will be very angry. But—he tried to deliver the cipher last night, and—"

"*Meredith* did?" Incredulous, the Squire sat down again. "But—he *fought* Stuart! He despises the Jacobites!"

Jeffery said, "Lance is his friend. And is half-demented, fretting about the cipher."

"God . . . bless him!" Lockwood turned away and became involved with his handkerchief. When he faced them once more, he said rather unevenly, "By Jove, but I'm deep in debt to Carruthers! I must go over at once and withdraw my challenge to the poor fellow!"

"No, sir!" exclaimed Jeffrey.

"You must fight him!" said Phoebe.

His eyes glassy, the Squire mumbled, "The . . . devil . . . !"

Sinclair was waiting in the stableyard, and walked to the house between his sister and Jeffery. He said in a low voice, "We've had to take two people into our confidence. His man, a good fellow, Phoebe, who fairly dotes on him; and the head groom. Baker lifted Merry down from his mare last night, and cleaned the saddle, so he had to be told."

"How is my brother?" asked Jeffery anxiously.

"Howell told me he passed a wretched night, and he looks it, but he's up and dressed. We've had a rare piece of luck in one sense." He held open the back door to the new wing, and they all passed inside. The hall was cool and deserted, and he went on softly, "Lambert and Otton have gone off somewhere, so they're out of the way."

"And Grandmama will not come down until after noon," said Phoebe.

Jeffery asked, "Is my mama about yet?"

"No. She really *has* caught my mother's cold and her maid brought word she would sleep late."

Phoebe thought, 'That should give us an hour, at least!'

Carruthers was sitting at the breakfast table, stirring coffee with his left hand, and reading the newspaper. He looked up as they came in, and Phoebe scanned him anxiously. He was excessively pale, and his eyes looked sunk into dark hollows. He came to his feet without apparent effort, but his smile was forced. The servants were in the room, and thus they exchanged formal greetings.

Hurrying to accept a chair beside him, Phoebe remarked, "You do not look well, Mr. Carruthers. Have you been sadly afflicted by mama's cold?"

"I fear I am a trifle indisposed," he admitted, sitting down carefully, "but colds seldom trouble me for any length of time. I only hope I may not be contagious to others. You were up early, ma'am. Had you a nice ride?"

"Went over to Birch Hill," said Jeffery, reaching for the marmalade but with his eyes very steady on his brother's haggard face. "Miss Ramsay was desirous of meeting Sir Malcolm again."

Meredith started, his gaze darting to Phoebe.

She said coolly, "You'd as well know, sir. I went to intercede with him about your wretched duel."

Meredith was astounded, and the effect her announcement had on the servants was such that he was able to dismiss them. When the doors had closed and they were alone, he demanded, "What the deuce have you two been about?"

Jeffery explained, "It was Miss Ramsay's idea, and there's not a bit of use your flying into the boughs, Merry. You look like the devil, and you will need a logical reason for a surgeon's services."

Meredith stared at him, then, comprehending, said with droll humour, "My God! Here I'd thought you were trying to protect me, instead of which you were arranging a duel for me!"

"In the course of which," said Phoebe, "we had to tell Sir Malcolm the whole story."

"The devil!" He jerked forward in his chair, the involuntary movement playing such havoc with his arm that whatever else he had meant to say was cut off.

Aching with sympathy, Phoebe reached out to clasp the hand that clutched the arm of his chair. He eased himself back, breathing hard, and turned to her with a quivering smile.

"The thing is," she said gently, "shall you be able to hold a pistol? Or fire it? Sir Malcolm was overjoyed to hear our news and is proud of, rather than provoked with, his son. But we stressed the need for speed."

Jeffery struck in, "His seconds will call on you at any minute.

Lockwood will demand the meeting take place at once. We thought it best.''

Carruthers looked dubious.

"You must name me and Ramsay as your seconds," Jeffery went on, "so that we can get your coat off fast afterwards. And we'll have old Linden for surgeon, of course."

"I'll not have him roped into this," said Carruthers sharply. "Even are we able to convince the rest of 'em that it's a—a legitimate duel, how do we explain away the pre-existence of bandages?''

Jeffery and Phoebe looked at one another. Phoebe said, "By having the duel very close by. And there—there must be no bandages.''

Meredith regarded her thoughtfully.

She said, anguished, "Poor Merry! I am so sorry, but—do you think you will be able to manage?''

Voices and several sets of footsteps could be heard in the hall. Low-voiced, Carruthers said, "Of course I will, clever girl. With the aid of that decanter. Sin—quick, if you please.''

Sinclair sprinted for the sideboard, poured a goodly portion from the decanter into Carruthers's half-empty coffee cup, and darted back again.

Meredith took a healthy swallow and coughed. "Gad!" he gasped. "I'll be a proper lushy one by the time all this is done with!''

The door opened and Conditt announced resonantly, "Sir Francis Hills. Major Coolley.''

The two gentlemen who came into the room were indelibly stamped County. Both wore riding dress and both had the ruddy complexions that spoke of the outdoor life. Major Coolley, a man of late middle age, bore himself with the upright carriage and ineffable air of authority of a soldier. Sir Francis Hills, some years younger, had earnest, rather prominent hazel eyes, a round face, and the beginnings of a paunch.

Standing, Carruthers performed the introductions and invited his guests to partake of breakfast, but drew back when Sir Francis advanced, hand outstretched. "Better not," he said, coughing convincingly. "Beastly cold.''

"Thought you looked rather puny," said the Major. "I say puny, eh, Hills?''

"Haw," said Sir Francis, eyeing Carruthers uneasily.

Conditt and a maidservant came in unobtrusively, and two more covers were set. When the servants withdrew and Sir Francis was busied with an egg, the Major lowered his cup and boomed, "Like a private word before we leave, Carruthers. Eh, Hills?"

"Aha," said Sir Francis.

They all stood as Phoebe came to her feet, Jeffery moving swiftly to pull back her chair. "I have things I must do," she said, smiling her sunny smile at them, "and shall leave you in peace, gentlemen."

They variously bowed, 'haw-ed,' and mumbled apologies, and she went out, drawing the eyes of both newcomers, so that Carruthers was enabled to lower himself cautiously into his chair.

"Dashed fine-looking gel, that," murmured Coolley, still gazing at the closing door. "Dashed fine, I say. Eh, Hills?"

"Yo," said his friend, having returned his attention to his breakfast.

Amused, despite his personal misery, Carruthers prompted, "How may I be of service, Major?"

"Eh?" said Coolley. "Oh. Yes. Frightfully sorry, Carruthers. I say, frightfully sorry. But Lockwood's raving. Wants to fight immedjit, don'tcha know. This afternoon. I say, this afternoon, in fact."

Sir Francis shook his neatly bewigged head. "Bad form," he remarked with rare volubility.

"Today is agreeable with me," said Carruthers. "Sooner the better."

"May we know your friends, sir?" asked the Major.

"I'll second him, of course." The deep, pleasant voice, sounding from the door that none of them had seen opening, caused Jeffery and Sinclair to jerk around in dismay.

Carruthers, his head alarmingly woozy, had the presence of mind to reach for his handkerchief. He was too dull-witted, however, to use his left hand and, having initiated the movement, was obliged to complete it. He buried his sweating face in the handkerchief and concealed his anguish by a series of coughs and sneezes that had his companions drawing back uneasily. "Sorry," he gasped, emerging again, having first carefully lowered his arm. He mopped his brow. "This damnable cold! Thank you, Brooks."

"Who the deuce are you fighting this time, Merry?"

"Lockwood. Couldn't get out of it. He struck me in the face. Twice."

Lambert took a chair and drew over a cup and saucer. "Bad

show," he observed, pouring coffee. "Still, you'd best postpone, old boy. You look positively green about the gills."

"Lockwood wants it this afternoon," said Major Coolley sternly.

"And I agreed," croaked Meredith. "Cold's getting worse, I can feel it. As well get the blasted business over with. Jeff—will you oblige?"

Jeffery said he would be proud to do so. Meredith struggled to his feet and sauntered to the door, handkerchief in hand. "I'll leave you gentlemen to work out the details," he said as stuffily as he could manage. "Pistols, Jeff."

Sinclair stood and went over to join him. As soon as the door closed, Carruthers said a feeble "Whew!" and staggered slightly.

Sinclair took his left arm and peered at him worriedly. "What a beast of a coil that Lambert should walk in at just that minute! *Now* how are we to manage?"

Carruthers sighed wearily. "Somehow. Come with me, will you, Sin? We shall have to find the lightest pistol I own."

Sinclair had observed the performance with the handkerchief, and had a fair idea of the price Carruthers had paid. He muttered, "How the deuce are you to lift it, much less aim and fire?"

"If the recoil knocks me down, it will look realistic, at least." Carruthers added with a wry grin. "We'd best all pray I don't go down *before* Lockwood fires!"

Phoebe stood on the front steps watching the carriage until it was lost to sight on the curve of the drivepath. By using the excuse that he had personal matters to discuss with his brother, just in case things went amiss, Meredith had been able to ensure that he and Jeff had the carriage to themselves. The fact that Lambert was going to officiate, however, added to the danger. *Somehow*, Jeffery had to cut the tight bandages away at the last possible moment and get Meredith to the duel site before any telltale stains appeared on his garments. *Somehow*, Meredith had to raise the loaded pistol and fire. They had thought at first it would be easier for him to delope, but although he had striven with all his might, he had been unable to lift his arm to the customary position to fire in the air, and had said he would simply aim wide.

The skies were dark and heavy with clouds, and Phoebe drew

her shawl closer about her, thinking miserably, 'He looked so ill, yet managed to wink at me. . . .' She bit her lip, plagued with dread of the outcome.

A loved voice enquired, "Do you feel inclined to talk about it, dear child?"

The Dowager Lady Ramsay stood close by, her wise eyes grave.

Phoebe hugged her. "Grandmama, I pray you will not tell Mrs. Carruthers, but—Meredith has gone to fight a duel."

Lady Martha was predictably shocked. "What, at *this* hour? These young fellows today have no sense of the proprieties!"

Phoebe gave a watery laugh, and the old lady said, "Walk with me, dearest, and tell me all about it."

And so Phoebe tucked her hand in the Dowager's arm, and they walked through the gardens while she offered the version of the affair that had earlier been agreed on.

For a little while Lady Martha was silent. Then she said, "I think you are become rather fond of your betrothed, after all. . . ."

Phoebe flushed. "After all, Grandmama?"

"Never think you fooled me, child," said the old lady, patting her hand. "I knew your heart was given to Lambert. What you and Carruthers were about, and why you agreed to wed him, I could not guess. I was only glad you *had* agreed, for I like the boy. Always have."

"Always? Have you known him long, then?"

"Long enough to know that he took the scars intended for his mother's face. I admired him for that. I met him in May for the first time in years. He was in Town with that rascal Roland Ma—Otton. I sent Roly off and had a long chat with Carruthers, but—Oh, what a beautiful cat! Does it live here?"

Their aimless stroll had taken them to the rear drivepath, where Satan sprawled under a large shrub growing against the wall of the Tudor wing.

"He belongs to Meredith, and makes poor Justice's life wretched." Knowing her grandmother's great affection for cats, Phoebe bent and attempted to cajole the animal from its hideaway. "Come and meet Lady Martha, you unsociable creature." Satan yawned, got up, took a step, arched his back, and sat down again. Phoebe reached for him, disturbing the branches, and sprang back with a cry of revulsion as dust showered down over her head and shoulders. Satan ran off, voicing his own outrage and stopping to shake various sections of him along the way, with equal parts of energy and indignation.

Phoebe exclaimed, "Oh! What horrid stuff!" and wiped an eye that stung unpleasantly.

" 'Tis all over you, love!" said my lady. "Run inside and change your dress. No, never wait for me. I will go and see the Armour Hall."

Phoebe entered the house by the nearest door and hurried to the first floor. Most of the servants were readying the house for tomorrow's tea-party, an event that she knew would have to go along without Meredith's presence. Ada did not respond to her call when she entered her suite, and she supposed must have been pressed into service elsewhere. The gloomy skies rendered her bedchamber dim, and she turned up the wick of her bedside lamp. Her shawl was covered with a heavy black dust. With a little "Ooo!" of revulsion, she shook it out.

A brilliant flash. A loud bang. She squeaked with fright and jumped away. The lampshade had shattered. The edge of her shawl was burning and full of splintered glass. She threw it to the floor, but before she could do anything more, she was pushed aside by a gentleman, dressed for riding, who stamped his glossy boot at the shawl.

"Water jug!" commanded Roland Otton, coughing from the smoke that billowed about them.

Phoebe ran to fetch it. He threw the contents over the shawl. Steam arose with a faint hissing. It smelled horrid, and Phoebe drew back, sneezing.

Otton strode to fling open casements and wave away the smoke. "Are you all right, ma'am? Did you drop the lamp?"

"Why, no. It is so odd. I was taking my shawl off and the lamp just seemed to explode."

Concerned, he scanned her. "You were not cut, I hope?"

"No, thank you." She dabbed at her stinging eyes. "But— only look at this horrid dust! 'Tis all over me! And black as pitch!"

He stepped nearer, his eyes sharpening. "So it is, by Jove! Come to the window, ma'am. Let's have a look at this."

The thought dawned that she was alone in her bedchamber with an infamous rake, to say nothing of a most dishonourable man, but the urgency of his manner alarmed her, and she asked anxiously, "What is it?"

He brushed some of the dust from her gown and, collecting it in the palm of his hand, moved it about with one slim fingertip.

Glancing up, his eyes narrowed, he asked, "Where did you come across this?"

"It is all over the bushes behind the Tudor wing."

"Is it, by God?" Without another word, he sprinted from the room.

Phoebe ran after him. Outside, Justice, who had been pondering the merits of chasing a provocatively sauntering Satan, brightened, and trotted beside Otton, the hope of a walk dawning in his canine mind.

Otton halted when he reached the Tudor wing, and began to investigate the shrubs. "No. Over there, sir," cried Phoebe, pointing. He went at once to shake the bush, bringing down a dark powdery rain.

"Curse and confound it," he muttered. "I don't like this."

"Oh, *do* tell me! What is wrong?"

"It is gunpowder, Miss Ramsay. A whole flask of the stuff, by the look of it."

"*Gunpowder?* But—if Mr. Carruthers was loading his pistol, why would he throw the powder out of his window?"

"A gentleman's second usually loads his guns and sets the triggers—though Merry will not use a sett trigger, come to think of it." Otton spoke absently, deep in thought. "If the powder was damp, or defective, it is logical that it should be discarded, but even Jeff would not have been so ramshackle as to fling it out the window. Unless . . . Ma'am, your pardon, but I've to ride at once. Jeff told me of the duel. Now, will you be so kind as to tell the grooms to saddle my horse?"

Not waiting for her reply, he ran back into the house, his manner so grimly purposeful, so foreign to his usual bored languor, that Phoebe picked up her skirts and sped to the stables.

A big, pleasant-faced young man with curly blond hair was busied at the feed bins and looked up in surprise when she ran in. He fairly leapt to do her bidding, wasting no time on questions.

Watching him, trying not to dwell on the ramifications of Otton's obvious suspicions, she asked in a distracted way, "Are you—I mean, is your name Henry, by any chance?"

He smiled at her over the back of Otton's tall chestnut horse. "Aye, miss. Henry Baker I be. And you are Miss Ada Banham's lady."

She nodded, and then Otton ran into the stables, a holstered pistol in his hand, and the long sword that Ada had called a colichemarde at his side. Baker led the horse out, and the animal whickered affectionately. Otton stroked the white blaze on his face and murmured something in a low caressing voice before he mounted in a supple swing.

Looking up at him, Phoebe said, "You believe someone tampered with Mr. Carruthers's powder-horn."

"I pray not, ma'am. The devil's in it that I doubt I'm in time. Stand clear!"

Henry drew her back. Otton lifted the reins and touched his spurred heels lightly to the chestnut's sides. "Come on, Rump," he said.

The horse's ears pricked up. Whether he knew his master well enough to be aware that something special was being asked of him, Phoebe could not guess, but it seemed to her that he did not gradually come to a gallop but was racing at full speed before ever they were clear of the stableyard.

Returning to the house, her heart was heavy. The duel was a staged deception. But that fact was known only to five people. If Otton's suspicion was correct, someone who believed the duel to be authentic had again tried to kill Meredith Carruthers.

"Merry!" hissed Jeffery, shaking his brother with reluctance but desperation. "Merry! For God's sake!"

Meredith blinked up at him. "Is it . . . over?" he asked, confused.

"Lord, but I wish it were! You're still in the coach, old fellow. Are you better? I'm most dreadfully sorry. I tried to be as careful as I could." He held the flask to his brother's pale lips. "We're at the spinney, but Linden's not here as yet. I told Lambert you were sleeping, and he went over to confer with Coolley and Hills. Merry, we simply *must* call it off! You cannot hope to—"

Meredith hauled his head up. "You'd be surprised, Jeff, what a man can do when his life is . . . is on the line. No, I'd best not drink any more brandy or I'll be too foxed to miss poor Lockwood."

Jeffery peered out of the window. "Here comes Linden now. Thank heaven! It's raining but very lightly. Can you get out?" He inspected his brother's sleeve, and groaned. "Try to keep your arm bent so the blood don't creep down your hand."

They descended into the drizzle, and Lambert hurried over and looked at Meredith frowningly. Jeffery led him away a few paces. Lambert asked uneasily, "Is he all right? Gad, but that cold has a grip on him."

" 'Fraid he's been hitting the brandy," said Jeffery by way of apology.

"Merry?" said Lambert, astonished.

"He hoped it might make him feel better. I think he's overdone it a trifle. Have you fellows measured off the ground?"

"Yes. We're ready. Only look at Merry's silly grin. Jove! What a mess!"

Jeffery retreated to his wavering brother and told him sternly to behave sensibly. Meredith hiccuped. Lambert sighed and went over to the other seconds.

Dr. George Linden, a gaunt man of about fifty years, his shoulders stooped with rheumatism, left his shabby coach and joined them, carrying his small bag of tools and complaining about the rain and the isolated location.

"Don't want the Watch here, Linden. I said, don't want—" began Major Coolley.

"Yes, we heard you, sir," said Lambert, looking uneasily at his principal. "Could we get started, please? Carruthers has a beastly cold."

"Should've thought of that before he interfered with my hunt," blustered Lockwood, slanting an oblique glance at his opponent. Even as he looked, Carruthers swayed slightly, then pulled himself up straight. Lockwood, a brave man, was suddenly more afraid than he ever had been in his life. A pistol was no weapon to be wielded by someone whose faculties were impaired. One sway such as that he had just seen could write his death warrant. He strode to his position and stood there, thinking of Lance and wishing he'd been able to see the boy just once more.

Jeffery, watching the right sleeve of his brother's dark brown coat, wondered if anyone else had noticed the darker mark near the elbow.

Meredith, the scene rippling before his eyes, gritted his teeth and prayed for the strength to lift the pistol that already seemed to weigh a ton.

"I shall count to three," called Major Coolley. "I say, I shall count to—"

"Well, for Lord's sake, just say—'one—two—three,' " snarled Lockwood, his nerves on edge. "Let's have no 'One, I say one,' and so forth!"

Affronted, the Major said with lofty disdain, "I shall then

202

drop my handkerchief. When I let it fall, you may fire. Do you"—he gave the Squire a hard look—"I say, do you understand, gentlemen?"

Lockwood growled an affirmative. Carruthers, guessing what the echoing voice had said, nodded.

"One . . . two . . ."

Jeffery held his breath.

"Three . . . !"

The white handkerchief fluttered down.

Drawing on every ounce of strength, Meredith dragged the pistol upward and fired. Through a thickening haze of pain, he saw a puff of smoke. If there was a recoil, he was past feeling it. Dimly, he heard the roar of Sir Malcolm's weapon and wondered, in a remotely interested way, why he had not heard his own. It really didn't matter. With a faint sigh of relief, he let go, and fainted.

Lady Martha had decided that the best procedure would be to manoeuvre Lucille Carruthers out of the way until the result of the duel was known. Aware that Meredith would be vanquished, Phoebe thought poor Lucille should be warned, but she could not betray her foreknowledge, and Lady Martha was quite confident that Meredith would neither kill Sir Malcolm, nor be gravely hurt himself; in fact, she fondly expected both the foolish creatures to delope. Secure in that belief, she argued that there was nothing to be gained by throwing Mrs. Carruthers into the vapours over something that would likely never happen, and she cajoled that lady to take her for a drive.

Phoebe went with her brother into the quiet library and told him about the powder and Otton's theories regarding it. Horrified, Sinclair said, "But, Phoebe, no one *knew* about the duel!"

"No one save Sir Malcolm and his seconds and those of us here at the Hall," she amended. "How can we know whom Sir Francis or Major Coolley may have told?"

He looked at her glumly. "They'd have had to act very fast. Still, it does sound ugly. I vow, old lady, we've brought ourselves into a very—"

Rapid hoofbeats could be heard. Phoebe's heart jumped convulsively.

"They're back!" cried Sinclair, and ran.

Phoebe followed. A surprised lackey made a sprint for the front doors and flung one open. Hurrying onto the steps, Phoebe saw Roland Otton's horse coming at great speed through the soft summer rain. Otton vaulted from the saddle and ran to the steps. "I was—too late," he cried breathlessly. "Gun misfired. They're bringing him home."

So it *had* misfired! Phoebe clutched her brother's hand. He asked, "How bad is it?"

"Not desperate, but nasty. Will you prepare the servants? Linden would like Miss Kraemer to help. She's a dashed fine nurse." He led Rumpelstiltskin around towards the stables, and Sinclair and Phoebe went together into the house. She found that she was crying, and wiped the tears away impatiently.

Sinclair put his arm around her. "Are you all right?"

"Yes." She smiled tremulously. "Just—so relieved. I never really thought he could manage it. I don't want to think about the other business. Hurry, dear, and tell the housekeeper, and I'll go and warn poor Howell, he's been fairly beside himself."

To a man, the servants were devoted to Meredith, and shock and dread of the outcome were rife, but they rallied, and by the time the carriage drew up at the steps of the Tudor wing, linen had been torn into bandages, lint and hot water and scissors had been prepared for Dr. Linden, and a piece of oilcloth covered by two worn sheets had been thrown over Meredith's bed to protect the fine linens.

Phoebe heard Conditt shout, "Here they come!" and she went to the head of the stairs in the family wing and stood waiting, gripping her hands together. Soon, she heard male voices and uncertain steps. Lambert's voice, saying "For God's sake, Merry! Let us carry you." And Otton, his tone sharp, "Leave him be!" Shadows appeared on the highly polished floor. Conditt, his voice trembling, said, "Upstairs, Master Jeffery. Everything's ready."

And then Meredith's voice, quiet but steady. "Do not look so distressed, please. I am very sure I shall live."

Phoebe's heart turned over. She heard a maid sob, the sound abruptly muffled. She saw him then, his dark head wildly untidy and uncharacteristically bowed, one arm across Jeffery's shoulder, the other in a neat sling, and his shirt and breeches a welter of scarlet splotches. She could not seem to breathe, and a lump rose in her throat, choking her. He looked up, and halted briefly, gazing at her. She managed, somehow, to smile through a blur of tears, and she saw a faint shadow of his quirkish grin dawn.

A strange heady joy swept over her, and at last, she knew.

She thought, in a proud, exultant triumph, 'So this is what it feels like. This is the *pig's trotter*!'

Otton closed the door softly and crept towards the great bed. Carruthers lay very still, his right arm heavily bandaged from wrist to elbow, and a bank of pillows on that side to prevent his turning onto it. He looked drawn and exhausted and quite defenseless. Otton tiptoed closer.

The maid sitting on the far side of the bed whispered, "He's not to be disturbed, sir."

He started. "Gad, but you gave me a fright! Didn't see you hovering there like a guardian angel, m'dear."

She blushed and giggled.

Carruthers's eyes opened. "Roly," he said, his voice less decisive than usual as he stretched out his left hand. "I knew you would come. Thank you."

Otton took the hand in a brief, firm clasp. "I was curious to discover if you still lived after all that butchering. Not feeling so merry just now, I'll warrant."

With a wry grin, Carruthers admitted that truth.

Otton perched on the side of the bed. "Cheer up. You'll likely feel much worse tomorrow. Second day's always the grimmest."

"Well! I never did!" uttered the maid, much shocked.

Otton regarded her with renewed interest. "Didn't you, by Jove! A virgin!"

The maid shrieked and threw her hands to flaming cheeks. Laughing weakly, Carruthers told her that the Captain would sit with him for a while, and that she could safely leave him. She peeped dubiously at Otton from between her fingers, and Carruthers went on, "Better go, m'dear. I apologize for my friend's vocabulary, but I assure you it will get worse if you stay, and I am quite unable to control him at the moment."

"That is perfectly true," said Otton thoughtfully, standing and strolling towards the girl.

"Roly!" protested Carruthers. "Let her be! She's a child only."

"A pretty child, methinks . . ."

The little maid fled, squealing, but with a sparkle in her big brown eyes.

Amused, Otton returned and took his seat again. "I think we

can narrow it to approximately forty people," he observed mildly.

Carruthers sighed. "I'm afraid I didn't fully understand what you were trying to tell us. Jeff said you believe my powder was tampered with."

"Not a doubt of it, my tulip." He embarked upon a succinct account of the gunpowdery shrubs, and went on, "Jeff loaded for you and swears he found no fault with the powder, and at all events would not have been so thimble-witted as to toss the contents of the flask out the window. Certainly, he'd have no logical reason for emptying the flask once more, after we'd returned."

"He did not. I asked Howell to bring it to me. It was full."

"Yes. Whoever discarded the original gunpowder then filled your flask with some mixture designed to do no more than spark. From the look of your pistol, I'd say it was largely soot. Assuming Jeff is *not* the guilty party—do not rend me, dear boy!—he innocently loaded your pistol with the sullied powder, tucked the flask into your box, just in case there was need to reload, and off you went."

"I see. And after we came home, my would-be murderer dumped out the faulty powder, replaced it with my own, and congratulated himself that I was shot because my pistol misfired."

"Shot, but not killed, unfortunately—as I've no doubt he had planned. Your old brainbox is working, I see. Sluggish, but prevailing."

Carruthers's arm throbbed so mercilessly that he was finding it very difficult to think at all. He knit his brows and said slowly, "I do not see that. Surely it would have been simpler to leave the useless powder where it was, and replace it at some later time. Must have been awfully risky to change it again."

"Yes, but don't forget that our villain didn't know we had rumbled the switch. Could he have popped some genuine gunpowder in the flask and it was tested and found perfectly satisfactory, we'd have been none the wiser, and . . ." He shrugged.

"And had it not been for you, Roly, a neat murder might have been disguised so as to seem a simple misfire." Carruthers moved restlessly, trying to ease his position. "It's damnable to know someone in my household wants me dead," he muttered fretfully. "Any suspicions?"

"As I said, at least forty. Any one of your servants could be

206

in the pay of some malcontent.'' He inspected the laces at his wrist and was silent.

Carruthers said wearily, "Go on. You've something churning around your fiendish brain. What is it?"

Otton looked at him uneasily. "You're properly pulled, and I've stayed too long. However, and to wit—the suspicions I cherish are mine own. You must develop your premise from the fact that if we rule out most of the servants, there are only five could logically have done the thing. Myself, Jeff, young Ramsay, Lambert, or your man.''

"What stuff! As though I would suspect you. And why would Lambert do away with me when he relies heavily on the allowance I make him? Howell's been with me for ten years. It certainly was not my brother, and as for Sinclair—gammon! The boy's decent as . . . as they come.''

"And that arm is giving you Hades, I see." Otton stood. "I'll go. Only came because I knew you'd be stewing.''

"Well, dammit, I'm still stewing! Roly—tell me what is in your mind.''

"Oh, very well." Otton settled one shoulder against the bedpost. "You say you do not suspect me. Why? You know that I'm after any loot I can lay my hands on and would not hesitate to throw you to the wolves did you stand in my way." Carruthers gave a derisive snort, and Otton sighed and went on, "Lambert seems an honourable man and certainly must value the allowance you make him. He dotes on your lady, however, and he may suspect you are winning her to a more kindly regard of your gruff and glummery.''

A different light brightened Carruthers's tired eyes. "Do *you* think I am?''

"Control yourself, Don Juan. What I think matters not. The thing is that if Lambert is 'one that loved not wisely but too well,' he might decide the world would rub along very well *sans* your disturbing presence.''

Breathing rather unevenly, Carruthers demanded, "The rest, please.''

"You will not like it, but . . .'' Otton hesitated, laid a cool hand on his friend's forehead, and scowled. "I thought so! Very well, Merry. Straight between the eyes, and then I'm off before Linden removes my head. Of us all, Jeff has the strongest motive. If you die, he stands to inherit the fortune and the lands—''

"Wrong. On both counts. My father made other bequests. And the estates are entailed."

"Yes, but does Jeff know that?"

Carruthers's triumphant grin faded.

"One of these years, my close-mouthed friend, you are going to have to tell that boy the truth of—"

"We do not discuss that now. Go on, Roly."

"You disapprove of his friends and his record at school, and have threatened him with expulsion to the colonies or to the cavalry. Now that, alone, is sufficient grounds."

Carruthers tossed his head impatiently. Otton could not know that Jeff, well aware that Lockwood had intended a near miss, would have had absolutely no reason to substitute soot for black powder. Unless . . . He frowned. Unless it was all a clever screen to direct suspicion at someone else. The powder on the shrubs could have been 'discovered' later, if Phoebe had not noticed it. Disgusted with such disloyal thoughts, he said, "Ridiculous! Is that all?"

"Not—quite. Jeff has seen you cuddling his—er, light o' love in your sacred spinney."

For a moment Carruthers stared in silence, then he muttered, "What the—devil d'you mean?"

"I mean, my sly rascal, our voluptuous villager. Rosalie Smith."

✨ *Chapter 15* ✨

Jeffery had supported his brother throughout Dr. Linden's temporary surgery at the site of the duel, and his garments were liberally marked with Meredith's blood. Lucille and Lady Martha returned home in time to see Jeffery's coat being carried downstairs by his valet, Dr. Linden following. Terrified, Lucille heard the word 'duel,' assumed Jeffery had been shot, and went into screaming hysterics, the uproar so alarming that Meredith heard and tried to get up. An irritated Linden returned to the sick-room and administered a heavy dose of laudanum. Lambert, attempting to speak with Phoebe, found her distracted and unable to spare him the few minutes he requested. He was obliged to return to the army post at Salisbury, and rode out, morose and silent, accompanied by Otton.

Late in the afternoon, Otton returned alone. Instead of going directly to the Hall, however, he turned off the lane some distance before reaching the lodge gates and dismounted in a clump of trees. He was expected, and Ben Hessell rose from the fallen trunk on which he'd been lounging, and snatched off his greasy cap.

"Well?" demanded Otton.

"Ain't no one seen no sign, sir," whined Hessell, "but young Carruthers was lotsa times with that there Catholic lordship. Glendenning. And Mr. Ramsay cries friends with a Mr. Devilley or suchlike, as is known to be—"

"Could you perchance mean *de Villars*?" interrupted Otton intently. "Mr. Trevelyan de Villars?"

" 'S what I said," Hessell grunted, annoyed.

Otton's dark eyes gleamed with excitement. "By Jupiter," he muttered. "I wonder . . . The last sight of Lascelles was near Guildford . . . I *wonder* . . ." He stood motionless and lost in thought, while Hessell's bitter eyes watched him with loathing.

"By God!" exclaimed Otton, driving one gloved hand into the palm of the other. "How blind! How stupid! That's it, of course!" He whirled on his startled hireling. "You've done well. If this goes as I think, there'll be a bonus for you. Now—in the matter of your other—er, employer. Have you found someone?"

Hessell nodded. "Ready and willing, guv," he said, adding with a sly leer, "and there weren't no need of you having to dirty yer nice clean hands."

Otton's eyes narrowed. "Excellent. Now listen carefully, and be sure you keep in mind who *really* employs you." He lowered his voice and gave crisp instructions. "If anything should go awry," he finished softly, "send someone to the stables at the Hall, and ask for Mr. Sorenson. Give him this." He held out a silver button on which was embossed the crest of the old and honoured house from which he had been banished. "Sorenson is my man of all work, poor fellow. He will get word to me, and I'll come. And—" His voice was suddenly menacing. "You will keep your mouth shut. You understand?"

"Not a blessed word won't spill outta Ben Hessell's gob, sir, I promise yer. Knock him right orf his high perch this will, and couldn't happen to a nicer gent. I owe him one. Ar, and more'n one, and—"

"Oh, stow your clack!" said Otton angrily. He turned away, but glimpsed the murderous glare that was slanted at him.

A faint ringing sound, and the point of a long, glittering dagger was at Ben Hessell's throat. He gave a strangled squeal and cringed against the tree-trunk behind him.

"D'you think I do not know what is in your mind, you poisonous slimy thing?" purred Otton. "It would amaze you to know how much blood is on my 'nice clean hands.' If you would not add yours—have a care! Now get on your way!"

"Yessir! Oh, yessir! I didn't mean nothing, sir!" And, smiling, bowing, touching his brow obsequiously, the big man fawned his way from sight.

Otton scowled after him. "Faugh!" he exclaimed. To have to use such a tool was repellent, but time was running out. He walked over to where Rumpelstiltskin grazed at a tuft of grass. The horse raised its head and nuzzled him affectionately, and he caressed the silken neck moodily. "*C'est la guerre*, Rump," he muttered. "And the trouble is, life is one long war." He mounted up and rode through the gates and up the drivepath to Meredith Hall.

Mrs. Carruthers was much relieved the following morning to learn that her eldest son had slept through the night and was feeling a great deal better. Her fears for his life had been extreme, but as soon as she knew he was in no imminent danger of expiring, her mood changed to one of resentment. It was, as she told Jeffery, most inconsiderate of Meredith to get himself shot the day before she had 'half the County' coming to his betrothal party.

With a gleam of amusement, Jeffery said, "I am very sure it was not Merry's intention to be wounded, Mama."

"Well, I must say I had thought him a much better marksman than that silly Malcolm Lockwood," she pouted. "And—he had the entire *year*, Jeff! Why must he fight a duel *now*? With his betrothed in the house, and that terrifying Grandmama of hers. It is too bad of him. It really is too bad!"

Her pique was eased when Phoebe came down for the party, enchantingly lovely in a Watteau gown of primrose taffeta embroidered in gold, the hoops very wide, her hair powdered and piled high on her regal head, and a gold filigree necklace at her throat. "Oh, but you will dazzle them all, my dear Miss Ramsay," she trilled, and when Phoebe replied shyly that there was "only one gentleman" she wished to dazzle, her cup was full.

An hour later, the long, graceful sweep of the Armour Hall was bright with taffeta and silk and satin, the weather having forbidden a garden party, as had been planned. Gentlemen bowed and postured amid the shields and lances, guarding the delicate blossoms of frailty entrusted to their protection. Ladies cooed and exclaimed and embraced, and noted with eagle eyes the incredible width of the new French panniers Lady Bentley-Harrison affected; the towering height of the wig worn by Mrs. Ursula Siddingham; the ruby gleaming dazzlingly on the white bosom of that scandalous widow, Mrs. Rosemary Monahan (believed to be the new interest of Sir Peter Ward). Justice, banished to the gardens, sat and gazed glumly in through the windows while his arch-enemy, serenely ensconced atop a tall chest, smirked at him in triumph.

Despite the fact that there were several military uniforms among the throng, a small group of gentlemen engaged in an irked discussion of the tactics employed by troopers who had searched their houses. "Like a pack of blasted baboons!" roared one angry octogenarian. Sinclair and Jeffery, resplendent in party finery, joined the group and learned to their increased unease that Colonel Fotheringay had pressed numerous civilians into the search, and had sent off to Southampton hoping to secure the hiring of a pack of hounds that had successfully run a fugitive to ground there. There were a few quietly uttered expressions of sympathy for the poor fellow who had so nearly escaped, only to be seized at the last moment, then a duchess arrived, creating quite a stir, and such dismal topics were abandoned.

For the next two hours a trio of musicians played discreetly, their melodies all but lost in the hum of talk and laughter, the clink of teacups and wineglasses, as the guests drifted about, chatting with this or that old friend, remarking on the beauty of the bride-to-be, and the unfortunate indisposition of the prospective groom. Brooks Lambert arrived in full regimentals and was immediately surrounded by admiring ladies. He was the essence of grace—"the epitome, my dear, dear Martha," trilled the Dowager Countess of Teignley, clutching her beloved Pekingese to her scrawny bosom, "of British young manhood. And so excruciatingly handsome into the bargain! Do you know, my love, a little bird told me that your lovely granddaughter had a tendre for him at one time. . . . Poor Carruthers . . . he had best look to his lady. . . ." And she smiled a hooded-eyed smile at her 'dear old friend' and crooked her gnarled fingers more securely about the handle of her teacup.

Phoebe was trying to concentrate on the attempted pleasantries of a rather inarticulate but likeable young clerical gentleman named FitzWilliam Boudreaux, who had escorted his patron, the Duchess of Waterbury. She had not seen Meredith, and her thoughts kept turning to him. A tingling sense of excitement pervaded her being. She knew, without glancing around, that he had entered the room.

As soon as she could do so without interrupting the reverend gentleman, she turned. Meredith was coming towards her. He wore a grey, excellently tailored coat, a silver-and-black waistcoat, and his hair was powdered and arranged in a becomingly tumbled style. Viewing him with the eyes of love, she thought him the most attractive man she had ever known, and saw the scars not at all, but she was angry: He was desperately pale, and the dark shadows under his eyes, the weary lines in his face tore at her heart. He carried his right arm in a sling, but when she stood and reached out to him, he clasped her fingers in his left hand and touched them to his lips.

Those standing nearby smiled fondly at the young couple: the

212

tall, striking man, the slender girl, radiantly lovely in the graceful gown.

"You are without a wit," Phoebe scolded softly. "You should never have got up so soon!"

He said as softly, "I would not have missed it for the world, ma'am. I wish I *were* a poet—it would take such a one to do you justice this afternoon."

She blushed and lowered her eyes. "For a man who lacks a silver tongue, you do surprisingly well, Mr. Carruthers." And raising her fan to hide her lips, she asked, "Have you discovered who tampered with the powder?"

"We are not sure it *was* tampered with, so do not be worrying for—"

"Foolish creature! I will worry until you are gone back to your bed. This is sheer folly."

Jeffery came over and said with a low voice and a wide smile, "Fotheringay has sent to Southampton for dogs. And they suspect Lance's true identity; the troopers are so thick about Lockwood's estate, you could scarce set a pin 'twixt 'em."

Meredith swore under his breath, smiled, and said audibly, "But how charming."

Affecting a giggle, Phoebe whispered, "What did you do with the cipher?"

"Never you mind, my girl. But—Jove, I'd rest easier were it safely delivered. We shall have very little time if—Oh, hello, Brooks. Escaped again, did you?"

"By the skin of my teeth," said Lambert disgustedly. "That blasted Colonel means to look under every weed from here to the Bristol Channel."

"Does he? Never say our abused countryside is being beaten again?"

"Thoroughly. I only slipped away for an hour. Phoebe, I must see you. I've grand news."

She looked at him regretfully. She had news for him also, news that must sadden the dear soul. "Very well, Brooks. Meredith—please! You have made an appearance. Your mama must be pleased. But you look very tired. Go back to your room, I beg you."

"I will," he promised. "As soon as you return. Brooks, you must not keep Miss Ramsay away too long. This party is in her honour, you know. We cannot both be absent."

Lambert nodded and offered Phoebe his arm. Taking it reluctantly, well aware of the puzzled glances that turned to them,

Phoebe said, "I want to talk with you also, Brooks. We can be private in the Hall of Mirrors, I think."

He led her there quickly, passing several maids and footmen who eyed them with curiosity, so that Phoebe's cheeks were quite pink by the time they reached the huge, echoing hall.

Lambert swung her to face him. "Grand news, love! I met your Aunt Hesther in Salisbury. She was just about to send off her footman with a letter for you, and entrusted it instead to me." He handed Phoebe a sealed letter and went on with exuberance, "It is from your mama, but pray do not read it now, for I've little time, and your aunt told me the gist of it. Sir Terence Glover is dead!"

Shocked, Phoebe exclaimed, "Oh, I am so sorry! Mama must be greatly distressed, for he has had a tendre for her forever."

"He must have," said Lambert with a grin. "Phoebe, he has left *everything* to Lady Eloise! Your aunt says it is in the neighbourhood of *eighty thousand pounds*!"

Her eyes became enormous. "Eighty . . . thous—My heavens!"

Catching both her hands in his, he said, "Do you not see, my darling? It means your family is no longer in straitened circumstances! Can I but win your grandmama's good opinion, they'll likely be willing to give me your hand now!" He swept the stunned Phoebe into his arms and bent to kiss her.

She pulled away quickly. "No, Brooks! I must tell you—" She broke off as the back door swung open. A flurry of wind blew the cloak of the girl who stood on the threshold. A girl of delicate beauty, her golden curls peeping charmingly from beneath her hood, her cheeks flushing with embarrassment when she saw them. "Oh! Your pardon," she stammered, dropping a curtsy. "I did not—I mean—forgive me!" And she fled.

"A regular little Fair, is she not?" said Brooks, amused. He tilted his handsome head as, distantly, a clock struck the half-hour. "Gad, I must be off, or Fotheringay will have my ears! What d'you think of my news?"

"Wonderful," she managed hollowly. "But I must—"

"Lord, that's right! You wanted to tell me something. Can you be very quick, m'dear? I'm treading on thin ice by even coming here tonight."

She looked up into his smiling eyes, and her heart sank. He loved her, and to hurt him was dreadful. What she had to say should not be tossed at him in so hasty a way, and the village girl's sudden appearance had made the moment even less opportune. She said, "I wish we had more time. Perhaps it had better wait."

"You're an angel to be so understanding." He pressed a quick kiss on her brow. "I will get away early in the morning. Can you meet me for a ride? I'll wait for you in that cluster of elms near the mound they think contains ancient artifacts. The one 'twixt here and Dewbury Minor. Do you know it?"

She said she did, promised to meet him there at seven o'clock, and let him kiss her hand before he left by the same door at which Rosalie had appeared. When she returned to the party, Meredith was nowhere to be seen. She was not surprised, and although she appeared bright and happy, as she had done earlier, her heart was heavy, and she was relieved when at last the party came to an end.

As soon as she could get away, she took her brother along to Lady Martha's suite and shared the news contained in her mother's letter. Lady Eloise had written in haste, having reached home to find Belinda already on the road to recovery. She was both devastated by her long-time admirer's demise, and astounded by his generosity. 'It will,' she wrote, 'make all the difference in the world to the family. The girls are assured of proper come-outs, and dear Sinclair can be off to University next term with no need to impose on Mr. Carruthers's good offices.' Sinclair was ecstatic. Lady Martha merely said, "Hmmnn . . ." and fixed Phoebe with a steady and disconcertingly penetrating gaze.

The company had stayed much later than was expected. The party was declared a resounding success by a jubilant Lucille, already entertaining plans for a large formal London ball, and dinner was little more than a light meal and a recapitulation of the day's triumph.

Jeffery announced that his brother had returned to bed, worn out by his short social fling. Phoebe was faintly shocked by his mother's obvious lack of concern. Lady Martha was also taken aback, but when she made a rather pointed comment, Lucille said confidently that they did not know Meredith. He was not the one, she said, to be troubled by a flesh wound, and would likely be fully recovered within a day or two.

Phoebe went up to bed feeling drained and dispirited. She was sure Sinclair and Jeffery meant to visit Lascelles, and she sat in bed trying to read until her brother tapped on the door at half-past midnight. "You will not believe it," he said in great excitement, "but Rosalie Smith was with poor Lascelles. It is

215

the grandest thing I ever heard. She and Lance and the Carruthers men grew up together, you know, and there is a great bond between them. But can you feature her being so brave as to take such a risk, and she was so grateful to Jeffery and to me, there was no listening to it. Carruthers told her—"

"Carruthers!" exclaimed Phoebe. "Oh, never say he was up again?"

"Well, er, yes. He did come over. He left before we did, however."

"I should hope so! He is foolish past permission! 'Twill serve him right if infection sets in!" Sinclair gave her a rather surprised look, and she blushed and enquired belatedly as to the condition of Lieutenant Lascelles.

"Oh, he runs a fever, poor fellow, and is fairly beside himself with anxiety for the cipher. Meredith promised that between us we will get it through, but I'll own I cannot think how he means to go about it."

Phoebe exclaimed, "*He* cannot go about it at all! Good heavens, does no one realize he is a mere mortal man? You saw that arm. He should lie in his bed for a week at the very least, much less be worrying—"

Sinclair interpolated solemnly, "It is all our heads at stake, old lady, and even were Meredith not greatly concerned with your own—which I begin to suspect he is—he'll move heaven and earth sooner than see any harm come to his family."

Phoebe fell asleep worrying about those ominous words. She did not sleep well and awoke to a dreary, overcast morning and the drearier prospect of breaking Lambert's loving heart.

When she went down to the stables, a chill wind carried the smell of rain and the clouds were darkening. Almost, she sent back upstairs for the cloak she had refused, but she did not intend to ride with Brooks, and it should not take long to tell him of her decision and return to the Hall.

Henry Baker had been warned of her plans and already had a frisky little chestnut mare saddled for her. He was troubled because of her insistence against an accompanying groom. Already taut with dread of the coming interview, Phoebe had no intention of allowing any other to witness it, and since Ada had hinted at the nature of the ride, Baker did not persist with his plea to escort her, but watched glumly as she rode out.

There were few travellers about on this grey morning. Phoebe passed a farm cart, the driver touching his brow respectfully to her; and some moments later she caught a glimpse of two dragoons riding on an early patrol. She reined up and kept out of sight until they had gone, then urged the mare to a canter. An occasional drop of rain had left its cold touch upon her cheeks by the time she reached the copse Lambert had designated. She slowed the mare again and entered the trees at a walk, her eyes searching. He was waiting in a small clearing, his bay tethered close by, and he came quickly to meet and lift her down from the saddle.

As usual, he looked the answer to every girl's prayer and he kept his arms about her, smiling down into her grave face as he exclaimed fervently, "At last! At last! How long it seems since we were alone and I was able to kiss my beloved without fear of—"

He bent lower. Striving to escape and to avoid his lips, Phoebe saw that even now they were not alone. An unexpected figure crept up behind Lambert; a tall, husky man, his features concealed by a raggedly cut mask, and one upraised arm holding a sturdy cudgel. There could be no doubt of his intent. Phoebe's scream of warning brought Lambert spinning round, his hand dropping to the hilt of his sword. He was much too late. The cudgel caught him above the ear with a solid thud and he went down without so much as a cry.

Before Phoebe could run, another man had grasped her. Her terrified struggles were brutally restrained. Her call for help was stifled by a rolled strip of cloth that was bound tightly over her mouth. Neither of her abductors said a word as she was tied hand and foot, then dumped unceremoniously into the back of a donkey-cart and a piece of oilcloth drawn over her. Dazed, terrified, half-smothered, she was tossed helplessly against the side as the donkey plodded over the uneven ground. Consciousness reeling, she clung to one thought—'Meredith . . .'

"I despise and abominate duelling," growled Dr. George Linden, tightening his grip on his cringing patient and taking up another instrument of torture, "and yet I do my humble best to mend the wounds of its thimble-witted adherents. Even when— be still!—even when they lie to me. In their teeth!"

Managing to snatch a breath, Meredith gasped, "Damned inquisitor! And—you know I'd not have . . . fought Lockwood had it not been—vital."

"Vital!" snorted the doctor. "You are healthy as any cart-horse, else you'd be in a raving fever and this arm would be

217

badly infected. This bone splinter should have come out yesterday, are you aware? But you'd already delayed and worn yourself down to the point I thought it best to allow you a day of rest before I poked about at you. And instead of resting, you cavort at a damnable tea-party! Do not move now, or you'll be sorry! Might a lowly . . . country practitioner enquire as to when you *did* take this wound, Carruthers?''

Carruthers flushed, lay as still as he could while enduring some more of the doctor's artistry, and at last said unevenly, "I'll pretend you did not—ask that, George.''

Linden laid aside his surgical probe and frowned. He was a fine doctor who could have made a name for himself in Town, but preferred the less remunerative practice of a rural district. He both knew and liked Meredith Carruthers, and the man was no fool. Given pause, he began to bathe the wound. "I can conceive of no reason why—'' His hand jerked. Carruthers swore ringingly, and Linden stared at him in consternation. "Merry! The troopers are thick as flies around Lockwood's estate, and there are whispers that Lance— You didn't— You wouldn't— Oh, *damme*! Never mind! Never mind!''

"You know I'd trust you with my life, but—''

"Spare me the favour!'' Linden took up his pot of black salve. "By God, I may despise duellists, but if there's anything worse, it's these damnable Jacobites! I've neither patience nor sympathy with the lot of 'em, and if I found one, I'd lose not an instant in turning him over to the nearest dragoon!''

With a twitching grin, Carruthers said, "I wish I may see it.''

"Do you! I served in Flanders, you may recall, and I shall never forgive the idiots who instigate such wholesale slaughter and suffering! And were any extra conviction needed, my favourite cousin bled to death in the mud of Prestonpans thanks to a Jacobite, and for want of a simple bandage such as this I now apply to your needlessly mauled arm. Speak not to me of the Jacobite Cause, Merry. I've not a shred of patience with it!''

Carruthers said quietly, "George, you cannot condone what is going on in Scotland.''

The doctor looked up at him for a moment, then his eyes fell. "You're a fool,'' he observed angrily. And wishing he were not so fond of the man, went on, "There's not a blasted bit of use telling you to rest, I'm well aware. But I wish you will make an effort to do so until another major catastrophe looms. Which,'' he went on gloomily, "in this house, will likely be five minutes from now!''

As it turned out, he was unduly pessimistic. It was one hour after Carruthers had made his slow way to his study that he leaned back in his chair, put down the list of proposed renovations for Castle Carruthers, stared up at Sinclair Ramsay's troubled face, and rasped, "How long ago?"

"Three hours. She was to ride with Lambert at seven, and she did not take a cloak because she told her abigail she meant to return directly."

Carruthers's eyes slipped past him to stare blankly at the rain-spattered windowpane. "With Lambert . . ." he breathed.

Sinclair leaned both hands on the desk-top and said intensely, "No, Meredith! My sister is better bred than that! Even if you believe it of her, can you suppose she would run off leaving Grandmama and me to face you?"

Carruthers hauled himself to his feet. "I can tell you, Ramsay, I'd a sight sooner think it than—"

The door burst open unceremoniously, and Ada Banham ran in, her face streaked with tears. "Oh, sir!" she wailed, running around the desk to hurl herself upon his chest. "I am so fearful for my mistress! It's that black cat! I knew it! A bad omen, if ever—!"

Her voice was growing very shrill. Carruthers, who had barely jerked the sling aside in time, managed to detach her from his cravat and said gently, "I understand your fears, but you do not help by maligning my cat, you know." She smiled tremulously, and he went on, "That's better. Now, tell me, Ada, which groom accompanied Miss Phoebe?"

"None, sir. Miss Phoebe was troubled and told my Henery— I mean, told Mr. Baker that she meant to ride alone." Wringing her hands, she sobbed, "If you was to ask me, some wicked man has seen how lovely she is, and she's . . . she's been took off to the desert, and sold to a wicked—"

Conditt interrupted this dramatic scenario, rushing in, crying urgently, "Sir! Come quick! It's Captain Lambert!"

To the best of his ability, Carruthers ran.

Jeffery and a sturdy lackey were aiding Brooks Lambert into the Great Hall. His tricorne was gone, his powdered head, spattered with crimson on one side, hung low, and his steps were dragging and unsure.

"The blue saloon—quickly!" called Meredith, gesturing to a hovering parlourmaid to open the door.

Lambert was conveyed inside, and lowered onto a faded sofa.

He lay back against the cushions looking very much the worse for wear.

Bending over him, Meredith asked, "Brooks, was Miss Ramsay with you?"

The long, curling lashes fluttered and Lambert looked up dazedly. "Phoebe?" And then, starting up in horror: "Phoebe! My God! I—" But he winced, clutched his head, and sank down again. "They took her!" he moaned, looking at Carruthers in helpless misery. "Those dirty bastards . . . took her!"

Phoebe awoke to cold and dampness. She was lying on a pile of leaves and bracken in a small, dirty room. The door looked solidly sturdy and the only window was set too high in the wall for her to be able to see anything but the leaden sky and one tree branch. A bucket stood in one corner, and a very rickety table held a chipped enamel bowl.

For a while she lay there, so bemused she could not seem to think coherently, but at length she began to wonder why she was here. The only answer that made any sense was that she had been kidnapped and was being held for ransom. She sat up, got to her feet, and went over to lean one ear against the door. She could hear snoring, but no conversation. She pressed on the door latch with nerve-stretching caution, and pushed. The door gave not an inch, and her heart sank to the awareness that it must be strongly barred on the far side.

Fighting panic, she bit her knuckle and turned to the window. She up-ended the bucket and stood on it, but she was not tall enough even then to see out. Perhaps, if she screamed . . . but the window was fastened at the top. She thought, 'What would Meredith do?' She picked up the bucket. Standing well back, she threw it with all her strength. It struck the window with a great crash, then bounced down inches from where she quailed with both arms over her face. Glass showered to the floor. She heard a throaty cursing and ran to the shattered window, screaming for help at the top of her lungs.

The door burst open. Screaming even more lustily, she glanced over her shoulder and saw a big man run in. Her vocal chords seemed to freeze as he came at her with terrifying menace, his shoulders hunched, and with the same hideous mask over his face that she'd seen just before Lambert was struck down.

"So yer awake, me fine Lady Mighty Muck," he leered. "Lovely voice yer got. An' if yer think it worries me—it don't.

Scream yer bloody head orf, mate—ain't no one'll hear yer. All yer done is let the rain in, which serves yer right.''

"What," Phoebe managed, finding her voice, "do you want with me?"

A grin twisted his thick lips, and his eyes travelled her lustfully. "How's about a little slap and tickle . . . ?''

She lifted her small chin another inch higher and, inwardly quaking, eyed him with what was, she hoped, regal scorn.

Another man entered, similarly masked, but of much smaller stature and almost skeletal thinness. He carried a tray on which was a thick earthenware plate containing some dark bread, cheese, a slice of beef, and an apple. The big man took the tray and offered it to Phoebe. "Not like what yer 'customed to, I 'spect, but it'll have to do, since our butler gone an' run orf wi' the washerwoman.''

The second man gave a neighing shriek of laughter. Phoebe ignored them both and turned her head away.

"Look at her, me cove," leered the big man. "All pride and pomp—like the rest o' the nose-in-the-air Quality. Eat yer dindins, Madam Queen, an' if yer a good gal, we'll bring some water, 'cause we knows as Quality folks likes ter be clean.'' He jerked a thumb at the bucket, and said with a sneering laugh, "I reckon yer knows what that's fer. We ain't got no fancy commode, but I reckon ye can fit yer little—''

"Animal! Take your filthy mind and your filthy mouth, and begone from my sight!''

He responded with a grin that he "allus did like a mort wi' spirit," then accompanied his cohort from the room.

Phoebe's seething disgust changed to despair as the sound of heavy bars being replaced came to her ears. She bowed her head into her hands, fighting tears. To weep seemed, in some remote fashion, to betray Meredith, and she sniffed, picked up the tray and, sitting on the inverted bucket, ate her simple meal. Surprisingly, the bread was not stale, the cheese of an excellent quality, and the beef tender. She was finishing the apple when the door opened again. The second man placed a tankard on the floor and, without a word, backed out.

The tankard contained ale. Phoebe was very thirsty and she sipped cautiously. It tasted foul, but she was sufficiently desperate to drink some. It was getting dark and the rising wind blew with chill dampness through the broken window. The ale warmed her, however, so that she did not shiver quite so badly.

It also made her drowsy. Yawning, and surprisingly carefree, she went to her improvised couch and curled up.

A long time afterwards, it seemed, she was vaguely aware of voices. She could not distinguish the words, and was so sunk in sleep that she was unable to rouse sufficiently to force her heavy eyelids open. She was lifted by strong but gentle hands and caught a whiff of pleasant masculine fragrance. As through a thick veil she glimpsed a snowy cravat. A gentleman, evidently. A distant corner of her mind thought, 'They are moving me,' and then she slept again.

✑ *Chapter 16* ✑

Carruthers sat his horse unmoving, so tired that the thought of climbing from the saddle was daunting.

" 'Ere we go, sir. Easy does it."

He blinked down into the crinkle-eyed smile of his head groom. "Hello, Baker. Any news?"

"Message come fer ye, sir," answered the groom in his soft Sussex voice.

Carruthers leaned gratefully on his strong arm, and Baker asked, "Did ye find any trace 'tall, sir?"

"Not a whisper, blast it! The others are still searching, but I'm pretty useless, so I came home. I'll have to call in the military now. No choice."

Baker shook his head. He was all too aware of how slow was the master's usually brisk stride, how drawn the strong face, and he walked with him all the way to the back door of the new wing.

At the steps, Carruthers took a deep breath and pulled back his shoulders. He clapped one hand on the groom's broad shoulder, and went into the house.

Distantly, a woman called excitedly, "The master's come!"

Conditt appeared and hurried to scan him. "Sir—you look—"

"Like the devil, I suppose." Carruthers nodded ruefully. "Feel like it, too. Where's the message that came?"

"We left it on the hall table for you, sir. I'll bring it up, if you will go to your chamber."

"Hell, no. How does Captain Lambert go on? Was Linden here?"

"The Captain has been sleeping, sir, but I believe his man is dressing him now. Dr. Linden was here and said the Captain

223

does not appear to have suffered a concussion. He was—er, not pleased to find you gone out."

"What would he suggest I do?" said Carruthers irritably. "Sit back and wait for Miss Ramsay to be shipped off as a . . . a slave? What have the ladies been doing?"

Conditt had dreaded this moment. "I'm afraid Lady Martha has been rather unwell, sir. The shock, you know."

Carruthers stared at him aghast, then turned about and went quickly up the stairs.

His scratch at the door of the Dowager's bedchamber was answered by her abigail, the big, raw-boned Swedish woman, a little bowed now with years, but still having rosy cheeks and bright eyes. Her face was worried, but she greeted Carruthers eagerly.

"Is that Mr. Meredith?" came a fretful cry.

He called, "Yes, ma'am. You permit that I come to you?"

"Yes, yes. Please."

He trod around the fine Chinese screen and took the gnarled hand tremblingly stretched out to him. The old lady scrutinized him with desperate anxiety. She was very pale and looked ill and older. He experienced a surge of rage that she must suffer, and said in his gentlest voice, "Alas, I have no news, my lady. I am sorrier than I can say."

Her eyes glittered with sudden tears, but she was a thoroughbred and said staunchly, "Not your fault. You must rest, lad. No use in all of us being laid low when—when . . . She *will* be found, won't she, Meredith? She *will* be all right?"

He stepped closer, bent, and kissed her on the forehead. "She will be found, ma'am. As God is my judge, I swear it!"

He felt less confident when he was sprawled in the armchair beside the glowing hearth of his bedchamber, a generous portion of brandy in his glass, and Howell pulling off his dusty riding boots.

"Well," sighed Carruthers wearily, "are you going to ring a peal over me?"

"Under any other circumstances, sir—yes. As it is . . ."

"Quite so. I fancy Mrs. Carruthers stayed by her ladyship?"

"She did, sir. She is resting now. Would you wish I send word?"

Carruthers passed a hand across his eyes. "Had I any good words to send. I do not, more's the pity. Ah—there you are, Conditt." He accepted the letter the butler offered. The hand was neat, but unfamiliar, his name misspelled, and the seal looking to have been compressed with a coin. Breaking it, he said, "My brother and Ramsay should return soon. If they've not found some trace, we—" He checked, his gaze fixed on the message.

You and Otton thought he was all tucked away so you could get the gold. Well, we got a better hand than what you thought. Fact is, we got 2 hands and 2 feet and all the rest of Miss Ramsey. We don't want to hurt her. What we want is Lasels WITH the poem. We know you got him.

You got till noon tomorrow. Then the lady will be sold for our expenses. She won't bring as much as what we'd have got from the reb. Still, it's better than nowt.

If you tell about this letter you won't never see her, and we'll tell all about her naughty little brother. When your ready to make the trade, run the royal banner up your flagpole and we'll send word where to fetch Lasels. The sooner the better for the lady. She's a pretty mort.

The hand Carruthers put over his eyes shook as violently as had Lady Martha's. "Lord . . . God . . . !" he whispered.

Lambert came in without benefit of a knock, his uniform cleaned and pressed, his face pale, and a bandage taped to the side of his head. "Is he awake?" he demanded of the alarmed Howell.

Carruthers lowered his hand and leaned back in the chair. Struggling for composure, he said, "I'm awake. How are you, Brooks?"

"I'm off for my troopers."

Carruthers stood, thanked his man and the butler, and dismissed them.

They bowed and departed, each man slanting a glance of intense resentment at the Captain as they passed.

As soon as the door closed, Carruthers said urgently, "We *cannot* have the military in this. Miss Ramsay is being held for ransom."

"The . . . devil you say!" And then, suspicion coming into his eyes, Lambert demanded, "How d'ye know?"

"A message came. It said in part that if we call in the military, Phoebe will be sold."

"I don't believe you! Where is this message? Let me see it."

Carruthers crumpled the letter in his left hand, strolled to the fire, and dropped it into the flames. He said coolly, "I burnt it."

Lambert's gaze flashed from the grave countenance to the curling letter amid the coals. Starting forward, cursing, he was restrained by a strong grip. "No, Brooks."

"What else did it say that you don't want me to see? Was it from Otton? When I get my hands on that—"

Carruthers's hand on his arm became a fist that seized Lambert's cravat and hauled him closer to a face so transformed by rage that he scarcely recognized it. "What," demanded Carruthers between his teeth, "has Roland Otton to do with this?"

Lambert tore free so savagely that Carruthers was staggered. "It was all a plot we contrived between us. He said he was trying to help me."

His eyes wide and staring, Carruthers whispered a hissing "Otton . . . !"

"Yes, my dear fellow?"

They both spun around at the sound of that drawling, insouciant voice.

Roland Otton, garbed in a deep-purple velvet evening coat, a great amethyst gleaming in his cravat and another on his right hand, his waistcoat a masterpiece and his knee breeches and lilac stockings devoid of the suggestion of a wrinkle, leaned in the doorway, swinging his quizzing glass on a silver chain. "I hear rumours you have made a mull of things, Lambert."

With an inarticulate growl, Lambert made a lunge for him, but Carruthers stepped between them. "Where is she?" he demanded.

Otton frowned a little. "You ask the wrong abductor, dear boy. I could not but pity Lambert's predicament, so I suggested he stage a kidnapping and a subsequent heroic rescue. I did not dream he would be so clumsy as to—"

"Clumsy, is it?" Lambert grabbed for his sabre. "By God, if I thought you had—"

"Be still!" thundered Carruthers, in a voice that startled both his hearers and would have purely terrified his mother. "Whom did you hire, Lambert?"

Flushing darkly, Lambert muttered, "One was a clod named Hessell, and—"

"Ben Hessell?" raged Carruthers. "You allowed Phoebe to fall into the hands of that crudity?" He rounded on Otton. "You damned treacherous hound!"

Otton drew back. "Now, my dear fellow, be reasonable. I

226

merely wrote the scenario. Lambert was in control of the actors and responsible for the welfare of the lady. How should I know he was unable to bring all to a successful conclusion? Now, before you murder me, pray tell me what has transpired.''

Controlling his wrath with a great effort, Carruthers said, ''The lady has been . . . really kidnapped. And is held for—ransom.''

''Far from pretending to strike me,'' Lambert put in, ''Hessell damn near broke my head.''

Otton pursed his lips. ''May one enquire why you stand here jawing? Get after the swine! They've likely not the brains to hide successfully. Call in dear old Mariner. Give him something to do.''

''They,'' gritted Carruthers, ''or whoever is masterminding this ugly plot, had the brains to send me a note warning that if the military are called in, Miss Ramsay will be sold. Among other things. Jeff and Sinclair, together with most of the men, are still out seeking her. There is no trace.''

''Then *pay* their damned blood money!'' raged Lambert. ''You can afford it! Whatever they ask!''

''There is that, of course,'' Otton murmured.

Carruthers snapped, ''There is not! They demand the rebel and his verse, which I cannot provide. Odd, is it not, Roly? The very thing *you* have sworn to come at.''

''Now, Merry, you surely do not think that I—''

''You have warned me you are a rogue, but I did not believe you capable of this kind of villainy.'' His eyes narrowed; he said murderously, ''I tell you now—if that girl is harmed, I'll have your slimy heart out!''

Otton murmured, ''Alas, how can I—''

Glancing to the side, Carruthers realized Lambert had gone. He sprinted to the door and along the hall. Leaning over the stair-rail, he shouted, ''Stop him!''

The two lackeys standing in the lower hall looked up at him in bewilderment. ''Stop who, sir?'' called one.

''Captain Lambert! Don't let him leave the stables! Get out there!''

They ran, Carruthers hurrying after them as best he could, but pausing on the drivepath to grip his arm and gaze helplessly at the horseman who was already cantering across the yard. Brooks Lambert eluded the men who plunged at him, and shouted, ''I don't know what else you were threatened with,

Carruthers. And I don't give a damn! The military are in this, as of now!'' And he was off at the gallop.

Coming up beside Carruthers, Otton murmured, "I really am sorrier than I can say, Merry. If—"

"Then get after him, blast you!" raged Carruthers distractedly. "If he brings in his men, there's no saying what that—that loathsome Hessell will do to her! *Stop him*, for the love of God!"

Otton looked gravely at the anguished face of his good friend, then ran for the stables.

It was a sickly smell, comprised of stale spirits mingled with dirt and sweat. Revolted, Phoebe opened her eyes. Vaguely came the awareness that she was in a different place, a cold, dim room built of stone slabs and with ancient iron braziers set into the massy walls. But the more immediate awareness rendered all others insignificant. Her crude abductor was leaning over her, his eyes red-rimmed and full of desire, his loose mouth breathing fumes of wine, his grimy hands prowling her body greedily. A wild rage burned through her. How *dare* he touch her so? Only Meredith had that right! With a cry of fury, she pushed him away and sprang to her feet.

He was on her like a wild beast, his big hands seizing her roughly. She clawed her nails down his face. He instinctively recoiled and the mask came away in her fingers, revealing the features of Hessell, the villager she had felt sorry for when Meredith had threatened to evict him from his cottage. She pushed him with all her strength and he staggered, his grip on her habit ripping the fabric so that it sagged downward, revealing the white blouse beneath.

Clutching his cheek and mouthing profanities, he sprang at her. She dodged desperately, crying out, and the emaciated man ran in, unmasked, his pock-marked face reflecting dismay. "Are ye daft, man?" he gasped. "You know what he said!"

Hessell checked and stood glowering at Phoebe and fingering his scratches. "See what she done ter me poor face, the bloody vixen!"

"I wouldn't want to be in your shoes when *he* sees it!" He seemed a cut or two above his fellow-conspirator and turned to say apologetically, "I'm sorry about this, miss, but we'll hang if we don't pull it off, so it's all the way, like it or not. I'll fetch you some vittles." He went into the adjoining room, calling over his shoulder for Hessell to watch what he was about.

"Aye, I'll watch it all right," sneered Hessell, his lustful eyes slithering over Phoebe.

Her knees shaking from the reaction, she went over to the heavy wooden bench and sat down.

"Ye're a pretty piece," said Hessell softly, "and ripe, I'll lay odds. What you need is a man, my pet. And what I'd like ter do is . . ." He proceeded to describe what he would like to do.

Phoebe tried not to hear the ugly words, but she began to feel soiled and sick, and thought in a near prayer, 'Meredith, my darling—come. *Please*, come soon!'

Carruthers woke abruptly. He was sprawling in the armchair in the library, a blanket over him, one branch of candles guttering and the fire still burning in the hearth. Momentarily confused, he started up and saw Conditt nodding in the wing-chair opposite. Memory rushed back shatteringly. He tossed the blanket aside.

Conditt started up and came to look at him anxiously. "Are you all right, sir?"

"Why in heaven's name did you let me sleep? Is there any word? Has my brother returned?"

"No to both, I fear, Mr. Meredith. And you *had* to get some sleep."

"What o'clock is it?"

Conditt went quickly to the mantel clock. "Just a little past three, sir." And moved by the despair he read in the shadowed eyes, he said, "They'll find her, sir. Have faith."

"Faith! The poor Scotswomen and children I saw ravished and tortured and slain by Cumberland's orders had faith, I don't doubt!" Carruthers gave a harsh crack of laughter. "Much good it did 'em! Has Captain Otton come back?"

"No, sir."

"Hah! And—my precious nephew?"

Conditt glanced to the window. Scowling, Carruthers paced over and looked into the night. A thin mist shrouded the court-yard, but faintly through it he could see a glow of distant lights. "What . . . the devil?"

"They've been at it since midnight, sir. Captain Lambert and his men. They've got torches and they've been beating all along the Cut. They must be nigh to the Quarry by now."

"Blast his hide!" It was not unlikely, thought Carruthers, that

229

Brooks would decide to search the Keep next. Lance must be brought to another hiding place.

As he'd anticipated, he had a battle on his hands when he told Conditt he meant to go outside for a breath of air, but at last he escaped, knowing the faithful man longed to accompany him, but having no intention of involving him in this treasonable tangle.

The air was clammy and cold, the mist wreathing upward and eddying about him as he walked towards the courtyard of the Keep. The few hours of sleep had restored him, physically, at least. His arm was a bit of a nuisance, but the only thing that mattered was Phoebe, and to be incapacitated and unable to join the search for her was nigh unbearable. Suppose Hessell was abusing her, terrifying her? And she, helpless and all alone! The thought made him writhe and he walked faster but found he was unable to escape the vivid horrors imagination painted.

He crossed the wide immensity of the courtyard head down and went blindly under the great arch of the main gate and across the drawbridge. It was very dark in that shadow and, coming out into the open again, he glanced up and halted.

A horse was standing with its front hoofs on the crumbling step; a tall chestnut. Even as he watched, Rumpelstiltskin shoved his nose at the partly open door and peered inside.

Excitement jolted through Carruthers. Otton was *here*! He certainly had made no attempt to stop Lambert, for Rump could have outrun the bay mare with little effort. Roland was here to search for Lance, unless—He stood motionless, his mouth setting into a thin, hard line. Moving with slow deliberation, he took off the sling and tossed it aside. With his left hand he eased from his pocket the pistol Conditt had insisted he carry. The fingers of his right hand closed around the grip and took the weight. The price paid was instant and sharp, but scarcely felt, for rage was a white heat that shut out all other awareness. He trod softly through the door and into the dank air of the Keep.

"I reckon as she knows who had her taken, sir."

"The devil!" Otton's black eyes flashed wrath as he faced his apologetic henchman. "I told you I was not to be mentioned in front of the lady. By God, Feeney, but she'd best *not* know, else you'll have a damned long wait for your pay!"

"Wasn't none of *my* doing, sir," whined the scrawny rogue.

"Hessell gets ugly when he's put down a drink or two. He was pawing the lady, and—"

"*What?*" With a shout of anger, Otton sprinted for the connecting door, forgetting the mask he'd cut out so carefully, his sword flashing into his hand.

He was in time to hear a loud smack and to see Hessell fall back a step from Phoebe's flushed fury, his hand pressed to a reddened and scratched cheek.

"Filth!" thundered Otton, advancing vengefully.

"Oh, thank God!" gasped Phoebe, hoping against hope that her suspicions were unfounded and that rescue was at hand.

Hessell, drunkenly uproarious, howled, "Cor, that's a good 'un! Don't thank yer Gawd fer *him*, lady! He's the one what—"

A shot rang out deafeningly, followed by another. Otton whirled as Feeney went down clutching his leg, and Meredith Carruthers threw down a smoking pistol and wrenched sword from scabbard. Otton backed away, his sword swinging to the guard position.

With an inarticulate snarl, Carruthers leapt to the attack. Retreating, parrying, blocking, Otton called, "Merry—now do not—Merry, can we . . . not talk?"

His answer was a sizzling quinte thrust that almost had him. He disengaged nimbly, drew in his arm, and attempted a beat on Meredith's blade. Thwarted, he danced aside, then essayed a lightning thrust in tierce. The swords rang together. Phoebe shrank, both afraid and fascinated. Hessell, grinning, was enjoying the furious battle, as hopeful of Otton falling as of Carruthers being the vanquished.

Crawling to the doorway, Feeney croaked, "*Help* him . . . you perishing fool! You want . . . to hang?"

Hessell scowled, but it was truth. He sought about and took up his cudgel.

Meredith parried a strong thrust with a prime parade; he raised his point to the left and, holding his sword with both hands, with the fort of the carte edge beat with all his strength on Otton's blade. Otton's weapon spun from his hand and he gripped his wrist, retreating.

Phoebe screamed, "*Merry!*"

From the corner of his eye Carruthers saw the cudgel whistling down at him. He flung himself to the side. The cudgel missed by a hair, but tore the sword from his grasp. He sprang even as Hessell swung up the cudgel again, and drove his left to Hessell's flabby midriff. The breath departed from the big man

231

in a rush and he sat down without grace, his tongue protruding and his eyes starting from his head.

Again, Phoebe screamed, and Carruthers whirled to find the point of the colichemarde at his throat.

"Meredith," Otton began reasonably, "I really have no wish to hurt you—"

His eyes slits of death, Carruthers panted, *"Saleté . . . !"*

Otton frowned, tensing. The sword point quivered forward, but was checked. He said, "You must know I'd not have allowed her to be hurt."

"You *scum!*" growled Carruthers. "You worthless . . . lying . . . treacherous *dog!*" And with each word, he moved forward on the balls of his feet, his shoulders a little hunched, crimson creeping unnoticed down his right hand. He was moving steadily but with such deliberate slowness that Otton, as steadily retreating, was unprepared when he suddenly jerked to the side. The sword whipped around. Carruthers ducked under it, then sprang. With his left hand he grabbed Otton's sword arm. His right fist clenched and came up from his knees to explode under Otton's chin. Hurled backwards, Otton collapsed and rolled to fetch up face down beside the connecting door.

And it was done. The lust to kill, which had both inflamed and strengthened Carruthers, faded. He became aware at last that his arm was all searing agony from shoulder to fingertips. Gripping it, he staggered, the room rippling before his eyes.

With a soft cry Phoebe started to him.

Hessell crawled to his feet and stood swaying and bemused.

Brooks Lambert ran across the connecting room, jumped Otton's feebly stirring form, and fired without an instant's hesitation. Hessell screamed and went down, crashing into Phoebe as he fell, his blood splattering her gown, his hands clutching frenziedly at her.

Sick and horrified, she shrank away, sobbing hysterically.

Unable to see much of anything, Carruthers sagged against the wall, reaction turning his limbs to water.

Lambert dropped his smoking pistol and swept the girl into his arms. "You are safe now, my dearest heart," he said, his deep voice husky with tenderness. "God forgive me, but you are safe!"

He carried the dazed Phoebe from the room as several troopers ran in, followed by Conditt and a frantic Howell. The troopers bent their attention on Feeney and Hessell. The servants rushed to their sagging employer and aided him outside.

232

Returning exhausted and heavy-hearted from their long and fruitless search, Jeffery, Sinclair, Boles, and their helpers saw bobbing torches in the castle courtyard and went to investigate. They encountered the dramatic little caravan. Despair became elation.

"By Jove!" exclaimed Jeffery, running to his brother's drooping figure. "You've had a bang-up good scrap by the look of you!"

Carruthers lifted a haggard but beaming face, his eyes blue and radiant. "She's safe," he murmured weakly. "By God, Jeff! She's safe!"

In all the excitement, no one noticed that Rumpelstiltskin and his wayward master had quietly slipped away.

Rousted from his cosy bed, George Linden was appalled to learn of Phoebe's ordeal. The girl was pallid and shivering. He pronounced her in a state of shock, gave the happily tearful Ada draughts and tablets and instructions, and embarked on the long trek to Carruthers's chambers. He was unusually restrained, and no blistering denunciations were levelled at his contumacious patient. He had already learned most of what had happened from a nervously babbling Phoebe, and he worked with quiet efficiency, Carruthers so sunk in exhaustion that the surgeon's efforts were scarcely felt.

Linden withdrew, engaged in a conference with Jeffery that left the youth pale and shaken, and started on the return journey through the buildings to seek out the Dowager. Although it was only six in the morning, she was wide awake and received him with bright eyes, an improved pulse and colour, and a breakfast tray that brightened his own eyes. They enjoyed a pleasant chat while he applied himself to the contents of the tray. When he departed, saying he would call in again later, he informed my lady that she was the only sensible individual in a madhouse.

Carruthers slept for twenty-six hours, awakening shortly after eight o'clock the following morning. He was drowsy and languid and perfectly willing to remain in bed, but he asked to be shaved, sure that soon or late he would have visitors. The first of these was Lady Martha, who crept in just after he had finished a light breakfast. Her gratitude was tearful and touching. He was, as she always had known, the perfect husband for her granddaughter. He was endowed with every virtue, his amused reminders of his sometimes sharp tongue and quick temper dismissed airily. Brooks Lambert may have carried her granddaughter to safety, but my lady knew very well who was the real hero.

By this time flushed and embarrassed, Carruthers asked about Phoebe and was assured she was peacefully asleep and would be brought to see him very soon. My lady stroked his hair fondly, beamed upon him, and departed.

Carruthers was dozing when the door opened again, and he looked to it with a leap of the heart.

It was, however, Brooks Lambert who trod softly across the carpet. "My very dear fellow," he said, having dismissed Howell by saying he required a private word with the master, "how may I ever thank you?"

Carruthers could think of several ways, but he said with a glinting eye that there was not the need. "What I did," he said minatorily, "I did for Miss Phoebe. And it would have been unnecessary but for your nonsense."

Lambert stood by the bed, smiling fondly down at him. "Merry," he said, "are you able to stand?"

Carruthers stared at him. "Of course."

Lambert pulled back the covers. "Then there is something you must see." He waited while Carruthers clambered from the bed, then led him to the window.

The castle courtyard was full of redcoats. A chill presentiment shivered down Carruthers's spine. "Your men?"

"Yes. We are to search the Keep. I thought I should tell you. . . ."

✑ *Chapter 17* ✑

Jeffery slipped into the bedchamber and stood hesitant for a
moment. Meredith was lying very still, his left arm across his
eyes. Half inclined to creep out again, Jeffery was shocked when
his brother lowered his arm. "Oh, gad! You're feeling dreadful.
I am sorry. I'll go."

"I'm all right. Are they gone?"

Jeffery trod closer to the bed and straddled a straight-backed
chair. "So you knew. Lord, but I thought I'd have a seizure
when I saw them prowling the Keep. Yes, they're gone, thank
God."

"Amen to that. But we must act, Jeff. If Fotheringay is able
to bring his damnable pack here . . . !"

"I know it. I daren't go near Lance, but Sin slipped over there
at dawn." He paused, looking grim.

"Fretting himself to flinders, is he?"

"He makes haste backwards, I fear. If Rosalie wasn't taking
care of him, I've no doubt he'd have dragged himself off by now,
and been taken. He's half crazed between anxiety for us and the
need to deliver the cipher. Lord, I hate to worry you with it
when you're so flattened, but—what the deuce are we to do?"

"Deliver that cipher! And I'm not flattened, Jeff. Just trying
to work out a plan."

"I wish to heaven we could forget the damnable treasure!
Neither you nor I are for the Stuart Cause. How in the devil we
are involved, I cannot fathom."

Meredith gave him a slow smile. "I fancy it is partly loyalty
to a good friend, who'd not fail us in like trouble; and partly
that these poor Jacobite families have suffered enough and have
a right to the return of their valuables."

"You're right, of course. Still, I wish Rosalie was not at risk."

"So do I. She's a brave girl. If we're discovered, we must shield her, at all costs."

"Absolutely! I told her yesterday that she should not involve herself. She just said, 'We're all friends, aren't we?' Bless her, what a grand—" He broke off as a clatter of hoofs and shouted commands rang out. Sprinting to the window, he swore. "It's a confounded colonel!"

Meredith sat up. "Fotheringay?"

"He's tall and thin. Walks as if the ground burnt his feet."

"That's him! Blast! They're bringing up the big guns!"

"Well, you're in no case to front one. I'll tell him you're too ill."

"He'd be sure to think it an evasion. No, I shall have to see the varmint, but be damned if I'll do it lying in bed. Help me over to the window-seat, there's a good fellow."

The ensuing interview was unpleasant. Colonel Fotheringay, tall, spare, with thin lips and hard dark eyes, entered unannounced, firmly closing out a spluttering and indignant Lucille. He was not a bullying man, but his words were snapped out, his keen stare never wavered, and Carruthers was subjected to such a barrage of questions that it was all he could do to keep his wits about him and reply without contradicting himself.

Surely, suggested the Colonel, it was odd that Miss Ramsay had said the kidnappers were peasants. Carruthers's confirmation of Miss Ramsay's statement brought a mirthless smile and the remark that it was damned arrogant of the clods to have hidden their victim in the home of her betrothed. Probably, offered Carruthers warily, this had been done because the Keep was the last place anyone would think to look and had already been searched by the military. The Colonel deplored the fact that a lady of Quality should have been so mauled by the fellows. "Scum of the earth," he said contemptuously. Carruthers agreed. "Odd, though," murmured Fotheringay with his thin smile, "not many peasants are skilled in swordplay. . . ." Beginning to sweat and not daring to name Otton, Carruthers described a fight in which he had been obliged to draw steel against Hessell's long cudgel.

"I believe you remarked you had entered the Keep on a whim," mused Fotheringay. "Is it your habit to carry both sword and pistol while in your home?"

"My life has been attempted a time or two of late, Colonel."

"So I heard. And confess myself astonished that no charges have been brought in that connection. Criminals, my dear sir, whatever their walk of life, must not be allowed to escape, else there's no telling where it may end. Take these damned Jacobites, for instance. You'd not believe it, but there are many sympathizers among the local aristocracy. Even so, I do assure you that they, and any who aid them, will be brought to book." The hard eyes challenged Carruthers's cool stare. "Not that it affects you, of course. I heard you conducted yourself well on the battlefield and that you have never—so far as we know—been in sympathy with Charles Stuart."

"I'm glad someone had a good word to say for me, sir. I fancy you will have managed to extract information from that rogue Hessell."

To his surprise, the Colonel's dark face flushed. "Unfortunately, he was presumed to be dead, and thus was overlooked for a brief period while the troopers turned their attention to the other rascal, Feeney."

Incredulous, Carruthers said, "You never mean Hessell was allowed to escape?"

"I'd not use just those terms," replied Fotheringay, stiffening. "He did get away, but in a dying condition, apparently."

"He appears to have been pretty spry. Still, you have Feeney, and—"

"Feeney tried to escape while being escorted to the post. He was shot."

Carruthers stared at him, and the Colonel seemed relieved when Jeffery came in and remarked pointedly that his brother looked "worn to a shade."

Fotheringay offered his apologies, thanked Carruthers for his cooperation, and took himself off. Very soon afterwards the troop went clattering down the drivepath.

Turning from the window, the brothers exchanged a grin.

"Phew!" sighed Meredith.

"Put you through the wringer, did he?"

"He's a shrewd man, and a good officer. I had to lie like a trooper."

"Do you think you convinced him?"

"Lord knows." Meredith sat down and settled his legs across the cushioned window-seat. "I suspect I'm no great hand at evasion."

Jeffery's handsome face became still. "Oh . . . I don't know. . . ."

Half-laughing, Meredith said, "Impertinent chub! When have you ever caught me at such tricks?"

Despite the knowledge that this was not the best time, Jeffery flung the gauntlet anyway. He said quietly, "Perhaps in the matter of Rosalie."

A second of taut silence. Carruthers, eyes bleak with anger, snapped, "Pot calling the kettle black?"

Flushing, Jeffery declared, "I would have been overjoyed had she returned my affection. But—I am not betrothed."

"Neither," said Meredith in a voice of steel, "is she likely to accept a slip on the shoulder from you."

"That ain't fair! My intentions are honourable, but I'm not supposed to notice when *you* carry on an *affaire* with her right under Miss Ramsay's nose?"

Meredith swung his legs down and faced his brother squarely. "I think you've said enough. In point of fact, you've said too damned much! Will you leave now—or shall I throw you out the door!"

"Why? Because I follow the precepts you and Mama have always taught me? Preach but not practice, is that it?"

Very white about the mouth, Meredith stood. Jeffery's head tilted upward. The droop of the mouth, the set of the jaw brought a softening to Meredith's harsh expression. He said, "I wish—" His lips closed, then he went on, "Rosalie has a special place in my heart. She always has; she always will. But—"

"But she is not a lady of Quality. I see." A new and icy hauteur in tone and manner, Jeffery said, "I came to receive my orders."

Meredith scowled at him. Then, sitting down wearily, he said, "Oh, very well. Try if you can get to Birch Hill. Poor Lockwood must be fretted to flinders. Tell him Lance is improving and that we must get him away—fast. He may be able to suggest some plan. If troopers stop you, say you carry a letter to the Squire from Lady Martha—she told me she was writing one, and I said you'd deliver it."

"Very good. Anything else?"

"Only—Jeff . . . Hell. No."

"I'll be off then." His back ramrod-straight, Jeffery strode across the room and went out.

Colonel Fotheringay's interrogation of Carruthers appeared to have been too much for the invalid. Three times Phoebe went with her grandmother to see him, but on each occasion they were met at the door by Howell, who told them regretfully that his master was fast asleep and would likely not wake for the rest of the day. Disappointed, and angered by Fotheringay's tactics, Phoebe knew also a vague unease. She passed the day with Lucille and her grandmother, went with them for a drive in the drizzly afternoon, and later had an anxious conference with Sinclair and Jeffery in the hushed privacy of the enormous state ballroom of the Elizabethan wing. Jeffery looked strained and told them that Meredith had sent him over to Birch Hill. "Jove, but I'd a time," he said ruefully. "There are troopers behind every blade of grass! Lockwood was so grateful for my news of Lance, it was pathetic. Merry had hoped he would have some idea of how to get Lance clear, but all he said was that whatever Merry decided to do, he'd back to the hilt."

Sinclair grunted. "Does he fancy we can keep Lance hidden here forever? When those dragoons were searching the Keep this morning, I expected to be hauled off to face a firing squad at any instant! Good thing Lambert was commanding, eh Phoebe?"

"Yes, indeed, for had he found poor Lieutenant Lascelles, I am very sure he'd not betray us."

"If he could have helped it," said Jeffery. "I'm only glad he don't know about the secret room."

Sinclair asked, "Do you know where your brother hid the cipher?"

"No. He wouldn't tell me." His lips tightened. "He was in one of his black moods this morning." In a lighter tone, he added, "And not a great deal more pleasant when I took my mother up this afternoon."

Phoebe looked at him sharply. "You saw Meredith this afternoon?"

"Well, Mama was anxious, you know."

She said nothing, and the little meeting broke up after various plans were put forth only to be rejected because of some flaw.

Returning to her chamber to change for dinner, she thought worriedly, 'He could see his brother and his mama, but he was too ill and too tired to see me. . . .'

Unperturbed by the drizzle, Colonel Fotheringay stood beside the village pond, watching in amusement the gnarled old hands that caressed his rangy mare, and listened to Joseph Smith's pipingly knowledgeable assessment of the animal.

"Foine deep barrel, allus likes t'see that, Oi does. And good straight legs. Jes' right in the back, too. Ye got y'sel' a nice little lady here, General. Nice."

"Colonel. You sound as if you know your horses, Mr. Smith."

"Ar. Well, Oi were part owner o' the smithy at one time, Oi were. Smith's Smithy, they useter call it." Joseph dug a frail elbow in the Colonel's side and cackled, and Fotheringay laughed dutifully. "Been doing a powerful lot o' riding these days, aintcha?" the old man continued with a sly twinkle. "Up an' down all England, Oi do hear. Does ye ever catch any o' they Jakeybite fellas?"

"Oh, many," declared Fotheringay, a steely look coming into the dark eyes. "To their sorrow."

"An' yer pleasure, eh?"

Fotheringay's colour deepened, and he shot a sharp look at the frail old villager. "You feel an empathy for these traitors, do you?"

Joseph took off his sagging hat, scratched his head cautiously, since his hair was not quite so thick as it used to be, and said craftily, "Maybe yes—maybe no." He giggled. "Seein' as Oi dunno what ye means."

"I mean that you feel sorry for the men who would have seized the throne."

"Whaffor?" asked Smith, more puzzled than before. "Your pardon?"

"What they want with the throne? Not much ye can do wi' a throne, now, be there? Take me, f'r instance. Was Oi to sneak a throne inter me cottage, it'd stick out like a sheep draggin' home a wolf by the throat. Not nacheral. Why," he went on, warming to his theme, "Oi do doubt as even Mr. Meredith up to the Hall could—"

Eyes glinting with irritation, the Colonel interrupted, "Mr. Smith, I am searching for an escaped rebel. A very special rebel. With a large reward on his hea—" Sensing a possible pitfall, he rephrased hurriedly, "With a large reward offered to whomsoever helps us find him."

"Be that so?" Joseph blinked respectfully at this impressive symbol of military might. "Why then, Oi reckon as ye'll catch him quick-like. Them rewards allus helps ye chaps bring home the bacon—'specially if ye cannot catch him yerselves. Oi heered as he was all smashed-up like. One would think it wouldn't be too hard fer a gert powerful chap like ye be, to—"

Controlling himself with difficulty, Fotheringay snapped, "It is your duty, sir, as a patriotic citizen of—"

"Good evening, Colonel," said a soft pretty voice.

The Colonel jerked around and lifted his riding crop in a polite salute to the little village beauty who approached, a basket of herbs on one softly rounded arm, and the hood of her cloak framing her gentle face. "Out in the rain, Miss Smith? I was attempting to persuade your grandfather to cooperate with us."

"I heard you, sir, but Grandfather knows nothing of such matters, and could not—"

"Well, that just shows how wrong ye be, Rosalie Smith," interposed the old man irritably. "Oi knows everything what goes on in Dewbury Prime, Oi does. *And* in Dewbury Minor," he added, drawing himself up to his full fifty-five inches.

"Now, Granddad—"

"Hush, girl! And let yer elders speak! Oi'll tell'ee summat, Colonel Foggerinhay," offered Joseph, his eyes suddenly cunning.

Dimples flashed beside Rosalie's ruddy lips. The Colonel, his own mouth a thin line, almost corrected that hideous mispronunciation, but decided he'd best not disturb the old fool's train of thought or it might never be restored, and one could not tell what he might have seen.

"*Oi* doan't know nought," Joseph went on, sidling closer to the officer. "But Oi knows a chap as knows more'n what he oughter, an' was ye t'keep a close watch on *him*, ye'd have that there bacon o' yourn in jig time!"

Rosalie stepped forward, uneasy, but the old man thrust out a claw-like hand to keep her away. "A big reward, he says, Rosie. New shoes fer ye, lass, and a new pipe fer me, maybe! Right, General?"

"Most assuredly. Who is this man, Smith?"

"No, no. He bean't a smith." Joseph peered around the drowsing village street as though Charles Stuart himself and two hundred Highland Scots lurked behind the cottages. "He be a—*parson*," he hissed.

To have been confined to his bedchamber for two days was galling to Carruthers, especially in view of the extreme danger hanging over his friend and his loved ones. That he had very little time to get the cipher through, and Lance safely out of England, chafed at his nerves. Hour after hour, he racked his brains trying to come up with a workable plan, but between the throbbing of his arm and the crushing weight of his own troubles he achieved nothing but a heightened sense of frustration. Towards evening he insisted that Howell help him get dressed, and he was sitting before a small fire feeling rather more like a functional human being when a sharp knock at the door was followed by the appearance of a grim-faced Jeffery. Howell left them, and Carruthers asked urgently, ''Are you not at dinner?''

''Yes, but the ladies have withdrawn, and I excused myself and slipped up here. We entertain only the Merritts and old Commodore Purcell tonight, at all events. The other guests sent regrets because of all the patrols lurking about. Merry—the most devilish thing! Large numbers of reinforcements have come into the district! The village fairly swarms with dragoons, and 'tis rumoured that by tomorrow, troopers will be posted along all roads and byways in a fifty-mile radius!''

''Lord, but they're hot after poor Lance! How do you know this?''

''Goodall came in from the village with that cloth his wife has woven for Mama. He was in a rare state; said it had taken him three hours to reach here, because he'd been refused the right to pass until the soldiers had searched his cart, and he had to wait an hour while they all but stripped some passengers from the Portsmouth Machine.'' He paused, then added, ''Did you know they're beginning to call them 'stage-coaches' now? In London—Oh, what rubbish I talk! Merry, it looks as though, if we're to get that cipher through, it must be tonight!''

Meredith swore. ''Jeff, get over to the Keep if you can, and bring back the cipher. I returned it to Lascelles after I failed with the dratted thing. Hurry, old lad. If what you heard is truth, we may have dragoons here again at any minute!''

Jeffery left at once, and Carruthers settled down to wait. Ten minutes crawled past. Twenty. At the end of half an hour, he decided that Jeff must have been obliged to return to the dining room. He dare not send down a request for him to come upstairs, and he waited in ever-growing impatience. At ten o'clock he judged the tea-tray would have been carried in. He sent Howell down to the withdrawing room with instructions to peep in and see if Mr. Jeffery was present. When the valet returned with word that Jeffery had apparently not returned, and that Mrs. Carruthers was ''most put out,'' Carruthers knew that something was wrong. He told Howell he would not require him for the rest of the evening. The faithful man hesitated, but Carruthers said he had a personal matter to discuss with his brother, who would likely come up soon, and could help him, if necessary, and the valet reluctantly went away.

Carruthers waited for a short interval, then managed, with a little difficulty, to throw a cloak around his shoulders. He slipped into the hall. A footman stood at his mother's parlour door, chatting idly with her abigail, but no other servants were in sight. He walked quickly and quietly along the hall and went down the side stairs and along to the back door.

Outside, the air was clean and cold. The cobblestones of the courtyard gleamed in the faint reflection of candlelight from the windows of the house, but the rain had stopped. The wind had come up, putting a deeper chill on the air. He thought, 'One might suppose it to be October rather than August,' and stood unmoving, eyes narrowed and searching. There was no sign of anyone, and he strode across the courtyard to the proud vault of the drawbridge. He crouched, his left hand grabbing for the pistol in his belt as he detected a shifting in the denser shadows by the moat.

Jeffery whispered, "Merry? Gad, but I thought you would never come!"

He sat with his back against the wall, accompanied by Satan, who uttered a friendly trill as Meredith put up the pistol and hurried forward.

"What is it? Are you all right?"

"The most nonsensical thing," groaned Jeffery. "I was running, and it was dark, you know, and—this damned cat jumped down on me from the drawbridge and fairly scared the wits out of me! I turned my stupid ankle on a slippery cobblestone, and be dashed if I can walk on it!"

Meredith at once knelt beside him. Satan, all innocent ingratiation, immediately began to twine around him, and Jeffery gave him a light swat and told him he was a blasted pest, and to be gone. The big cat shot off with an irked yowl. Meredith groped in the dark for his brother's ankle and ran his left hand over it gently. "Lord, it's swollen! What a fool I am, to have waited about, doing nothing. I thought you'd been obliged to go back to the guests."

"Not your fault. Is it—broken?"

"Jupiter, does it feel that miserable? I'd guess it was sprained, but I suppose one of the smaller bones could be broken. If I give you a hoist, can you stand?"

With his aid, Jeffery managed to get up and balance himself

243

against the wall. He leaned on his brother's good arm and hopped along painfully. "I wasn't able to get the cipher for you," he said. "Lance was properly miffed when I asked for it. He insisted he'd *never* given it to you, and that he would not do such a thing. He says it is *his* responsibility, and that he'd given his word never to let any other take it. He became so agitated I finally just left the silly fellow."

"He was half delirious when he let me take it. Perhaps he has no recollection of having done so. I fancy we'll have a fine time prying it out of him now." They struggled on, and Meredith gave a breathless laugh. "A fine pair of rescuers! I ride into an ambush, and you trip over your feet."

Jeffery chuckled, but after a minute said awkwardly, "Merry, I'm sorry about—what I said this morning. I chose the deuce of a time to—"

"Oh, stubble it! I must get used to the notion that you're a man now, and—"

Satan shot past, Justice in hot pursuit, baying furiously.

"Curst animals," grunted Meredith. "That uproar will bring someone! Here we are, Jeff. Now when we get inside, I—"

Phoebe, still wearing her evening gown, swung the door open. She held a lighted candle but set it down as she ran to help Jeffery on the other side. "I thought it was Sinclair," she said. "He came to my room in search of Jeff, and when we couldn't find either of you, he started over to the Keep. Where shall we take him, Merry?"

He nodded to a closed door. "In here. It was the butler's study when this wing was in full use, but is seldom opened nowadays."

The room was panelled and neat and smelled of beeswax polish. Meredith guided Jeffery to a chair. "Look after him for a minute, will you? I'll find Sinclair."

"I'll go," said Phoebe.

"No. It's raining. I can—"

She said with fond exasperation, "*Will* you stop taking everything on your shoulders, love!" and, appropriating his cloak, swung it about her and ran into the night.

For a moment he stared rather blankly at the closed door, then he drew the curtains and lit another candle. "Now let's have a look at that ankle."

They had scarcely begun to examine the injury than Phoebe and Sinclair came in, supporting the fugitive between them.

"Another cripple," remarked Sinclair ironically.

Lascelles sank weakly into a chair.

Meredith exclaimed, "Lord! Where was he?"

Sinclair answered, "Halfway across the courtyard, looking properly drunk."

"Lance, you idiot," said Meredith, peering into his friend's thin face. "What did you think you were about?"

"Thought I was stronger . . . dammit!" Lascelles gave a wry smile. "Still, I am—am going along better now."

Sinclair gave a derisive snort.

Phoebe, who, much to Jeffery's embarrassment, had been inspecting his ankle, said, "I think nothing is broken, but it is a nasty sprain, and should be bound."

"We'll haul him upstairs in a minute," said Meredith. "Lance, things are getting too sticky. You must let me—" He jerked around as, again, the door was flung open.

"So here you are," said Lucille fretfully, holding Justice's collar. "Did you hear all the barking? I—" She stopped, her bewildered gaze travelling the four young men who, with varying degrees of difficulty, had stood at her coming. Behind her, Lady Martha whispered, "My . . . dear God!"

"L-Lancelot . . . ?" quavered Lucille uncertainly. "But— you are hurt, and, poor boy, how very ill you look. Wh-why do you wear Meredith's new coat? Why are you all . . . in here, so quietly? I—I do not—Aah!" A hand flew to her throat and the colour drained from her face, leaving the twin spots of rouge in bright relief against her pallor. "Merry! Lance was always wild, but—He *cannot* be—You would not *allow* him here, if . . ."

Carruthers said softly, "I'm afraid he is. And I would. He is my friend."

"And I am your *mother*! And—oh! You have involved *Jeffery*! And—and our *guests* in this ghastly business! Are you run quite *mad*?"

He did not reply but moved quickly to grasp Lascelles's arm as that unhappy individual made for the door. "Sit down and behave yourself," he ordered gruffly, thrusting him back into the chair.

Sinclair said in a clear, firm voice, "You mistake it, Mrs. Carruthers. I involved Meredith. He did not involve me."

Lucille stared at him miserably.

Lady Martha fixed her grandson with a cool stare. "Are you in sympathy with the Stuarts, Sinclair?"

245

He hesitated. "Say rather, I help where I can. And I mean to help Lascelles, or Lockwood, in any way possible, ma'am."

She nodded, accepting that.

"As do I," said Jeffery.

Lucille wailed and dissolved into sobs. "They are just boys, and—and have no understanding of the horror they br-bring down upon us all. But—but *you* know, Meredith! How *could* you allow it?" She turned her anger on Lascelles. "Do you see what you have done? Why must you come here, and—"

Unspeakably wretched, Lascelles shrank, and pleaded, "Merry—for the love of heaven, let me—"

"Run headlong to sure death?" Carruthers said with stern implacability. "Mama, if you ask me to deliver Lance up to be hacked to pieces in front of a yowling mob, the answer is no!" The autocratic lift of his hand quieted her remonstrance. "My apologies, but talking will pay no toll. Lance, there is no question but that you are too weak to essay a wild ride, even were there no soldiers hunting you. We've about run out of time. I'm afraid it's tonight or never. Give me your blasted cipher and—"

"No!" His white face ravaged, but proud and determined still, Lance cried, " 'Fore God, have I not endangered you sufficiently? And never mind that rubbish about my having given it you before, for I'd not sink so low. It is *my* responsibility. *My* risk." He gave his friend a smile that spoke volumes. "Because you and your brother were so insanely loyal as to risk your necks for me, I am rested and clean and have eaten well. I have not the words to thank you—and the Ramsays, for what you have done. But—'tis enough. I shall do, now."

"For about three miles—maybe," observed Meredith.

Sinclair muttered, "Or three minutes!"

"Is that cipher as important as you believe," said Meredith, "you'd as well destroy it now as try to deliver it yourself. You'd be taken within the hour." He shook Lascelles's shoulder gently. "Lance—have some sense. You *know* how weak you are. You'd simply not get through a countryside swarming with dragoons."

Lockwood muttered, "So I am to stand back and allow you to risk your life for a cause you despised. I thank you! I am not such a poltroon!"

Phoebe said, "Lieutenant, I honour you for your courage, but—is there perhaps someone who could come here for the cipher?"

"No!" shrieked Lucille.

Lascelles stared at her, bitting his lip in agonized indecision.

Meredith prompted coolly, "Well, Lance?"

"There is . . . perhaps. But—"

"I'll go and fetch him," said Sinclair.

For the first time looking directly at Phoebe, Carruthers saw her blanch, but she said nothing. Almost imperceptibly, the hard line of his mouth softened.

Lucille flew up and ran to grip his hand. "Meredith, you *must* not let him go! Don't let him bring a Jacobite here! Do you *want* us all to die by the axe?"

Her fear was intense and perfectly legitimate. Appreciating that, Carruthers put his arm around her and said repentantly, "I am indeed sorry to cause you such anxiety, my dear, but we must pray that—"

She intervened with the fury of terror, "There is no need for prayers! Always you have vowed you love me, but *now*, when our lives are at stake, it becomes very clear that you would willingly sacrifice Jeffery and me for your traitorous friend, who has brought about his own downfall! And why you should—"

"Have done, ma'am!" Lady Martha had restrained herself for as long as she could, and now said explosively, "Your son is head of his house and has arrived at a decision. It is one that I personally applaud, for a man should stand by his friends."

Moaning in despair, Lucille subsided into her handkerchief.

Carruthers slanted a grateful look at the old lady.

Lascelles stood and said humbly, "Ramsay—you have been so good. I—I wish to heaven I might ride in your stead. God go with you!"

Flushing, Sinclair gripped his frail hand. "Tell me to whom I must go."

Lascelles bent to murmur in his ear.

Carruthers said, "You will wish to say your farewells to your ladies, Sin. I'll go and see about a mount for you."

He went outside and made his way to Baker's quarters. The groom was still up and soon had Elbow Grease saddled. Sinclair ran into the barn booted and spurred, and Carruthers wished him luck, and asked softly, "Are you clear as to your route?"

"Aye. I know where the village lies." Sinclair mounted up, exclaiming, "Jove, but I was surprised when Lascelles spoke the name of the man I'm to bring! I'd never have suspected that one!"

"At least," said Carruthers whimsically, "should you be intercepted, you will have no difficulty inventing reasons for fetching him here."

✑ Chapter 18 ✑

When Carruthers returned to the Tudor wing the little group was still gathered in the butler's study. His mother sat drying her tears, Phoebe was folding a tablecloth, and Lady Martha was knotting a tight bandage she had bound about Jeffery's ankle. He stood as his brother entered, and said with a flourish, "*Voila!* I am restored! We have with us a physician *par excellence!*"

"Yes, and you will be the better for keeping off that foot, lad," said Lady Martha. "It's a nasty sprain."

Phoebe asked anxiously, "Is my brother away, Mr. Carruthers?"

"Yes, ma'am. Pray try not to be overset. He is up on one of my fastest horses, and if he keeps his wits about him will likely have little trouble."

"What is he to say should he be stopped?"

Carruthers glanced at Lady Martha.

Rolling an unused strip of linen, she said, "Oho! So I'm the excuse, am I? What is it? Am I ill, or merely dead?"

He smiled. "Certainly not the latter, ma'am, but sufficiently ill to—"

The door clicked open. Rosalie Smith stood on the threshold, her hood fallen back, her cheeks bright from the blustering wind. Loathing the shameless hussy, Phoebe thought with a pang, '*Has* she to be so very pretty?'

Lucille said in dismay, "Whatever are you doing here at this hour, child? Oh, my heavens! Something else is wrong! And why not? The whole world has gone mad!"

The girl's hazel eyes had flashed to the fugitive. She said an anxious "Lance!" and started towards him.

Even more swiftly, Carruthers moved to intercept her. "He's asleep," he said, taking her hand in a caressing way that brought

248

a frown to Jeffery's face. "I fancied you safe home long since. Why are you come back?"

She glanced apprehensively at the others, and Meredith said, "Never worry, m'dear. Everyone here knows about our fugitive."

"It is only," said Rosalie, in her shy, cultured little voice, "that there are so many troopers come. They are everywhere, and Lance is so desperate to deliver his message, I was afraid he might try something silly."

Carruthers drew up a chair for her. "Has that confounded Fotheringay been frightening you?"

"No." She gave a mischievous smile. "He is gone away, thank goodness."

"He is? Do you know where?"

Dimples peeped beside her mouth. "I do, because it was my wicked grandfather's doing."

Fascinated by her every movement, by every inflection of her soft voice, Jeffery asked, "What has the old gentleman been about? More of his fables?"

"Yes, indeed. He is *such* a rascal! Only think, he has convinced the Colonel that a pure *et sans reproche* gentleman is in fact a go-between for the Jacobites, and that if he is watched, he will soon or late lead the way to the fugitive and those who shelter him." She gave a little gurgle of laughter. "Oh, Merry, I wish you might have seen the Colonel's face as he rid out. So grimly determined! I wonder he did not withdraw all the troops and straight away go and arrest the poor creature."

Jeffery chuckled. "What a trickster Joseph is."

"And now a great celebrity at The Meredyth Arms, and cannot stop laughing about it, which is really very naughty of him, having directed suspicion to a man of the cloth!"

Carruthers was suddenly breathlessly still, and Lascelles, who had been lying back, watching Rosalie through half-closed eyes, jerked himself upright. "Who?" he cried, patently horrified.

She looked from one taut face to the other and said with an uncertain smile, "Don't worry—'tis the last gentleman could ever be involved."

"Who?" demanded Meredith.

"Why, Father Charles Albritton, the new curate who—"

Groaning, Lascelles bowed his face into his hands.

Carruthers turned pale, stood and muttered, "Well, that's *properly* dished us!"

"What is it? Oh, what is it?" cried Lucille nervously.

Phoebe gasped, "N-never say it . . . it really *is* Mr. Albritton?"

Lucille let out a shriek. Lady Martha, very white, said threadily, "Then—my grandson rides to his death. . . ."

Struggling up, Lascelles said, "I'll go after him at once!"

"Noble of you," Carruthers muttered cynically. "God forbid you should ride to *my* rescue in your present state!"

"Of course he cannot go!" Jeffery stood also. "Have a horse saddled, Merry. I'll take a short cut and—"

"No!" Lucille threw her arms around him. "You're hurt! And besides, it's too dangerous! Meredith will go!"

Phoebe was sick with fear for her brother, but she gave a gasp at this, and despite her own terror, Lady Martha pursed her lips disgustedly.

No less appalled, Jeffery said, "The deuce, Mama! You are forgetting that Merry has a wound and—"

"No, but—but he is so strong," she babbled frantically. "And always he knows just what to do and—and rescues us from our little predicaments. He won't let us down, will you, Merry, dearest?"

His eyes empty, he answered, "I trust not, Mama. I'll go, of course."

"Like hell!" Jeffery freed himself from his mother's clinging arms and said wrathfully, "Will you for once give me credit for having a *little* backbone? No, Mama! Be still, if you please!" Flushed, he snarled at his brother, "*Always*, it is you! *You* know what is best; *you* will provide; *you* will advise us! Well, now it's *my* turn! I've a slightly sprained ankle. You've a wound Linden has warned me is badly inflamed. Do you fancy I mean to sit here like—like a cowering weasel while—"

Lady Martha intervened sharply, "Do you stand here, arguing, neither of you will be in time to save my grandson!"

"Very true," agreed Meredith, starting to the door. "But we're a poor lot. Sinclair has a good ten-minute lead over two cripples."

"*I* am not crippled," declared Phoebe. "And I can ride as fast as either of you!"

"Through countryside a'swarm with ragtag soldiery and bounty hunters? I think not, madam! Jeff—we'll ride together." Ignoring his mother's heart-broken cry, Meredith turned to Rosalie. "Run to the stables, love, and find Henry Baker. Tell him to saddle Rogue and Mouser at once." She flew, and he said to Lady Martha, "My man knows of this. Will you please go and ask him for dark cloaks and a brace of loaded pistols for my brother and me?" She went out at once, Phoebe accompanying her.

Jeffery limped over to his mother and took her into the hall, talking to her gently.

Lascelles, the picture of dejection, sat with his fair head downbent. Carruthers turned from watching Lucille walk away, and went to place a comforting hand on his shoulder. "My poor idiot, do not look so distraught. It was not your intent to involve us. A poor thing friendship would be were we loyal only when times are good." He smiled into the strained grey eyes that lifted to meet his own. "Now stop being a block, and give me your damned cipher."

Lascelles froze, staring at him.

"You just ran out of choices," Meredith pointed out. "We cannot bring Albritton here now, short of inviting Fotheringay along. Your only hope of delivering your message is to entrust it to me."

Briefly, Lascelles struggled with conscience, then he sighed. "Yes. You've the right of it. But—dammitall, Merry, if anything happens to you—God! How shall I live with myself?"

"I sympathize," said Carruthers drily. "Come *on*, man!"

Lascelles stood and unbuckled his swordbelt. The dark leather was overlaid here and there with strips of tooled pigskin, and from beneath one of the strips he pried a carefully folded scrap of parchment. Carruthers already knew the hiding place, but did not betray that knowledge. He had not read the cipher the first time he carried it, but now, when Lascelles handed it to him, he scanned it, and read,

III

Odd, how gently they come home,
Wooing peace once more.
Riding off they were not so.
Is it ever thus with war?
Frequently, it seems mankind
Terrifies or trembles.

"Is that all?" he muttered. "A frippery thing like that, to cause so much of death and grief?"

Lascelles gripped his shoulder. "If they catch you with it, Merry, you will likely know both!"

* * *

Mounted on Spring, and facing Meredith's livid fury with unshaken calm, Phoebe said, "You do but waste time, sir."

"And you are ridiculous," he fumed, jerking Rogue's head up as the big black made a grab for a recklessly sauntering Satan. "You can only delay us, ma'am. You will be unable to keep up through the country, and at the speed we must ride, and—"

"My brother's life is at stake," she countered. "And I do not propose to leave it in the hands of what you yourself named two cripples. If I am not allowed to ride beside you, Meredith, I shall follow."

Her face, under the little black hat with the large blue feather, was determined. Carruthers dared delay no longer. He started off, flinging at her over his shoulder, "Very well, but if you fall behind, you will be abandoned, I warn you!"

She did not doubt him and, for all her brave defiance, her heart was beating very fast as she guided Spring across the yard and out through the gates. Anxiety for Sinclair was uppermost in her mind, but nagging in the background was another fear; it had its roots in the fact that Meredith had refused to see her this morning, and that although he had come downstairs tonight, he had obviously avoided her. How eagerly he had gone to take Rosalie's hands; how ardently smiled down at her. Phoebe trembled to the dread that he had been comparing his two ladies, and that his regard for the lovely country lass was proving the stronger. In the next instant she was recalling his kisses; the tender moments that even in memory could cause her cheeks to flame. Those had not been the actions of a man regretting his bargain, had they?

Thus the anxieties of Miss Phoebe Ramsay, galloping through the windy darkness, a gentleman on each side of her, in a desperate race to avert tragedy.

For as long as they were on his lands, Meredith set a breakneck pace, but some half-hour after leaving the Hall, he slowed, turned off the lane they had followed for some moments, and led them up a long, gradual slope. It was all Phoebe could do to see their way, for the moon was frequently hidden by fast-scudding clouds and she felt at times that she was riding headlong through a black tunnel, only her faith in Meredith enabling her to continue at such a rate. The horses were all blowing now, and she was breathless. She wondered how Jeffery was managing and, knowing how relentlessly a sprain aches, she peered at him. His face was shadowed, but he was riding well.

They were coming into wooded country, and Meredith called, "Careful here. Stay close behind me, ma'am."

She thought of his earlier threat to abandon her to her own devices, and smiled to herself, but guided Spring closer to the big black, and Jeffery pulled in beside her.

"My Lord!" he exclaimed, looking about. "You never mean to take Phantom Pass?"

"Only way," grunted Meredith. "He has too good a start on us."

Jeffery muttered something Phoebe did not hear but that was definitely apprehensive. Then they were cantering. They came out of the trees onto a broad plateau. The moon slid from behind the cloud-rack to allow a glimpse of a strange, deserted landscape. For as far as the eye could see, there was no sign of cultivated land or human habitation, and on the jumbled irregular slopes and hollows, great boulders stood up like silent, menacing sentinels of this macabre place. The turf beneath them was coarse and springy, concealing low spots and rabbit holes, and twice Spring stumbled. Meredith led them at a steady, mile-eating speed, the black horse guided with an unerring hand around the grassy areas that Phoebe at first thought level land and only at the last instant saw were depressions filled with taller grasses.

She heard a frightened snort from Mouser and glanced around to see the grey plunging, Jeffery barely retaining his seat. "Are you all right?" she called anxiously.

"Look out, dammit!" cried Meredith, angered. He grabbed her reins, wrenching Spring back, then jerked his head at the depression alongside, into which the mare had almost wandered. "Quicksand, Miss Phoebe! *Now* do you see why I didn't want you with us?"

She stared at the treacherous ground in revulsion, and said a small "Oh."

"Oh, indeed," he muttered and turned to his brother. "How goes it, aged youth?"

Jeffery replied airily, "Very well, thank you, gaffer."

"Let's get on then. And this time, ma'am, keep your eyes on me. Jeff will manage, but if he don't I shall not stop, for he can find his way out by daylight. You understand?"

It was for Sinclair, and despite the hurtingly brusque tone, she could only be grateful. "Yes," she said meekly. "I understand."

They went on. And on. Up and down and around. In and out of strange, narrow little gorges, hemmed about with rocks. A wild gallop over a stretch of open grassland, only to be waved to a plunging halt by Meredith, who must, she realized, be holding the reins in his right hand despite the sling.

Jeffery was panting distressfully. "What . . . is it?"

"Troopers! See there, below us. Damn! I didn't expect them here. We'll have to go over the top!"

"Merry! You are not serious?"

"Oh, am I not? Here we go—God save us all!"

He turned sharply to the left, riding at a trot and picking his way with care. Looking ahead, Phoebe gave a gasp of fright. The land soared to a majestic escarpment. Surely, he did not mean to attempt that climb? It was not possible! The slope was too sheer, too barren!

Jeffery gasped out, "Merry—have you ever . . . gone over the top?"

"Twice. It's not easy. Especially with a game ankle. You'd do well to turn back now, Jeff, unless you feel up to a climb and a scramble down."

Jeff said nothing, but stayed doggedly with them.

Very soon the horses were scrambling for a footing. Phoebe clung to the pommel, watching Meredith anxiously and worrying about Jeff. The latter worries were justified first. She heard a muffled shout and a frightened whinnying, and looked back to see Mouser scrambling up and Jeffery sprawling.

Meredith halted. "Jeff," he panted, "you gave it a jolly good try. You must go back, old fellow."

His brother strove gamely, gripped his leg, and sank back. "Just have to—rest . . . for a bit. Go on, Merry. I'll catch up."

"Nonsense! You'd break your neck going down, even if you did reach the top. Go back!" And without so much as a word to Phoebe, he urged Rogue forward again.

For the rest of her life, Phoebe was to be troubled by occasional nightmares of what followed. The wind, which had been steadily rising, was a gusting gale by the time they scrambled onto the summit. Her relief and amazement at having survived the climb were short-lived. The furtive moon illumined a sheer, boulder-strewn slope, the surface deeply fissured and broken so that she despaired of being able to negotiate it, much less get the horses safely down. They had dismounted soon after Jeffery's tumble, and Meredith, who had been leaning wearily against Rogue, now came over to her.

"We'll rest for a minute," he said breathlessly. "How are you?"

"Frightened," she admitted. "How can the horses get down this awful cliff?"

"Hopefully on their own. Surer than the devil, I cannot carry 'em."

She smiled. "Merry, is your arm a great nuisance?"

"It is a great nuisance to be half-crippled tonight, I don't mind telling you." He was scanning the slope behind them. "I cannot see Jeff—can you?"

She turned to look, and was staggered by a howling blast. Meredith grabbed her as an unearthly screaming filled her ears. The wind was so strong she could scarcely draw a breath, and she buried her face in his cravat. The screaming persisted. The horses fidgeted and whinnied nervously. "What is—that hideous noise?" she shouted.

"Nobody knows. Wind through the rocks, perhaps. The locals think it's the souls of the dead. That's why none will come this way. Among other things." He grinned at her. "We'd best get on. Don't try to lead Spring." He went to the mare's head and stroked her, murmuring softly, then said, "She'll follow me. It's the big fellow I'm concerned about." He gripped Phoebe's hand tightly, "Nothing ventured . . ."

They started down, but had gone only a short distance when Phoebe slid a yard. Her heart in her mouth, she screamed. Meredith jerked her backwards and she sat down hard and without elegance. He knelt beside her and she was in his embrace, sobbing into his cravat. "Oh—I cannot! I didn't think—Merry—I am terrified of high places!"

He said with breathless indignation. "This is the very deuce of a time to tell me that, Miss Ramsay!"

She peeped up at him contritely. "I know what you are thinking. I 'had to come.' I'm so sorry."

"I'm not," he shouted above the howl of the wind. "My brother has left us, poor lad. If I should be the next casualty, your brother's life will be in your hands, ma'am. Besides"—he smiled—"my pets are limited to Justice and Satan. Lacking a tame dragon to fly you down, you've either to go on down, or back up and then down the other side. Sorry, m'dear, but that's the best I have to offer."

Despite his teasing manner he was very pale, and his left hand

255

gripped his hurt wrist from time to time. He needed her, and Sinclair needed her—would she ever forgive herself if she let them down? Her little chin came up. She said, "Let us try again, then," and forced herself to stand up.

He clasped her hand once more. Her knees were trembling, but she concentrated on the fact that this man who tried to guide her and balance himself with one arm in a sling was striving so for her dear brother's sake. Meredith led her in a sideways, snaking descent, so that their progress was slower, but a little less hair-raising. "Do not look any farther than your boots," he shouted, and she obeyed, conquering one step at a time, her breath ragged, her heart pounding with fear.

She gave a shriek as Spring came down very close, snorting her fright, but managing to keep upright to an extent, although she was practically sitting and sliding. Unable to stop, she shot past and vanished into the darkness.

Waiting, holding his breath, Meredith heard no threshing about, or the terrible equine screams he so dreaded. "One down safely," he muttered.

They were about halfway down when Rogue at last attempted the slope. They heard a thunderous scrambling, a great rattling of loose shale. Meredith pulled Phoebe into his arm and stood with his back to the rain of stones. The black fairly whizzed by. There came a wild neighing and the unmistakable sound of a fall. Phoebe felt Carruthers's hand tighten bruisingly on hers, but he said nothing and they struggled on. It became an endless nightmare of fear and effort. She was preparing to beg him to rest just for a minute, when she felt a difference, and with a gasp of astonished triumph realized that they were on level ground. "We're—down!" she cried.

He said a curt "Bravo!" and left her, hurrying to Spring, who stood grazing. He was running his hand down the mare's legs when Phoebe discerned another shape against the darkness. "Merry!" she cried joyously. "There's Rogue! He's standing!"

"Praise the Lord!" he breathed. "Stay with Spring. I'll get him."

Rogue was trembling and there were some superficial cuts on his side and shoulder where he had fallen, but by some miracle no bones were broken and both animals appeared to have escaped serious injury.

Carruthers took a minute or two to quiet the big stallion, then he tossed Phoebe into her saddle. His own mount was an awkward effort that dismayed her. They were off at once, however, keeping clear of the roads and lanes, cutting across country, past cottages that gradually became more frequent, the blustering wind helping to drown the sounds of their going.

The moon escaped its cloud net at last and revealed tossing trees, a large branch down across a lane ahead, and a horseman riding fast along that lane and taking the obstruction without check.

"It's Sin!" called Phoebe. "Merry! It's Sin!"

He said, "And the village only a mile or so off!" and was away and onto the lane at a pounding gallop.

The wind sent his cloak billowing out and whipped Phoebe's hair into a flying mane. She leaned forward in the saddle, urging Spring to greater efforts, marvelling at Carruthers's endurance and horsemanship, her eyes fixed on him and the striving stallion, her ears filled with the blustering wind, the pound of hoofs, the creak of saddle leather. Sinclair glanced back, then rode faster.

'Sin,' thought Phoebe desperately, 'can't you feel it is only Merry and me? Stop!'

The distant spire of a church was visible now, a deeper black against the sky. There would be troopers there, waiting. Her nerves tight with dread, she saw Rogue seem to stretch out, as though before he had been merely trotting. Meredith was crouched low, as one with the powerful animal, and they pulled ahead until she was left some distance behind. She saw Sinclair glance back again, and saw also, with a gasp of horror, the moonlight gleam on a pistol in his hand.

Faintly borne on the wind came a shout. Sinclair turned more fully, then he was slowing, wheeling his mount. Phoebe gave a sob of thankfulness and came thundering up as the two men met.

"Carruthers!" cried her brother. "What the—*Phoebe*!"

"Troopers—ahead!" panted Carruthers. "Off the road . . . quick!"

His back propped against a tree, his long legs stretched out before him, Carruthers watched Phoebe as she came towards him, holding up her habit and treading with care. The wind had died away, early sunlight was brightening the little clearing, and the cloudless skies gave promise of a warm day. Phoebe's habit was mud-stained and there was a tear here and there; her boots were scraped and her dashing hat gone. He was glad of that, because the red-gold of her untidy hair was caught by the sun and shone like a flame around her grubby face as she sank to her knees beside him.

"Are you feeling better?" she asked, searching his wan features anxiously.

"Better, but thwarted and most unheroical, alas," he replied.

She said gravely, "You will never convince me of the latter, sir."

A dark flush stained his beard-stubbled cheeks. He said with a rather forced laugh, "What? Though I failed you in the matter of the dragon?"

"It is small wonder you were so exhausted, Merry. At all events, it is as well we had to rest, else we might have blundered right into those wretched soldiers. I wish I might change the bandages on your arm, but—"

"Do not fret, ma'am. It is no trouble, I assure you."

"Then why do you hold the wrist so?"

He released his hold hurriedly. "Is Sin coming back yet?"

"No. But I did see the troopers again. They are in the hollow over there"—she nodded to the northeast—"watching the road. One has dropped off to sleep, I think, for I could hear snoring, but the other two are smoking and grumbling."

"They'll have something to grumble for if Fotheringay catches them lounging about when they're supposed to be watching for such evil conspirators as ourselves."

She leaned closer to push back the hair that curled untidily on his brow, but he shrank away from her touch. She felt rebuffed and looked at him searchingly, but his eyes avoided hers. Stifling a sigh, she asked, "Merry, whatever are we to do? Even if we *could* get the cipher to Father Albritton, the Colonel suspects him now. It might well be that we would deliver his death-warrant."

"I know. I've been thinking about it; not very successfully, I'm afraid. I don't think I'd shine at this rebel game."

Phoebe lifted one hand cautioningly as she heard a soft rustling among the undergrowth. Sinclair came into the clearing looking tired and glum and declaring that it was impossible to get near the church without being seen. "Troopers everywhere, blast it all! What the devil are we to do?"

"Think," said Carruthers.

They did.

"I've a grand notion," exclaimed Phoebe. "Why don't I—"

"No!"

"But, Merry, I could say I'd come to see him to arrange our wedding, and—" She stopped in new anxiety.

Sinclair also had seen the white teeth clamp onto Carruthers's lower lip. "Bad, is it, Meredith?" he said sympathetically. "We must get him home, Phoebe."

"For Lord's sake, stop maudling over me," Carruthers snapped, glaring at him. "I shall—" and he paused, tilting his head to listen to the faint, musical sound that echoed distantly. "What the devil *is* that? I've been hearing it this half-hour and more."

"What? Oh, it's the stonemason. He was working busily when I looked into his shop just now. See the little place just next to the graveyard? I hate to give up, but—"

"Stone . . . mason . . ." mused Carruthers. "How were you able to see into his shop?"

"The troopers all are on the other side, around the church. Why?"

Excitement brought a glitter to the pale eyes. "At what is he working? Could you see?"

Mildly irritated by this irrelevancy, Sinclair shrugged, "Oh, an angel or some such thing. There were gravestones lying about as well. What matter?"

"Ah . . ." breathed Carruthers, throwing Phoebe a twinkling glance.

Sitting back on her heels, she stared at him, awed. "Merry—you would not dare!"

He grinned. "Sometimes, m'dear, 'tis the thing right under your nose that you do not see."

"I doesn't see how I can be a-doin' of it, marm," said Mr. Vardy.

The morning was scarcely begun, but it was already warm. The sun's heat was not responsible, however, for the plump little stonemason's distressful mopping of his round face. He eyed the young widow with increased alarm as her sobs became even more heart-rending. A pleasant little thing, he thought, for all that her face—what he could see of it—would have been the better for a wash. She wasn't common, though, for her country voice was soft when it wasn't weeping, and there had been no screeching at him when he'd told her he couldn't start work on her late husband's gravestone today. The skirt she wore looked good-enough quality, if a bit tore, but her shawl might have been cut from some old garment, and she held it so close that he couldn't see her hair at all.

"It ain't as I mean to be disobliging, marm," he explained reasonably. "It's this here angel, d'ye see? I be late with it already, and—" He gave a yelp and recoiled as the widow emitted a heart-broken wail.

"I do have been savin' and savin', and working s'hard, sir," she gulped. "I got the money now, as the man at church had said 'twould cost. I swore to my Sam on his deathbed as he'd have a marker over him 'fore his next birthday. And that be tomorrer, sir! I doan't ax as ye finish it. If ye could just get the words drawed on the stone, and if the vicar could say 'twas fitting, that'd please me—me darlin' Sam." Her sobs increased in volume, and the good stonemason shrank as she reached out to him pleadingly.

How fortunate it was, thought Phoebe, that she had put on her black riding habit. How even more fortunate that Meredith had worn his black cloak, so that they'd been able, with the aid of Sin's pocket knife, to cut the lining into this makeshift shawl. And above all, how fortunate that this innocent little man's wife did not work with him in his dusty shop, for a woman would have seen at once the excellence of the material of her skirt, and guessed the value of the heavy silk from Merry's butchered cloak. "Could-couldn't ye . . . *please* . . . ?" she begged.

"Oh, Lor'," groaned poor Mr. Vardy, so unnerved that he snatched off his scratch-wig and wiped the top of his head. "Whatcha say yer husband's name was, me dear?"

"Ch-Charters."

He frowned. "Be blowed if I reckernize the name . . ."

"We're from Father Albritton's home parish," explained Phoebe, well coached by Meredith. "Over by Ashdown Forest. But Sam often passed this way and he thought it so pretty he was fair set on being buried here. And the other clergyman said as 'twould be all right, and that Father Albritton, knowing Sam, would see everything was done proper."

"Ar. Well then, that's likely why I didn't know the name," said Mr. Vardy, adding with a reluctant sigh, "Let's see your words, missus."

Eagerly, Phoebe thrust out the paper they had drawn up, and Vardy peered at it, mouthed out the words silently, and pursed up his lips. "Oh, sir," she babbled, "I'd be s'grateful! Sam's officer writ that out, and Sam allus liked it, he did. I—I let him down something drefful, not havin' his marker up 'fore this.

But—I does all the washin' I can take in, and what with the preserves I bottles, and all the little ones—seven I got, sir . . . and . . ." she sobbed heart-rendingly.

And the end of it was, of course, that following a few more feeble and rejected suggestions, the beleaguered stonemason accepted the widow's carefully hoarded coins, promised to "get right at it," and was overwhelmed when she snatched up his grimy hand, pressed a kiss on it, and went, weeping, from his life.

"Bless me soul!" he gasped, lifting the marker she had chosen. "Fancy that, now! Poor little dear!"

In the dimness of the ancient Church of St. John, in the equally ancient village called Wilmington West, an intrusive ray of sunlight awakening his fair head to a gleam of gold, Father Charles Albritton rested a calm blue gaze on his visitor. "I cannot think of what you suspect me, Colonel," he murmured, "but may I tell my housekeeper to set a cover for you?"

The afternoon had grown warm and sultry. Fotheringay was hot in his uniform and harbouring a suspicion that doddlish old fool of a villager had hornswoggled him. "I think I have not accused you, Reverend," he grunted. "But I know you priests are always ready to help the underdog, no matter how well justified his chastisement."

Albritton said in his gentle voice, "Our first and greatest Teacher left us an example of mercy."

"If all men were merciful to criminals, Father, this world would contain more thieves and murderers than honest citizens!"

"Then it is a thief or a murderer you suspect me of concealing?" A smile hovering about his mouth, the young priest said, "I do assure you, sir—"

Fotheringay left the frayed leather chair and stamped over to the window of the small office. Looking outside, he interpolated, "I have not said I suspect you of concealing anyone."

"You have had me stripped and searched. You have kept me a virtual prisoner in my own church since yesterday afternoon. One must assume—"

"Who's this fellow?"

Albritton unwound his tall figure from the wooden settle and stood to face the man who waited, hat in hand, at the open door. "Good afternoon, Vardy. Never say the angel is completed?"

261

With an uneasy glance to the glowering officer, the villager replied, "I put it aside early 's mornin', sir. Account o' the widder were s'anxious to get the stone on Mr. S. Charters."

Perplexed, Albritton stared at him. He knew no one recently deceased by the name of S. Charters. In fact, the only S. Charters he could remember was that awful Professor Samuel Charters, who'd taught classical Greek at Eton, and—He fought to conceal an instinctive start. Charters was inextricably linked in his mind with Tio Glendenning and Merry Carruthers, both of whom had run so hopelessly afoul of the professor's horrid temper in the matter of the piglet. 'Tio!' he thought, his breath catching in his throat. And, very conscious of Mariner Fotheringay's disgruntled presence at his elbow, he said, "Poor woman. Better late than never, I suppose."

"Aye. Wants you t'be sure 'tis all right, she does. Could ye come, sir?" Plump and perspiring, he wiped his face with a hideous red-and-purple kerchief.

Fotheringay rasped tartly, "I am talking with Father Albritton."

"Ar. I see that. Thing is—"

"I'd better go," said Albritton. "Is the lady still here, Vardy?"

"No, sir. An' glad o' it I be. Weeping something drefful. And one thing I cannot abide is a drippy female. I'd like to know which grave it is, sir. One o' they unmarked ones by the hedge—eh?"

"Yes, I believe so. You will excuse me, Colonel?"

"Come with you," said Fotheringay. "Matter of fact, I'd like to drop in at your shop, Vardy. I've been considering a monument for my late uncle's grave. Like to have a look at your angel."

Vardy's heartbeat quickened. So did Albritton's, only for a very different reason. He managed somehow to preserve his demeanour, and they all went out into the warm afternoon sunshine.

From a certain quiet little clearing on the side of the hill above the village, three pairs of red-rimmed eyes watched the church.

"Why the deuce did it take him so blasted long to go over there?" Sinclair muttered fretfully.

"Could he have completed it?" asked Phoebe. "I told him to be sure to bring Father Albritton out to see it when he'd roughed it in."

"I wonder it didn't occur to him to ask Albritton to look at the parchment before he started work on the stone," said Carruthers. "We'd have been properly in the soup."

Phoebe said, "Oh, he did suggest that. I told him it was what my dear Sam had wanted, and I really hoped that once Father Albritton saw it already on the stone, he'd not object."

Carruthers chuckled. "Clever girl! He's certainly been chipping away for hours, and I fancy he has to work with—"

"Here they come!" cried Sinclair. "Oh! Egad! That damnable Mariner Fotheringay's with them!"

Phoebe gave a moan of apprehension, and Carruthers muttered, "I pray I've not ruined the entire business. It was all I could think of."

"Damn sight more than I could've thought of," said Sinclair loyally.

"You *did* tell him to include the number?" asked Carruthers. "Lance said that was vital."

Phoebe nodded, nerves tight as the three small distant figures walked into the cluttered yard of the stonemason's shop.

"Charles," sighed Carruthers, "I hope your friend God has His hand over you this afternoon—or your friend Carruthers may have laid that fine head of yours on a very bloody block!"

"It ain't easy to work with stone," Mr. Vardy was saying as he led the way into his dusty little shed. "And the lady being so fussy . . . But, there. Saved up all her pennies, poor creature. I shouldn't grumble. She said as you'd remember her husband from your home parish, Father, and—"

"So this is your angel!" Fotheringay paused to admire the large and grieving figure by the entrance. "Impressive. How much d'you get for something like this?"

Brightening, Mr. Vardy left the silent clergyman and hurried to offer Colonel Fotheringay a bargain rate.

The wrangling voices faded, and Albritton stood motionless, staring at the small stone slab on which had been carefully etched:

SAMUEL CHARTERS
III

Odd, how gently they come home,
Wooing peace once more.

Riding off they were not so.
Is it ever thus with war?
Frequently, it seems mankind
Terrifies or trembles.

"Robber!" exclaimed Fotheringay wrathfully, stamping away from the protesting Vardy. "Fifty sovereigns, indeed! Never heard of such a thing!"

The clergyman turned to him at once. "Oh, I don't know, Colonel. It requires a lot of skill, you know."

"What about *that*?" demanded the Colonel, throwing a contemptuous gesture at the small stone plaque.

"Why, that do be a simple job, sir," explained Vardy. "Only two pun' ten. Course, it ain't hardly started yet, as you can see. What d'ye think, Father?"

Moving towards the door, the clergyman shrugged. "A bit pretentious," he said, his face somewhat pale. "But if that's what the poor woman wants . . ."

"Pretentious, indeed," agreed Fotheringay, scowling at the slab. "Samuel Charters, Third! Good Gad! Some of these blasted peasants give themselves airs!"

"Oh, how I wish you might have seen it, Grandmama," cried Sinclair exuberantly, as they gathered together in the withdrawing room that evening, an envious Jeffery perched on the arm of the sofa beside his mother and Phoebe seated near Lady Martha, who hung on Sinclair's every word, her eyes alight with excitement. "You could all but feel Fotheringay's frustration when they came out of the stonemason's, and in jig time he and his troopers had gone clattering off!"

Phoebe smothered a yawn and said sleepily, "Father Albritton was grinning so broadly that we could see it, even up on the hill."

"And went straightaway back into the shop," her brother added. "He knew! No doubting."

"Well done! Oh, well done!" exclaimed the old lady, beaming at the conspirators as though she were part of their scheming.

"I only marvel that you were not killed, going over the top of Phantom Hill," said Lucille, shivering. "I am very grateful you had the good sense not to try and follow them, Jeffery."

He flushed. "So am not I!"

"It must have been horribly difficult for you, Meredith," said my lady, eyeing the quiet Carruthers with some unease. "I hope you have not overtaxed your strength."

He straightened. He was extremely pale, but he grinned at her brightly. "It was worth every minute, ma'am. It is done! We've to get Lance to another hiding place, but I've already thought of one will serve well enough till we can whisk him to safety in France. The worst of it is over now, and at last we can have done with this silly masquerade!"

Phoebe's heart gave a lurch.

Lady Martha said curiously, "Masquerade?"

Meredith chuckled. "I think we should tell them now, Miss Ramsay. This has gone on long enough."

Dimly, Phoebe knew that Sinclair was looking at her, his fine face very intent, and that Mrs. Carruthers had begun to fan herself nervously. She felt icy-cold and suspended, as though awaiting a blow that came, with slow inexorability, to slay her.

"I am very sorry that it was necessary for us to deceive you," said Meredith, smiling around at three puzzled faces and carefully avoiding the other two, "but we had little choice. You see, Lady Martha, when your granddaughter and I were discovered in the Pineridge basement, we had been hiding poor Lance. There was no compromising behaviour between us. No mutual and overwhelming surge of passion, or anything of that nature. In point of fact, we neither of us wanted this betrothal, since we both have interests—ah, elsewhere. But—"

Lucille dropped her fan. "Meredith! What are you saying?"

"Why, that there really was no betrothal, dear Mama. It was an embarrassment merely that we could not explain without endangering us all, so—"

"So now," put in Lady Martha, her voice hard and cold, "you wish to break the engagement?"

"But, my dear ma'am, there *was* no—"

Sinclair interposed a grim "Phoebe, you say nothing. Is it your wish to terminate your betrothal to Carruthers?"

Remote, frozen, Phoebe thought, 'He doesn't want me. He enjoyed a dalliance, nothing more.' Achingly, she remembered saying after he had kissed her in the old Keep, "You take advantage of the situation." And his reply, "Of course." He had been honest with her from the start. He'd said he had no wish to marry. But she had come to think . . . Only she was wrong. He did not want her.

"Phoebe . . . ?"

Sinclair was staring. They all were staring; all so angry. She looked at Meredith and found him watching her in an amused way. She must not betray the fact that her heart was shredding into hurting little pieces. She must not make more of a fool of herself than she already had done. In a voice that sounded as if it came from a thousand miles away, she said, "Sin, you know how I felt when we were forced into this . . . deception."

"Deception . . ." whispered Lucille, white to the lips.

Lady Martha got to her feet and marched to stand directly in front of Carruthers, who at once stood to face her. "I think I cannot accept this," she said. "It has seemed to me that you and my granddaughter—"

"Shared a kindness for each other?" he interrupted. "Why, so we do, ma'am. I admire Miss Phoebe greatly. Only—as I told her from the start, I do not want her for—my wife."

Lucille uttered a shriek and burst into tears. Sinclair jumped up, scowling.

Phoebe said, "It is perfectly true, Grandmama. And Mr. Carruthers was aware from the start that I—loved Brooks."

Lady Martha glared at her. "Yet from what your mama told me, and certainly since I came, for ten days you have been looking at him as if he was some young god; and he's been looking at you as if you wore a halo and wings. Now you say you do not care for each other! All well and good, but—how d'you mean to get out of it without scandal is what I'd like to know!"

Meredith gripped his arm. He looked very tired and haggard. "I expect we cannot," he said. "I'm afraid I shall have to be jilted."

Lucille succumbed to screaming hysterics.

By ten o'clock next morning, the valises and portmanteaux had been packed and the horses poled up. A pale but composed Miss Phoebe Ramsay, a tight-lipped Mr. Sinclair Ramsay, and a flushed and furious Lady Martha Ramsay had entered the first carriage. Ada Banham had said her farewells to a stricken Henry Baker and gone, scattering tears, into the second carriage. Now, with a cracking of whips and rumbling of wheels, they departed, leaving behind a Meredith Hall that seemed echoingly quiet, and servants who trod softly and looked solemn, knowing that very soon the newspapers would carry news of the broken betrothal and that once again they would be obliged to defend the honour of their house against the jeering staffs of all the neighbours.

Jeffery's attempt to speak with his brother met a level stare that froze him to the marrow. He faltered into silence and went off defiantly in search of Rosalie Smith.

Emerging from her suite an hour later, her eyes red from weeping, but with rage strengthening her, Lucille found no sign of her quarry. She knew where to look, however, and made her way up the hill girded for war.

She found him leaning against the crumbling Gothic wall, his back to her as he gazed down at the whispering stream. Alone, silent, hostile, antisocial; his father all over again. The sense of her own ill usage brought stinging tears to her eyes and she ran up behind him, saying on a sob, "How *could* you, Meredith? How *could* you? You knew what it meant to me, and now . . . Oh! We will be laughingstocks! Shunned! And just when I had so hoped we might at last . . ."

She did not finish her denunciation for, wearily, he turned to her and she saw his eyes. The years rolled back. She was young again, kneeling beside the grave of her slain lover, knowing her heart had been buried with him.

She reached out. "Oh—my *dear*," she said tenderly. "My *very* dear . . ."

For an instant, Meredith stared blindly at her. Then, with a muffled sound that was neither groan nor sob, yet something of each, he walked into her arms.

∽ *Chapter 19* ∾

"It's unnatural," stormed Sir George Ramsay, glaring across the breakfast table of his London house, and slamming down his copy of *The Gazette*.

"Oh, dear," his wife sighed. "Is it Mr. Pitt? Or are they slandering poor Walpole? Or has the Prince of Wales done something outrageous again?"

"For pity's sake, don't be such a thimble-wit, Eloise," he snapped. "It is our daughter I refer to. There's no pleasing the gal, I vow! She yearns, she sighs, she wilts"—he gave an exaggerated impersonation of a lady wilting—"for Brooks Lambert, but gets herself compromised by Meredith Carruthers. We manage to rescue her from that stew, only to have her quarrel with Carruthers. Though, mind you, Eloise," he interrupted himself, eyebrows bristling, "I consider *his* conduct thoroughly reprehensible, and have no doubt he is now beyond the pale, socially, at least."

Phoebe kept her lack-lustre eyes on her plate and said nothing.

"You have got egg on your cravat," said Lady Eloise, glancing at her mulish-looking son, and her just as mulish-looking mother-in-law.

"Being a generous, fair-minded father," Sir George went on, ignoring his wife's irritating observation, "I have told her she *may* wed Brooks Lambert, and does she brighten? Is she grateful?" Silence following this pained enquiry, he snarled, "It would be gratifying was the head of this house to be informed exactly *why* this betrothal was terminated, and whether it is my bounden duty to call that cad out!"

"Fiddle-faddle!" exploded his formidable parent. "If any calling out was needed, young Lambert would have—" She closed her lips as a footman trod discreetly into the room and proffered an ivory-and-gold salver to her granddaughter. "Callers? At this hour?" she snorted.

Phoebe stared down at the card, losing all her colour. Lady Eloise, deeply worried about this quiet stranger who had replaced her sunny-natured daughter, asked "Dearest? Is it someone you do not wish to see?"

"Oh, no, Mama," said Phoebe breathlessly. "P-pray excuse me."

Lucille Carruthers, a vision in gold silk, waited in the morning room, and came to her feet as Phoebe hurried to greet her.

"Good day, ma'am. I did not know you was in Town. How very kind in you to call. May I offer you a cup of tea, or—"

"Nothing, I thank you." Lucille resumed her seat on the blue velvet sofa. "I was afraid," she said timidly, "that you might refuse to receive me. Under the—the circumstances. But I brought Rosalie to Town to shop for her bride clothes, and—"

Phoebe gave a gasp, and blanched.

"Oh, good gracious," said Lucille. "I had thought you knew. We met your brother in the Strand—did he not mention it?"

Forcing her numb lips to move, Phoebe said that Sinclair must have forgot. Somehow, she managed a smile. "I am to be wed soon myself, so I can guess how happy Miss—Miss Smith must be."

"Oh, she is in alt, sweet child, despite the difficulties. She has loved him all her life, you see, but never dreamed they would be able to wed."

"How lovely," said Phoebe, a ghastly smile distorting her lips while a claymore transfixed her heart. "I had heard M-Meredith was ill. I trust he is recovered."

Watching her from under her lashes, Lucille murmured, "My son will never pamper himself, you see. Infection set in, and he was very ill for a few days." She saw terror in that white, lovely face, and her heart was wrung. Looking up, she said quietly, "He is much better, my dear. Physically, at least. But I did not come here to speak of Meredith, but of myself."

Phoebe watched her wonderingly. Lucille gripped her reticule hard, and said, staring at it, "You see, I did not quite finish my—my story, when I was telling you about my husband. You will remember I said that Paul found out about Edvard?"

"Yes. But—oh, ma'am, I know how painful it is for you to speak of it. Pray do not—"

"But, you see, I must tell you the—the whole. I neglected to tell you that . . . there is a joke about the Hoagland family. It is

269

said that—none of the wives can for long escape the . . . the Hoagland Double." Her cheeks very pink, she said, "I prayed I might be spared, but—within a year of meeting Edvard I—I was in the family way." She heard Phoebe's shocked little gasp, and not daring to meet her eyes, rushed on, "I gave birth to twins. I knew that my husband would guess at once, if he saw the babes, so I swore my maid and the midwife to secrecy, and put one of my dear children out for adoption. Paul did not suspect, and as time passed, his visits became infrequent. If he did come, his servants came first so as to prepare for him, and I had time to send Jeffery to visit friends. Only . . . on the day he scarred Meredith, he arrived unexpectedly. He entered the Great Hall just as Jeff was running down the stairs. My son was almost six years old. Paul had not seen him for two years, and instead of a babe, he saw a very fair child. He took one look, and knew. Luckily, Nurse saw Paul's face, and she hurried Jeffery into a carriage and took him off for a drive." She paused, and after a small, tension-charged silence, finished in a very small voice, "*That* was—was why Paul was so enraged, you see."

"Oh . . . my!" whispered Phoebe. "How very dreadful for you. Did you ever see your other twin again, ma'am?"

Lucille smiled shakily. "How kind and understanding you are. Yes. I thought I was being so clever, you see. The family with whom I placed my little one were not happily situated in Town. Grace, although only five years my senior, had been my companion, and her husband, John, was born on the Carruthers estate. He had charge of Paul's horses and was often brought to Town when Paul was courting me. His marriage was—ideal, save that they were not blessed with children. I knew they would be good to my babe, and they were indeed. Eventually, I persuaded them to return to the village, and I gave them funds to start a little business." Meeting Phoebe's look of disbelief, she continued, "They are dead now, but always kept my secret. Even their families believed the child was their own. My—my daughter is grown, of course, and—"

"Oh! My dear God! *Rosalie?* Poor Meredith is so deep in love and does not know the girl is—"

Lucille said gently, "But—he *does* know, my dear. He has known for years, which is why he has always taken a great interest in her. A sadly misinterpreted interest, which is my fault. I straitly forbade Meredith to reveal the truth to a living soul. I so—so *dreaded* more scandal. I knew if the facts came out, people would censure me even more, for allowing my

270

daughter to be brought up a commoner. And that all the terrible stories about Paul would be revived again. I''—she wrung her hands—"I just could not *bear* it! Merry begged me to let him tell Jeff, but I refused and so he—dear loyal soul, kept my secret.''

Hopelessly confused, Phoebe stammered, "But—if he *knows*, he could not have been—I mean, she cannot be his—Well, then, they *cannot*—Oh! I do not *understand*! You just said Rosalie is to be wed—and that she has loved him all her days.''

"And so she has, my dear. It was because of his son's devotion to a village girl that Malcolm Lockwood forbade their marriage and he and Lancelot parted in anger.''

"*Lascelles . . . ?*'' said Phoebe, still bemused. "But—but if Rosalie loved *him*, why did she not show it? I'd have thought—Oh!'' She clutched Lucille's hand. "Did she remain silent for fear Sin and Jeffery would not help Lance?''

Lucille nodded. "The little minx was afraid that if they guessed she and Lance were long promised, they might not continue to take such risks for his sake. She was wrong, and it was naughty of her to lead those two poor boys on, but—when the life of the one you love is at stake . . .''

"Yes. Who could blame her? But—she knows the truth about herself now? Jeffery knows?''

"I could not remain silent after I realized how Meredith—Well, I went to see Malcolm Lockwood. The soldiers tried to keep me out, but Lambert was there, dear boy, and I told him I meant to tell the Squire what I thought of him for hurting Meredith. He let me pass, and when we were alone, I confessed the whole to Sir Malcolm. He was—very kind, and at once gave his consent. Lancelot and Rosalie will be wed as soon as they are safely on French soil.''

"Oh, I am so glad!'' cried Phoebe. "Only . . .'' Her brow puckered again. "Why did Meredith let me believe he loved her?''

Lucille said helplessly, "My dear, I do not know. All I can tell you is that when my dear Edvard died, life became to me an intolerable burden. Each morning, I woke to despair, and the future loomed cold and dark and empty. Meredith says little and keeps very busy with our tenants and our properties. But sometimes I see a look in his eyes, and—oh, dear Miss Ramsay, I fear he lives in that same terrible despair that I knew!''

* * *

Brooks Lambert stood very still in the green saloon, staring incredulously at Phoebe's beautiful, troubled face. After a long moment, he echoed, "Not *marry* me . . . ? But—why? I thought your papa had withdrawn his objections? The termination of your betrothal to Carruthers has been published. I—I do not understand."

Miserable because she was hurting him so, she said, "Brooks, dear, I am indeed sorry. But—but . . . I *cannot* wed you. You see—"

He seized her arms and said in a voice she scarcely recognized, "Has that sneaking swine come around begging you to take him back? Has he dared to—"

Irked, she pulled free. "Do you mean Meredith Carruthers?"

"Yes, by God! If I thought he'd dare—"

"I have not seen him since we left the Hall. But it makes no difference. I wish I could say this without hurting you, but—you see, I—I love him. I shall never marry anyone else."

He stared down at her, his face unreadable. Almost whispering, he said, *"You . . . love . . . Carruthers?"* He laughed harshly. "Lord alive, but this is rich! *You*—beautiful, kind, graciousness personified; and that—that scarred, brusque, unpolished dog? My poor darling—you are *ill*!"

There was a twist to the fine mouth that she had never seen; a sneer in the voice, and, in those deep blue eyes, a little flame that appalled her. She stepped back. "I think you must forget, Brooks, that the man you just spoke of in so disgraceful a way is your kinsman, who has supported you these—"

"He is rich," he grated, advancing on her so that she drew farther back, a little frightened. *"That's* the truth of it, eh? It's his money you want!" He grasped her arms in a pounce that brought a shocked cry from her. "Well, I'll not hold that against you, love. *We* shall be rich, I promise you. Richer than your wildest dreams! You've no need to throw yourself away on that cur, for—"

"Let me go!" she stormed, angry now. "I would love Meredith Carruthers had he not a penny! He is the bravest, most caring, truly honourable man I ever knew! I *love* him! And he loves me. And I think you had better leave, Brooks."

His face was flushed and suddenly far from handsome. "Do you *really* think that, Miss Phoebe?" he jeered. "Then allow me to tell you something. I'll not go. And you shall not marry that worthless clod. By an accident of birth, *he* inherited a for-

272

tune, and *I* was doomed to the life of a poor relation! He threw the poor dog a bone . . . a pittance!''

Horrified, scarcely able to credit this transformation from his usual gallant charm, she struggled to be free. "You are despicable! Merry had no need to give you a penny! You never have known squalor or want, but many men born to those conditions have fought their way to success, and many men born to wealth have squandered their way to poverty. Merry fights always to improve the lot of his people! To cherish his mama and guide his brother, when it would be so much easier to shrug and turn away! Oh! You are hurting me, Brooks! If you do not let me go, I shall scream for help.''

He released her, but watched her with such brooding disgust that she wondered she could ever have imagined she would marry this bitter, vengeful man. Walking to the door, shaken as much by the realization of what she had so narrowly escaped as by this terrible confrontation, she said, "Please do not call here again.''

In his normal, pleasant voice, he said, "Phoebe, he will not marry you.''

With her hand on the latch she replied, "If that is so, then I shall never marry. Goodbye, sir.''

He moved very fast, to throw one arm across the doorway. Smiling down at her, he said silkily, "Then Carruthers's head will be on a spike on Temple Bar within the month.''

She stood utterly still, staring up at him, feeling the blood drain from her cheeks.

"*And*—your so dear brother's,'' he purred. "And *his* so dear brother's.'' He laughed softly. "That would break the heart of his stupid flibbertigibbet of a mother. I fancy your family is made of—er, stronger stuff, eh, my love?''

Stunned, her mind seeking numbly to comprehend, she allowed him to pull her back and close the door. "You—you went to him . . . ?'' she whispered. "That day after I was k-kidnapped . . . My God! Did you arrange *that*, too?''

"Not as it went. Otton and I staged it so that I could 'rescue' you and win over your beloved grandmama. But Otton wants the Jacobite treasure, and he suspected Meredith was hiding the courier. He kidnapped you in an attempt to force Carruthers to give up the cipher.'' He shrugged. "Oh, well. Many a slip. I was luckier. You see, I knew about the secret room. I went there, looking for you, and found Lockwood, fast asleep.''

"And so—you blackmailed Meredith.''

His eyes gloating at the memory, he said, "I brought my troop into the courtyard—do you recall? And I went up and told the dear fellow he had three minutes to choose between life without you—or death for just about the lot of you!" He chuckled. "Lord, shall I ever forget the look on his face! He was so maddened he actually tried to attack me, would you believe it? I had to be a little rough with the fool, which delayed me a trifle. But he really had no choice. I had him"—he put out one long, well-shaped hand and, slowly, closed it—"where I had wanted him for years. Life has its moments, my love. Life has its moments!"

"Why?" she whispered. "You don't love me. I doubt you have ever loved anyone but yourself!"

He frowned aggrievedly. "I did love you, m'dear. But—more to the point, my Aunt Ophelia admires you tremendously. She's extreme wealthy, you know. You will recollect my telling you I was her heir. I did fail to mention one little qualification—I inherit only if *you* become my wife. My dearest girl, you do not look happy." He bent over her as she sank into a chair. "I promise to be generous and attentive. I have other—er, playmates, I'll be honest. But—you shall always come first with me."

Sick, aching with grief, she thought, 'Merry . . . my poor darling . . .'

Lambert chucked her under the chin and when she jerked her head away in revulsion, he said softly, "Meanwhile, I shall offer you the same choice I gave Meredith. The decision, my love . . . is yours. . . ."

It was rare that Lady Martha joined her son and his wife for breakfast, but the following morning was bright and the sun crept under her eyelashes early. She lay in bed, troubled, and at length rang for her abigail. An hour later, she went downstairs in search of company. Her decision was not altogether salubrious; Sir George was in a quarrelsome mood as a result of the good offices of a 'close friend' who had whispered to him of the rumours that were abroad regarding his daughter's broken engagement. "They'll have more to titillate 'em when they read today's *Spectator*," he snarled. "And considering this is supposed to be a time of joy, to look at the inhabitants of this house would convince any—" He glanced irritably at the lackey who crept in and went around the table to offer the tray and the card it held. "What the deuce d'you want?" demanded Sir George.

"A morning caller, for Lady Martha," the lackey notified the chandelier.

"So it has started," she said, reaching for the card. "My personal friends know perfectly well I seldom rise before noon, and none but a gabble-monger would come as soon after—" The cup in her hand jolted, sending coffee splashing. "Ah . . ." she whispered, turning the card over and reading the brief message while her son and Lady Eloise watched curiously.

"Well?" demanded George. "Which of your tabby friends wants to hear all the grisly details?"

To the lackey, Lady Martha said, "You may show the gentleman to my parlour, Dennis, and tell him I shall join him in ten minutes."

"Gentleman?" echoed Sir George. "What gentleman?"

Sailing to the door like a frigate in a fine breeze, his mother threw over her shoulder, "My new lover!" and was gone, leaving him to splutter and glare at the departing and grinning lackey.

Captain Roland Otton, strikingly handsome in dark brown velvet and gold brocade, bowed low as my lady entered her private parlour. "My felicitations, ma'am," he murmured.

"For what?" she barked, surveying him with distaste.

"Why, for having found me." He ushered her to a chair as though she were a guest in his house, rather than he in hers. "How did you manage it, pray? I had fancied my flat well hidden."

She shrugged impatiently. "The never-failing source."

"The servants? Ah. Even so, it was unwise for me to come here. Reputations must be considered."

Her lip curled. "Thank you, but I believe my good name will survive."

" 'Tis my own I worry about," he declared demurely. "I am a dedicated villain, my lady. I do not *help* people."

She stared at him. "Well, if ever I heard such rubbish! I collect that is your grandfather's verdict. I like Muffin, but he holds himself too up, which causes him at times to be a heartless old curmudgeon."

Otton's dark countenance had become very still. "No, ma'am," he said gently. "I really cannot permit that you speak of him so. I had supposed very few people knew of my—er,

275

former identity, but my grandfather was—is—perfectly correct in his assessment of my character. Have I your leave to sit down?"

She gestured to the nearest chair, which he occupied, managing to do so gracefully, although it was a straight-backed and uncomfortable article.

"I am disgusted with you, Mathieson," said my lady unequivocally. "Because of your 'character,' as you call it, at least one and possibly two men are dead."

"Forgive," he corrected again, "if I beg that you call me by the name I now use. And as for your accusation, I will accept responsibility for one, although Ben Hessell is an evil animal and may yet live. Still, they both were, as am I, greedy for gold. They knew, as do I, the risks involved."

She leaned forward, her fierce eyes piercing him. "To steal Phoebe was a cruel and wicked thing to do, which you know very well."

"But of course. What would you expect of so depraved a character?" He smiled on her, the fine black eyes twinkling, one chiselled white hand lazily swinging the silver chain of his quizzing glass.

"Lud!" uttered my lady, baffled. "What a dreadful waste."

"Well, it was," he agreed, deliberately misinterpreting. "However, to cry over split milk pays no toll, I've learned, so let us to business. How much are you prepared to pay?"

"Pay?" she said, blinking. "I had hoped to enlist your aid out of your friendship for Meredith Carruthers."

"Dear old Merry." He touched a slight discolouration still visible under his chin. "I bear him no ill will because he near broke my jaw after I had spared his life. Now, tell me of your nefarious plot, but keep in mind, dear Lady Martha, that I am a poor soldier. My services run high."

Despite herself, a twitch of amusement disturbed the set of my lady's stern mouth. "What makes you think I enlist your aid in a 'nefarious plot'?"

He spread his hands. "Why else would you come to me, ma'am?"

The Dowager smuggled her morning caller out of the house through a side door, but when he came around to Clarges Street, Otton could see no sign of the link boy he had hired to walk Rumpelstiltskin. He frowned a little. Surely, the wretched urchin would not dare . . . But then he saw Rump some distance off, a man bending over his hoof, another man watching closely, and the link boy nowhere to be seen. Scowling, Otton began to run. Coming up with the pair, he cried angrily, "What the devil are you doing to my horse?"

The big fellow, who'd been inspecting the hoof, straightened. "Lucky for you I spotted him, sir."

"Baker!" exclaimed Otton. "The deuce! I left Rump in the charge of a link boy. What happened?"

"Your horse picked up a stone, sir. I got it out, never fret, but the boy tried it first, and Rump savaged him. He's in the coach."

With a dismayed curse, Otton swung open the door and started up the step into the dim interior. Without warning, the roof fell in, and for a while he forgot his troubles.

Carruthers wrung out the rag with his left hand and thrust it at Otton, who sprawled, moaning, on the shabby sofa in the small, dismal parlour. "Lady Martha was willing to help me, no questions asked," he said, seating himself in a droopy armchair. "She found you, and hired you, which was a ruse to get you here."

Indignant, Otton exclaimed, "That evil old lady! How could she have looked me in the eye, knowing I was to be brutally attacked? You could have called on me without breaking my head, Merry!"

"No. You'd not have come."

Otton eyed him thoughtfully. In the nine days that had elapsed since their last disastrous encounter, Carruthers had become thinner. He looked hunted, his eyes dark-rimmed pools of ice, grim and without a gleam of the humour that had formerly lurked there. "I think you are right," murmured Otton. "I wonder if I should charge you with assault and battery . . ." He listened to Carruthers's profane response with amusement, then raised a languid hand. "Softly, Merry. Softly. My poor head. Have you any wine in this ghastly place? Where is this ghastly place, by the bye?"

Baker, who had been standing quietly beside the door, responded to Carruthers's gesture by crossing to a small table containing a bottle of wine and some chipped mugs. He poured a generous portion of Madeira into two of these, and carried them over.

Carruthers said, "Pour one for yourself, Henry. I am much beholden to you."

"Not so am I," muttered Otton, accepting the mug. "Where is Rump?"

"At the corner stables. I've rented a small flat near Ludgate Hill. Roly . . . I need you. For old times' sake—will you help me?"

Otton had never known this proud man to plead. He found himself unable to meet the desperation in the grey eyes and looked away, saying lightly, "Seems to me, my lad, as if you're past helping. Why did you provoke the luscious Miss R. into jilting you?"

Carruthers gazed into his mug and answered slowly, "I had no choice. You knew that we were hiding Lance. . . ."

Otton sighed. "Would I had known where. Some little cubbyhole in your great Keep, I fancy?"

"Yes. It seems that years ago, when my papa was in his cups, he took my charming nephew to the secret room. While I was searching for Phoebe, Lambert was also searching. He remembered the room, and he found Lance, sleeping."

Otton groaned. "Then—damn him!—he has the cipher!"

"He was not interested in one verse of a four-verse poem. What he has—is me."

"Not our noble Lambkin?" Otton lifted his brows. "Blackmail? Dear me!"

Carruthers said tonelessly, "He came to me when I awoke. I was given three minutes to make a choice. If I gave my sworn oath to terminate my betrothal to Phoebe, he would say nothing about Lance. If I refused, he would feel duty-bound to arrest Lance. And Jeff . . . Sinclair . . . and me."

"Good God! You makebait! You should've shot the bastard out of hand."

"I'll admit I attempted to take him on." Carruthers gave a mirthless snort. "He levelled me *sans difficulté*. I doubt I was up to the heft of a pistol at that moment, even had I kept one under my pillow. Besides, it was quite useless. Beautiful Brooks had the Keep surrounded by his troopers. Lance would have been taken, beyond doubting."

Otton shook his head, marvelling. "To think he actually threatened the brother of his beloved! I'd never have given him credit for such ruthlessness. Certainly, he knew you would all have been executed."

"Certainly. And the estates confiscated, which would have

left Mama destitute—if she survived her grief, which I doubt. To say nothing of the tragedy to the Ramsays."

Otton was silent for a moment, staring at him. "By God, but he had you in a vise! But—did he not cut off the hand that feeds him?"

"You forget, Phoebe is now in the way of being an heiress."

Otton pursed his lips. "Hmmnn. What a splendid actor he is. Loathed you for years, and hid it so well. You realize, Merry, that he was behind all the attempts on your life."

"I realize."

"It is your inheritance he's after, my tulip. Lock, stock, and barrel. He'd have lost the lot were you chopped up for high treason. On the other hand, if his scheme had succeeded, and you'd been slain in the duel, or our devious Hessell had removed you from this sphere with his trusty musket the day—Whoops!"

Carruthers growled, "You *knew* it was Hessell?"

"Clumsy of me, but no point in denying it now. Yes. I caught him, red-handed, as it were."

"And failed to warn me—my good *friend*!"

"Deplorable, I know. But I'd a use for him, and I did stipulate that his continued freedom depended upon his poor aim was there to be another touch at you."

"You are too good," said Carruthers sardonically. "Do you chance to know if Lambert intended Jeff's death, eventually? He's not aware, I think, that my half-brother does not inherit."

"True. I fancy Jeffery was destined to survive you by only a year or two at most, before meeting with an—er, unfortunate 'accident.'"

Carruthers swore softly, but with a fluency that caused Otton to blink. "I agree," he said sympathetically. "I do draw the line at some things, and I'll admit blackmail sticks in my craw."

"Then—help me!"

"How? You gave him your *word*—no getting out of that, old fellow! He's got you. I'm sorrier than hell to say it, because the slimy toad don't deserve your dainty lass, and—I think you are—ah, somewhat smitten, no?"

Meredith balanced his mug very carefully on the arm of his chair and stared at it. The strong hand trembled, but his voice was steady. "I love her more than my life," he answered.

"Pity. Lady Martha seemed to think Phoebe may at one time have reciprocated your feelings."

The dark head jerked up. Carruthers snarled, "She *does*! *Present* tense!"

Otton put down his mug. "I am a wounded man, and if you raise your hand to me, I shall scream for aid." The twinkle left his eyes. He said quietly, "Merry—did you see this morning's *Spectator*? Phoebe is to marry Lambert. The announcement hinted at a small private ceremony to be conducted within a very few days due to his military—"

Carruthers sprang up, sending his mug crashing to the floor. Chalk-white, he snarled, "She would not! She *would* not! Dear God! Not *him*!" He flung away, suddenly, his voice breaking, his head bowed low, and a hand across his eyes.

Otton exchanged aghast glances with Baker. "My dear fellow," he cried, deeply moved by his friend's anguish, "how can you blame the girl? You convinced her you do not love her. She has been courted by your clever nephew for some time, I believe. And—she does not *know*, Merry!"

For a moment, Carruthers continued to stand with head down and shoulders hunched over. Then he turned, his eyes suspiciously bright, and asked unsteadily, "How—how much, Roly?"

"My tulip—there's *nought* to be done! Your oath—remember? Unless—do you desire me to remove Lambert from this vale of tears?"

"He thought of that, and has left a sealed document with his solicitor to be opened in the event of his death."

Otton shook his head. "Clever clod. And you have broken my poor head for nothing."

Carruthers jerked over a straight-backed chair, straddled it and, regarding Otton steadily, said, "Roly, I have a plan, but I cannot manage it alone. You are the *only* man who could help me to carry it off. How much?"

All business, Otton sat straighter. "Information."

"If you mean the cipher, it has already reached its destination."

"Hell and damnation! Very well—the name of the man to whom it was delivered."

Carruthers's heart sank. He said, "I cannot."

"You and your damned integrity! You're sworn to secrecy?"

"Yes. But 'twould make no difference. I'll fight for my happiness, Roly. But not at the cost of a good man's life."

"Then you're a fool! You worship the girl—it's writ all over you."

Carruthers gripped the top of the chair until the bones of his left hand shone white, but when he spoke it was to whisper again, "I cannot!"

"*You* cannot! What of her? She is pining away! You should only see how pale and sad—"

Springing up, Carruthers shouted wildly, "Damn you! D'you think I've not thought of that? Nigh gone mad, thinking of it?" He paced up and down the room, then repeated a tormented "No! I tell you, I *cannot*! Oh—never mind! Go, blast your eyes! Go! I'll manage—somehow!"

Otton came to his feet, clutched his head, then started to the door.

Baker, grim and scornful, blocked his way.

Carruthers grated, "Let him pass, Henry."

Baker stepped aside.

His hand on the latch, Otton checked and turned to lean back against the door. "A bargain rate," he proposed with a faint grin. "Only tell me the name of the town to which you delivered your cipher. Only that, Merry, and I'm your man."

Carruthers drew a quivering breath. "God forgive me," he muttered. "I'll compromise to this extent, and no further. We went over the top of Phantom Hill."

Exultant, Otton cried, "North! *North*, by God! And I was so sure it was east!"

Watching him tensely, Carruthers asked, "You'll do it, then?"

"Deuce take it—no! I asked for the town! You gave me a direction only!"

"You damned, soulless, mercenary—Hell! Five hundred guineas!"

"A thousand!"

Meredith bit his lip, "Done!"

Henry Baker said, "Lor'! I'm glad you're not *my* friend, Cap'n!"

A fitful breeze tossed the tree-tops and blew up the waves, setting the small boats to bobbing in the cove, and causing the yawl to rock uneasily and strain at its anchor chain. The air was chill in this quiet cove of the Dorsetshire coast and held the smell of rain, and although the moon was not yet up, flares were lighted on the beach so that the two men who stood watching from the bluff could see the sailors carrying the large trunks and crates to the longboat.

Lambert said redundantly, "Wind's coming up."

His cloak flying in that same wind, Otton moved closer. "You

281

chose these bullies, my Lamb. Are you sure they are to be trusted?''

"Very. I'm not all wool upstairs, y'know. Told 'em this was a cargo of guns for a secret force preparing to start hostilities in France. They'll not dare risk seizing a military cargo. Besides which, I've a few fellows on board, in addition to your own, to make sure no one tampers with the crates.''

The last item was loaded, the longboat was pushed into the tide, and the sailors started to row out to the yawl. Half an hour later, the sails having disappeared into the night, Otton clapped a hand on Lambert's shoulder and said triumphantly, "We're rich men, Lambkin.''

They walked side by side up the slope, the wind billowing their cloaks, and a few drops of rain falling on their faces as they approached the small tavern set back among the trees.

Lambert murmured, "I can scarce believe it is done.''

"And well done. Which is why I needed you. Only a soldier could have brought that cargo to the coast and aboard the vessel without it was searched.''

"Lord God! If they *had* searched!" Lambert laughed shortly. "A far cry from weapons, eh? When you first told me you'd got your hands on a shipment of that Jacobite gold, I'll own I did not believe you.''

"But—when you saw it, that was sufficient proof, no?''

"Jove, but it was! Did you ever see such a haul? All those encrusted golden bowls and silver plates! The gems! The jade! The gold coins! Bags and bags of the lovely things!''

"Enough and to spare for us both.''

There *was* enough, but Lambert had already decided that it would be much nicer not to have to share with this adventurer. Otton didn't deserve it. He was truly a nasty fellow to so treat his friend, for there was no doubt but that Otton had got his hands on the treasure by betraying Carruthers. Just to guard against trickery, Lambert had given his men secret instructions, as a result of which, instead of the yawl sailing for the secluded beach near Boulogne that Otton had designated, she would put in to land some ten miles to the north. And quite unknown to this dandy beside him, he had booked passage for himself and Phoebe on a private and very expensive yacht that would sail at midnight. A fast vessel that would reach France's coast before the yawl, and with a crew able and willing to off-load the yawl's priceless cargo. He and Phoebe would be married on board, and with luck he'd get back before his special leave was up—a wealthy man. Two birds with one stone, by Jupiter! Otton was peering at him. "Oh—more than enough," he agreed, realizing that he had failed to answer.

Otton drawled, "What d'you mean to do with your share?"

"Buy an estate. But first, I shall have my marriage announcement framed, and send it to my dear uncle for a memoir." He chuckled. "I'll have no more need of him, or of his beggarly allowance. Were it not for the fact I shall own the Hall someday, I'd inform on the swine and have done. I'd have been so damn delighted to see both Carrutherses hauled off to the Tower."

They crossed the neat yard of the little tavern, and Otton halted. "I wish you'd not brought the girl here. If she sees me, she's liable to set up a screech."

"She'll do what she's told, never you fear. And by this time tomorrow, she'll be Mrs. Brooks Lambert, and couldn't testify against me if she wanted to."

"She could testify against *me*, friend, so I'd as soon be on my way. I'll call on you when you return to Town."

They made some preliminary arrangements and then parted on the step, Otton heading to the stableyard, and Lambert running lightly upstairs to the room where he had left his bride-to-be.

⤝ *Chapter 20* ⤞

Lambert entered the private parlour without benefit of a knock. Phoebe was sitting at the window, and she turned the sad and faintly contemptuous face that he had privately promised himself to change. He put off his cloak, unbuckled his sword-belt and tossed it aside, then pulled her to her feet. "Well, lovely one, my business is concluded. Almost. We are going to be richer than I'd dreamed. That will not grieve you, eh?"

She said nothing, but turned her face when he tried to kiss her, so that his salute landed upon her ear, instead of her lips.

Smiling, he took her chin between his fingers. They bit deep, and she winced despite herself as he forced her head around. "You must behave nicely, my love, or I might tell your admired ex-fiancé to have that black devil of a horse shot. Or something equally delicious. He is quite helpless, you know, and must do whatever I command. And my commands . . . may very well depend upon your cooperation."

And so she let him kiss her and submitted to his hungry mauling, although shame brought the tears streaking silently down her cheeks, and she wondered dully how long she must endure life with him before she was allowed to die.

Lambert drew back. "Alas, but you've much to learn, sweeting. Now, I've a charming peculiar in London might teach you . . ." He chuckled. "*That* would be a novel set-to. My mistress advising my wife in matters of the bedchamber."

"What a slimy slug you are, Brooks."

Phoebe's grieving heart gave a great leap at the sound of that deep voice.

Lambert whirled around, enraged.

Carruthers leaned just inside the closed door, watching him with disgust.

"Now *damn* your eyes," growled Lambert. "You'll regret this, I promise!"

"Oh, Merry . . ." whispered Phoebe. "*Why* did you come?"

Recovering somewhat, Lambert jeered, "He came to our wedding. There's a notion! Come with us, dear Meredith. Watch me take your beloved to wife." He laughed tauntingly, "Jove, but I'd like that!"

Carruthers did not glance his way, his full attention on Phoebe's tears, her agonized eyes and wringing hands. "Why did you agree to wed him?" he asked. "Don't you know what kind of rubbishy thing he is?"

Lambert's gaze narrowed. "It is going to be a great pleasure to school you, Carruthers. You had everything—except the thing you most want. But your love wants me—don't you, dear one? She *always* has wanted me."

Phoebe gave him a swift look of loathing. Returning her eyes to Meredith, she answered brokenly, "I—have no choice, my heart."

Despite what he already knew of Lambert, that anyone naming himself a gentleman should blackmail a lady was beyond belief. Astounded, Carruthers whispered, "Lord . . . God . . . !"

"If your prayers are done," grinned Lambert, "you can get out."

Carruthers stared at him blankly.

Stepping closer, Lambert said, "You're going to pay dear for all those years when you lorded it over me."

"I was—" began Carruthers.

The words were cut off as Lambert flailed a back-handed blow that slammed across his mouth and sent him reeling. Phoebe gave a little whimpering cry and closed her eyes for a second. Lambert glanced at her. "Do you want to see him kneel? He will if I tell him, won't you, dear Meredith? Prove me right. On your knees, you cur!"

Carruthers's head came up slowly. His mouth was cut and a narrow line of crimson streaked down to his chin. But he was smiling. It was such a smile as froze the blood in Phoebe's veins, and caused Lambert to step back a pace, instinctively.

"You unspeakable vermin," said Carruthers softly. "I'll see you in hell first!"

Lambert sprang at him, fist clenched.

Carruthers waited calmly until that whizzing blow was well launched, then swayed lightly aside. Lambert's knuckles rammed into the wall, and he howled. Carruthers laughed with unholy joy, and leapt in. A flashing jab, a blazing uppercut, and Lambert measured his length on the floor. Carruthers bent, grabbed him by the collar of his splendid uniform, and hauled. "Up, *canaille*," he panted. "I've scarce begun."

"You've . . . *finished*," gasped Lambert, scrabbling upward. "You brainless oaf!" He jerked a finger at the white-faced Phoebe. "You just wrote her brother's death-warrant! Hit me again, and yours will go to the Tower with him!"

Phoebe bit her knuckle in terrified despair.

Carruthers took a deep breath and stepped back. "When you inform, foulness, you must be sure to tell Mariner Fotheringay what you've been about today."

Dabbing a handkerchief at his lips, Lambert paused, his eyes fixed and wary.

"For instance," Carruthers went on, his own eyes a blaze of steel, "will you explain why you hired a ship to transport Jacobite gold out of England?"

Lambert tensed, but said, "You would have a difficult time proving that, friend, and would be yourself answering to an inquisitor in the Tower, long before—"

"Did you know, Brooks, that Roland Otton has a cousin named . . . Jacob Holt? Ah—you do recognize that estimable name. He is a man as hungry for promotion as you are hungry for money. A letter was sent to his solicitor this morning, with a note that it is to be handed to Holt in the event of the arrest of any member of the Ramsay or Carruthers families. The letter it refers to is addressed to you, Lambert, and written in deep gratitude by one Captain Lancelot Lascelles. He is rather wordy, I fear, in thanking you for having enabled him to escape in exchange for a share of the treasure."

Lambert said nothing, only his eyes were deadly, and he seemed to the breathless Phoebe to crouch a little, like a wild beast readying to spring.

Carruthers went on, "It should be simple enough for Holt to find witnesses to prove that you did, in fact, smuggle traitor and treasure out of England. Now what, noble soldier, would Mariner make of that little foray? Do you fancy your golden head would adorn Tower Bridge within one week? Or would they chastise you longer before decapitation set in? A month of . . . questioning, mayhap?"

Lambert said in the same hushed, guarded voice, "I did not take the treasure. Otton did."

"But *you* provided the boat, Lambert. *You*, rightfully mistrusting Roly, hired the bullies. It was by *your personal* orders that the troopers were discouraged from searching the cargo. A cargo, my poor chap, which contained more than my family valuables, and—"

Lambert stiffened. "*Your* valuables?"

"Well, not *all*. Some of it was donated by Lockwood. But who's to know that? And in case you fear that Otton will steal it, I should tell you that half the 'crew' are my people. Including my brother, by the way, though you'd never recognize him. Do you not see, Brooks? I paid Otton to approach you, knowing that someone of—shall we say, colourful repute, must tell you of the 'treasure' else you'd not believe it. And do you remember those two big chests? Only a token shelf of valuables, Lambert, and below, something infinitely more valuable. In one, Lance; and in the other, his lady, Rosalie Smith. Why, how very pale you are become! Console yourself. You have, almost single-handedly, saved a rebel's life."

White to the lips, Lambert rasped. "You lie! Damn your dirty soul to hell! You lie!"

"Oh, no. Lies seldom serve, I've found. I assure you that Lance and his lady are at this very moment en route to a new life in La Belle France. All thanks to you." Carruthers's smile faded. He said curtly, "And we are thus at what is, I believe, called impasse. You are hoist by your own petard, you murderous bastard, and—"

Torn between hope and dread, Phoebe had been watching Lambert. She saw his face convulse into a mask of hatred so maniacal that it appalled her, and she gave a scream of warning.

Carruthers also had seen that changed expression, and he hurled himself gladly to meet the berserk charge. They met head on. Half-demented with rage and frustration, Lambert had astonishing strength. Carruthers, with bitter scores to settle, was equally inflamed, and the two tall men fought in a brutal trading of punishing blows, the petrified girl darting from their path as they plunged about the small room, sending furniture crashing. Hurled back, Carruthers evaded a following blow and sent home an uppercut. Lambert staggered, but in desperation flung a wicked swipe at the barely healed arm that sent his hated kinsman reeling and, half-blind, to stumble over a broken chair and go down.

Wheezing, mouthing obscenities, Lambert was on him, hands clamping around his throat. Carruthers, unable to breathe, a red haze swimming before his eyes, brought both fists up and, with a supreme effort, slammed them outward, breaking Lambert's hold. He threw a right to that classic jaw and crawled free, but Lambert staggered up and rammed a boot into his ribs, shatteringly. Carruthers doubled up, choking. Snatching up a leg of the smashed chair, Lambert raised it high, croaking, "You're dead, damn you! I lose—but it'll be worth it to beat your brains out!"

With a sob of terror, Phoebe ran to grip his upraised arm and cling with all her might. Lambert uttered a slobbering snarl and thrust her away, but she hung on until he tore her loose, hit her, and sent her flying.

Carruthers fought his way to his feet. The chair leg whizzed at him. He stumbled clear, then struck with the heel of his right hand in a solid chop that landed just above and behind Lambert's flying elbow. The chair leg dropped from the numbed hand, but Carruthers had paid a price also, and he swayed, sickened with pain. Lambert sent a left straight for the jaw. Carruthers partially blocked the blow, but it landed hard enough to send him to one knee. Phoebe was not getting up. Fear sent wrath searing through him. He was up even as Lambert aimed another savage and unheroic kick. Avoiding the gleaming boot, Carruthers drove a left jab to the midriff. Lambert said, "Ooosh!" bent in half, and went zooming into the door. It burst outward just as the host and a waiter ran along the hall.

" 'Ere! 'Ere!'' cried the host frantically, then jumped clear as Lambert sailed past, plunged into the railing, and took it with him down into the vestibule.

Carruthers charged out, sprinted along the hall and halfway down the stairs, the wails of the host and the waiter drifting after him. That miserable coward had hurt Phoebe! He'd dared to raise his hand to her! He leapt the banister and ran across the vestibule. Lambert came at him, a heavy, branched coat rack held battering-ram fashion, and murder clearly written on his bloodied face. Carruthers had to dive for his life. The coat rack grazed his back and slammed into the glass base of a tall old grandfather clock. Lambert swung his coat rack high. The grandfather clock toppled and fell, pinning Lambert and coat rack. Carruthers reeled over, clambered on top of the horizontal clock, and knelt there, laughing gaspingly, while Lambert howled profanities.

The host and the waiter ran up and grabbed Carruthers, pulling him away. He cried out and clutched his arm, but with sanity returning.

The host swung up a club, his square face red and enraged. "I could love yer, fer fightin'—and laughin' even when yer hurt. But, by Gawd, sir, I'll *brain* yer if yer makes a move," he shouted. " 'Swelp me if I don't! *'Swelp* me!"

Two housemaids crawled out from under the counter, and a farm wife peered from behind an overturned armchair, surveying the carnage in awed disbelief.

Dizzy and shaking, Carruthers staggered back to look down at Lambert. Tears of helpless rage streamed down the distorted, unhandsome countenance. "Someday!" sobbed Lambert. "As God be . . . my judge! I'll even . . . the score! You and—and that stinking . . . reptile, Otton! *Some*day . . . !

"Were I you," gasped Carruthers, swaying drunkenly, "I'd get . . . back to duty. You've . . . many lies to invent to . . . account for having forbade your men to—to search that vessel."

Lambert groaned, tried to pull the clock clear, and fainted.

The host came up, also weeping. "Oh, sir! *Whata* fighter yer is! But—lookat me *stairs*! Lookat me *clock*! Lookat—"

Carruthers fished in his pocket and drew out his purse. He could not see clearly, but his bruised fingers managed to hand it over. "Sorry," he panted.

The host sniffed, and drew his sleeve across his eyes. "Ar. Well—"

Carruthers was already weaving to the stairs. "Send me reck-reckoning. . . ." he croaked, and began to toil up the steps that now seemed two miles high.

"Merry," quavered a beloved voice.

He halted, groping blindly for the wall.

Phoebe sat at the top of the stairs, a chambermaid peeping around the corner at her. A red welt across her cheekbone was darkening to a bruise, one eye was swollen, her hair hung in a tangled mass, her gown was torn at the shoulder. And on her face was a radiance that made his heart ache with love.

"Oh, my . . . dearest," she sobbed, reaching down to him, but quite unable to move. "You are so battered, and you will have an awful black eye. And—oh, heavens! you've made your arm bleed again! Are you in much pain?"

"Yes," he said, grinning at her despite a split lip. "And—oh, God, Phoebe . . . it was worth every . . . second!"

He thought he told her how much he loved her, but could not

be sure. He dragged his failing body on until he could reach her shoe. The last thing he remembered was kissing it. . . .

Lady Martha Ramsay tiptoed into the bedchamber, stopped abruptly, and hurried to the bed. Her eldest granddaughter lay there, giggling like a schoolgirl, and clutching a letter to her breast.

Lady Martha smiled at the lovely, happy face, and for the hundredth time sent up a quick, grateful prayer.

Sinclair came in, Belinda behind him. "Is she weeping?" he asked anxiously.

Belinda said, "Mr. Carruthers has turned up his toes. Dead as a mackerel, is what it is!"

Running to join them, Julia said, "Belinda, you little beast! She's laughing! Phoebe—how wonderful it is to see you so happy!"

Phoebe sat up. "Thank you, dear." Her glowing eyes embraced them all. "My *very* dears," she amended. "How are my bruises today?" Belinda ran for the mirror, and while they all chorused eager assurances that the evidences of the battle were almost faded away, she peered at herself. "It will do," she said judicially. "Sin, are you off somewhere? You look very grand."

He glanced down at his new blue coat and answered shyly, "Well, er—as a matter of fact, I'm going to Glendenning Abbey with Jeff. Old Bowers-Malden thought Jeff might like to see the place, since he's so interested in architecture, so Tio's driving us down."

Phoebe said, "I thought Lord Horatio was terrified of his noble sire."

"I suppose he is, in a way. I must say the old boy was very nice to me, though. Phoebe, you'd not believe how pleased Meredith was when Jeff told him what he really wants to do. Proud as a peacock! And cannot do enough to help."

"How *is*—Mr. Carruthers?" enquired Phoebe demurely.

"Fine as fivepence! But—I gave you his letter. Doesn't he say—"

"Nothing about himself, which is very typical. Was he . . . did he seem—"

"He was laughing like a gondolier when we left."

Phoebe blinked. "He was? Why?"

290

"Oh, it's that fellow Otton. It seems he made Meredith pay before he would help him, and—"

"Disgraceful!" said my lady. "Perhaps his grandfather is right about him after all!"

"And he had just sent Merry back his bank draft with the most crazy letter, saying he is thrown into despair because he finds he values Merry's friendship more than the money, and is convinced he is a candidate for Bedlam. He said the only thing that consoles him is that he stole something from the 'treasure,' so perhaps his villainy is not wholly ruined."

Phoebe laughed. "Poor fellow. His faith in himself is quite shaken, I am sure. Well, have a nice time, Sin."

He thanked her and headed for the door. "You'll forgive me if I rush off? I don't want to offend the Earl. You'd not credit it, but he's most frightfully interested in bats. I think I may do some reading on them at University. . . ." He waved and went out, closing the door with a bang.

"Bats!" snorted Julia, sitting on the end of the bed. "If you ask me, he's so smart today because he's hoping to see Glendenning's little sister!"

Belinda, more single-minded, asked, "Phoebe—why were you laughing? Isn't that Mr. Carruthers's handwriting? Oooh!" she pounced on the small, flat case. "A present! May I look?" It was opened, even as she spoke.

Phoebe said a redundant "You may. But it's not in there." She held out her wrist, and they crowded around to inspect and admire.

The bracelet was of intertwined gold ropes, and in the centre a flat oval on which was a beautifully enamelled broadsword, a dainty rose lying across it.

"It is part of the Carruthers crest," said Phoebe, touching the red rose with one gentle fingertip.

"Oh, it's lovely," said Julia. "And he sends you a rose every day! So romantic."

"What does he have to say?" asked my lady.

Phoebe took up the letter again and gazed at it, her eyes very tender. "If you will all swear not to tell, I'll read it. Well . . ." She blushed. "Some of it."

They all settled down on the bed in eager anticipation.

"My dear Miss Ramsay," Phoebe began, *"I am glad to know you are feeling well again. I have managed, my adored—*Er, well, I'll skip the next few lines. Let's see. . . . Ah! *Our courtship was never really that, was it? And if ever a lady deserved*

291

the most ardent courtship a clumsy tyrant can manage, you are that lady. I therefore mean to come and court you, best beloved, so soon as the scandal has died down a little. And also, because I want to allow you time to stop and consider, and to be very sure of your own heart. Lord knows, I am not worthy of you, but I don't want to win you because you have a foolish notion of gratitude, or being indebted, or some such fustian.

"I hope you will accept the small gift, and even if you should decide against accepting the man who sends it, wear it in remembrance of some wonderful hours amongst the many that were less than wonderful.

"Yours, et cetera,
Carruthers."

She looked up, her great eyes twinkling.

The four ladies looked at one another.

" 'My Dear *Miss Ramsay* . . . ?' " murmured Julia.

"Men!" said Belinda.

"Men!" they echoed, and giggled together as ladies will when they connive to the downfall of some hapless male.

Fred Boles gazed up at lofty vaulted ceiling and massy walls and pursed his lips. "Seems like an awful great waste to me, sir."

The shadows gone from around his eyes and the sling from his arm, Carruthers said with a grin, "My contribution to the heritage of England. We all owe her a great deal, you know. You go to your lunch, Fred, but let me know when my brother returns, will you? Think I'll wander around the old place for a bit."

Boles nodded and went off, smiling to himself because the master was back to his old self; was, in fact, happier than he'd ever seen him, as though the burdens he carried on his broad shoulders had been immeasurably lightened. "Love!" he muttered, rolling his eyes at the sunny heavens. "Cor!"

Left alone, Carruthers strolled the length of the Great Hall, lost in thought. She must have received his letter yesterday. Would she accept the bracelet? More to the point, would she accept *him*? He frowned, the glow fading from his eyes. She was so *very* beautiful. If she had been merely pretty, or even rather plain, he might stand a better chance. The gentlemen had fairly flocked around her at the Pineridge Summer Ball. Just because he had shared those hectic ten days with her and had been able (thank God!) to circumvent Brooks Lambert's vicious schemes did not give him the right to expect she would choose him. There were so many men who were better-looking, more adept in the art of flattery, and—he smiled wryly—poetry. . . .

He walked down to the outer hall and stood contemplating with unseeing eyes the square of light on the floor that shone from the hole in the ceiling through which invaders had been doused with boiling pitch. He gave a startled gasp as something shot through that aperture to bounce off his head. A rosebud lay at his feet, a dewdrop on one of the leaves gleaming like a diamond. Staring at it, his breath was snatched away.

In trembling eagerness, he jerked his head up and beheld an upside-down but lovely face, framed by the crumbling opening; great eyes soft with love, ruddy lips curving to a tender smile, glorious hair unpowdered and hanging in a red-gold cloud about her.

He breathed, "Phoebe!" and was running madly to the broken old steps and sprinting along the narrow upper passage.

Phoebe had intended to wait, dazzling him with her white gown and long hair (just like the Lady Clemency's), and the red rose she held. But she was overpowered and began to run too, arms outstretched. His heart bursting, Carruthers caught her to him and held her crushed against his chest, his cheek pressed to the cool, silky tresses, his eyes closed in an ecstasy of bliss. He could scarcely endure to break that embrace, even to kiss her, but he managed it, drawing back at last, dazed with delight, when she murmured that she really must breathe, and that ribs had their uses.

He looked down at her loveliness and knew that if she had refused him he would have been lost in the dark for as long as he lived. In a voice husky with emotion, he said, "You little wretch! You have spoiled all my plans to court you."

"I couldn't wait," she said simply, snuggling her face into his cravat.

He kissed the top of her head. "How did you know I was out here?"

"Your mama told me. We're all here, my love. The whole lot of us came. And I think I have never seen Mrs. Carruthers look so happy."

"Nor her son so bewitched. . . . Phoebe, my love, my life— will you marry me?"

She leaned back her head and looked up at him. "With pride and joy, and all the love that—"

He gave a wild shout and snatched her to his heart.

After a while, they wandered out of the old Keep, Meredith's arm tight around her and her glowing head against his shoulder. Phoebe paused on the drawbridge to glance back at the great pile. "Darling, shall you really rebuild it?"

He ran a finger along his jaw line. "I'd rather thought to raze it. Dreadful waste of land, and—"

"You wicked liar," she told him fondly.

He chuckled, looking down at her, a clear blue flame in his eyes that made her pulses leap madly.

Justice came padding up, tail wagging. Satan jumped over the wall, dealt the hound a swat, tore under his stomach, and raced off sideways. Justice gave his humans a long-suffering look.

Meredith patted his head. "We're all bedeviled, old fellow," he said. "You by a Satanic feline. Me by . . ." He paused, his dancing gaze turning to Phoebe.

"By what, sir?" she demanded with mock outrage.

Had the convex wing across the courtyard been a ship, it must have tilted down, so many beaming individuals crowded every window, watching the lovers.

Very aware of the audience, Meredith did not answer, bending to Phoebe, his eyes igniting her soul. She lifted her face eagerly, but when he sought her lips, she whipped the rose between her teeth.

Laughing, he removed the obstruction. "My adorable . . . little shrew," he whispered.

Phoebe slid both arms around his neck, and with his lips a breath away, murmured, "Beloved . . . Tyrant . . ."

The sun shone benignly on them and drew sparkles from the dewdrops on the blossom that lay at their feet. A great red rose.